I0656323

VICTIM STATEMENTS

(COLD AND FROSTY MOURNING)

The 3rd in the Kenny Hughes Memorial Trilogy

JUDY FORD

COPYRIGHT

Victim Statements

(Cold and Frosty Mourning)

Published by Bernie Fazakerley
Publications

Copyright © 2021 Judy Ford.

No part of this book may be used, transmitted, stored or reproduced in any manner whatsoever without the author's written permission.

All rights reserved.

ISBN: 978-1-911083-80-1

DEDICATION

Dedicated to

SAMM (Support After Murder and Manslaughter)

SAMM is a national charity supporting friends and families after their loss of a loved one to murder and manslaughter.

You are not alone…

CONTENTS

MAP OF SHOTOVER COUNTRY PARK

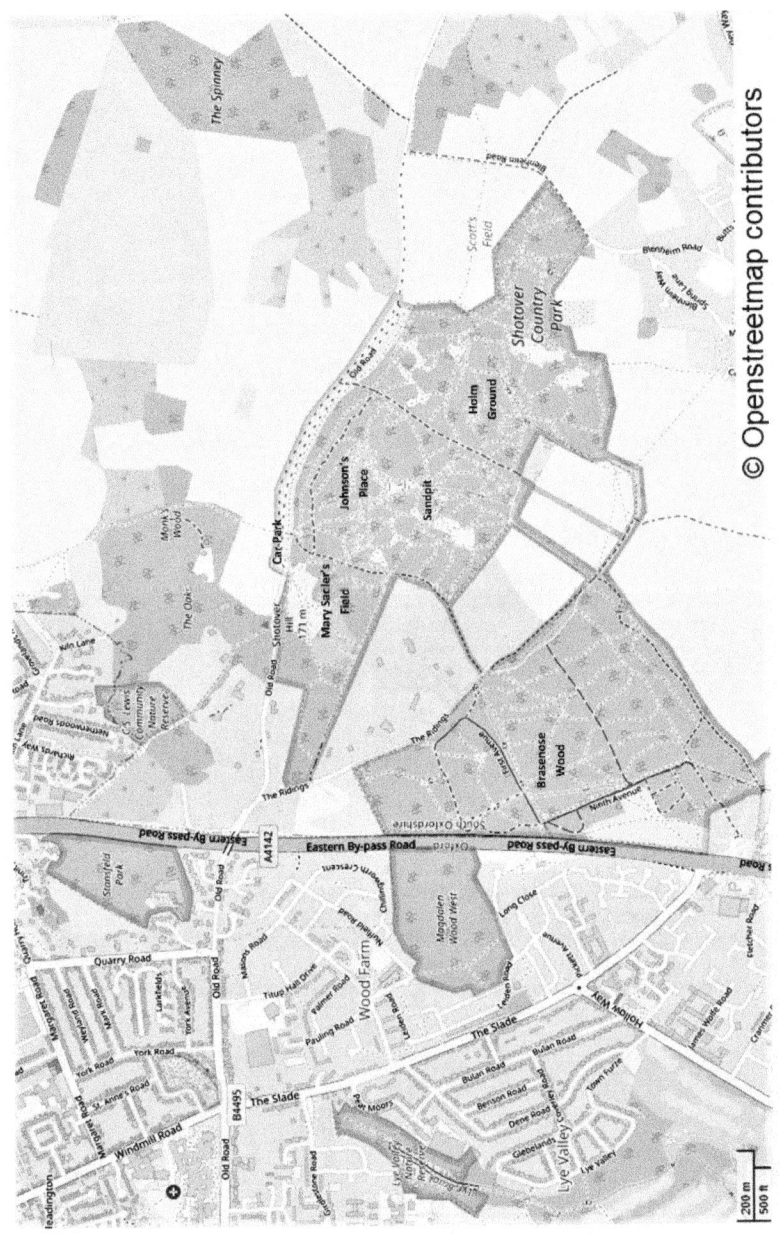

© Openstreetmap Contributors. This map was produced using data available under the Open Database License

1. LET'S GO FLY A KITE

'It's grown! It must be as tall as me now.' Chrissie strode across the grass towards a lanky rowan sapling, which stood tall compared with the stout bamboo cane to which it was tied. It was still just a single stem with feathery leaves spaced out along its length, but it was certainly flourishing. The finely-serrated leaflets fluttered in the breeze and the top of the tree swayed and bowed. It was always windy up here on Shotover Hill.

'I suppose it will have done. We can't have seen it for nearly four months.'

Gavin hurried to catch up with his wife. It was Saturday 4th July 2020 – Freedom Day as the popular press described it. The day that places of worship, pubs, restaurants, hairdressers and non-essential shops were at last allowed to re-open after the COVID-19 lockdown. An emergency measure that had initially been put in place for three weeks, in an attempt to stem the spread of this deadly new virus, had lasted for far longer than anyone had dared to suggest that it might. Now, at last, they could visit the place where they had buried Kenny's ashes six months, and half a lifetime, ago. For the first time since March, they could visit the tree that they had planted in his memory and remember the happy times when they had come up here with him while he was growing up.

They stood together in front of the tree, holding hands, each thinking their own thoughts. It had been a tough six months since that December day when they had been summoned to the hospital where Kenny was undergoing emergency surgery following a murderous attack. It had seemed so cruel at the time not being able to say a final goodbye; but ever since March the news had been full of stories of relatives unable to be with their dying loved-ones. Their experience wasn't so abnormal anymore. Perhaps it never had been.

Gavin turned and walked over to a wooden bench, which stood in the shade of a large oak tree. He put down the bag that he had been carrying and reached inside.

'What've you got there?' Chrissie asked, coming over to join him.

'D'you remember the kite we made for Kenny for his seventh birthday?' Gavin pulled out a piece of brightly-coloured fabric made up of sections of blue and yellow cotton material sewn neatly together. 'You made the sail and the tail, and I did the spars and the line.'

VICTIM STATEMENTS

He reached into the bag again and took out two lengths of thin dowel. He slipped them into pockets at the corner of the kite, carefully fitting the thin cord that ran through a hem round the edge of the fabric into slots in the ends of the dowels. He held it up and shook out the long tail, made of a length of ribbon with multi-coloured bows tied into it at intervals. Finally, he attached a reel of thin string, pulling it firmly to check that it was secure.

'I found it in the loft when I put away the Christmas decorations. One of the spars was broken, but apart from that, it was still in pretty good nick. I mended it and now I thought I'd give it an outing. This was where we took it for its maiden flight.'

'Yes, I remember,' Chrissie smiled. 'You had a great time, but Kenny got upset because he couldn't get it to stay up.'

'Well let's see if I've still got the knack,' Gavin smiled back. He carried the kite out into the centre of the field and put it down on the grass. Then, letting out the cord as he went, he walked backwards into the wind. When he judged that the line was long enough, he stopped and gave it a jerk. The kite lifted off the ground, bounced a short way along the grass and then flopped back down again.

'Shall I give it a lift?' Chrissie called from the bench.

'If you like.'

Chrissie got up, walked across the field and picked up the kite. She held it high above her head. 'Ready?'

'Yes. Let it go … now!'

Chrissie launched the kite into the air above her head. It rose then veered downwards again before Gavin got it under control, pulling the string rhythmically to make it climb higher. As the wind took it, he let out the line, still pulling gently to maintain the tension. Soon it was soaring upwards as he continued to allow the reel to turn in his hands. He craned his neck and screwed up his eyes to watch its swooping flight against the brightness of the sky. There was something satisfying and therapeutic about collaborating with the wind to keep the homemade craft airborne.

Chrissie returned to the bench and sat down on it. She gazed out over the grass and shrubby trees at the view of Oxford and, beyond the sprawl of Cowley, to the distant Berkshire Downs. Were there more bushes now than there had been when Kenny was a boy? Or perhaps this wasn't the spot where they had stood looking down on the city, competing to spot familiar landmarks. Had that been further on, on the other side of that hedge, in the next field? What a pity she hadn't thought to bring their binoculars. Kenny had never grown tired of that special moment, each time they came here, when he managed to bring them into focus on their own house, three miles away in Rose Hill.

Gavin seemed to be engrossed in his kite-flying. Perhaps that was his way of communing with Kenny. Chrissie smiled as she reached into her handbag and got out her knitting. It was very pleasant up here in the warm July sunshine – one of those days that reminded you of the hot, dry summers of your childhood! And for once, they neither of them had any pressing tasks waiting to be done – or at least nothing that could not wait until tomorrow.

'Hi there!'

Chrissie looked up as a family group approached across the grass. It was their friends Wayne and Dean with their two boys Carl and Harry. A moment later she was engulfed by a barking bundle of black-and-tan fur as Star, their German Shepherd Dog pup, recognised her and bounded over to deliver her own exuberant greeting.

Dean gave a piercing whistle at which the dog immediately turned and raced back to his side.

'Good girl!' Carl praised her, patting her on the shoulder. 'Are you ready for a game?'

He held up a rubber ring high above his head and gazed down sternly at Star, who sat down and looked up at him expectantly. She knew that she had to sit still and wait or he would not throw the ring for her to retrieve.

'Hasn't she grown!' Chrissie exclaimed. 'She's hardly a puppy anymore.'

'Yes, she is,' Harry corrected her earnestly. 'She won't be fully grown for ages yet, and we've got loads of things we've still got to teach her before she can be a police dog.'

Dean was a volunteer puppy socialiser with Thames Valley Police, and Star was being fostered with them until she was mature enough to be assessed as suitable (or not) for a career in the Dog Division. It was a responsibility that both boys were keen to share – and both were convinced that, with their help, she would be successful.

VICTIM STATEMENTS

Wayne went over to the bench and sat down at the opposite end from where Chrissie was seated. They were probably a bit less than two metres apart, but it was out-of-doors so the risk must be reduced, mustn't it? They both watched as Carl threw the ring and Star raced across the field after it, her ears flopping as she bounded over the grass. She brought it back and sat down in front of the boy, looking up adoringly as she waited patiently for him to take it from her.

'Good girl!' he declared. 'Give!'

He took hold of the ring and Star released it. He was about to throw it again when his younger brother shouted in protest.

'It's my turn now! Give it to me!'

As if he had not heard, Carl raised his arm ready to send the ring flying across the field again, but Dean intervened.

LET'S GO FLY A KITE

'No Carl. Harry's right. You have to take turns. Give the ring to him.'

Chrissie smiled at this little altercation. As a teacher, she was familiar with the challenges associated with caring for youngsters. It had always been a source of regret for her that Kenny was an only child, but at least she had not had to cope with sibling rivalry and the impossible task of always being demonstrably fair to every family member.

'Are the boys back at school now?' she asked Wayne. 'Or will they have to wait until September?'

'No, we're still home schooling,' he replied. 'They're neither of them in the right years to be back in. Not that we'd really feel comfortable about them going back yet anyway. I know kids aren't supposed to be badly affected by the virus, but you never really know, do you? My parents both had it back in May and Mum still isn't right. Dad says she sometimes sleeps almost all day and just cleaning the floor makes her so breathless she needs to go for a lie down.'

'I'm sorry to hear that. I suppose it's this "long COVID" that they've started talking about.'

'Yes. That's what Dad says it must be. The funny thing is: he got it worse than she did, but he's back to normal now and she's still so tired and breathless. It doesn't make sense.'

'Nothing much seems to make much sense at the moment,' Chrissie sighed. 'We're just plodding on from day to day hoping things will get sorted somehow in the end.'

LET'S GO FLY A KITE

'I know what you mean,' Wayne nodded. 'We've given up on planning for the future. There doesn't seem any point when we don't know what things are going to be like in a month or two. Our main concern has to be keeping the boys in the best place possible mentally, and Star has been a real godsend in that respect.'

They watched as the two boys played with the young dog. After a few minutes, Harry got bored with the repetitious game of throwing and retrieving the rubber ring and he wandered towards Gavin, staring up at the kite as it hovered far above them.

'Hello PC Hughes,' he said politely. 'What's that?'

'It's a kite,' Gavin smiled back at him. 'Haven't you seen one before?'

'No. How does it stay up like that?'

'It's the wind. I'm not sure exactly how it does it,' Gavin confessed, 'but you have to keep pulling on the string to keep it taut and then the wind keeps it up in the sky.'

'Is that hard?'

'Not really. If it wasn't for this coronavirus, I'd let you have a go, but we'd better not get too close.'

'OK boys!' Dean called. 'Who wants to go to the sandpit?'

He clipped a lead on to Star's collar and headed off down a path that led into woodland at the side of the field. Carl and Harry scampered excitedly after him. The natural sandpit with its tiny stream (perfect for experimenting with dams) was a favourite place for the boys to play.

Chrissie looked enquiringly towards Wayne.

'No, I'll stay here. I'd only slow them down,' he said in answer to her unasked question. 'It's OK,' he added, seeing an expression of concern crossing her face. 'I'm getting used to my limitations now. I've realised that trying to do everything I used to be able to do just makes me tired and cranky and annoys everybody else too. There are plenty of things I *can* do with the boys and it's much better for them if I stick with those.'

'Well, that's a wonderful attitude to have,' Chrissie said warmly, 'but I still think it's a pity you still can't … Well, it does seem unfair … Hit-and-run drivers are despicable. The least they could do is to stop and face up to the consequences.'

'That's all water under the bridge now,' Wayne shrugged. 'And thanks to your husband and his colleagues, the driver was found.'

'It was only a youngster, wasn't it,' Chrissie said thoughtfully. 'So, I suppose it wasn't so surprising they panicked and didn't stop. I know how reluctant the kids in my class are to own up to things sometimes. But still … knowing they'd hit someone …!'

'And who knows?' Wayne continued, anxious to stem Chrissie's flood of concern for him. 'Apparently, this one-sided weakness may still improve some more. My neurologist keeps talking about the plasticity of the brain and how no one knows how long recovery from head injuries can continue. I don't suppose I'll ever get back on the rugger pitch, but you never know, perhaps by this time next year we'll all be able to ride out here on our bikes instead of coming in the car. I gave it a go in the park the other day. The boys thought it was hilarious, the way I was wobbling about, but I managed to stay upright – just!'

LET'S GO FLY A KITE

'That's great! I do hope-' Chrissie broke off at the sound of her phone ringing in her bag. She dropped her knitting on the bench beside her and reached inside. She glanced down at the screen and then swiped it to answer the call. 'I'm sorry, I'd better take this.'

Wayne nodded and then, not wanting to listen in on a private call, he got to his feet and wandered over to speak to Gavin. Chrissie watched him striding across the grass with his funny lop-sided gait as she listened to a familiar voice. It was Yvonne Whittle, another mother who had lost a son to the murderous activity of the Butler gang.

'Chrissie?' she asked anxiously. She always sounded apologetic on the phone, as if she expected to be rebuffed. 'I hope this isn't a bad time?'

VICTIM STATEMENTS

'Not at all,' Chrissie assured her. 'I'm just sitting here in the sun with my knitting while Gav's off flying a kite.' Yvonne said nothing, so she went on, 'What is it? Is something wrong?'

'There's this letter come through the post today ...'

'What sort of letter?' Chrissie asked. 'I mean, what was it about?'

'It's from a lawyer – at least I think that's who it is.' Yvonne sounded even less sure of herself than usual.

'Is it about the trial?' Chrissie demanded at once. 'Have they fixed a date? We haven't heard anything!'

'No. It's nothing to do with that. Its ... Well, you see, we didn't have the money for Harry's funeral. We never knew how much they cost! And we didn't want .... We wanted him to have a decent ...'

LET'S GO FLY A KITE

Chrissie felt a pang of guilt as she realised that, at the time, she hadn't given a thought to this other family who were also grieving the loss of a son. She hadn't known Yvonne and her husband Trevor then, but even so, they ought to have gone to the funeral to show solidarity with …. But Yvonne was speaking again. She pressed the phone closer to her ear and tried to concentrate on what she was saying.

'Trev didn't want to worry me about …. Well, to be honest I was in too much of a mess at that stage to take it in if he *had* told me. So, he took out this loan. I thought it'd all come out of our savings: we had nearly two thousand in the building society, saving for when Trev's taxi needs replacing. I never knew that wasn't enough!'

'And the letter?' prompted Chrissie. 'Was that about this loan?'

'Yes! It says we're in arrears on the payments and … I can tell you exactly: I've got it here. It says "unless the outstanding sum is received within thirty days of the date of this letter, we will have no choice but to take legal action." What does that mean exactly? What's going to happen? We don't have the money to pay. Trev hasn't been earning since Lockdown started and the agency's only been paying me eighty percent while I'm on furlough, and the internet's been costing more since Leo's been home schooling, and-' Yvonne's voice rose and Chrissie was afraid that she was becoming hysterical.

'Let's try to keep calm and think it through.' She hoped that she sounded firm but not patronising. Craig, their lodger, had sometimes accused her of treating everyone like a child in her class. 'It says you've got thirty days from the date on the letter. Can you see when that was?'

'The seventeenth.'

'Of June?'

'Yes.'

'Then that means they won't do anything until the seventeenth of July, which is a fortnight off.'

'But we haven't got the money!'

'How much is it – if you don't mind telling me?'

'It says "two thousand four hundred and seventy-three pounds". Trev says he only borrowed two thousand and he'd paid some of it back before … but the interest's been mounting up and there's something here about debt collection fees and surcharges for late payment and

… He'd have paid it all back by now if it hadn't been for this coronavirus.'

'I think you need some proper debt counselling.' Chrissie was starting to feel out of her depth. 'Have you tried Citizens Advice?'

'No. How would I …?

'Their number will be in the phone book or you could Google it or – tell you what,' Chrissie added hurriedly, suddenly thinking of the potential for an unwary user to stumble across sites on the internet that might make her situation even worse. A novice like Yvonne could easily be taken in by unscrupulous "advisors" offering to consolidate her debts into one easy-to-pay loan, or some other scam. 'I'll do a bit of digging and ring you back with some numbers of people who'll give you advice without charging anything.'

LET'S GO FLY A KITE

'Would you?' Chrissie could feel the relief in Yvonne's voice. 'I'm sorry to be a bother; I just didn't know who else to ask.'

'Of course! It's no bother. I'm sure there must be someone out there who can he-.' She broke off suddenly as a thought struck her. 'You *have* had your compensation from the CICA, haven't you? That should've covered most of the funeral costs.'

'I don't think so. What's that? Trev did everything to do with the funeral. Like I said, I wasn't up to thinking about money when Harry was killed.'

'It's the Criminal Injuries Compensation Authority. Someone should've told you about it and helped you to apply. We got two and a half thousand for Kenny's funeral. Mind you, it only came through last week due to "delays in the system caused by COVID", which is only an excuse because we sent the form off back in January.'

'There was someone came round – family liaison, I think she said she was – with lots of forms to fill in. Would that be it?'

'Yes, probably. Did you send them off?'

'She came back for them, but Trev told her we could manage and we didn't want charity. That's what makes me think they were to do with money.'

'I think you ought to fill in the form,' Chrissie advised. 'It's not charity; it's just what you're entitled to. Tell Trevor it's like compensation because the police didn't keep Harry safe the way they should've done.'

'I don't think we've still got the forms,' Yvonne faltered.

'Don't worry. I expect I can find them for you – or Gavin will. There's probably an online version that may get the money quicker. I'll ask Gav and get back to you. But you still need to talk to a debt advisor to find out what you can do about that threatening letter in the meantime, while you're waiting for it to come through.'

'OK, I'll try.' Yvonne still sounded unsure of herself. 'But I don't think Trev … I think he didn't want to admit the forms were too complicated for him. He might not like it if I …'

'Let's cross that bridge when we come to it,' Chrissie declared decisively. 'I'll talk to Gav about it and I'm sure we'll be able to help. Now, how are you in yourself?' She knew that Yvonne's main way of coping with stress was to turn to alcohol.

'I'm doing OK – or I was until this letter came. Are you sure they can't come round and take our things away?'

'If the letter says thirty days, then they can't be intending to do anything before that,' Chrissie told her firmly. 'The main thing is to get proper advice now, so you can do something about it before then. Try not to worry. I'll talk to Gav and get back to you this evening, OK?'

She ended the call and put her phone back in her bag. Then she gazed across the field to where Gavin was in conversation with Wayne – at a distance of two metres, of course! He had wound in the kite and seemed to be pointing out elements of its construction to the young man. Perhaps he was advising him on how to make one for the boys. Then Gavin put the kite down on the ground and demonstrated how to launch it.

LET'S GO FLY A KITE

Chrissie smiled as it soared up into the sky again. No, she wouldn't interrupt his pleasure by asking him about Yvonne's money worries. There would be plenty of time for that during the drive home.

Perhaps half an hour later, she looked up from her knitting at the sound of young voices approaching from the woods. Harry scampered across the grass to Wayne, who was sitting on the bench again, reading a book. He scooped his son up onto his lap and hugged him. Then he pointed up at the kite, which was still flying high. 'Would you like to help me make one of those? Then we could all come up here and fly them together.'

'Yes please! When?'

'Well, I'll have to buy the stuff first,' Wayne smiled back. 'But, maybe next weekend. We'll have to wait and see.'

VICTIM STATEMENTS

They sat together watching. Gavin was starting to wind in the kite. Star was lolloping across the grass, running awkwardly with a muddy stick in her mouth. She came up to Wayne and sat down in front of him, gazing up expectantly.

'What's that you've got there?' he asked.

Star thumped her tail against the ground, continuing to watch him in case he decided to reach into his pocket for the treats that she knew he was carrying.

'It's just some stick she unearthed in the woods,' Dean told him, coming up and snapping the lead on to Star's collar. 'Drop it now, Star. It's time to go home.'

At the word "home" the dog got up and turned towards the car park, but she did not drop the stick. Carl stepped forward and stood in front of her.

LET'S GO FLY A KITE

'Give!' he commanded sternly.

Star hesitated. The stick was clearly a trophy that she did not want to leave behind.

'Give!' Carl repeated, taking hold of the stick by one end.

Star growled low in her throat and tightened her grip.

'Bad Star! Give! Now!' Carl said in a louder voice.

Star opened her mouth and released the stick.

'Good girl! Well done!' Carl patted her on the shoulder and looked towards Wayne, who fished in his pocket and brought out a dog treat. He handed it to Carl who presented it to Star. 'Good girl!' he repeated.

'Can I have that stick?' asked Wayne. 'It looks a bit odd to me.'

VICTIM STATEMENTS

Carl handed it over. Wayne held it, weighing it in his hand and frowning in puzzlement. Then he pulled up a handful of grass and wiped off some of the mud that coated its surface.

'I'm not sure this is a stick,' he said at last. 'It doesn't feel right. The weight's wrong for its size and look at the ends.'

Dean peered down at the object in his husband's hand. It was about fifteen inches long and about an inch thick in the middle, but much thicker at either end.

'I see what you mean,' he said slowly. He took the object from Wayne, holding it in the middle and twisting it round to look at it more closely. 'That end in particular looks almost like…'

'The ball in a ball-and-socket joint?' suggested Wayne.

'Ye-es,' Dean nodded. 'It's a bone, isn't it? Not a stick.'

'That's what it looks like to me.'

'A bone? asked Carl excitedly. 'D'you mean Star's found a body? Like in Midsomer Murders?'

'No,' Wayne said hastily. 'It'll just be from an animal.'

'What sort of animal?' demanded Harry.

'I don't know,' Dean confessed. He looked towards Wayne. 'A deer d'you think? It's big.'

'What's that you've got there?' Gavin had finished bringing the kite in to land and was standing next to Chrissie with it folded in his hand.

'Just something Star found in the woods,' Dean told him. 'We think it's a bone of some sort. We were just trying to think what sort of animal it could've come from.'

'Can I have a look?'

VICTIM STATEMENTS

Gavin put the kite down on the bench and Wayne passed the bone across to him. He stood staring down at it, wiping the mud off with his hand.

'Daddy Dean said it's from a deer,' Harry informed him.

'Yes, maybe,' Gavin murmured. He continued to stare down at the object in his hand. His mind was racing, trying to think of the best course of action.

'What do you think happened to it?' persisted Harry.

'I don't know, son.' Gavin smiled down on the boy momentarily before turning to Dean. 'Could you take me back to where she found it?'

'Yes, I suppose so.'

'Star can take you,' Carl piped up. 'She's going to be a police tracker dog. She'll show you – won't you Star?'

LET'S GO FLY A KITE

Gavin turned to Wayne. 'Can you keep the boys here while we go and have a look? You can give them a go with the kite if you like.'

'OK.' Wayne stared back and then nodded. 'Do you think there'll be any more – bones I mean?'

'I won't know until we look.'

'I want to come too!' protested Carl. 'I want to see Star finding the bones.'

'No Carl,' Wayne said firmly. 'You stay with me. Don't you want to fly the kite?'

'I'd rather find the body,' insisted Carl sulkily.

'No one said anything about a body. PC Hughes just needs to check that there's nothing there that needs reporting. Isn't that right Mr Hughes?'

Wayne looked towards Gavin, who nodded. 'That's right. If it's a deer that's been killed, that could be illegal shooting and we'd need to investigate. And whenever there's a crime scene you have to have as few people walking over it as possible so we don't destroy evidence.'

'Footprints and things?' asked Harry.

'That's right,' Gavin nodded. 'So it has to be just me and Daddy Dean and Star, I'm afraid.'

'You'll enjoy flying the kite,' Chrissie put in. 'I've got some hand sanitiser in my bag and a disinfectant spray. I'll spray the kite before you touch it, and then you boys had better put some sanitiser on your hands too, just to be on the safe side.'

Dean led the way back through the trees with Star on a short leash. Gavin followed carrying the bone. He wasn't an expert, but he had seen human remains before and this looked strikingly similar to a thigh bone that had been unearthed in the back garden of a man who had later been convicted of concealing the death of his elderly mother and claiming her pension for more than a decade.

'I think it was round about here that she picked it up,' Dean said, stopping and waving his arm round in a broad sweep to indicate an area of leaf mould to the left of the path.

'Do you think she'd be able to take us to the spot?'

'I doubt it. She's only a puppy. She hasn't been trained to do that sort of thing yet.'

'Oh well!' Gavin pushed forwards under the low-hanging branches, his eyes fixed on the ground, looking for any sign of disturbance or any more sticks that might turn out to be bones.

VICTIM STATEMENTS

Star watched for a few seconds and then pulled at the lead, eager to join in this new game. Dean let it out and allowed her to have her head. She bounded after Gavin barking excitedly. Her humans did not usually take enough interest in important things like sniffing under trees or digging in leaf mould. Then she quietened down and walked purposefully forward, her nose twitching. She pushed past Gavin, who had stooped down to examine a hole in the ground beneath a large beech tree. A few feet further on she stopped.

Dean hurried to catch her up, but before he could reach her, she had begun digging. Leaves and earth shot out behind her as she scrabbled in the soft ground with her strong front paws. The two men watched expectantly, wondering what had made her choose this particular spot for her excavation.

'Hang on!' Gavin had spotted a small, pale-coloured shape in amongst the debris that was piling up in Star's wake. 'I think that might be something. Can you hold her back for a bit?'

Dean stepped forward and took hold of the dog's collar. He pulled her away from the hole that she had dug. She whined in protest but eventually accepted defeat and lay down with her head on her paws.

'Have you found anything?' Dean called to Gavin.

'I think so.' He held up a small creamy-coloured object. 'I think this is another piece of bone.'

He got down on hands and knees and started digging in the soft soil with his fingers. It was slow work and he could feel Star's resentful gaze on him as if to say, 'let me do it. I'm better at it than you!'

Dean waited, wondering how long this was going to take. It was time they were getting home.

'Oh my God!' Gavin stood up and beckoned Dean to come closer. As he peered down into the shallow trench that Gavin and Star's combined efforts had excavated, his heart gave a lurch. That round shape with black, earth-filled eye sockets was not part of an animal skeleton; it was a human skull!

'OK,' Gavin said from behind him, business-like now that this was clearly a police matter. 'You'd better get back and take the kids home. Tell Chrissie that something's come up – work – and she should go home too. I'll make my own way back later. Don't talk to anyone about this; we've got to preserve the scene until the forensics people have been over it.'

For a few moments, Dean stood transfixed, unable to take in what he had just seen. Then he nodded and turned to go back, jerking the lead to let Star know that she should follow him.

Gavin took out his mobile phone and called for assistance. Then he stood there beneath the trees, staring round, mulling over in his mind what to do next. It was important to guard the scene to prevent any of the dog walkers, joggers and other visitors to the country park from trampling over the evidence or disclosing the find to the press or social media; but would the uniformed officers, who were now on their way, be able to locate him if he remained where he was?

He made his way back to the path through the woods and positioned himself where he could see back along it to the car park. Straining his ears, he could hear the sound of a car moving across the gravel surface. He hoped it was Dean driving the boys back home, safely out of the way before the forensic investigation began. A pair of runners came past, swerving wide to avoid coming too close to him. Gavin watched them go and then sat down on a fallen tree trunk and prepared to wait.

2. DEM BONES, DEM BONES

'I do feel we ought to try to do something for the Whittles,' Chrissie said, as she passed the gravy boat to Gavin. 'It's dreadful for them to be in debt just because of having to pay for their Harry's funeral.'

Gavin poured gravy over his leg of lamb with roast potatoes, and then passed it on to Craig, their lodger. Sunday lunch was still a traditional one in the Hughes household whenever Gavin was off-duty. After several months of extended shifts and reduced rest days, the number of police officers self-isolating through having come into contact with the virus had reduced, and he was enjoying the luxury of a whole weekend free of work commitments.

VICTIM STATEMENTS

'I'll have a word with Family Liaison and ask them to pay another visit,' he promised, 'but I gather Trevor's never been very keen on having them round there.'

'That's why I was wondering if *we* could do something – help them fill in the forms for compensation or get them some proper debt counselling or even-'

'I'm not that good with forms myself,' her husband put in quickly. 'There were so many people wanting to help when Kenny died that I just left it all to them. I can't even remember who it was that dealt with the CICA claim. I suppose it was probably the guy from the Police Federation, but there was that woman from the pension scheme who sorted out Kenny's death-in-service lump sum too ... and Pam Gregson from the custody suite, I think she helped with some of the paperwork … To be honest, I don't remember much about it. It's all just a bit of a blur, looking back.'

'Couldn't we just give them the money?' Chrissie suggested. 'To stop the interest carrying on mounting up. We don't really need Kenny's lump sum, do we? I mean, it's not as if he had any dependents or anything.'

'I don't think Trevor Whittle would like that,' Gavin objected. 'He'd think we were being patronising. It'd be like we didn't think they were capable of supporting themselves.'

'But it's not that,' Chrissie insisted. 'It's like you said just now: after Kenny was killed, we weren't in any fit state to sort out all those forms and things, but all sorts of people rallied round to help. Why didn't Yvonne and Trevor have people doing the same for them?'

VICTIM STATEMENTS

'Well, according to DC Ray, who was their Family Liaison Officer, one reason was Trevor didn't want anyone from the police interfering in their affairs,' Gavin told her with a sigh. 'He's his own worst enemy sometimes! Anyway, that's not the point. He's just not going to accept a handout from us, so you might as well forget it.'

'Well then, what about all that money people sent in for Kenny?' demanded Chrissie, unwilling to let go of her desire to do something practical to help Yvonne and her family and to do it immediately. 'People donated because they were shocked at the way he was killed. Surely, they'd want to help the Whittles too? I mean, the boy was only killed because he was the one person who might have told the police who it was who was driving the car that killed Kenny.'

DEM BONES, DEM BONES

'I don't know.' Gavin was still dubious. 'I think Trevor would still think it was charity. Anyway, it's not for us to decide. We agreed that the money ought to be given to Police Care[1], so we wouldn't need to worry about how to use it and nobody could say we were profiting from people's generosity.'

'Maybe in hindsight that was a mistake,' Chrissie grumbled. 'We ought to have thought about the Whittles. It's all very well for us: we've had the whole force rallying round to help us – and the public too! Not that I'm that keen on the way Kenny's face keeps popping up on the TV and in the papers. You'd think

---

[1] Police Care UK is a charity that provides support to serving and retired police officers and their families.

they could at least let us know beforehand, wouldn't you?'

'If you're so keen to help these Whittles, why don't you just give the money anonymously?' Craig asked.

'What? A couple of thousand pounds in used fivers, pushed through their letterbox in a brown envelope?' asked Gavin with a chuckle.

'I was thinking more: find out who they owe the money to and pay *them*. The way these loan sharks pile on the interest, they could owe twice as much before that stuff you're talking about from your criminal injuries compensation, or whatever it is, comes through. You know what those bureaucrats are like!'

'He's right Gav,' Chrissie agreed. 'That's the main thing, isn't it? Stop the interest mounting up while the compensation comes through! Couldn't we offer to *lend* them the money? That wouldn't be charity and –'

She broke off at the sound of the telephone ringing in the hall. Gavin got up and left the room to answer it, glad of an excuse to avoid any further discussion of the Whittles' financial plight. He was as sympathetic as Chrissie towards their situation, but her persistence in the naïve assumption that she could somehow put everything right for them was beginning to irritate him.

'Hello? Gavin? I hear you've found a body for us!' It was the unmistakably cheerful voice of DCI Jonah Porter. Gavin had heard that he was back at work, now that the government had decided that it was safe for people in the highly vulnerable "shielding" group to venture out of their homes again.

VICTIM STATEMENTS

'The Chief Super has assigned the case to me,' Jonah went on. 'I think she's decided I can't do much harm with a cold case like this, even if I am a bit past it. So now, I want you to tell me all about it. I gather it wasn't really a body as much as a heap of bones?'

'I don't really know that much,' Gavin hedged. 'You'd do better talking to Ruby Mann: she's the Crime Scene Manager.'

'I know,' Jonah sighed, 'but she won't speak to me. I'm only supposed to be working Tuesdays to Thursdays and someone's got at her to refuse my calls except when I'm on duty. That's what I meant about giving me a cold case: I'm obviously no longer to be trusted with anything that might be time-critical.'

'Then shouldn't I do the same?' Gavin asked, smiling to himself and shaking his head at his colleague's efforts to subvert

DEM BONES, DEM BONES

a system designed to prevent him from overworking.

'How's Chrissie doing?' Jonah's abrupt change of subject caught Gavin by surprise. He grunted something incoherent, but the senior officer carried on, 'I heard she was there when you found it. She's not too shaken up by it, I hope?'

'No, no, not all; she's fine,' Gavin stammered, still unsure what this was all about.

'That's good. I was afraid it might have been a bit of a shock for her, not being used to that sort of thing. Which of you was it who actually found the human remains?'

'Neither of us really. It was the dog.'

'I didn't realise you had one.'

'We don't. It wasn't ours it was …,' Gavin trailed off as he remembered that

VICTIM STATEMENTS

Jonah knew Wayne and Dean very well. It was their small engineering company that was responsible for designing his state-of-the art electric wheelchair.

'Yes? Go on! What about the dog?'

'Did you know that Dean O'Brien is one of our puppy socialisers now?'

'Yes. I gather it's all been a great success. Don't tell me it was Star who found the body?'

'It was. She dug up one of the leg bones, and then I unearthed the skull, and then I called for backup and left it to the SOCOs to dig up the rest.'

'Well, well, well! I must give Wayne and Dean a ring,' Jonah said happily, 'to check that the boys are OK,' he added, hearing Gavin's intake of breath at the remark. 'Just another pastoral call, like this one. Taking an interest in everyone's welfare.'

DEM BONES, DEM BONES

'If it's welfare you're talking about, what d'you know about debt counselling and criminal injuries compensation?' Gavin challenged, suddenly seeing an opportunity for getting help with Chrissie's anxiety over the Whittle family.

'Haven't you got all that sorted yet? Don't tell me you have to wait for the trial before they'll –'

'*We* have,' Gavin interrupted him, 'but Chrissie's worried about the Whittles. She's got pally with Mrs Whittle these last few months – with them both being mums who've lost a son – and now she's heard that they're finding it hard to pay back a loan they took out for the funeral. I gather they never got round to filling in the forms for compensation, and now –,' he broke off at the sound of voices from the other end of the line.

VICTIM STATEMENTS

'There you are, Jonah!' it was the unmistakable Liverpudlian tones belonging to Jonah's personal assistant, Bernie Fazakerley. 'Are you coming out with us or what? It's a beautiful day out there. You're not going to … oh! I see!'

'Just having a quick call with Gavin.' Jonah sounded defensive. He might be a senior police officer with authority over the likes of humble PC Gavin Hughes, but Bernie's remit to take care of his well-being extended to taking whatever steps were necessary to prevent him from pushing himself beyond what his body, weakened by a spinal injury more than a decade earlier, could stand.

'Pumping him for information about those bones he found? What are you like? Forget it. They'll keep until Tuesday.'

DEM BONES, DEM BONES

'No.' Gavin couldn't help smiling at the affronted tone in Jonah's voice. 'That wasn't what we were talking about at all. Gavin was asking of we could help Mr and Mrs Whittle with the forms for claiming compensation to pay for their son's funeral.'

'Mr and Mrs Whittle? That's the boy the Butler gang killed before Christmas, right? And they've not put in their claim yet?'

'They couldn't cope with the paperwork on top of everything else,' Gavin interjected, 'and now they're in debt, and Trevor Whittle's a taxi driver, which means he hasn't had any income to speak of since March.'

'If it's Criminal Injuries Compensation you're talking about, I don't mind having a look at it with them,' Bernie offered. 'It's a long time ago now, and I expect the forms have all changed, but I sorted that out for Peter when Angie was killed, so at least I've been there before.'

'Would you? That'd be great. Chrissie thought I could do it but ...'

'And doesn't the foodbank have a debt advisor they could talk to?' Bernie went on. 'Have you suggested they talk to them?'

'Chrissie said something about telling Yvonne to try Citizens Advice. I don't know if they'd want to go to the foodbank. Trevor doesn't like the idea of accepting charity. If we mention that to him, he may think Yvonne's been telling Chrissie that he can't feed his family. He's a bit old-fashioned that way.'

'Anyway, we ought to let you get on,' Bernie said firmly, seeing Jonah opening his mouth to ask another question. She had not been taken in by his claim that his telephone call had nothing to do with the "Shotover Skeleton" as the media were already calling it. 'We're probably keeping you from your Sunday dinner. Feel free to pass my number on to Yvonne Whittle and I'll be happy to do whatever I can.'

Recognising that protest would be futile, Jonah terminated the call with a movement of his finger on the keypad attached to the arm of his multifunctional wheelchair and then immediately started keying in another telephone number.

'Who're you calling now?' demanded Bernie. 'Not Andy Lepage or the SOCO team, I hope?'

'Nothing of the sort,' her friend smiled back. 'O ye of little faith! This isn't work. I just thought, now that we're allowed to meet with other households at home, we might invite Wayne and Dean to come over with the boys. They liked playing in the tree house last summer, and the lads can give the chair a service at the same time. It was due ages ago, but we kept putting it off because of Lockdown.'

'Yes,' Bernie conceded, still suspicious that Jonah was up to something, but unable to work out what. 'That's a good idea.'

Carl and Harry were delighted with the prospect of spending the afternoon at the house where Jonah lived with Bernie and her husband Peter. The large garden was perfect for all sorts of games and, as Carl explained loudly in the car on the way over, it would be good experience for Star to meet someone in a wheelchair.

DEM BONES, DEM BONES

'PC Stanton said she needs to be ready for anything. I bet she'll be surprised to see a man moving around sitting down!'

'Yes,' Dean agreed from the driving seat, 'but do you think *you* could stay sitting still instead of bouncing around like that? Have you both got your seatbelts fastened properly back there?'

They turned into the drive of the large house in the Headington area of Oxford – less than a mile, as the crow flies, from where Star had made her grisly discovery. Dean parked the car and went round to the back to release her from her cage, while Wayne opened the doors for the boys to climb out. Carl ran up the ramp to the front door to ring the bell, but before he could do so, Bernie appeared through the side gate and ushered them into the back garden.

VICTIM STATEMENTS

'We thought it would be better to stay out of the house,' she explained. 'It's such a nice day, there's no need to go indoors and it's supposed to be a lot safer meeting people out in the fresh air.'

They followed her round the side of the house to where Peter and Jonah were seated on the patio. Jonah greeted them enthusiastically.

'Come and sit down!' he called out. 'You can all sit round the picnic table and we'll stay over here, two metres away like good law-abiding citizens.'

'What would you boys like to drink?' Bernie asked, when they had all settled down on the two wooden benches on either side of the table. 'There's orange juice or lemonade – or I can make a brew.'

DEM BONES, DEM BONES

Once his minder was safely out of earshot fetching refreshments from the kitchen, Jonah turned to address Carl.

'I hear Star has started her career as a search dog. Tell me about how she found the bones.'

'She just went off into the trees and came back with it,' Carl told him, beaming with pride at being singled out by such an important police officer. 'You knew it was something special, didn't you, Star?'

Hearing her name, the dog leapt up from where she was lying under the table and put her front paws up on Carl's lap barking excitedly.

'Down, Star!' Dean said sternly. 'Down!'

The puppy bounced away across the patio, continuing to bark excitedly. Carl slipped off the bench and went after her. Dean stood up, ready to help, but holding back to give his son a chance to assert his authority over the wayward canine. The boy grasped hold of Star's collar with one hand and pressed down on her shoulders with the other. She continued to writhe and bark for a few seconds before finally giving in and settling down in a crouching position with her head resting on her large front paws.

'Good girl!" Carl praised her.

'I expect she's bored,' Dean told him. 'Why don't you take her for a run round the garden – if that's OK with you?" he added looking towards Peter, who nodded his acquiescence, waiting until the boys were some distance away before rounding on Jonah.

'What's all this about?' he demanded. 'Are you telling me it was Star who found those human remains over on Shotover?'

DEM BONES, DEM BONES

'So, when did you realise what it was she'd found?' Jonah asked, addressing the young men as if Peter had not spoken.

'It just looked a funny shape to me,' Wayne told him, 'but we assumed that, if it *was* a bone, it must be from some wild animal'

'Until PC Hughes started acting like there was something wrong,' Dean added. 'And then he unearthed the skull and that was when I realised it wasn't just ...'

'So, it was Gavin!' Peter suddenly put two and two together. 'You devious old ... Just wait till Bernie finds out what you've been up too; that's all I can say!'

'Oh yes!' As he spoke, Bernie herself rounded the corner of the house carrying a tray of glasses. 'What's he done now?'

VICTIM STATEMENTS

'It turns out that it was their dog that unearthed that skeleton yesterday,' Peter told her. 'Gavin must've let on when they were talking earlier and that's why he was so keen to invite them over this afternoon – not that we aren't very pleased to see you,' he added hastily, turning back to Wayne and Dean. 'It's just that Jonah's supposed to be taking it easy and only working the three days a week that he's paid for – and not all the hours God sends!' he finished, directing a hard stare in the offender's direction.

'I'm not working!' Jonah protested. 'We're just having a friendly chat about something interesting that happened yesterday – just the same as anyone might do. How're the boys?' he went on, studiously ignoring the black looks that Bernie was giving him. 'They don't seem traumatised by the incident.'

DEM BONES, DEM BONES

'Not at all!' Dean laughed. 'They just think it's exciting. They didn't see much – only the big bone that Star found, and that didn't look anything much – certainly nothing to give anyone bad dreams about. Carl's a bit cross that we wouldn't let them help dig up the rest of the skeleton, but he's so proud of Star for finding it!'

'What happens now?' asked Wayne. 'With the body, I mean.'

'Well, they'll have cordoned off the area to stop anyone getting in and destroying evidence,' Jonah explained. 'And they'll be going over it all with a fine-tooth comb looking for the rest of the skeleton. It could take days, or even weeks, depending on whether they're still all there together or if they've been scattered around by scavenging animals, for instance. Then, once they reckon they've found all the bones-'

'Will they join them all together to make a real skeleton?' None of the adults had noticed that Carl was back, standing behind his fathers and hanging on every word of their conversation.

'Yeah!' Harry piped up. 'The toe bone's connected to the foot bone, the foot bone's connected to the ankle bone-'

'The ankle bone's connected to the leg bone!' Carl joined in, singing raucously and shaking his limbs in a sort of dance, while Star leapt around excitedly, enjoying this new game.

'That's enough, boys,' Wayne said firmly, taking hold of Carl and sitting him down on the bench. 'Settle down and drink your juice.'

DEM BONES, DEM BONES

'And then afterwards, I'll show you the tree house,' Bernie promised.

'And in answer to your question,' Jonah said, ignoring signals from Peter to drop the subject, 'no, they won't join the bones together. Someone called a forensic anthropologist will look at them to try to work out what sort of person they belong to, and a forensic pathologist will look to see if the bones tell them anything about how whoever it was died.

'And then what?' asked Carl.

'Then the hard part starts,' Jonah told him. 'That's where the police come in. We have files on all the people who've been reported missing, going back years and years. We'll have to look back at them all and try to work out if any of them fit with what we know about the bones that Star found. The scientists will probably be able to tell us whether it was a man or a woman – or it could even be that there's more than one person buried there, we don't know yet – and they may be able to make a guess about what they might have looked like, but the chances are they'll be lots of different people that it might be. So, then we'll have to ask more questions and talk to more people and ... well, generally nose around being busybodies until we get the answers we need.'

'It usually takes a long time,' Peter added. 'It'll probably be months or even years before we know what happened.'

'And sometimes we never find out,' Jonah nodded.

'But Supercop here prides himself on being like the Mountie who always gets his man,' Bernie joked, 'so he'll be like a dog with a bone until he gets to the bottom of it all.'

DEM BONES, DEM BONES

'Woof!' Star got up from under the table, where she had been lying, panting after her run across the grass, and started pawing at Dean's leg.

'Look at that!' Harry squealed with delight. 'She wants to help too!'

'No,' Dean shook his head with a laugh. 'She just heard the word *bone* and thinks we must be offering her one. I brought a teething toy with us to keep her from chewing the furniture in Bernie's house. It's in the car. I'll go and get it for her.'

3. A POLICEMAN'S LOT

Gavin's shift began early the next day, but evidently not as early as the working day for the young journalist who was lurking in the street outside his house when he emerged through the side gate, pushing his bike.

'PC Hughes?'

'Yes? Can I help you?'

'I do hope so,' the young man gushed. 'I gather you were the one who found the body on Shotover Hill. What can you tell me about it?'

'Nothing, I'm afraid.' Gavin smiled back, trying not to betray his impatience. 'There'll be a press release when there's anything to say about it.'

'But you actually found it, didn't you? How did that happen?'

A POLICEMAN'S LOT

'As it said in the papers, a member of the public found it while they were walking their dog,' Gavin informed him firmly. 'And that's all I'm allowed to tell you. Now, I've got a burglary to attend, and I'm sure you have things to do too, so perhaps you wouldn't mind …?'

He pushed his bike past Chrissie's car, parked on the drive, and swung his leg over the saddle. The young man stood for a few moments looking dissatisfied, then, seeing that Gavin was waiting for him to move before setting off, he turned and started walking away. Apparently satisfied, Gavin pushed off and cycled past him, giving a friendly wave before taking the first turning on the left.

Once he was out of sight behind a tall hedge, he stopped again, got out his mobile phone and dialled his own home number.

'Chrissie? I just thought I'd warn you: there's a journalist hanging around outside wanting to ask about the Shotover business. I don't know whether he knows you were there too, but he may try to collar you when you go out anyway. Just be ready to give him the brush-off – and you'd better warn Craig not to say anything too.'

He ended the call, turned his bike round and pushed it back to the corner of the street. Sure enough, there he was, walking nonchalantly past the end of their drive.

Gavin smiled. He didn't fancy the young man's chances if he accosted Chrissie when she set off for her work in a school for children with special educational needs. She had no love for journalists, especially not since enduring the media circus that had accompanied Kenny's death. Although the press had been overwhelmingly supportive following the murder, that hadn't lessened the violation of their privacy during the most traumatic time of their life together. And as for Craig! Well, he wouldn't stand any nonsense from a wet-behind-the-ears reporter like that one, especially if he looked as if he posed a threat to Chrissie. Just so long as it didn't turn physical – they could do without Craig getting accused of assault …

He pedalled purposefully along, heading for the Cowley Road area where the burglary had taken place. It was in the next street from where Stella Gilbert, the young PC whom he was supervising, lived; so he had arranged to pick her up on the way. He also hoped to pick her brains about the neighbourhood and any other recent criminal activity there.

Stella was waiting for him outside the Victorian terraced house where she lived with her grandmother and half-brother.

'I don't know anyone in that road personally,' she told him in answer to his queries, as they walked along together pushing their bicycles. 'I think quite a few of the houses have been converted into student accommodation. I haven't heard of any other burglaries recently. Gran would know – she hears all the local gossip!'

'This is a Mrs Langdon, living alone, who went to the bathroom in the night and noticed the light was on downstairs. When she went down, she found a window open and called 999. There was nobody available to attend and, with the intruder having gone, it wasn't a priority, so we're going to be the first officers on the scene, and we can expect her to be upset that it's taken us five hours to get to her.'

'Only five hours? So, when you say "in the night" you really mean early this morning?'

'That's right. The call was logged at three twenty-seven.'

'So, not even five hours,' Stella commented, looking down at her watch. 'I've heard stories of people waiting longer than that for an emergency ambulance!'

'You've got to remember that she's on her own and someone's broken into her house and messed with her things.'

'Unless she left the light on and the window open herself,' Stella suggested. 'It sounds like a scatty old lady getting confused to me!'

'Well, we'll soon see. This is the house.'

Gavin fumbled with the gate at the entrance to a small front garden, surrounded by a low brick wall. Eventually, it swung open, creaking on rusty hinges. There was a red-and-black tiled path leading to the front door. The rest of the garden was covered with uneven paving and almost filled with three wheelie bins in assorted colours. He pressed the bell and stood back to wait for an answer.

A minute or two later, Stella saw the net curtains twitching in the bay window. A face peered out momentarily and then vanished again. She could hear footsteps inside the house. Finally, the door opened and an elderly woman looked out at them. Her hair was dyed auburn with grey roots growing out. She would no doubt be pleased that hairdressers were now once more permitted to take appointments.

'You took your time!' she greeted them. 'I suppose you'd better come in.'

'Thank you, madam,' Gavin answered politely, wiping his feet carefully on the mat before entering. 'I'm PC Hughes and this is PC Gilbert. I'm sorry that nobody was available sooner. We're rather hard-pressed at the moment with the coronavirus pandemic.'

'Well, I suppose now you're here, you'd better come through.'

They followed her down a dark hallway into the kitchen, which was a single-storey outrigger at the back of the house.

There's where they got in,' she said, pointed towards the traditional-style sash window, now closed. 'When I came down it was open at the bottom.'

Gavin wandered across to it and examined the fastening. It refused to move when he attempted to twist it round into the locked position.

'Was this how it was when you went to bed last night?' he asked mildly, conscious that this question might sound like an accusation that she had brought her misfortune on herself through inadequate security.

'Yes,' she confirmed. 'I sometimes open this window at the top, but never at the bottom. That's how I knew someone had been in.'

'I see,' Gavin nodded. 'Can I have a look at the outside now, please?'

Mrs Langdon opened the back door and Stella followed Gavin out. She watched as he examined the woodwork of the window. The paint was peeling and the wood beneath gave way when he poked it with his house key. Putting his gloved hands flat on the glass, he pushed upwards. As he applied more pressure, the window slid up and soon he was able to get his fingers under it and open it fully.

'It's easy enough to see how someone could've got in,' he murmured. 'They wouldn't even need a jemmy.'

'Aren't you going to dust it for fingerprints?' Mrs Langdon called from the kitchen doorway.

'Well, I *could* ask forensics to send someone round,' Gavin said apologetically, 'but they're very busy at the moment, so I doubt if it'd be for a while. And these days, most criminals – even youngsters – know all about all that, and they wear gloves.'

VICTIM STATEMENTS

He looked down at the ground beneath his feet. 'No chance of footwear marks either, with so much concrete about. I'm sorry, Mrs Langdon, but it's always very difficult to find the perpetrators of this sort of crime. There's nothing here to tell us who it was – certainly nothing that would stand up in court. Now, if you can give me a list of anything that's missing, we can do our best to see if we can get any of it back for you.'

'How can you do that, if you don't even know who took it?' demanded Mrs Langdon scathingly.

'It all depends how identifiable it is,' Gavin explained patiently. 'If you mark items such as TV sets, videorecorders, computers and so on with your post code, then it'll be hard for them to be sold on. Then they may be dumped when the criminals realise, or if they're amateurs, sometimes they even try to flog them and get caught that way. Jewellery's another thing: we have a good relationship with various businesses that buy second hand stuff and they let us know if someone brings in something suspicious. Perhaps we can all go back in and we can sort out that list?'

'I think I must've disturbed them,' Mrs Langdon told them when they were back in the kitchen. 'They didn't take much. If you'd come as soon as I rang, you might have caught them before they got away.'

'So, did you hear them moving about in the house?' asked Stella.

'I didn't realise till afterwards, but that must've been what woke me up. I went to the bathroom, and then when I came out, I saw the light was on downstairs; so I went down and then I saw the window had been forced.'

'It was brave of you to go downstairs when you thought there was a burglar down there,' Stella said innocently, still unconvinced of the existence of the intruder.

'I didn't think about that at the time,' Mrs Langdon admitted, flashing a look of annoyance at the young officer. 'I thought I must've left the light on – although that's something I never do.'

'Getting back to what was stolen,' Gavin put in gently, getting a notebook out of his pocket. 'If you could just take me through the items and I'll write a list.'

'Well, I haven't been over the whole house, so there might be some things I haven't noticed …'

'That's alright,' Gavin assured her. 'Take your time. You can let us know about anything else later. Just tell me about what you know about now.'

'We-ell,' the householder seemed surprisingly reluctant to be pinned down on the question of her exact losses. 'Like I said, they must've run off before they had time to find much. All that's gone – as far as I can see – is some cash from the kitchen drawer.'

'Could you show me?' Gavin enquired.

Mrs Langdon walked over to a drawer and pulled it open. She took out a square biscuit tin of the sort that contains "traditional highland shortbread" and opened it. 'There was close on nine hundred pounds in here. Now look!'

Gavin and Stella looked. The tin contained a few one- and two-pound coins and some smaller change, totalling no more than ten or twenty pounds in all.

VICTIM STATEMENTS

'It was my holiday money,' Mrs Langdon explained. 'I put something away out of the housekeeping each week.'

'I see.' Gavin handed the tin back to her. 'And when did you last look inside?'

'Friday, after I did the weekend shop.'

'And the money was all still there then?'

'Yes, of course. I know you think because I'm old I must have dementia and I'm imagining it all, but I know there was someone in here last night and they've taken my savings.'

'Yes. I'm sorry, madam, I just need to get everything down straight in my notes.'

'There's not much mess,' Stella observed. 'It looks as if whoever it was knew where to look. Who else knew that you kept money in that drawer?'

'Well, no one – no one except my son, Robert.'

'You haven't had anyone round recently – doorstep sales people, meter-readers or anything like that?' suggested Gavin.

'Now you mention it, I did have a plumber in to fix the kitchen tap last week. I suppose he could've looked in the drawer while he was here.'

'Can you give us his name?'

'I can't remember. I got it out of one of those free newspapers they keep pushing through the door these days.'

'Did he give you a receipt, perhaps?' Gavin coaxed. 'That would have his business name on it.'

'Yes, I'm sure he did. That would be in here.' Mrs Langdon pulled open another drawer and took out another tin. This one had a photograph of Caernarfon

Castle on the lid and the caption "Croeso i Gymru!" She opened it and small pieces of paper fell out on to the work surface.

'Here it is! SJ Evans, Plumbing and Heating. I remember now, he called himself Steve.'

'Excellent!' Gavin smiled. 'I'll just note that down.' He wrote the name and telephone number in his notebook and then handed the receipt back to Mrs Langdon. 'Now, I'll give you a crime reference number so that you can claim on the insurance and, unless there's anything else you want to tell us, we'll get out of your hair. Oh! One other thing: is this a rental property or are you the owner?'

'What business is that of yours?' Mrs Langdon asked sharply.

'It's only, that window's in a bad state. It needs attention to make it secure. We could write a report for you to give to your landlord. They're obliged to do repairs to keep the house safe.'

'Well, there's no need. It's my own house. I've been living here nearly sixty years. It'd have been our diamond wedding next week if Jim hadn't had his heart attack.'

'Then can I suggest you get someone to look at that window for you? Really it needs replacing. A modern one with double-glazing might save you money on your heating bills too. Now here's what you need for your insurance. I'll go and file a report and we'll be in touch if–'

'Mum!' Gavin broke off at the sound of a man's voice in the hall. Mrs Langdon took the piece of paper that he was holding out to her as she passed him on the way out of the kitchen to greet its owner.

VICTIM STATEMENTS

This turned out to be a grey-haired man, nearly as tall as Gavin but less muscular – plump rather than well-built. He gave his mother a peck on a cheek and then strode past her to speak to the police officers.

'So, you found time in your busy schedule to come out to an old lady who's had her house broken into, did you?' he snarled sarcastically. 'I don't suppose there's much chance of you finding the vermin who did it, is there?'

'I'm afraid not, sir,' Gavin replied politely. 'I've given your mother the information she needs to make a claim from the insurance and I'll arrange for a community support officer to come round and give her some advice on security. And now, we'll leave you to–'

'Not so fast.' The man set his feet wide apart and stood with his arms folded barring the route to the front door. 'I want to know why it took you so long. My mum called you at three something this morning-'

'Three twenty-seven,' Stella added helpfully.

'– and now it's …'

'Eight forty-two,' Stella filled in for him as he pulled out his phone to check the time.

'That's right. My eighty-three-year-old mother was left quaking in her bed, fearing for her life, while you lot … I've come all the way over from Abingdon, I'll have you know!'

'I'm sorry, sir. We have to prioritise our resources.'

'And how come a vulnerable old lady in a house on her own isn't a priority? When I told her to ring 999, I never thought it'd take this long for anyone to come out to her.'

'As I said sir, I can only apologise that we don't have the resources to attend every call right away.' Gavin reflected to himself that, if he was so concerned about his mother's welfare, Robert Langdon could have come over during the night himself. "All the way from Abingdon" was in reality a mere twenty minutes' drive, especially now that the pandemic had reduced the traffic so much, but he remained polite and professional. 'Now, I need to go and file the information that your mother has given us, so that the break-in can be investigated fully, and I have two more households to visit this morning as well, so if you wouldn't mind stepping aside?'

A POLICEMAN'S LOT

'Come on, Robert,' Mrs Langdon urged. 'Come and sit down and I'll put the kettle on.'

After a moment's hesitation, Robert Langdon moved out of the way to allow Gavin and Stella to make their way to the front door and out into the morning sunshine.

'What do you think really happened?' Stella asked as they unlocked their bikes. '*I* don't think there was a break-in at all. I think she left the light on and the window open herself and forgot about it. Old people do that sort of thing, don't they?'

'What about the money?'

'She put it somewhere else and forgot about it. Or maybe her son borrowed it or she spent it. Didn't you hear what he said? She only rang for the police because he told her to. She obviously rang him first and he didn't want to get out of bed to come to her, so he told her to ring us. She's probably doing it all the time and he just wanted to shut her up!'

'Maybe, but we can't possibly be sure of that. And we can't rule out that someone really did break in and take the money.'

'So, are you going to investigate this Steve Evans guy – the plumber?'

'*I'm* not going to investigate anything. That's not our job. I'm just going to write my report and leave it to CID to decide what to do about it.'

'It's a bit hard on him if he's under suspicion just because some old bat can't remember where she put her savings,' Stella muttered. 'What was she doing having nine hundred pounds in cash lying around in the house anyway?'

'I know, I know,' Gavin sighed. 'We can only advise. We can't make people do the sensible thing. Let's hope for her sake that she has just misplaced that money. There's no way we're going to get it back for her and I doubt the insurance company will pay out either. They'll probably agree with you that she shouldn't have kept so much cash in the house. Now, on your bike! We need to pay a visit to the Whittles, to offer some more advice that will probably be ignored!'

'It looks as if Mr Whittle must be working,' Stella said, pointing at the empty space on the drive where a silver taxi usually stood.

'Yes. Yvonne told Chrissie that business was looking up,' Gavin agreed.

'I'm glad Trevor's out. That will make things much easier.'

'What is it we're here for?' Stella asked as they approached the front door of the modest post-war terraced house, built by the council but now managed by a housing association.

'A spot of Family Liaison,' Gavin told her. 'Chrissie wants me to help them with getting compensation for Harry's death.'

'I thought there were officers from CID who specialised in that. Won't they have had someone assigned to them?'

'Yes, but Trev didn't get on with them and they've rather fallen through the net, according to Chrissie. Yvonne rang her at the weekend worried about a loan that Trevor took out to pay for the funeral, and I promised Chrissie I'd call round and offer to help.'

A POLICEMAN'S LOT

He knocked on the front door and then stood back to wait. Glancing up at the house from further down the drive, Stella saw a face looking out at them from the front bedroom window. It was Leo, the Whittle's thirteen-year-old son. She waved and smiled, but his only response was to move away from the window.

The door opened and Yvonne Whittle looked out. Gavin studied her appearance carefully. She was casually dressed in a lavender-coloured short-sleeved top over dark purple trousers with an elasticated waist. Her hair was parted in a straight line over the top of her head and held back in a neat bun at the nape of her neck by an elastic band concealed beneath a gauzy purple scarf. It moved gently in the draught from the door making the silver pattern printed on it glint in the morning sunshine.

VICTIM STATEMENTS

Turning his attention to her face, he noted that her eyebrows had been plucked into graceful arches above her deep brown eyes, which appeared tired and were a little bloodshot, but he was relieved to see that they did not have the glassy look that they took on when she had been drinking. It looked as if her cry for help to Chrissie had been her first, rather than her last, resort when she realised what financial trouble they were in.

'Oh! Hello!' she looked enquiringly up at Gavin then across to Stella and back.

'This is just a routine visit,' Gavin told her, 'to keep you informed about the situation regarding the trial. You may have heard that Oxford Crown Court re-opens today.'

'No. I hadn't heard about that.' Yvonne shook her head, making the pendulous earrings that she was wearing shake and tinkle. 'Does that mean the men who did it will be put back in jail now?'

'No, I'm afraid not. They're still out on bail. And I'm afraid that it may still be quite some time before they come to trial, because of the backlog of cases. I just wanted you to know that things are starting to move in the right direction at last.'

'Thank you. It was kind of you to think about us.'

'Not at all. You have a right to be kept informed. And there was something else,' Gavin added, detecting a slight movement as if Yvonne were thinking of closing the door again. 'Chrissie told me you'd been having some trouble filling in some of the forms we gave you. I can get you some help with that.'

VICTIM STATEMENTS

'You'd better come in.' Yvonne retreated into the house. Stella pulled out a face mask from her pocket and held it up towards Gavin with a questioning look on her face. Wearing face masks was not yet compulsory except on public transport, but government guidance had shifted in the last few weeks and it was now considered advisable in enclosed spaces. Gavin shook his head silently, judging that anything that might increase Yvonne's anxiety or impede communication was to be avoided. Stella put the mask away again and followed him through the front door.

She looked up at the stairs. Some six months ago, Mrs Whittle had returned from her early morning cleaning job to find her older son's body hanging from the bannisters. It must have been the first thing she saw when she opened the front door. Stella pictured the scene in her mind: Yvonne coming in, wearing her winter coat because it was a cold day in December, maybe with it already half off because she only had a short time before she'd be going out again to her next job, stopping in her tracks as she saw Harry's legs dangling in front of her, then running forward to help him and finally realising that there was nothing she could do for her firstborn son.

'Come through here.' At the sound of Yvonne's voice, Stella pulled her mind back to the present and followed Gavin through a door on the left into the lounge.

'Excuse the mess. I haven't had time to tidy up after Trev and Leo had a boys' night in watching the football last night.' Yvonne darted round the room picking up crisp packets and drink cans. 'Sit down both of you. Would you like some tea?'

'Better not,' Gavin said quickly. 'Social distancing – you know!'

'OK.' Yvonne stood hesitating in the doorway. 'Do you mind if I just take these to the bin?'

'That's fine. Go ahead.'

They sat down at either end of the sofa. While they were waiting for Mrs Whittle to return, Gavin looked round the room. Now that Yvonne had removed the debris of the previous night's snacks, it looked tidier that he had seen it before. There was a pile of magazines stacked neatly on a shelf beneath the television set – not spread out across the chairs as if their readers had not had the energy to put them down, but had simply allowed them to drop where they were sitting. The low table in front of the settee was empty – not overflowing with assorted bits and pieces. Things were looking good. The discovery that her family was in debt had not (yet) sent her back into that dark spiral of alcoholism and depression.

'I looked out these forms.' Yvonne was back, holding a sheaf of papers in her hands. 'But I don't think all the bits are here anymore.'

She laid them out on the table in front of Gavin and then sat down on a chair at the other end of the room. Gavin looked down at the papers. He saw that some of the boxes had been filled in, but most were still blank. The pages were all jumbled up, leaping from 3 to 9 and then back to 1 – or was that the first page of a different form altogether?

'I tried ringing Citizens Advice, like Chrissie said,' Yvonne told him, while he was still trying to make some sense of the paperwork, 'but I guess they don't work at weekends.'

Gavin looked up.

'Look, I'll be honest with you: I'm not much good with these things myself, but I know someone else who can help you to fill them in. If I give you her number, will you ring her?' He reached into his pocket and took out a small piece of card on which he had written down Bernie's name and mobile number. He put it down on the table and, after a moment's hesitation, Yvonne reached out and picked it up.

'Bernie Faz – Fayzay – what does that say?'

'Fuh-**zack**-er-lee. Bernie Fazakerley. She's married to an old friend of mine. His wife – that is his first wife – was killed by a gang of youths. That was years ago now, but Bernie did the forms for him to get compensation, and she's offered to do the same for you, if you'd like.'

'Bernie's a funny name for a woman.'

'It's short for Bernadette, but everyone calls her Bernie. Just give her a call. You'll like her.'

'I don't know.' Yvonne slipped the card into a concealed pocket in the front of her trousers. 'Some of the questions on those forms are very … very *personal*, if you know what I mean. I'm not sure Trev would like me talking about them with a stranger.'

'But this is money you're entitled to,' Stella said earnestly, leaning forward and putting out her hand towards Yvonne's, then remembering social distancing and hastily withdrawing it. 'You've been through an awful time and you owe it to yourself to take what's yours to – to – to make it just a little bit less absolutely awful. Do you see what I'm getting at? It's your right to have compensation and you shouldn't let some stupid forms stop you getting it.'

'Stella's right,' Gavin said gently. 'And I'd add to that that you wouldn't just be doing it for yourself. Think about Leo: he must know something's up. Seeing you worried about that money's bound to make him worried too.'

'My gran always says it was looking after me and my brothers that kept her going after my mum died,' Stella chipped in, suddenly remembering and hoping that this might be a helpful remark.

'You lost your mum?' Yvonne looked at Stella as if noticing her for the first time.

'It was a long time ago,' Stella said quickly. 'I was hardly old enough to remember. I'm just grateful to my gran for taking us on.'

'OK.' Yvonne turned her attention back to Gavin. 'I'll give your friend a ring about the compensation, and I'll have another go with Citizens' Advice. I have to pick my moments though: Trev would get mad at me if he knew I'd told anyone about us owing money. He'd think I was making out he wasn't man enough to look after us. You know how it is.'

Gavin nodded silently. He and Chrissie had always enjoyed the benefit of safe public sector jobs providing a combined income in excess of their modest needs, but he understood the insecurity felt by men on low wages whose self-respect depended on their ability to provide for their families. It must have been difficult for Trevor Whittle over the past few months when their only income had been from Yvonne's furlough payments topped up with various benefits – always assuming that they had navigated the complex application system! Perhaps he ought to ask Bernie to check out Universal Credit as well as Criminal Injuries Compensation when she spoke to Yvonne.

'So, you won't let on to him about me ringing Chrissie, will you?'

'No, of course not, and when you've got the forms filled in and sent off, you can tell him that you got a follow-up from Family Liaison while he was out, and they insisted on putting them in for you,' Gavin suggested.

Yvonne nodded. 'Yes. I'll do that. He'll be pleased when we've got the money. It's just … he doesn't like to think we need to beg for anything. You know what I mean?'

Gavin nodded again. He got to his feet to signify that they were leaving. Stella followed suit.

'And how's young Leo?' Gavin asked, glancing up the stairs, as they stepped out into the hall. 'It must be boring for him on his own all day.'

'Yes,' Yvonne nodded. 'He's been very good about it, but it *has* been hard for him. He's meeting up with some of his mates later, to play basketball in the park. That is allowed now, isn't it?' she added anxiously, suddenly aware that she could have got her son into trouble if this would be breaking the COVID-19 regulations.

'Yes. That's right,' Gavin confirmed, hoping that he had remembered the rules correctly. There was something about "close-contact team sports" still being banned, but he wasn't sure exactly what that meant and he would certainly have been hesitant about trying to prevent Leo and his friends from enjoying their game. 'Outdoor sport is allowed from today.'

VICTIM STATEMENTS

They walked down the drive and out into the road. Looking back, Gavin saw Leo's dark brown face at the bedroom window, staring out at them with anxious brown eyes. Was he worried about his mother? She had seemed more together than she had usually been since the earthquake of Harry's shocking death, but was that just a front that she had put on for their benefit?

'Where to now?'

He turned away abruptly to address Stella's question. 'Lewes Road. I want to call on Wayne and Dean to check that the boys are both OK after finding those bones the other day.'

It turned out that the boys were excited, rather than traumatised, by their discovery. Gavin and Stella found them sitting at a table in the garden with their school books. Star was in her run chewing busily on a raw bone. They looked up hopefully when Dean led the visitors round the side of the house to join them, sensing an opportunity for a break from their studies.

'Hello PC Hughes!' called out seven-year-old Harry. 'Come and look at my picture! I'm writing my news for Mrs Taylor. It's all about Star and how she found that skeleton in the woods.'

He held up an exercise book to display a drawing of a dog, recognisable as Star by the black-and-brown colouring, with a large bone protruding from either side of its mouth.

'Very good!' Gavin said, wondering what the boy's teacher would make of his story. It must be quite rare for "What I did at the weekend" to involve finding a mysterious body hidden in a shallow grave in the woods.

'Have you found out how it got there?' demanded Carl, looking up from his latest mathematics works sheet. 'Was it a murder?'

'No,' Gavin told him solemnly, trying to dampen down the boy's enthusiasm. 'These things take time. First, they have to find all the bones, and then some clever scientists will have to look at them and do tests to find out how long they've been there. They could be really, really old bones, from hundreds of years ago. If they are, then there won't be any point investigating because everyone who knew them will be dead.'

'What will happen to the bones then?' asked Carl.

'I don't exactly know,' Gavin confessed. 'If they're very old indeed then they might hand them over to a museum for clever people to study to see if it tells them anything about how people used to live in the olden days.'

'Will they put them in a glass case?' Harry asked, 'like those funny black heads[2] we saw when we went there?'

'No, I don't think so. They'll just keep them in the back somewhere until they've finished with them and then I expect they'll just bury them somewhere – in a proper grave in a cemetery.'

'And if they're *not* very, very old?' persisted Carl.

'Then they'll have to try to find out who the bones belong to and how they

---

[2] The *Shuar Tsantsas* or shrunken heads, which were displayed in the Oxford Pitt Rivers Museum for many years, were removed from public view in September 2020, following an ethical review.

died,' Gavin told him, 'but like I said, it'll take a long time.'

'Why?' Carl sounded disappointed. In the television crime dramas that he was fond of watching, the whole case always seemed to be completed within a matter of days.

'These things just do,' Gavin told him. He was beginning to wonder if it had been a bad idea to call round. All he had done was to re-ignite the boys' interest, which was already greater than was healthy. He consoled himself with the thought that at least they weren't having nightmares about their experience. Either the care that he had taken to avoid them being present when any clearly identifiable human remains were unearthed had paid off, or they were just less sensitive to such things than he had feared.

A POLICEMAN'S LOT

'Aunty Bernie said Uncle Jonah will find out what happened,' Harry told him earnestly. 'She said-'

He broke off as Gavin turned away, bending his head to listen to a voice coming through on his police radio. 'I'm sorry, boys, we're going to have to go. There's been an incident reported and we're needed. That's a great picture of Star. I'm sure your teacher will like it.'

4. POST MORTEM

Jonah, too, was frustrated at the slow pace of developments. Bernie had stood firm throughout Sunday and Monday, refusing to drive him over to view the crime scene for himself while he was officially off-duty.

'Tuesday will be quite soon enough,' she insisted. 'You can't do anything until they've found enough of the bones to have a chance of telling how many bodies there are and how long they've been there.'

Jonah pulled a face and toyed with the idea of making a break for it and going over there on his own in his all-terrain electric wheelchair. It was less than a mile to Shotover if you cut along the path through the CS Lewis Nature Reserve. The battery would definitely last out to get him there and, if it packed in on the way back, he could telephone for Bernie to come and rescue him. Why did she have to be so awkward about it all, anyway? Just because, technically, it wasn't a working day, it was unreasonable of her to expect him to forget about such an interesting case.

After plotting his escape in his mind for about twenty minutes, wiser counsels prevailed and he resigned himself to another day at home. If he did start out on his journey, it would not be long before his absence was noticed. Bernie and Peter would feel obliged to abandon whatever activities they had planned and come after him. They had already given up so much of their freedom in order to look after him, the least he could do was to stick by the rules. He did not often dwell on his disability, but now he silently raged against the injustice of the bullet that had rendered him dependent on technology and his friends' goodwill to live anything resembling a normal life.

For the tenth time, he punched Ruby Mann's number into the keypad on the arm of his chair and asked her for an update on the search of the crime scene. She sighed, and he could picture her eyes lifted skywards as she informed him that they had recovered a few more bones that morning and had now extended their activity to a wider area covering the whole of that part of the woodland. She had someone preparing an inventory of everything that they had found, of which she would upload a copy for him to look at in the morning. No, there was nothing of particular note to report yet.

POST MORTEM

By mid-morning on Tuesday, the bones had been transferred to the mortuary. Forensic anthropologist, Penelope Black looked up and smiled when the door opened and Bernie came in, holding it wide to allow Jonah's chair through. Detective Sergeant Andy Lepage followed them in and closed the door behind him.

'It looks as if it's just one body,' she told him. 'The skeleton is fairly complete. There are just some of the smaller bones missing: fingers, toes one or two of the vertebrae. The SOCOs are looking for them, but there's been some animal activity which may have dispersed them.'

She held up a rib and pointed out serrations on one edge, which she identified as the tooth marks of small rodents.

'What can you tell me about them?' Jonah asked.

'It's an adult female. Quite small: I'd estimate 155 centimetres – that's about five foot one in old money. Probably European ancestry, but could be Asian; I'd be amazed if she turned out to be African, the nasal aperture is quite wrong.'

'And how long since she died?'

'Difficult to say with any accuracy.'

'Care to hazard a guess?'

'Not really.'

'Go on! Force yourself.'

Penny sighed. 'Well, she'd certainly been in the ground for some time. I'd say ten years minimum, could well be more – several decades maybe.'

Jonah said nothing but continued to look up at her hopefully, so she went on.

'The soft tissues have decayed completely, as have any clothes that she may have been wearing when she was buried. The bones are discoloured from lying in the soil and some of them have cracked, which suggests they've been there for a good long time. As I showed you, there has been gnawing by rodents and there's some root growth through some of the bones. All of these things point to the body having been there for a long time. Exactly how long is impossible to tell. We've taken some samples of the soil and leaf mould from the scene because the composition of the soil affects the speed of decomposition, but it's unlikely that the results will narrow down the window.'

VICTIM STATEMENTS

'So, if we're going to look back through the Missing Persons files, how far do we need to go?' enquired Jonah.

'That depends more on how far back you think it's worth investigating,' Penny said. 'As far as the science goes, there isn't really a limit I can give you, but there could be other considerations.'

'Such as?'

'Well, the question I'm asking myself is "why wasn't it found before?" There can't have been anyone digging around in that part of the wood since the body was put there. So, how long has it been left alone? Are those trees wild ones or were they planted, and if so, when?'

'I think Shotover is ancient woodland,' Bernie said. 'I'm pretty sure I read somewhere it used to be part of a royal forest.'

'But a lot of work's been done since they made the country park' Jonah pointed out. 'I suppose that could give us a bit of a fix on when the latest is that a body could have been put there. It's still going to be like looking for a needle in a haystack if we can't get any better idea of what sort of person we're looking for. How about doing a facial reconstruction?'

'It'd be expensive,' Penny told him, 'and it'd take time.'

'Hmm,' Jonah pondered. 'Yes. I suppose we'd better leave that until we're sure we need it. What about DNA?'

'It can be done, but it's not straightforward getting DNA from bones. It'd be expensive, and it'd take time.'

'And not much use until we've got something to compare it with,' Jonah finished for her. 'OK then, what else have we got? Dental records? What's the state of her teeth?'

'Better than I might have expected, given the length of time since death. The skull and mandible are both intact and a majority of the teeth are still in situ. The SOCOs have retrieved a couple of the ones that had fallen out and they're sifting through the soil in case there are any more. So, as soon as you've got a possible identification, we ought to be able to confirm it from her teeth.'

'As soon as we've got one,' Jonah echoed. 'Isn't there anything to get us started? No personal effects of any sort near the body?'

'As I said, whatever clothes she had on have decayed or been taken by animals; even synthetic fabrics are popular with mice and rats for nest-building. However, there were a couple of things you might like to have a look at.'

Penny led them over to a bench at the side of the room and picked up a plastic evidence bag. She held it up in front of Jonah's face.

'This buckle could have been on a belt that she was wearing, maybe off a coat? It looks mass-produced, but if you can find out when they started making them, it might give you that "earliest possible" date that you're looking for.'

'OK,' Jonah nodded. 'Can you send me some photographs? And what about this fabric that's attached to it? Does that tell us anything?'

'I'm no expert,' Penny answered, 'but I know a man who is. I'll get them to have a look at it and see if they can come up with anything.'

'Good. Now we're getting somewhere.'

'The other thing that may interest you,' Penny said with a note of triumph in her voice, 'is this!'

She picked up another evidence bag and, smiling broadly, held it up for Jonah to see, conscious that she had saved the best find until last.

Jonah peered at the bag, trying to make out what the small object inside it was. It comprised two small rectangles of some metal joined together by a short chain. Cuff-links! Or rather, a cuff-link. Not something that you saw very often these days: most shirts had buttons on their sleeves. Cuff-links were only for formal attire, such as you might wear with a dinner jacket. But then, Oxford was a place where formal occasions were happening all the time: college gaudies, Schools dinners, Commem Balls, …

Bernie took the bag from Penny's hand and smoothed it out so that the object inside it was easier to see clearly. 'I recognise that crest: it's the Lichfield College arms.'

She held it out towards Jonah, who peered closer and saw a black shield with a smaller red-and-white shield inside it topped by a  similarly-coloured bishop's mitre. The college motto on a tiny scroll beneath it was too small to read, but Jonah remembered it from a previous investigation: veritas liberabit vos – the truth will set you free.

'The other half looks as if it's something to do with rowing,' Bernie murmured. 'The college rowing club perhaps?'

Jonah studied the image on the other rectangle. 'LCBC,' he read out slowly, struggling to make out the tiny letters beneath a pair of crossed oars, their blades black with a red-and-white ornamental cross near the ends. 'Lichfield College Boat Club is my guess. I'd say this belonged to a club member.'

'But it's an odd thing to find with a *woman*'s body,' Bernie pointed out.

'And are we sure it *was* with the body?' asked Jonah, looking towards Penny.

'Well, according to Ruby, it was found in amongst the bones. Her team took photographs. If it wasn't on the body when it was buried then the chances are it was already in the ground and the body was put in on top of it – but what are the chances of that?'

'So, you don't think it could have been dropped later, by someone just walking through the woods?' Jonah pressed her.

'I couldn't rule it out, but I'd be surprised.'

'And who goes walking in the woods in a dress shirt?' asked Bernie scornfully.

'We're talking about students here,' Jonah observed drily, 'anything's possible. After a night of carousing in the college bar, I wouldn't put it past the boat club to drag themselves over to Shotover for a midnight romp!'

'The Captain of Boats and his girlfriend up to a bit of hanky-panky in the bushes; things get a bit rough and she ends up dead?' suggested Bernie.

'And, in his sozzled state, he just covers her up with leaf mould and gets out, hoping she won't be found,' Jonah finished for her. 'It's a possibility, don't you think?'

He looked up at Penny who nodded. 'Yes, it's a possibility. My guess is that she was quite young when she died, so a student would certainly fit.'

'How young?' Jonah pounced eagerly on this snippet of information.

'Late teens, early twenties probably, but could be a bit older. I'm mainly basing this on dentition. She has two wisdom teeth not yet erupted and there was very little wear on her incisors. She also has only a couple of fillings. That all points to a youngish person, and that's also consistent with my examination of the other bones.'

POST MORTEM

'OK,' Jonah nodded, 'we seem to be getting somewhere at last, but the big problem is narrowing down the time window. Are you sure you can't be a bit more specific about the time of death?'

'Not at the moment. I'll go back out to the scene this afternoon and investigate the soil horizons. That may help with getting an idea of the time-frame.'

'Soil horizons?' queried Andy.

'The soil in a wood is made up of various layers,' Penny explained. 'When a body is buried, the digging disturbs these layers and they get mixed up: subsoil from lower down may end up on the top of the pile and so on. That means we can tell approximately where the top of the soil was at the time of burial. After the grave is filled in, leaves and other debris continue to accumulate on top – that's particularly true in a woodland setting such as this one. That may give us an idea of how many years have passed since the body was buried, but it'll still be very approximate.'

5. A RUM DO

Yvonne sat at her dressing table staring into the mirror. Her hair was a mess but she didn't have the energy for the lengthy process of de-tangling the tight curls. She reached into a drawer and pulled out a long rectangle of red-and-yellow patterned fabric. She unfolded it, estimated the central point and held it up behind her head. Then she brought the two ends round to the front and crossed them over, pulling them tight so that her mop of black hair was gathered up inside the folds of fabric. Finally, she took the ends back down and round the back of her head tying them together firmly at the nape of her neck. A bit of pulling and tucking ensured that all the frizzy locks were covered.

VICTIM STATEMENTS

She studied her reflection in the mirror again. That was better! At least she no longer looked as if she had just crawled out of bed. She dropped her eyes to her makeup bag, but the effort of choosing lipstick and eye shadow was too much for her in her present low state. She contented herself with applying moisturiser to her face and neck and then brushing on a little powder.

After these exertions, her first instinct was to lie down on the bed for a rest, but she knew that if she did, she would drift off to sleep and before she knew it the morning would be gone and Trevor would be back expecting his lunch, for which she needed to get out to the shops to buy bread. She forced herself to get to her feet and go downstairs.

Just as she reached the hall, two letters dropped through the front door.

She carried them through to the kitchen and put them down on the working surface next to the kettle while she made herself a cup of tea. Leo, sitting at the table with a bowl of Honey Monster Puffs in front of him, looked up as she entered and seemed to be studying her face. Yvonne forced a weak smile and asked languidly, 'what are you planning to do today, Leo?'

'Dunno,' he shrugged, shovelling the last of his cereal into his mouth and slipping off his chair. 'I've got some homework to do first – Geography.'

Yvonne watched him go, pulling the kitchen door closed behind him as if he wanted to shut her out of his life. A few moments later she heard his footsteps going upstairs to his room. She didn't see much of him these days. He always seemed to have school work to do –

except when he was outside practising his basketball shots. She ought to show more interest in him – talk to him about all that homework – check he was alright. Was he missing Harry as much as she was? The boys had never seemed to get on that well when he was alive, but …

The kettle boiled and she poured water on to a teabag in the mug that Harry had brought home from primary school the weekend of Mother's Day eight or maybe nine years ago. The picture that he had painted on the plain white surface was almost all worn off now and, unless you knew what it said, you wouldn't be able to tell that round the back were the words "For Mum" with three kisses.

He had been a sweet little boy back then – everybody said so – and always eager to please her. She wandered over to the fridge and added milk to the mug before plucking out the teabag and squeezing it between her long elegant fingers with their neatly trimmed nails. In fact, Harry had always tried to be a good son. He'd done his best to live up to Trevor's expectations; it was just that he wasn't academic. He'd worked hard at his GCSEs. It wasn't his fault that the results had been so disappointing.

She discarded the teabag in the bin and then carried the mug and the letters over to the table. She sat down, holding the mug in both hands and staring down at the envelopes. She could leave them for Trevor to open when he got back; but then he might not tell her what was in them and she would be left worrying. If they were more demands for money that they did not have, it would be better to know.

VICTIM STATEMENTS

She put down the mug and reached out slowly for the first letter. Turning it over she recognised the familiar return address of the housing association that owned their house. Trevor always paid the rent from their joint bank account. He hadn't mentioned any difficulty with it – her furlough pay from her morning cleaning job just about covered it, didn't it?

She tore open the envelope and started reading. There was a long paragraph – intended to be friendly – about how the writer understood the difficult time that everyone was going through and assuring them that the association would be sympathetic towards tenants requesting a temporary "holiday" from paying rent. However, after that there was a table setting out the rent due each month, the amount that they had actually paid and the cumulative shortfall. The letter concluded with advice on claiming benefits to help with rental payments and an assurance that there was no question at this stage of any action to evict tenants who had fallen into arrears.

Trevor hadn't told her that they were behind with the rent. He didn't want to worry her, she supposed. But if he'd concealed that, what else might he be keeping from her? She sipped her tea and braced herself to open the other letter. It was addressed to Trevor, so perhaps she should leave it for him; but it looked official, so … she turned it over. The address on the back was vaguely familiar, but she couldn't remember where she had seen it before.

She put down her mug and started to open the envelope. Then she hesitated and put it back on the table. She would leave that one for later. Trevor might come back any time. Right now, she ought to take advantage of his absence to do what she could to sort out their money problems. She carried her mug out into the hall and picked up the landline telephone. She dialled the number on the card that Gavin had given her and stood waiting for an answer. She could hear it ringing out and then a voice with a strong Liverpool accent told her that "Our Bernie" wasn't able to take her call right now, but if she liked to leave her name and number after the tone, she would call back as soon as she could.

Yvonne replaced the receiver without leaving a message. She could never think what to say, and in any case, she didn't want this "Bernie" calling later when Trevor might answer the phone. She stood in the hall, listlessly wondering what to do next. She must go out and get that bread for their lunch. She'd better make a list of things they needed from the supermarket.

She picked up the pen that they kept next to the phone for taking messages and then wandered back into the kitchen and sat down at the table again. The back of the envelope from the housing association would do to write on. She turned it over and made a start: bread, milk, eggs, what were they going to have for dinner? Trev liked the chicken curry that she sometimes made from a Trinidadian recipe that his grandmother had given her. If she made it for him tonight, maybe afterwards he would be feeling mellow enough to discuss with her how they were going to fix their finances, instead of batting away her anxieties with assurances that he had everything in hand.

She finished her list – and her tea – and got up, ready to go out. But then her eyes lighted on the unopened envelope still lying on the table. On a sudden impulse, she snatched it up and tore it open. It was another letter from the debt-collection company seeking to recover the loan that Trevor had taken out to pay for Harry's funeral. There was something about fees for having defaulted on payments due. Then there was a table, showing interest charges each month and displaying the total accumulated debt as just short of three thousand pounds.

Yvonne gasped and held her hand over her mouth. This was worse than she had thought, even in her worst nightmares. How could the debt be increasing so fast? Wasn't there anything they could do to stop it? She collapsed back into her chair and sat there with her elbows on the table and her head in her hands. What was happening to them? How could they ever get out of this hole that seemed to be growing deeper and deeper all the time?

'Is it OK for me to go out to the park now, Mum?' Leo stood in the doorway holding a basketball between his hands. 'Charlie and Aidan are meeting up there for a practice.'

'OK. Just mind you're back by lunchtime.' Then, as an afterthought, 'but what about that Geography homework you said you had?'

'I've done most of it. I'll finish it when I get back.'

'OK. Just see that you do or your dad'll be cross.'

VICTIM STATEMENTS

'Don't worry. I've got it all under control.'

'I'm glad someone has,' Yvonne muttered under her breath as her son headed off through the front door whistling merrily.

However, the interruption had stirred her from the paralysing fear instilled by the letter. She would have to talk to Trevor about that later. Right now, the important thing was to fetch supplies so that they would be able to eat.

In the supermarket, Yvonne pushed her trolley round the one-way system. She picked up garlic and onions from the fresh vegetables section, but the lime that she needed for her curry recipe didn't seem to be there, so she chose a lemon instead. Next came the chilled food section where she picked up a two-pint bottle of milk. Then round to the frozen food for a small pack of chicken breasts. The bread was further on in an aisle shared with other bakery products. Bags of doughnuts were on special offer, so she picked one up. Leo would enjoy that with his lunch. She looked down at her trolley and then at the list on the back of the envelope. She had everything. Now how did you get out?

She carried on following the arrows on the floor, passing snacks and soft drinks and then cans of beer and bottles of cider. She turned into the next aisle (wines and spirits) and discovered that she was at the end of the queue for the checkouts. She stopped obediently on one of the pairs of footprints painted on the floor, waiting for the line of shoppers to move.

As she waited, she allowed her eyes to wander over the shelves. One particular bottle caught her attention: Golden Hind West Indian Rum, gold lettering in an old-fashioned font beneath a picture of a galleon in full sail. That was the brand that her father used to drink, sitting out in the sunshine (when there was any!) in the tiny garden of their London flat when she was a child. He used to say that it reminded him of his home back in Trinidad.

Not that he could have been old enough back then to be drinking rum! He was only five when his parents brought him to London, settling first in Brixton and then later in Hackney, where Yvonne had been born and raised. Most of his stories of life back on that island paradise (as he described it) must have originated in his imagination more than his memory. Had he and his siblings really wandered barefoot through the sugar plantation, breaking off pieces of young cane and sucking out the sweet juice? Had they really attended school out of doors with just a thatched canopy above them to provide shade from the apparently continuous sunshine? Of course, that couldn't be strictly true – what about the rainy season?

She reached out her arm and picked up the bottle, turning it round in her hand to study the label, her eyes becoming misty as she remembered. At least Dad had died before Harry's murder. He would have been devastated at the thought that his little grandson had been strung up by his neck like a horse thief in those old westerns that he used to watch on TV. And he would have been mortified at the way that Harry's name had been associated in the news reports with the production of illegal drugs.

She became conscious of the woman ahead of her in the queue looking at her, and hastily put the bottle down in her trolley. You weren't supposed to put things back on the shelf once you'd touched them, in case you contaminated them with coronavirus.

The queue moved and Yvonne stepped forward two metres. Now she was standing next to the vodka. This had been her favourite source of comfort in those weeks following Harry's death, when the pain had been so unbearable whenever she was sober. A dash in her breakfast tea had set her up for the day – or at least enabled her to drag herself as far as the sofa in the living room where she would while away the endless hours in front of soap operas and game shows – anything to take her mind off the picture in her head of him hanging there in the hall and the emptiness in her heart whenever she remembered what it had been like when her two boys were small.

She hadn't had a drink for weeks now. It was good to know that she wasn't really addicted. Things had got a bit out of hand back in December, but anyone would have needed something to get them through what she'd been through. She'd proved now that she was in control. She'd got herself back on track. If only there wasn't that letter to worry about – and the rent – and the long, long wait for the trial of Harry's killers!

'That's over the limit for contactless,' the woman at the checkout told her when she held up her credit card.

VICTIM STATEMENTS

Yvonne stared down at the groceries that she had already packed in bags ready to take home from the store. She couldn't remember adding that bottle of vodka to her trolley. She pushed her card into the chip-and-PIN machine and typed in the numbers. Her heart fluttered as it suddenly occurred to her that they could already have reached their credit limit. That was something else that Trevor always took care of. What if he hadn't –? But it was alright: the till whirred as it printed a receipt and the shop assistant told her that she could remove her card now.

Back at home, she stowed the spirits in the drawer with her underwear, telling herself that it wouldn't do for Leo to come across them. He was just at the age when he might be tempted to experiment with drink. She caressed the rum bottle dreamily, thinking of her father as she did so. It was exactly ten years since he died – perhaps that was what had sparked off her memories of him. She could picture it like yesterday: another hot July day, just like today; her sister had rung to call her to his bedside, but the boys were too small to be left alone or to make the journey by bus and train to the London hospital where he lay dying. By the time Trevor got back to look after them, it was too late. A nurse tried to console her by saying that he was unconscious and probably wouldn't have known she was there anyway, but however well-meant, it didn't help. She was his oldest child and she should have been there with him!

VICTIM STATEMENTS

She removed the seal on the top of the bottle. She would just have a tiny sip in remembrance of her father before going back down to get the lunch ready. She fumbled in the drawer for the small glass that she kept there, but before she could pour out any of the amber liquid, she heard the front door opening. She immediately abandoned her plan and pushed both bottles as far into the drawer as she could, carefully arranging the underclothes to conceal them from anyone who chanced to look inside.

She went to the top of the stairs and came face to face with Leo on his way up carrying the basketball.

'Oh, it's you! I thought maybe your dad was home.'

'He is too. He got back the same time as me. He's in the kitchen. He's in a rush for his lunch, 'cos he's got another job booked.'

'That's great! Work must be picking up then. Put that away and then come down and we can all have lunch together.' Yvonne squeezed past her son and hurried down to join Trevor in the kitchen.

Yvonne dried the last plate and put it back on the pile in the cupboard. She hung the tea towel up on the rail above the radiator and looked round the kitchen. It looked clean and tidy – very different from those dreadful days a few months ago when she didn't have the energy to wipe the table clean or brush up crumbs from the floor. She was really on top of everything now! Trevor was starting to get work for his taxi again and Leo seemed determined to do well at school – or at least he spent a lot of time shut up in his room with his homework.

She looked up at the clock on the wall. There was time for a coffee and a sit down before she needed to start making the curry. Or maybe …? It was Dad's anniversary, after all. She would have a tiny shot of rum to remember him, and have a look through those old photographs that she always meant to sort out and never got round to.

She found the box of photographs in the bottom of the wardrobe and put it on the dressing table while she searched in the drawer for the glass. Then she remembered: she had stopped keeping it there, after she'd started to suspect that she might have a drink problem, to make it harder for her to drink secretly in her bedroom.

She carried the bottle of rum and the box of photographs down to the living room and put them down on the coffee table. There were small glasses in a display cabinet next to the window – family heirlooms that used to belong to her parents. Just the thing for drinking a memorial toast to her father!

She poured the drink and held the glass up allowing the sunlight shining in through the window to light it up for a few moments as she pictured him in her mind, smiling at the sight of her walking down the aisle with Trevor as they left the church on their wedding day. He had been so proud of her that day – or so he had told her. She sipped the liquid slowly at first and then put back her head and emptied the glass in a single swallow.

VICTIM STATEMENTS

The rum slid smoothly down her throat and gave her a warm feeling in her stomach.

She fastened the top back on the bottle and set it down on the table next to the box of photographs and … the letter! There it was! That horrible letter telling Trevor that he owed more money than they could ever hope to repay! He must have picked it up from the kitchen table and brought it in here to read. He hadn't said anything about it, although he must have realised that she had read it. He didn't want to discuss it. Was that all he was trying to keep from her? Were there other things – other debts perhaps – that he wasn't telling her about?

Her heart began to pound in her chest and she instinctively reached for the rum bottle and poured herself another glass.

A RUM DO

Two hours later, Leo put his head round the door, hoping that the room would be empty and he could use the TV screen for one of his video games. He stopped short when he saw his mother slumped on the sofa, glass in hand. His first instinct was to back out before she noticed him there, but then something stopped him. He stood unable to move, his heart pounding and his mind racing. She'd been OK for weeks now. He'd got used to the idea that she was better, that she'd learned to cope with losing Harry, that life was going back to normal again.

'Leo?' Yvonne, sensing him there in the doorway, twisted round to look up at him

The glazed look in her eyes as she tried to focus on him shocked him into speaking. He strode forward into the room and stood over her, staring down with a mixture of distress and anger. He snatched at the rum bottle lying on the coffee table, but with remarkably fast reactions for someone who appeared half asleep, Yvonne grabbed it first and held it tight to her chest.

'Mum!' he shouted in her face. 'I thought you'd stopped all this.'

'It's just a little drink to remember your granddad,' she told him, speaking in the slow, careful manner of a drunk who is determined to appear sober. 'It's his tenth anniversary today.'

'Oh Mum!' Leo made another unsuccessful lunge towards the rum bottle. 'Stop this! Granddad wouldn't want to see you like this.'

'What do you know about it?' Yvonne got unsteadily to her feet, still holding the glass in one hand and the bottle in the other. 'You don't understand what it's like to lose your dad. He was … he was …'

Leo watched in dismay as her face crumpled into tears. She swayed and seemed about to fall. He put out his hand to help her, but she pushed him away. She steadied herself with a hand on the back of the sofa as she made her way to the door.

'What's Dad going to say when he comes back and sees you like this?' he called after her as she ambled out into the hall.

Leo stood there listening to her footsteps ascending the stairs. He heard them padding across the landing and then there was a click as the bedroom door closed. He sat down heavily on the sofa, no longer interested in the games console. All that he could think about now was his mother – or rather his mother and the trouble there would be when his father came home and found her like this.

He looked down at the table in front of him. There was a shoe box lying there, half full of old photographs. Some of them were spread out on the table, two had fallen on the floor. He leaned forward and began putting them away in the box. Dad always blamed Mum if the house was in a mess.

In amongst the photographs, there was a letter. It looked new – not yellow and faded like the pictures. Did it belong in the box with them? He unfolded it and glanced down the page, taking in the name of the debt collection agency and the figure **£2,995.62** printed in bold. His heart gave a lurch as he read the words "legal action". Were Mum and Dad in trouble? Was that what the police were doing at the house yesterday? Would they go to jail if they didn't pay?

He sat staring at the letter, unable to move. The clock on the mantlepiece (inherited from his rum-drinking grandfather) ticked away the seconds. A delivery van passed the window and pulled up next door, bringing their neighbour's groceries. A dog barked in the road outside.

Leo jumped at the sound of the telephone in the hall. At first, he ignored it. Then, hearing movement above, he got up and went to answer the summons, worried that his mother might come down to take the call. Whoever it was, it would be better if they did not speak to her in her current state. It might be the social worker who had visited back in January, anxious to check the welfare of the family following Harry's death. They'd fended her off then, managing to conceal Yvonne's drinking habit by a concerted effort from all three of them, but may she have suspected? Might she be ringing now, trying to catch them out?

'H-hello?' he stuttered nervously.

'Hi. I think you tried to ring me earlier.' It was a woman's voice, speaking in a strange accent in which "earlier" was pronounced "airlier". When he did not reply, she went on, 'I'm Bairnie Fazakerley; is that Mrs Yvonne Whittle?'

'N-no. She's not here – I mean she's not well. She's in bed. You'll have to ring again later – no, tomorrow.'

'Oh! I'm sorry to hear that. It's not COVID, I hope?'

'No, it's not COVID, it's … it's just a bad headache – a migraine.' Leo remembered hearing their neighbour, Mrs Prentice, telling his mother how her daughter suffered from these debilitating attacks.

'I'm sorry,' the woman repeated. 'Could you …? Is that Leo I'm talking to?'

'Ye-es,' Leo said cautiously, wondering how this strange woman knew his name.

'I'm a friend of Chrissie Hughes.' She appeared to have read his mind. 'She told me about you. She gave your mum my number so I could help her with something. Could you tell her that I've got some ideas and I think we'll be able to get things sorted out for her?'

'Yes. OK.'

'Good. Thanks then. Bye!'

6. THE MISSING LINK

There was light rain spotting the windscreen when Bernie pulled into the small yard that served as the car park for Lichfield College. With the college closed and most of its staff either furloughed or working at home, there was more space than usual and she was able to find a place with ample room behind the car for Jonah to exit in his wheelchair. They made their way round to the porter's lodge and Bernie tapped on the sliding glass panel to attract attention.

'Can I help you?' A bespectacled man in his forties slid open the window and peered out at them.

Bernie held up Jonah's warrant card and her own ID. 'We're from Thames Valley Police,' she told him. 'We'd like to ask you about this.'

THE MISSING LINK

She put the evidence bag containing the cuff-link on the counter and pushed it towards him. He reached out and picked it up, holding it in front of his face and peering in suspiciously.

'Do you recognise it?' Jonah called up, craning his neck to see the porter's face.

'That's the Lichfield College crest,' the man answered, 'but it's not one of the ones we sell now. I can show you one of those.'

He disappeared into the gloom of the lodge, returning a few moments later holding a small presentation box containing a pair of cuff-links. Bernie took it and showed it to Jonah. Each link comprised a copy of the Lichfield College shield attached to a hinged bar to enable them to be pushed through the shirt cuff and then fastened.

VICTIM STATEMENTS

'We sell a lot of them to visiting alumni,' the porter told them. 'It's quite a good fundraiser – especially when they all come back for the Gaudy. Not that there'll be one this year,' he added gloomily.

'We thought these ones might belong to the college boat club,' Bernie said. 'Do you know anything about that?'

''Fraid not,' the porter shook his head. 'Not my remit, I'm afraid. You need to speak to the club president, but he's not here. They sent all the students home before Easter.'

'If you could give us his name and home address?' Jonah suggested, smiling up amiably.

'I'm afraid not, sir. We can't go handing out that sort of personal information willy-nilly.'

THE MISSING LINK

Jonah considered the situation. There were processes that he could go through in order to make it a legal obligation to reveal the information, but that would take time and involve paperwork; or he could go above the porter's head and speak to the college senior management, but was it worth doing either of these when the owner of the cuff-link most likely left the college a decade or more ago?

'This could be quite old,' he said at last. 'It might not be the same as the boat club use now. Is there anyone who would know about that? Or do you have a college museum or anything like that where there might be memorabilia like this?'

'Old Bernard might be able to tell you about it. He's been here for donkey's years. There's not much about the college he doesn't know.

VICTIM STATEMENTS

'And could we speak to him, please?' enquired Jonah.

'Not today, I'm afraid. It's his day off. We only have a skeleton staff on duty at the moment. He'll be in tomorrow, if you'd like to come back then.'

'And there's nobody else who might know anything?' Jonah pleaded.

'Not that I can think of.' The porter shook his head. 'You come back tomorrow and speak to Old Bernard. If anyone can help you, it's him.'

'I suppose that will just have to do.' Jonah's tone was disappointed. 'I'd be grateful if you could contact the rowing club president and ask him to get in touch.' He looked towards Bernie, who took out a business card and handed it over to the porter. 'Tell him it's needed for a murder enquiry.'

THE MISSING LINK

There seemed to be nothing more they could do at the college, so they returned to the car and Bernie drove Jonah to the police station to meet with the rest of the team investigating the case.

It was the first time that Jonah had gone into work since before the lockdown started back in March. It seemed at once familiar and yet eerily different. The large open plan office had been rearranged so that all the desks were facing in the same direction. More than half of the workstations were unoccupied to promote social distancing. Normally, when Jonah entered, he would have been engulfed by colleagues leaping to their feet, eager to tell him about developments in the case and new leads that they were following up; but now they all stayed in their places, wary of moving about the room for fear of coming close enough to someone else to transmit the virus. More than half of them were wearing face masks.

Bernie opened the door but did not follow Jonah inside. 'You don't need me here, do you? I'd like to have another go at ringing Yvonne Whittle. Chrissie said it was better to talk to her during the day when Trevor's more likely to be out. I'll use your office, if that's OK?'

'Right, fine,' Jonah answered absently, his mind fixed on the quest for the identity of the Shotover skeleton. 'See you later.'

Bernie closed the door behind her friend and headed briskly along the corridor to his private office. Once inside, she sat down at the desk, took out her mobile phone and dialled the number from which Yvonne's missed call had come the day before. It rang out for a long time before anyone answered.

'Hello?' the voice sounded older, but no less tentative.

'This is Bernie Fazakerley. I was hoping to speak to Mrs Yvonne Whittle?'

'Yes. That's me.'

'I think you tried to ring me yesterday. Chrissie Hughes told me she'd given you my number. She said you'd like some help with the forms for claiming criminal injuries compensation.'

There was a long pause. Bernie wondered whether Yvonne was still listening or perhaps she didn't want to answer for fear of being overheard.

'Is this a bad time? I can ring again later if that would be better.'

'No. That's OK. I just don't know…'

'I've had a look at the information on the CICA website. You're definitely entitled to claim for funeral expenses and you ought to qualify for some other things too, but I need information from you to fill in the online application. It might be easier if I could call round. Would that be OK?'

'I don't think … I'd have to ask Trevor first. He doesn't like other people knowing about our business. He wouldn't like anyone else to know…'

'Well maybe we can do it over the phone then,' Bernie said hastily, afraid that Yvonne might abandon the whole idea if it meant confiding in Trevor. 'I can go through the questions and you can tell me what answers to put.'

'Yes, thanks, but not right now. Trev's only washing the car. He might come in and want to know who I'm talking to. Like I said, he doesn't like other people knowing our business.'

'OK. When would be a good time for me to ring again?'

'I don't know. It all depends when Trev gets a callout. He drives a taxi – did Chrissie say? – and he hasn't been getting much work since this pandemic started.'

'Yes, Chrissie told me that was the main reason he couldn't pay back the loan. That's another thing: have you managed to get any debt advice yet?'

'I tried ringing Citizens Advice.'

'Did they help?'

'I never got through.'

'Well, I've got another number you could try. It's the Oxford Church Debt Centre. They specialise in helping people like you and Trevor. Have you got a pen and paper to write it down?'

Bernie heard the dull thud of the telephone receiver being put down, followed by some rustling sounds. Then the line went silent for a while before eventually Yvonne's voice came through again.

'Hello? Are you still there?'

'Yes. I'm here. Are you ready for that number?' Bernie dictated the number of the helpline and reiterated her offer of help with the application, but when she tried to set a date for another call, Yvonne suddenly became agitated.

'I'm sorry, I'll have to go now,' she gabbled. 'Thanks for ringing.'

'OK. Ring me again and we'll fix something up. Maybe it would be easier for you if you come round to our house?'

Bernie sat staring at the phone in her hand. The line had suddenly gone dead. She guessed that Trevor had come in and Yvonne had slammed the phone down to prevent him overhearing her conversation. Had she heard Bernie's final invitation? Would she ring again to set up a meeting?

The rest of the day passed without any call from Yvonne. Bernie wondered whether to contact Chrissie to let her know what had happened, but decided against it. Chrissie would probably feel obliged to do something, and really it was up to Yvonne to accept the help that they had offered to her. Besides, it suited her if she didn't get a call while Jonah was on duty, because she had to be ready to take him to wherever the investigation might require at a moment's notice.

The next day, it took them back to Lichfield College to interview Bernard Malpas the head porter. He was expecting them and came out of the porter's lodge to speak with them more conveniently.

'Chief Inspector Porter! Welcome to Lichfield College again. Darren tells me you've got a pair of cuff-links you'd like me to cast my eye over.'

Jonah remembered the elderly porter from an earlier case in which a dead man had been found in the Fellows' Garden[3]. He smiled back at him and Bernie held up the evidence bag containing the link.

'It's not a pair, just one link,' Jonah told him, 'and we're hoping you might be able to give us an idea of who it may have belonged to.'

---

[3] You can read about this in "A Secret Gardener?", © 2020 Judy Ford, ISBN: 978-1-911083-62-7

THE MISSING LINK

'Let me have a look.' The porter took the bag and studied the contents carefully through his half-moon spectacles. 'Ah yes!' he murmured. 'I remember these. It's a good while back, though, not long after I started here.'

'So, that would be ...?' Jonah enquired.

'I joined the staff in seventy-eight, so probably the early eighties.'

'And who might have had them?'

'The president of the boat club had connections to some jeweller's company and he arranged for them to be made. They weren't on general sale – just for members of the club. You see the cross-oars and initials LCBC? That means Lichfield College Boat Club. I don't know if they still sell them to members. I haven't seen any of them for years, but then there's no reason why I would: it's all down to the boat club, nothing to do with the college.'

'But it couldn't be any earlier than 1978?' Jonah pressed him.

'No, definitely not. I remember the first consignment arriving. It was delivered here – to the porter's lodge. It was a registered parcel and we had to sign for it.'

'And do you remember any more batches coming?'

'No.' Bernard shook his head. 'But that doesn't mean there weren't any.'

'No, of course not.' Jonah paused in thought. 'And can you tell me the name of this club president with the jewellery connections?'

'Now there you have me!' the porter pursed his lips and moved his head slowly up and down. 'No, I'm sorry. I can see him there, like it was yesterday, opening the parcel and holding up a pair of these cuff-links, very pleased with himself, and boasting about how clever he'd been getting them made.'

'So, he thought highly of himself, did he?' Jonah asked, pouncing on these words. 'He liked to show off?'

'Yes, I suppose that just about sums him up,' Bernard agreed. 'He liked to get himself noticed. I remember he nearly got sent down for some escapade on May Morning. I forget the details. His dad came and had a talk with the Master and it all blew over.' He sighed and shook his head. 'But the name just won't come. I'll be worrying about it all day now.'

'Don't do that,' Jonah said, 'but if you do remember, please let us know. It could be important.'

Bernie stepped forward and exchanged the evidence bag for one of

Jonah's business cards. 'There's a number to ring there.'

The porter stepped back into the lodge, leaving Bernie and Jonah in the archway that connected the outside world with the main quadrangle of the college.

'What now?' asked Bernie.

'We need to find out more about the members of this boat club,' Jonah declared, 'and especially the president who got those cuff-links made.'

'The link won't necessarily be one of his,' Bernie pointed out. 'It needn't even belong to anyone he knew. For all we know, it could have become a tradition for the boat club to get them made every year. All we know for sure – and even that depends on Old Bernard being right about the ones he saw being the first – is that it couldn't have got there any earlier than 1978.'

'I know,' Jonah agreed testily. 'It doesn't really narrow the time window very much, does it? But it's all we've got to go on – which is why I want to find that boat club president. Surely there must be some college archives where they keep records of college clubs. Where would they be?'

'Maybe try the college library?' suggested Bernie, 'or the Master's secretary?'

'Hi there! Long time, no see.'

While they were still hesitating over their next move, a tall woman in trousers and a polo shirt had approached them from across the quadrangle. Bernie spun round to see who was speaking to them and immediately recognised Professor Paula Wellesley, Fellow of Lichfield College and holder of the Robert Boyle Chair of Physics.

VICTIM STATEMENTS

'Hello Paula How are you?'

'Fine,' she smiled back. 'Just off for my first non-essential shopping trip since lockdown started. What brings you here? If you're looking for Martin, he's working at home, like most of the dons. It's only me, the Master and a few overseas students still in college.'

Unusually for academics in modern times, Paula lived in a suite of rooms in the college and did not have another home to retreat to when the "stay-at-home" order came into operation. She knew that Dr Martin Riess, Fellow in Geology, was a close friend of Bernie and Jonah.

'No,' Bernie told her, 'this isn't a social visit: we're working. Jonah's in hot pursuit of the other one of these.'

She held up the evidence bag and Paula studied its contents.

THE MISSING LINK

'A missing cuff-link?' she queried, raising her eyebrows and smiling quizzically. 'Isn't it a bit over-the-top to have a Detective Chief Inspector hunting for lost property?'

'Ah! That's just it!' Jonah broke in. 'Whose property is it? That's the question!'

'And the answer?' Paula continued to smile.

'Possibly a murderer,' Jonah told her, 'or possibly just a rambler who dropped a cuff-link.'

'I don't think I'd go rambling wearing one of those,' Paula observed, 'so I suppose that must point towards the murderer theory. What makes you think that?'

'This was found among human remains in a shallow grave,' Jonah explained. 'Of course, it may have nothing to do with it, but ...'

'The Shotover skeleton? Are you investigating that? But I thought you'd retired?'

'He persuaded them to take him back part-time,' Bernie grinned, 'and this case is just right for that. When a body's been in the ground for decades there's no desperate rush to identify it within minutes or hours.'

'I have a whole team working on it. They don't stop just because I'm forced to take a few days off every week.'

'See what he's like?' Bernie shook her head censoriously. 'A total workaholic! We should have realised that retirement was never going to work.'

'You don't happen to know how we'd find out about members of the college rowing club from the nineteen eighties, do you?' Jonah looked up at Paula, treating her to one of his most endearing lop-sided smiles.

'You could try Graham Weldon.'

'The name sounds familiar. Who is he?'

'He's a tutorial fellow – Chemistry.'

'And student accommodation tutor?'

'Yes, I think he is; how did you know?'

'I've come across him before, now you've reminded me. He was there when your old bursar was killed.'[4]

'Anthony Bridgefield? He was no loss to the world!' Paula snorted. 'So, you investigated that, did you? I never knew.'

---

[4] See "Awayday (which don did it?)" © 2014, Judy Ford, ISBN: 978-1-911083-06-1

'But to get back to the boat club,' Jonah cut in. 'Why do you say Professor Weldon might be able to help us?'

'He was an undergraduate here *and* he rows. I'm not sure how old he is, but nineteen eighties sounds about right. I hope you're not going to tell me that he killed the woman in the woods; I quite like Graham.'

'High praise indeed!' commented Bernie, who knew that Paula had a low opinion of the male sex generally.

'You wouldn't happen to know his home address, by any chance?' wheedled Jonah.

'No. I think it's Summertown or maybe Wolvercote, but ... I think I've probably got his mobile number in my contacts, though.' Paula took out her phone and started scrolling through names on the screen. 'Yes, here it is!'

THE MISSING LINK

She held it out towards Jonah, who leaned forwards in an attempt to see the numbers. 'Can you read it out to me?' he said at last, 'to save us getting too close.'

Less than an hour later, they pulled up outside an impressive Edwardian terrace in north Oxford. The small garden of the house belonging to Professor Graham Weldon and his wife, was paved over, and the wall had been removed to allow two cars to be parked on it. Bernie stared at the narrow gap between the vehicles, and the steep steps leading up to the front door, and then she twisted round in her seat to speak to her passenger.

'No chance of getting your chair in there. Probably best if I ask him to come out and talk to you in the back of the car.'

Jonah nodded his acquiescence. 'Yes. Go ahead.'

He watched as his assistant climbed the steps and took hold of the old-fashioned brass door knocker. His wheelchair was firmly strapped sideways inside the back of the modified car, so he had a clear view through the side window. He waited impatiently as the seconds ticked by with no response from inside the house. What was taking the man so long? They had telephoned ahead, so he knew they were coming.

At last, the door opened and Graham Weldon appeared. His steely grey hair was longer than Jonah remembered it being when they last met – probably the result of lockdown closures of barbers and hairdressers – and his broad figure seemed even more massive. He was dressed in casual trousers and an open-necked shirt. Bernie was speaking to him now and gesturing towards the car. Then she turned and came back down the steps. The man stepped out of the house pulling the door closed behind him. They both squeezed through to the road and came round to the back of Bernie's car.

She opened the rear hatch and indicated to Professor Weldon that he should sit on a flap-down seat just inside. It was on the opposite side from Jonah in his wheelchair, making it easy for them to converse while maintaining social distancing. Then, leaving the back door open, she walked round to the side of the car and got back into the driver's seat.

'I gather you studied at Lichfield College as an undergraduate?' Jonah began. 'When exactly was that?'

'Seventy-nine to eighty-three,' the don replied promptly, 'but why do you ask?'

'And you were a rower – a member of the college boat club?' Jonah continued, ignoring the question.

'Yes, but why do you want to know?'

'We've found something that we think belonged to another member of the club, probably from a similar era.' Jonah glanced towards Bernie who went back round the outside of the car to hand the cuff-link in its evidence bag over to Weldon for his inspection.

He took it from her and held it up in front of his face, pushing his long hair back from his eyes to see better. He studied it intently without speaking.

'Have you seen anything like this before?' Jonah enquired, impatient at the lack of response.

THE MISSING LINK

'Yes.' Weldon looked up with a puzzled frown on his face. 'I've got a pair of these myself as it happens.'

'Really?' Jonah gave a little yelp of excitement. 'How many other people had them? How can we find out who they were? Do you have their names? Can I see yours?'

Weldon answered the last question first, smiling at Jonah's sudden eagerness. 'I can try and dig them out for you, but it's a long time since I've worn them, so I'm not sure where I've put them. As for who else had them: it was quite a select few. The president of the club had them made on a whim and then more or less forced all the first and second crew to buy them off him. I think it was probably a couple of dozen pairs. That was one each for the sixteen rowers, two for the coxes and then the other six for various club officials and basically any members who'd pay.'

'Do I detect a certain lack of enthusiasm on your part for the venture?' suggested Jonah.

'That's putting it mildly,' Weldon confirmed. 'The president that year was a typical Public-School toff – an old Etonian who looked down on the hoi polloi. His dad owned the company that made them and he bragged about what a good deal he'd got for us. It didn't seem like such a good deal to me, but then I was surviving on a local authority grant with no big allowance from Daddy to pay for fancy dress!'

'Do I take it you didn't get on with this president?' Jonah asked. 'What was his name, by the way?'

'Julian Palmer, and you're right: I can't say I had much time for any of the boat club committee. They were all self-important idiots from posh boarding schools who saw being up at Oxford as a bit of a lark. I don't know why I didn't leave – except that I liked the rowing and I was quite good at it.'

'And you say that all the members of the boat crews had a pair of these cuff-links? Can you give me any more names?'

'Let's see … Julian rowed stroke in the first eight that year, and then there was a chap with big ears at number seven …'

'And what year was that, by the way?' Jonah cut in as Weldon trailed off in thought.

'Eighty-three. I was in my final year and so was the fellow at number seven … He had a funny name … what was it now? … I know! Peregrine – that was it! I can't remember his last name though. All the others were second years, I think.'

'Any other names?' persisted Jonah.

'Number six had long red hair that flapped about when he rowed,' Weldon replied, pushing his own hair back behind his ears. 'I was number five, so I got quite used to watching it! I can't remember his name though. It was a long time ago, and like I said, we didn't have much in common apart from the rowing, so we haven't kept in touch.'

'Is there anywhere we could get hold of a list of boat club members from 1983?' Jonah enquired. 'Does the college keep records?'

'Well, the Alumni Office would have a list of all the undergraduates that year. I might be able to identify them from that. Or the college archives might have lists of the crews for Eights Week each year, I'm not sure.'

'And how would we go about looking in those?'

'The archives are in the library. I could show you, I suppose. Not today, though, I'm due in a webinar in Budapest in half an hour – virtually, of course. How about tomorrow?'

'Thanks.' Jonah glanced towards Bernie who stared back warningly in a silent reminder that he was not on duty the following day. 'We'll talk to the librarian and the Alumni Office and see what they can dig out for us. If we need your help again, we'll be in touch. So, just to recap: the people who had a pair of these cuff-links were the first and second eights, including the coxes, and the boat club committee – anyone else?'

'Now that you mention it, a couple of years later the treasurer complained that there were still some of the links knocking about that hadn't been sold. Julian had left by then and the new committee were more interested in getting the club finances fixed than showing off their finery at the Eights Week dinner. I think we voted to put them on general sale to raise funds.'

'That widens the field a bit,' Bernie muttered.

'I thought you were in your final year.' Jonah sounded puzzled. 'How come …?'

'I stayed on to do a DPhil,' Weldon explained. 'I'm a glutton for punishment!'

'And how many of these spare pairs were there "knocking around"?'

'It can only have been two or three, now I think about it. The vast majority went to the 1983 boat crews. That treasurer was a bit of a fuss-pot. The chances are they'll have found people in the club willing to buy them, once they knew about them.'

The college librarian was eager to help, and readily supplied lists of names for the rowing crews from 1970 to 2010. Armed with these, Jonah next contacted the Alumni Office. The administrator with whom he spoke via a video link from his office was less cooperative. She explained with exaggerated patience the importance of confidentiality and her obligations under the GDPR[5]. Jonah

----

[5] General Data Protection Regulation: an EU regulation transposed into UK law by the Data Protection Act 2018, which puts

smiled sweetly and used his most persuasive tones, but she was adamant, conceding only a promise to send out an appeal to the 1983 rowing crews asking them to contact the police.

'We should have warned Weldon not to mention the cuff-links to any of his rowing buddies,' Jonah muttered after he ended the call. If the owner of the missing link gets wind of the fact that we're looking for its partner, he'll know we're on to him and start destroying any evidence there may be linking him to the death of the woman in the woods.'

'On the other hand,' Andy Lepage pointed out brightly, 'if he gets worried

---

responsibilities on people and bodies that hold personal data not to share them except within strictly-defined parameters.

that we're after him and makes any moves to cover his tracks that could work to our advantage. If he's frightened, he may make mistakes and draw attention to himself.'

'Let's hope you're right,' Jonah agreed. 'So now what? We do at least have one name. Andy, can you start tracking down this Julian Palmer? It should be simple enough with what we know about him: old Etonian, Oxford graduate, family in the jewellery business …'

7. LONG WEEKEND

Working only three days a week during an interesting case did not suit Jonah's energetic nature at all. Lying on his front, while Bernie applied a dressing to a pressure sore that had begun to develop on his left thigh as a result of spending too much time sitting in one position in his wheelchair, he mulled over in his mind what they knew so far, and made plans for taking the investigation forward.

'Hurry up, can't you?' he demanded. 'I want to give the lab a push to get on with that DNA test on the bones.'

'I'm sure they're doing it as quick as they can,' Bernie told him firmly, 'and it's not as if you'll be able to do anything with it until Tuesday.'

'Maybe not, but Andy might. I've told him to focus the trawl of missing persons files on the early eighties, with particular reference to anyone with connections to the university, especially Lichfield College. If any of them happen to have DNA saved, that could give us an identity for our skeleton.'

'But is that likely, back then?' Bernie gently rolled him over and busied herself with re-attaching the special sheath that connected his penis to the tube leading to his urine bag. 'I thought DNA was much less advanced in those days.'

'You never know,' Jonah answered petulantly. Bernie recognised that he was frustrated at being kept at home while his team were busy working on the case. She tried to think of something to distract him.

'Eddie's bringing the kids over this morning,' she told him. 'Under the latest relaxation of the regulations, Peter's allowed to look after them again now so that Eddie can work at home better. I thought we could take them for a socially-distanced walk to the Nature Reserve – once you've had your physio,' she added firmly. 'You somehow managed to get out of it yesterday and that's probably contributed to you getting that pressure sore.'

'Alright, alright,' Jonah muttered. 'No need to go on about it.'

Bernie fetched the hoist and carefully transferred him into the strange contraption that was Jonah's functional electrical stimulation machine. She settled him into the padded seat, strapping him round the chest and over the shoulders to prevent his body from toppling over or twisting round as he exercised. Then she attached electrodes to his skin to enable the machine to stimulate his muscles in sequence so that the limbs that he could no longer control himself would receive a thorough workout.

Next, she stretched out his legs in front of him and positioned his feet on two metal plates, strapping them in using Velcro fastenings. Then it was the turn of his arms. She gently bent his fingers around two hand grips, securing them with more Velcro.

'OK,' she declared. 'You're good to go.'

She switched on the power and stood watching as Jonah's legs moved backwards and forwards in turn as if they were jogging slowly. His arms moved back and forth in time with his legs. A monitor displayed the speed and force of his movements and his heart rate and breathing.

'OK,' she murmured after a few minutes. 'That's the warm-up done. Now let's see how you perform under pressure.'

She adjusted the settings and Jonah's limbs began to move faster. His breathing became more rapid too and a few drops of sweat appeared on his forehead.

'Your cardiovascular function seems pretty good,' Bernie observed with satisfaction. 'I was afraid the two days off might have set you back.'

Jonah, however, wasn't listening. He was still thinking about the case.

'I've set Monica and Alice tracking down the rowers. They're usually quite good at internet searches … Of course, that's something I could do myself,' he added, after a few moments' thought.

'Maybe I will, after you've got me out of this contraption.'

'Oh no you don't!' Bernie said emphatically. 'You're going to have a proper weekend off and give Andy and Monica a chance to show what they can do without you breathing down their necks all the time. They need the experience. How're they ever going to get promotion if you never let them do anything?'

'They get plenty of chance to shine!' her friend protested, 'and when Andy gets round to taking his inspector's exams, I'll be the first to recommend him for promotion.'

'And Monica?' Bernie asked, suspiciously.

'She's not ready yet. She's fine with the theory, but she hasn't got … you need to have a *feel* for the job – to instinctively know what will get people to talk. And she's more interested in furthering her career than being a good police officer.'

'Are you sure that's completely fair?' Bernie challenged with a grin. 'Couldn't it be that you're sore because you discovered that she was sucking up to you because she thought you'd be able to get her promotion and not because she fancied you?'

'Nonsense! I'm simply making an objective assessment of the relative capabilities of my two detective sergeants. Now, are we done here? I think I heard a car on the drive. If I'm going to be roped in to entertain Peter's grandkids, I at least want to be properly dressed before they start climbing all over me.'

LONG WEEKEND

As Bernie had hoped, the arrival of four-year-old Ricky and three-year-old Abigail provided a sufficient diversion to keep even Jonah's mind off the police investigation for the rest of the morning – apart, that is, from a surreptitious phone call to the forensic lab asking for progress on the DNA test. In the presence of Ricky's irrepressible exuberance, no adult could concentrate for long on anything other than answering his constant questions and thinking up new things to keep him occupied, while his little sister charmed everyone she met with her green eyes and radiant smiles.

There was a moment of misgiving during their walk through the CS Lewis Nature Reserve when Bernie noticed Jonah giving a wistful look towards the path that led to Shotover Country Park, only half a mile away. She quickly called the children over to look for mini-beasts in a pile of logs. Ricky shouted with excitement at the sight of an armadillo woodlouse which curled up into a tight ball when he poked it with his finger. Jonah gave a final look of longing towards the path to Shotover and then obeyed the little boy's call to "come and look, Uncle Jonah!"

When they got home, Peter prepared the lunch, with the "help" of the two children, while Bernie emptied Jonah's urine bag and checked the dressing on his pressure sore. Then she left him to his own devices while she fetched in the washing from the line in the garden. When she returned, she found him engrossed in something on the computer screen attached to his chair. He looked up and grinned.

LONG WEEKEND

'They've managed to get a DNA profile from the bones,' he announced, 'but so far, all that does is to confirm that they're female. I've told Andy to double-check all the missing persons files to see which ones have DNA records we can check against it.'

'As if he wouldn't have done that off his own bat!!' Bernie snorted. 'What're you like? How many times do I have to spell it out to you? You – are – off – duty – today! You ought to be pleased: you never enjoy the spadework anyway. Just sit back and enjoy your weekend off while the others do all the tedious stuff. Then, on Tuesday, you'll be able to go back in and look at all the data they've gathered and apply your genius to solving the case with a single wave of your incredible brain!'

Peter called them into the kitchen for lunch before Jonah could think of a suitably caustic reply. Abigail was already sitting on the booster cushion that raised her high enough to reach the large wooden table in the centre of the room. Ricky waited until Jonah had positioned his wheelchair at the end of the table and then climbed up on the seat next to him and clamoured to be allowed to give him his food.

Over the years, they had experimented with various splints and mechanical devices to enable Jonah to feed himself, but without success. His natural impatience with such trivialities as eating – unimportant compared with catching criminals – made him unwilling to stick with any new contraption for long enough to master it, and any benefits in terms of independence were negated by the inevitable need for someone to clean him, his clothes and the surrounding area following each messy experiment.

'Please!' begged Ricky, leaning across the table and pulling the salad bowl towards him. 'I'll be very careful.'

Peter put out his hand and moved the bowl back. 'That's up to Uncle Jonah,' he told his grandson firmly. 'He may prefer to have Aunty Bernie doing it like usual.'

Jonah looked at Ricky, who gazed back with soulful brown eyes. In truth, he would very much prefer Bernie's ministrations. Her experienced eye enabled her to time each mouthful to fit in with his chewing and swallowing. She could be relied upon not to force food too far into his mouth or to spear his gums with the fork. But then he remembered Lucy, Bernie's daughter, only nine at the time of his spinal cord injury. She had been so pleased and proud to be allowed to help him in that way, and she had become very adept at doing so.

He smiled at Ricky and nodded his head. 'OK, Ricky, you can have a go. Would you like to start by buttering some of that lovely fresh soda bread that Granddad Peter's made for me?'

After lunch the children asked to play in the attic rooms where Bernie had stowed away many of Lucy's old toys. Peter went with them, leaving Bernie and Jonah alone together, downstairs in the living room. Jonah looked towards Bernie with his most winning smile on his face.

'How about we pay Professor Weldon another visit and see what else he can tell us about the other members of the boat club? He may remember more about them now that we've got a list of their names to jog his memory.'

'Absolutely not! If that corpse was put there back in 1983, another few days waiting for you to be back on duty isn't going to make any difference, is it? If you want to do something useful, have a think about what we can do to help the Whittles with their money problems.'

'You've told her you'll help. What more *can* we do?'

'That's what I'm asking you. If you're so clever, why can't you come up with some ingenious plan to get them back on their feet? I can't think why she hasn't rung.'

'Perhaps she's doesn't like to. Why don't you ring her?'

'I don't want her to think she's being bullied.' Bernie flung herself down into an armchair and stared out through the French windows at the sunny garden. 'And she doesn't like talking on the phone if Trevor's there.'

'I could ring,' Jonah volunteered. 'Then, if Trevor answers, I can make out it's just a routine police call keeping them informed about progress in the prosecution of the Butler gang.'

'Has there been any?'

'No, but there's no harm in reassuring them that the trial will go ahead once the backlog of cases starts to be cleared – better than letting them think we've forgotten all about them.'

'OK. I suppose you might as well have a go. Try and persuade her to come round so I can show her the details I've downloaded. I'll find the number for you.' Bernie took out her phone and started scrolling through her contacts.

'No need: I've already got it from when we were investigating Harry's murder. You go and make us some tea and I'll give her a call.'

'OK.' Bernie got to her feet. 'Oh! And ask her to bring those solicitor's letters she's had, when she comes. I'd like to see what they *really* say. She may be panicking unnecessarily.'

When she returned with the tea, Bernie found Jonah still busy on his phone. He hastily ended the call when she entered the room, but not before she had heard him telling Andy to keep him informed if anything interesting turned up in the missing persons files. She stared at him coldly and raised one eyebrow in disapproval. He smiled back with the guilty expression of a child caught in the act of disobedience but confident of his parent's indulgence.

VICTIM STATEMENTS

'Yvonne says she'll come round on Sunday afternoon,' he told her. 'Trevor and Leo are going out somewhere together, so she'll be able to slip away without them knowing. And she's going to bring both of the letters *and* the receipts for the funeral.'

'Gavin! What brings you – oh! I see.' Bernie looked past the burly police officer, standing outside her front door to see a smartly-dressed black woman standing on the drive nervously clutching a black leather handbag. It reminded her of the first time that she had seen Yvonne Whittle, huddled next to her husband on two of those uncomfortable plastic seats in the reception area of the police station. Would she remember her from that encounter, when she and Trevor had come to report that their son Harry was missing and discovered that he had been arrested for his part in a cannabis-growing business? Probably not: as personal assistant to the DCI, Bernie would have blended into the background, no more notable than the paint on the walls.

'I gave Yvonne a lift,' Gavin explained. 'It's over three miles and the buses are hopeless. It'd have taken her an hour to get here on her own.'

'Yes, of course,' Bernie flushed with annoyance a herself for not having thought of this. She ought to have realised that the only car that the family would have was Trevor's taxi. 'I should've thought of that before I suggested her coming round. Thank you for stepping in.'

She waved towards Yvonne, who looked back apprehensively from beneath a large purple hat with a wide satin ribbon around its crown. 'Hi there, Yvonne. I'm Bernie. Thank you for coming over. Let's all go round the back. The gate's open. Follow me.'

She led the way round the side of the house into the large back garden. Both of her visitors were wearing face masks and Gavin had a tube of sanitising gel in his hand.

'Go on round,' she urged them, standing back, waiting to close the tall gate behind them. 'The others are all round there on the patio.'

Gavin led the way. Yvonne followed, holding her bag pressed tightly against her chest. When Bernie came round the corner of the house, she found them standing on the edge of the paved area behind the kitchen and living room, staring out at the huge expanse of lawn and trees.

'It's like a park!' Yvonne breathed in awe.

'Peter said it was a big garden,' Gavin added, 'but I hadn't expected something quite like this.' He had visited the house on several previous occasions, but this was the first time he had seen round the back. 'There's acres of it!'

'No,' Bernie smiled, 'it's just under an acre. It looks bigger than it is because it's broken up by the bushes so you can't see it all at once. Mind you: it sometimes feels like acres when it comes to keeping it tidy. It's more than we can handle in the summer when the lawn keeps growing and the weeds keep multiplying!'

VICTIM STATEMENTS

She turned to Yvonne. 'Let me introduce you to everyone. This is my husband, Peter.'

Yvonne looked towards Peter, who smiled back and raised his hand in a socially-distanced greeting.

'Peter used to be a police officer too,' Gavin informed her, 'but he's retired now.'

'As should Jonah be,' Bernie added. 'You've met him before, but he's off-duty now, so try not to think of him as DCI Porter the –'

'– the incompetent fool who failed to give your son proper protection as a potential witness to a murder,' Jonah finished for her. 'I know it's just words and it doesn't make things any better for you, but I won't ever forgive myself for that.'

'I – I – I'm sure you did your best,' Yvonne stammered in evident discomfiture.

'And this is my daughter, Lucy,' Bernie continued, raising her voice slightly to cover Yvonne's embarrassment. 'She's just back from university. I drove up to Liverpool to fetch her yesterday, so she wouldn't have to come on the train.'

'Hello.' Yvonne looked towards Lucy. 'What are you studying?'

'Medicine,' Lucy replied promptly. 'I'm hoping to become a forensic pathologist – eventually!'

'Oh! You must be very clever.'

'I don't know about that. I did have quite a lot of help. Mike Carson – he's a pathologist here in Oxford – helped me a lot with preparing for the interviews.'

VICTIM STATEMENTS

'Sit down,' Peter urged, pointing towards two garden chairs spaced well apart. 'I'll go and make us all a drink, while Bernie has a look at those forms with you. Come along Lucy! You can help carry things.'

Peter and Lucy disappeared indoors. Yvonne stood staring after him for a second or two then suddenly seemed to recollect herself and subsided into one of the chairs. Gavin sat down too and removed his face mask. He looked more normal now, but still somehow very different from Bernie's picture of him in her head. Had she never seen him out of his police uniform before?

'What would you like to see first?' Yvonne asked, rummaging in her bag. 'I've brought those solicitor's letters, like Inspector – like Jonah said, and I've got the receipts for the funeral and …'

'Let's take a look at those letters first,' Jonah said briskly. Or – Gavin! Could you hold them up where I can read them, while Bernie takes Yvonne through the application form for her compensation?'

Gavin carefully replaced his facemask and sanitised his hands before taking the documents from Yvonne and carrying them over to where Jonah was waiting, next to the table at which Bernie sat with her laptop computer in front of her.

'OK,' Bernie said, turning to Yvonne, 'now, I've made a start, but there are a whole lot of personal details about you and your family that I don't know. You have to do it online now – there isn't a paper form anymore. I can do that with you now if you like. Shall we do that?'

'Er … yes … yes, I suppose so. What do you need me to do?'

VICTIM STATEMENTS

Bernie lifted the lid of the laptop and clicked the mouse to open a web browser. 'Let me just find the right page and I'll be able to tell you the list of things it says you need to be able to tell them. … Let me see … Yes! Here we are! The date and location of the crime, the name of the police station where it was reported, your crime reference number – Jonah's already given me all of those. It says they may need your GP's name and address, but I think that'll only be for people who were injured and then treated by their doctor, so let's leave that for now. Details of previous applications: are you quite sure that your husband didn't ever make an application for compensation before?'

'Well, like I told Chrissie, I wasn't in a good place after Harry died. I left everything to Trevor. But I don't think he ever finished filling in the forms. I mean, if he had, he wouldn't have had to take out the loan, would he?'

'OK. Never mind about that then.' Bernie could see that Yvonne was on the verge of deciding to abandon the whole idea of claiming. 'So long as you don't know anything about it, that's all that matters. Let's get started. She clicked on a large green button on the screen, labelled "Make a claim".

'It says, "Are you applying for someone who died of their injuries?" That's pretty straightforward.' She selected "Yes" from the options available and clicked "Continue". This took her to a new page where she was asked to create a user account.

'It says I've got to register before I can apply,' she told Yvonne. And it's asking me for an email address and a password. Do you have an email address?'

'I don't think so.'

'Let's see …,' Bernie pondered what to do next. 'I could try doing it all in my name with my email address, but things might get complicated if we do that. And anyway, I'm not sure I like the idea of me having control over your affairs like that. I mean, you hardly know me.'

'So, you can't help after all?'

'No – Yes – I'm sure I can help: I just need to think about it. Oh! Here it says if you don't have online access or need help you can ring their Customer Service Team. Why don't we do that?'

'I don't know…,' Yvonne murmured looking very uneasy. 'I'm not good on the telephone.'

'And they won't be working on a Sunday, anyway,' Bernie muttered. 'I know! At least, I think I do. You do have internet access at home, don't you?'

'Yes. We got it put in for the boys, and Trev uses it for the taxi business.'

'Good. So, if I set you up with a free email account from Google, we can register that with the criminal injuries people and you'll be able to receive any emails they send to you.'

'How? Will I need a computer?'

'Have you got a mobile phone?'

'Yes. It's here somewhere.' Yvonne fumbled in her bag again. Bernie was relieved when she brought out a smartphone. She had had momentary misgivings as she imagined that Yvonne might still only have a basic phone with no data capability.

'You'll be able to receive emails on that,' she told her. 'Ask your Leo to connect it up to the WiFi for you. He'll know how to do it. If you hand it over to me, I'll get it connected on our system while you're here, and then I can set things up for you.'

It took some time, but eventually, with much passing back and forth of the phone, accompanied by ritual hand sanitising, Yvonne was equipped with both an email address and a user account for the CICA.

'Keep those passwords safe,' Bernie advised as Yvonne carefully tucked away the small piece of paper where she had written them down. 'You'll need them to log in again in the future. I've saved them to your phone, but if we need to log in on my laptop again, you'll have to type in the password.'

'Why don't I write them down for you to keep too?'

'Because you shouldn't share your passwords with anyone else, in case they log in and do something you wouldn't want them to do. Now let's have a go at filling in this application, shall we?'

'Before you do, would you like to hear what I think of these letters?' Jonah asked.

'Yes please.'

'Well, the good news is that they're not from a solicitor; they're from a debt collection agency, which is different. And they haven't actually started legal action yet. This is just to make you scared so that you pay up. On the other hand, it may well be true that the agreement that your husband signed included provision for them to add charges as well as interest if payments are missed. The threat to take you to court is fairly meaningless at the moment, with the backlog that the courts have got due to COVID. However, it's important to get the debt paid off because the interest and charges will just keep mounting if you don't.'

'Will this compensation be enough?' Yvonne asked anxiously.

'Maybe,' Bernie answered. 'Probably,' she amended, seeing the scared look on Yvonne's face. 'It all depends exactly what you can claim for when we fill in the application. The funeral expenses ought to be covered, but not the interest on the loan. But there are others things to take into account. You should be compensated for the trauma to you and your family in addition to paying for the funeral.'

'And meanwhile, you may be able to do other things to sort out the debt,' Jonah added. 'Have you tried ringing the debt advice line that Bernie told you about yet? They should be able to help you. They may be able to tell you where you could get a loan at lower interest to pay this one off without waiting for the compensation to come through.'

'Or they may have other ideas,' Bernie added. 'They may be able to negotiate with the loan company on your behalf, for instance.'

'No, I haven't rung them yet,' Yvonne admitted. 'It isn't easy finding a good time. I don't want Trevor to know. But I will get round to it,' she added earnestly.

'Good,' Bernie smiled back. 'Now, let's see what we can do with this online form, shall we?'

8. A QUESTION OF IDENTITY

Back at work the following Tuesday, Jonah felt that he had had a double-breakthrough. Not only had the SOCOs (who were still combing the crime scene for clues to the identity of the body) found what appeared to be an important piece of evidence, but also (and this was perhaps an even greater triumph, during these days of stringent budgets and metaphorical belt-tightening) Chief Superintendent Alison Brown had finally agreed to his request for a facial reconstruction to be made from the skull.

He smiled as Andy Lepage held up the evidence bag containing a lanyard with a plastic ID card attached to it. 'Marieke Cornelissen,' he read out, 'Staff Nurse. Now we're getting somewhere!'

'Possibly, sir, and possibly not.' Andy was more cautious. 'It was found some distance away from the body, and look at the date on it.'

Jonah peered closer. 'I see what you mean. It says it expired in 1995, which is a decade or so later than we were thinking of, based on when we believe the cuff-link was made. But there's no reason to think the cuff-link was lost right away. Remember what the porter said about the official college cuff-links: they're popular with alumni returning to Oxford after they've left. Maybe one of the boat club members wore the cuff-links to a gaudy, years after he bought them.'

'So, are you thinking that, while he was here on a visit, he took this nurse up on Shotover Hill for a roll in the leaves, something went wrong and she died, and then he buried her there?' suggested Andy.

'Something like that. I suppose he could have killed her elsewhere and transported the body, but then you'd think he'd have got rid of the ID badge more efficiently, instead of leaving it lying around near the body. Either way, it seems likely that our unidentified corpse could be Marieke Cornelissen. What do we know about her?'

'Nothing yet, sir. This has only just come in.'

'Well get on to the hospital and find out what they know about her. No, on second thoughts, I'll do the hospital; you go through the Missing Persons files to see if she was reported missing. The card doesn't say when it was issued, so it could be 1995 or a few years earlier.'

'Right you are, sir.'

A QUESTION OF IDENTITY

'Our ID badges expire three years after they're issued,' the helpful woman from the hospital HR department told Jonah. 'So that would mean that she started her employment here in 1992 or earlier. What was the name again?'

'Marieke Cornelissen.'

'How do you spell that?'

Jonah carefully spelled out the name a letter at a time.

'Well, I can tell you that there's nobody of that name working here now,' the woman informed him after a short pause.

'And what about back in 1995?'

'I can have a look for you, but …'

There was a long pause. Jonah could hear the sound of typing on a computer keyboard. Then, 'I'm sorry. There's nothing on the system. We did a major review of our records back in 2017 when we were preparing for GDPR. We got rid of the files on any staff who'd left more than a certain number of years before that.'

'You mean you can't even confirm that she worked for you?' Jonah demanded. 'What about if she applied for another job and her new employer wanted to know about her time here?'

'If it was back in the early nineties, it would hardly be relevant, would it?' the woman pointed out. 'Look, I'll talk to my supervisor if you like. I know we've got a load of paper records archived somewhere off-site. Maybe there'll be something about her there.'

So then they were back to playing a waiting game. Jonah patrolled the open-plan office looking round irritably, interrupting members of his team in their work to demand progress reports. They would look up wearily from a Missing Persons file or the transcript of a telephone call, shaking their heads and telling him that there was nothing yet.

It was not that they did not have any information to go on. If anything, there was too much. Dozens of members of the public had rung in with theories about the identity of the body or news of suspicious behaviour in the Shotover area which, "now that they came to think about it" might have been connected with the its disposal. Up until the finding of the lanyard, they had been prioritising evidence from the mid nineteen eighties; now they had to go back and study anything that had come in relating to the period from 1992 to 1995, which was when Marieke must have lost her ID card.

Was the corpse in the copse Marieke Cornelissen? Or could she simply have dropped her ID card nearby in a completely unrelated incident? If so, it should be possible to track down where she was now. Since she was a nurse, the chances were that, after she left Oxford, she would have moved to another hospital. Jonah set his team contacting NHS trusts across the country in the hope that Marieke might now be working for them.

Was it time for a public appeal for news of her? It might get results, but it would also put ideas into people's minds that she was mixed up in the murder. If she was a completely innocent party who simply happened to have dropped her lanyard while on a walk in the country park, it would be unfair to associate her with this crime. Public perception, once formed, was very difficult to change.

'I need to see Professor Weldon again,' he announced suddenly. 'I want to ask him if anyone from the boat club was going out with Marieke Cornelissen. And I want to show him the list of rowers and see if it jogs his memory. He surely must know more about them than he's told us so far.'

Graham Weldon, however was not available for a meeting. When Jonah rang, his wife answered the telephone and told them that he had developed symptoms of COVID-19 overnight and was now in bed with a cough and a high temperature.

Jonah expressed sympathy and wished the professor well, asking her to pass on the message that he would like to speak to him when he was well enough. He was about to ring off, but Mrs Weldon stopped him.

'He'd been going to ring you,' she said. 'He had something he thought you ought to see.'

'Oh?' Jonah's face brightened. He had resigned himself to waiting for several days – or longer – before being able to get any information from the professor.

'Well, two things actually. There are his boat club cuff-links, which he tells me are important to you. I can vouch for them both being here, safe in their box. I'll send you a photo if you like, with a time-stamp on it to prove it's current.'

Jonah decided that he liked this efficient woman. 'Yes please, if it's not too much bother while your husband's ill. Just knowing that he has them is useful to us. We're trying to track down everyone who had a pair.'

'So I gathered. I understood from what Graham told me that anyone who had a pair and can't demonstrate that they've still got them both is under suspicion.'

'Well, let's just say that they'd be someone we very much wanted to talk to,' Jonah said evasively.

'And the other thing,' Mrs Weldon went on, 'is a document containing information about the purchase of the cuff-links for the college boat club. Graham said you'd be interested to see it.'

'Really? Tell me about it.'

'I can scan it and send that to you as well, if you like.'

'That would be extremely helpful.'

'Then I'll do that. It's the minutes of one of their committee meetings. It turns out they were all up in a box in our loft. Graham spent a whole afternoon up there hunting for them. He has no idea about filing and archiving!'

'He kept them; that's the main thing,' Jonah said eagerly. 'That's the sort of attitude I like – much better than this idea of shredding everything as soon as you can, that everyone seems to have got ever since the Data Protection Act came in.'

'Retention of personal data beyond when it is needed is a serious matter,' Dorothy Weldon said stiffly. Jonah wondered what her job was. It sounded as if she were well-versed in data protection legislation: an administrator at the university, perhaps? No – that was a sexist thought; she was just as likely to be

CEO of her own business or a lawyer or doctor.

'Yes, of course,' he agreed out loud, 'but the minutes of meetings are more like historical documents, aren't they?'

'Anyway,' she went on, 'he showed me the minutes of the Hilary term meeting in 1983, which includes an item on the purchase of two dozen pairs of custom-made cuff-links for the rowing eights and committee members.'

'Excellent!' Jonah crowed. 'So, there were just twenty-four pairs made. And your husband has one pair, which leaves us with just twenty-three more people to find. Once you're both out of self-isolation, I'll need to see the cuff-links and I'd like to take away the minutes as evidence, but meanwhile, if you could send pictures of them both, that would be immensely helpful. There's an email address on the card that I gave your husband.'

'Yes. I've got it here,' Dorothy Weldon confirmed. 'I'll scan the document and send it right away.'

'Thank you. And I hope Professor Weldon makes a full recovery very soon.'

Jonah looked towards Bernie triumphantly. 'That's quite a breakthrough. The minutes of the meeting will have the names of the committee members on them, and they may have other information about what was going on in the club at that time. And, if nothing else, at least we don't need to worry that there could be dozens of those cuff-links out there.'

'I'm more concerned about the question of whether Professor Weldon could have been an asymptomatic carrier of COVID-19 when you met him last week,' she replied drily. 'I think we ought to go home right away and start self-isolating ourselves.'

'He kept his distance,' Jonah argued, 'and we had the door and windows of the car open while he was in with us.'

'But nobody knows if that's enough to prevent transmission,' Bernie objected. 'All that anyone knows about this coronavirus is that it seems to be remarkably easy to pass on. Anyway, quite apart from all that, government advice is that everyone should work at home if they can – and you certainly can co-ordinate this investigation from home, so that's where you ought to be!'

With very bad grace, Jonah agreed to work at home for the rest of the week. The moment that Bernie let him in through the door, he was heading for his private sitting room, intent on chasing up the hospital HR department over their failure to get back with more information about Marieke Cornelissen.

It turned out that a brief summary of her employment record had been filed away in the hospital archives. This comprised: her name (Marieke Johanna Cornelissen), previous names (none), payroll number, pay grades (D on appointment in 1989, rising to E in 1994), date of birth (5th March 1966), positions held (staff nurse, mainly working on male surgical wards), leaving date (May 1995), reason for leaving (resigned).

'Not much to go on,' Peter remarked when Jonah showed this information to him when he came into his room to tell him that their evening meal was ready.

'It tells us that she left the hospital two months before her ID card expired,' Bernie pointed out, 'and it *doesn't* say anything about her failing to turn up for work one day. So, if she was killed and buried up on Shotover, my guess is it must have been after she'd stopped working for the hospital.'

'Wouldn't she have had to hand her ID back before she left?' asked Jonah.

'Yes, but I bet people don't always.'

'If the last shift she did was on nights, there may not have been anyone to hand it back to,' Peter suggested, becoming interested despite his determination not to get involved in police work now that he was retired – or to encourage Jonah in his monomania.

'But why would she be wearing her lanyard if she wasn't working for the hospital anymore?' demanded Jonah, 'and that belt buckle they found looks just like the ones that nurses used to wear. I was hypothesizing that she was still in her uniform when she was killed.'

'Always assuming that the body *is* Marieke Cornelissen,' Peter said drily, 'but what if it isn't? What if she just happened to go for a walk in the woods, after she'd left the hospital? Maybe she was taking the last of her annual leave before her contract ended. Nurses often have leave still owing when they finish; it's so hard to find a good time to take it while they're there.' He spoke from experience: his first wife had been a nurse, as were both his daughter and daughter-in-law.

'And she may not have been wearing the lanyard,' Bernie chipped in. 'It could have been in her handbag, and she dropped it when she fished in it for a tissue or a lipstick or whatever else it is that women keep in their handbags.'

A QUESTION OF IDENTITY

Bernie prided herself on never having owned or carried a handbag, which she considered to be a mark of female subjugation to male expectations. As a result, her pockets were always bulging with credit cards, mobile phone, face mask, sanitiser and other essentials of twenty-first century life.

'Or the lanyard may even have been the cause of her death,' Jonah mused as he followed Peter through to the kitchen. 'If we follow the hypothesis that she went with a member of the 1983 Lichfield College rowing team for a romp in the woods, maybe they were into sadomasochism of some sort. Maybe she gave him the lanyard to tie round her neck and he went too far and strangled her.'

'And I suppose, if she'd already left her job, that would explain why there wasn't any outcry when she didn't go in the next day,' Bernie added.

'What about friends or her landlord or all the other people who must have expected to see her around, though?' asked Peter, heaping rice onto plates and adding steaming home-made curry from a pan. 'Didn't anyone report her missing?'

'Not that we've been able to trace so far,' Jonah admitted. 'And the hospital didn't keep a record of her address, so we can't check up when she left there and whether she took all her things with her.'

'If her boyfriend was the type that gets a kick out of half-strangling his partner, don't you think she was probably living with him?' suggested Lucy. 'The way you're talking, he sounds like the sort who wouldn't like to let her out of his sight any more than he had to.'

A QUESTION OF IDENTITY

'Mmmm,' Jonah swallowed the spoonful of curry and rice that she had inserted into his mouth as she spoke. 'I suppose, if he was the jealous type, he may have driven all her other friends away from her, which would explain the lack of any missing person report.'

'If she was living with a member of the rowing club, that must narrow them down to the ones who were living in or near Oxford at the time,' Peter pointed out.

'You're right,' Jonah agreed in a tone that somehow implied that he hadn't expected Peter to come up with such insight. 'We need to find out where they were all living between when they graduated and 1995. What a pity professor Weldon is out of action for a couple of weeks! At least his wife is on the ball. She sent the pictures of the cuff-links and the minutes of their committee meeting promptly enough. Perhaps I could email her with a photograph of Marieke Cornelissen's ID card and that list of boat crew members and ask her to-'

'Oh no you don't!' Peter interjected. 'She's got enough on her plate nursing her husband and worrying that she may be going to go down with coronavirus too. You can't go pestering her to show him photographs and lists of names! I keep telling you: those bones aren't going anywhere; it doesn't matter if it takes a few months to find out who they belong to.'

As the days dragged on with little or no progress in the case, Jonah began to think that Peter's estimate of a few months might have been over-optimistic. Suspecting, from her name, that Marieke Cornelissen could be a Dutch citizen, Jonah contacted the police in the Netherlands. They agreed to help, but told him that Cornelissen was not an uncommon name and, without more to go on, it was likely to take some time, especially with their ranks depleted by illness and with extra duties imposed by the pandemic. He was lucky, however: COVID-19 cases were right down now and it looked as if the crisis might be nearly over; so, they would do their best to trace her for him.

Bernie, meanwhile, was wondering how Yvonne had got on with the debt advice centre and her application to the Criminal Injuries Compensation Authority. She had expected a call from her once she had news on any progress.

Had she still not rung the centre? Had her application not yet been acknowledged? Was her failure to make contact because Trevor's taxi business was doing so badly that he was at home all the time and she could not telephone without him being aware of it? Or, on the contrary, was it that he was now bringing in a steady income and their debt problem was beginning to recede?

'I've just thought,' Peter said as they cleared the breakfast table on Saturday, 'if we're self-isolating we can't help Father Damien with marshalling arrivals at mass tomorrow. I'd better give him a ring and let him know. I should have thought of that before.'

'How long are we supposed to self-isolate for?' asked Lucy. 'I mean, does the clock start when you found out about

Professor Weldon having symptoms or when you met him?'

'It must be the day we met him, surely,' Bernie said. 'Since if we did pick up the virus from him, that's when the incubation period must have started. So, two weeks from then brings us to next Thursday.'

'So, we could have passed it on to people at church last Sunday!' Peter exclaimed in dismay. 'I never thought of that. I'd better warn Father Damien.'

'Won't that just get a whole lot of people worried unnecessarily?' objected Jonah. 'Think about it rationally: neither Bernie nor I have any symptoms nine days after we were exposed – if we were exposed at all – to the virus. The chances are we're both perfectly clear and no danger to anyone.'

VICTIM STATEMENTS

'I have to admit I'm with Jonah there,' Bernie agreed. 'There's no point spreading panic just because there's a theoretical chance that we were infectious last Sunday. We were being careful about social distancing – which is more than some other people were doing – and it's only chance that we even know about Professor Weldon being ill.'

'We aren't even legally required to self-isolate now,' Jonah added, 'because he hasn't had a positive test. He may just have an ordinary throat infection or a bad case of hay fever.'

'So, I'd play it down with Father Damien, if I were you,' Bernie continued. 'Tell him this is just precautionary and the chances are there's no risk at all.'

'But *why* hasn't he been tested yet?' demanded Lucy. 'He ought to have got a test as soon as he developed symptoms.'

'Of course, he *should*!' Bernie snorted, 'but we've got Boris's[6] "world-beating track and trace system", haven't we? You can't expect people with COVID symptoms to get tested, just like that, can you?'

'I think you'll find it's called "test and trace" now,' Jonah informed her. 'And it's a government IT system, so what could possibly go wrong?' he added sarcastically.

'It doesn't really matter, does it?' Peter sighed. 'We'd just better all do the responsible thing and keep away from anyone outside the family until two weeks after Bernie and Jonah met the prof. All

---

[6] Alexander Boris de Pfeffel Johnson was the UK Prime minister during the 2020-21 COVID-19 pandemic.

being well, it's all just a false alarm, but we'd all feel dreadful if anyone did catch COVID from one of us, wouldn't we?'

He made his phone call, following Jonah's advice to play down the risk and emphasise that they were all well and there was no cause for alarm. He was still fending off Damien's offer to bring them supplies of food during their voluntary incarceration when Bernie's mobile started to ring. She took it out and looked down at the screen.

'It's Chrissie. I wonder if she's heard from Yvonne.' Bernie went out into the hall so that she could speak without interfering with Peter's conversation. 'Hi Chrissie. How're you doing?'

'I hope this isn't too early. We're going out in a few minutes and I wanted to ring you today.'

'Not at all. We're always up early to get Jonah up. This is practically mid-morning for us!'

'I was wondering if you'd heard anything from Yvonne Whittle recently?'

'No. I was thinking of ringing *you*, but I assume you haven't either?'

'No. I don't like to ring her, because I've only got their landline and I'm never sure if Trevor…'

'I was expecting her to let me know how she got on with the debt advice people,' Bernie told her, 'and we'd half agreed to meet again so she could show me how much Universal Credit they're getting. I'm pretty sure she won't have claimed everything that she's entitled to. And I was hoping to talk to her about putting in another compensation claim: for the trauma she experienced finding her son's body the way she did. I've been doing some research about that, and I'm sure she has a right to compensation for that, in addition to the claim we've already put in to cover the funeral costs.'

'I hope she's alright,' Chrissie said anxiously. 'Maybe … Do you think DCI Porter could call round – as the Senior Investigating Officer – and check up on the family under the guise of keeping them in the loop with the prosecution?'

Well, certainly not this week. We're self-isolating after someone he interviewed went down with COVID symptoms. Maybe Gavin could call on her?'

'Yes. Yes, I'll ask him. I hope you're all OK?'

'We're fine,' Bernie assured her. 'Well, apart from Jonah going round like a bear with a sore head because he wants to be out there, pressing ahead

A QUESTION OF IDENTITY

with identifying that body you found over on Shotover Hill!'

9. TWO STEPS FORWARD, ONE STEP BACK

There was still no news from Yvonne Whittle the next day; so, Chrissie persuaded Gavin to fit a visit to the house in Chichester Road into his routine patrol of the area on Tuesday morning. As they walked along the pavement in the sunshine, nodding, as they passed, to residents tidying their gardens, Gavin became conscious that Stella seemed hyper-alert, jumping at every little sound or sudden movement. It was months since he'd seen her so much on edge like this. Had something happened to bring back memories of the day she had watched Kenny being crushed against a wall?

As they turned a corner, their ears were assaulted by loud music blaring

TWO STEPS FORWARD, ONE STEP BACK

from a car with all its windows open to let in air to combat the sweltering heat. Instinctively, Stella pressed herself back against the privet hedge which separated the houses from the pavement, cowering away from the noise.

Gavin slowed his stride, but took care not to stop and stare. Seconds later, Stella had recovered herself and, walking briskly, caught up with him.

'How're you sleeping?' Gavin asked a few minutes later, trying to sound casual. 'This hot weather's no good for me.'

'Not that well,' Stella admitted. Then, after a pause, 'Does it show?'

'You seemed a bit jumpy this morning, that's all; and I wondered if …'

'I wish the trial was over!' Stella declared, as if changing the subject. 'I can't stop worrying that I'll make a mess of giving evidence. It'd be awful if they got away because the jury didn't trust what I said. I dreamt about it, last night. The defence lawyer kept firing questions at me and I just kept talking nonsense and everybody was laughing at me.'

'It doesn't all depend on you,' Gavin told her firmly. 'And anyway, there's no reason to think you'll mess up. It'll all be fine – you'll see.'

'I suppose so.' Stella sounded unconvinced.

'It's this stop-start business that's getting to you,' the burly police officer went on. 'Chrissie and I feel the same. They said the trial would be in the spring; then they said no new jury trials; then they closed the courts altogether; then they let the Butlers out on bail; now the court's open again, but still no date …'

TWO STEPS FORWARD, ONE STEP BACK

'I'm sorry. Of course, it's worse for you and Chrissie. I'm just being silly.'

'No, you're not. You're bound to be nervous about testifying for the first time.'

'Thanks.'

They walked on in silence. Then Stella confided in a low voice, 'I'd like to be able to forget what I saw, but I know I mustn't because I need to be able to tell the court exactly what it was like, so that they'll convict Shane Butler. So, I keep running it through in my mind to make sure I've got all the details right.'

'Don't do that,' Gavin urged anxiously. 'There's no need, and it won't help. You've got your written statement. You can read that to refresh your memory before you go into the witness box. Until then, just push it all to the back of your mind and try to forget about it.'

'I don't like to. I owe it to Kenny to –'

'Kenny wouldn't want you having nightmares on his account.'

'I know – it's just …' Stella sighed. 'It's such a big responsibility!'

They continued walking and soon the Whittles' house came into view.

'It looks like Mr Whittle's out,' Stella observed. 'His taxi's gone.'

'Yes,' Gavin agreed. 'I hope that means his taxi business is looking up.'

As they walked up the short drive to the front door, Gavin looked up and saw Leo's face at the bedroom window. He smiled and raised his hand, but the boy vanished without acknowledging his greeting. He knocked on the door and then stepped back to wait. There was no sound from inside. Looking up, he spotted a slight movement of the curtains in Leo's bedroom. He must be watching them from in hiding.

Gavin knocked again. This time he heard the sound of footsteps on the stairs and then there was a shadow visible through the frosted glass in the front door. Someone was fumbling with the lock. Finally, the door opened and Yvonne peered out at them, bleary-eyed and blinking in the strong sunlight.

Her hair was unkempt, matted on one side and sticking out in a bushy mass on the other. She was wearing a pale blue dressing gown beneath which protruded bare legs ending in pink slippers.

'Good morning, Mrs Whittle,' Gavin greeted her. 'How are you?'

'We're doing alright.' Yvonne swayed a little and clasped hold of the door frame to steady herself. 'Well, I'm feeling a bit rough, if I'm honest,' she confessed when Gavin said nothing in response. 'It was Harry's birthday yesterday – no, the day before – it *is* Tuesday, isn't it?'

'Yes,' Gavin confirmed. 'I'm sorry to intrude at such a difficult time. I just wanted to check that you're getting the help you need with the compensation and … stuff,' he finished awkwardly, not liking to mention the family's debt problem or, still less, Yvonne's drinking.

'Don't worry about us,' Yvonne replied evasively. 'Trevor's been getting more work this week. He's out now, in fact!' she added with a rather false-sounding brightness.

'Bernie was expecting to hear from you,' Gavin told her. 'She thinks you're entitled to more than you've claimed for. She'd like to meet up with you again.'

TWO STEPS FORWARD, ONE STEP BACK

'I don't want to be any bother. She must be busy, looking after her – her – that detective in the wheelchair.'

'She's spent a lot of time looking into your entitlements,' Gavin persisted gently. 'You don't want her to have wasted all that, do you?'

'That's very kind of her, but I'm sure we don't need any more help. Like I said, Trev's working again now, and I've been told I'll be off furlough and back at work in August. We don't need any handouts.'

'It's not handouts, Mrs Whittle,' Stella chipped in, frustrated at Yvonne's evasion. 'It's only what you're entitled to. You and Trevor pay your taxes, don't you? This is just giving you some of that back.'

'PC Gilbert is right, Mrs Whittle,' Gavin agreed. 'Every citizen has a right to compensation when they're injured as a result of crime. Your taxes pay for that, the same as they pay for having a police service to prevent crime. We didn't prevent Harry being killed, so you're entitled to compensation.'

Yvonne stood staring at them for a few seconds before answering. 'OK,' she said at last, 'I'll give your friend a ring, later.'

'Do you think she's been drinking again?' Stella asked as they continued their foot patrol of the neighbourhood.

'Quite likely. I didn't know about the boy's birthday. I can imagine it setting her back – all those memories!'

'Isn't there anything we can do? I mean ... isn't there something someone could do to help?'

'I dunno,' Gavin sighed. 'One thing I *am* going to do is to give Bernie a ring.'

They walked on until they came to the end of the road. At the junction there was a small triangle of grass with a bench and a litter bin on it. Gavin sat down and took out his phone.

'Gavin?' Bernie's unmistakeable voice came through loud enough for Stella to listen in. 'How're you doing – and Chrissie?'

'We're both fine. I'm ringing about Yvonne Whittle. Chrissie says you were wondering why she hadn't been in touch.'

'Yes, I was expecting her to call me to set up another meeting. I'm sure she hasn't claimed half of what she could.'

'Yes, well … I just wanted to let you know… I've just come from there. She told me it was the boy's birthday at the weekend. That's probably why she hasn't felt up to phoning you.'

'Oh! Of course. I understand. I'll back off for a bit. Thanks for telling me. I can't meet her until next week anyway – we're self-isolating.'

'Oh?'

'Jonah interviewed a potential witness in connexion with that body you unearthed, and now he's gone down with COVID – the witness, I mean, not Jonah!' she added hastily.

'Absolutely!' Jonah chipped in. 'I'm still fighting fit and ready for anything.'

'Well, anything except sitting back and taking things easy for a bit,' Bernie retorted.

'Did you see the appeal we've put out for information about Marieke Cornelissen?' Jonah went on.

TWO STEPS FORWARD, ONE STEP BACK

'I'm not sure that I did.' Gavin sounded puzzled. 'Who is he – or she?'

'She *was* a nurse at the John Radcliffe from 1989 to 1995,' Jonah told him. 'We found her name badge in the leaf litter near your body, and nobody seems to have seen her since she quit her job twenty-five years ago.'

'So, you think it's her body buried in the woods?' Gavin queried.

'That's the sixty-four-thousand-dollar question, isn't it?' Jonah chuckled. 'It could be her, or she could have killed someone else and buried the body, or she could have nothing at all to do with the case and just be a careless nurse who dropped her ID card during some shenanigans in the woods. That's why we're appealing for people to come forward and tell us anything they know about her – either before she lost it or afterwards. So far, we know hardly anything about her apart from her name.'

'It's a funny one,' Gavin observed. 'It sounds foreign.'

'It's Dutch,' Jonah confirmed. 'We've been on to the police in the Netherlands, but they made it pretty clear that they had better things to do with their time than hunting for random females. So, we're pinning our hopes on the public appeal. There must be *someone* around who remembers her.'

Indeed, there was, but it was not until a week later that Cheryl Richardson called the incident room number and told her story to Jennifer Moorehouse, a member of civilian staff. Jennifer immediately put her through to Jonah.

'I used to work with Marieke, years ago,' she told him. 'We were both nurses at the JR. I'm sorry I didn't call you before, but we've been working flat out. This is my first day off in a fortnight.'

'Not to worry,' Jonah reassured her, 'as my PA keeps telling me, we're investigating a body that's been lying in the ground for probably a quarter of a century, so a few days isn't going to make any difference.'

'You think the bones you found in the country park belong to Marieke then?'

'We don't know. All we do know is that her hospital ID card from 1995 turned up close to where they were buried. It could just be chance. The bones may have already been there for years before she went there, or the body may only have been buried there after she dropped it. That's why we've appealed for information. If she's still alive, we'd like to speak to her, and if not, we'd like to find some data to enable us to confirm that those are her bones.'

'I see.' There was a long pause before the nurse went on, 'I'm not sure how much help I can be. I only knew her for a few months. She said she was leaving to go travelling, but I don't really know any more than that. I don't have a forwarding address for her or anything.'

'That's fine. Just tell me anything you can remember about her, however trivial. It all helps to paint a picture that could make it easier for us to find her. Let's start with something basic: we guessed from her name that she might be Dutch – is that right?'

TWO STEPS FORWARD, ONE STEP BACK

'Yes. She came from Rotterdam.'

'Now that's really helpful,' Jonah said encouragingly. 'We've asked the Dutch police to help, but they told us it was like looking for a needle in a haystack. At least what you've just told me reduces the size of the haystack somewhat. Now let's see … you don't happen to know what her address was when she was living in Oxford?'

'No. I do remember she used to walk to work, so I guess that means it can't have been far from the JR.'

'Presumably she was renting? Do you know if it was a house or a flat? Or if she was sharing with someone else?'

'No, I'm sorry.'

'Never mind. What about boy friends? Or did she have any other close friends that you knew of?'

'Yes, yes she was seeing someone. What was he called now?' Cheryl paused and Jonah could hear her breathing as she tried to remember the name. 'No, I'm sorry, it won't come. I do remember he was at the university.'

'A student?' Jonah asked eagerly. 'Or a member of staff?'

'I'm not sure, she just said he had a room in one of the colleges.'

'Which one?'

'I don't know. I'm sorry. I don't know their names very well. It was one of the old ones in the centre. She said his room was like a monk's cell.'

'Good, good, that's very useful. Now what did she say about where she was going when she left? You say she intended to travel – was she going with her boyfriend, do you know?'

'I think so. Well, I assumed they were going together. I'm not sure whether she actually *said*. I'm sorry.'

'And did she say anything about where they were going – or where they were going first, if they were travelling?'

'She said a lot of things. She wanted to see the world.' There was another long pause. Jonah waited patiently and was rewarded when Cheryl continued, 'She did mention South Africa, I remember. Yes, I'm almost sure that was where she said they were off to. I think he had family there – or maybe she was the one who did. I don't know, but there was definitely some reason they'd decided to start there.'

'Excellent!' Jonah declared warmly. 'You've been a great help. Now, is there anything else that you can remember about her – anything at all?'

'I don't think so. It was a long time ago. I'm sorry.'

'Yes, of course. Well, if you do remember anything else, please do let us know. And thank you for ringing – you really have been very helpful.'

Jonah ended the call and swung his chair round triumphantly to look at Bernie. 'We've got something to go on at last! I'll get on to the South African police right away and someone can try to find the place she was living when she was in Oxford. It must have been in Headington somewhere – probably a rented flat. It's a pity we don't know for certain that her boyfriend was at Lichfield, but it's a reasonable assumption that he was and that he was the owner of the cuff-link.'

'Except,' Bernie pointed out, 'that all the people who had a pair of those cuff-links were at Lichfield ten years earlier than when Marieke Cornelissen was going out with this lad, who may or may not have been living in Lichfield college rooms. If her university boyfriend did drop the cuff-link then he must have come back to Oxford after graduating and either done a postgraduate course or become a live-in member of staff. And in that case, he could have been at any of the colleges, not necessarily Lichfield.'

'I suppose you're right,' Jonah agreed grudgingly. 'It just all seemed to fit together so nicely. Anyway, the first job is to ring the South African police and ask them if they can find any record of her arriving there in 1995.'

VICTIM STATEMENTS

The South African police were polite, but appeared less than enthusiastic about a request from a British police officer for them to search for information on a Dutch citizen who might, or might not, have arrived in their country a quarter of a century earlier. They pointed out to Jonah that they were in the middle of a pandemic and that, while cases and deaths might be declining in the UK, the opposite was the case in South Africa and it was putting an extreme strain on their resources.

Jonah presented himself at his most charming, but the senior officer to whom he spoke was firm: they would note the details that he had given and, when circumstances allowed, they would pass them on to their immigration service, who might be able to help; but enforcing an unpopular night-time curfew and a ban on alcohol sales was quite enough for his workforce to deal with at the moment, depleted as it was through COVID-19 infections.

'You can see his point,' Bernie said, observing the dissatisfaction in Jonah's face as he ended the call. 'You can't expect them to view this as a priority when they're struggling to contain the virus. I've been having a look at the international data: things are just kicking off big-time in South Africa.'

'He told me Cornelissen is quite a common name among Afrikaners too,' Jonah told her gloomily, 'so we seem to simply have increased the size of the haystack again!'

'No,' Bernie laughed. 'This is a second haystack with a different needle in it. The Dutch needle is Marieke's past history; the South African one is where she went when she left Oxford.'

However you chose to describe it, progress in the case moved at geological speed during the ensuing days and weeks. Jonah's team searched in vain for any record of where Marieke Cornelissen had lived when she was in Oxford. The public appeal for information about her attracted no further responses. The facial reconstruction was stuck in a queue behind more urgent cases. Enquiries at all the Oxford colleges failed to identify Marieke's boyfriend. Professor Weldon's condition worsened and, on admission to hospital, it was confirmed that he did indeed have COVID-19; it would be some time before he could be shown the list of names. Neither did any of the other members of the Lichfield 1983 rowing eights come forward in response to the email that had gone out from the Alumni Office.

As the family's self-imposed isolation continued, the national response to the virus became increasingly chaotic and difficult to comprehend. While the chancellor continued to encourage people to assist restaurants and pubs to recover from the dire effects of the lockdown on their businesses by eating out, new local lockdowns were imposed in Greater Manchester, East Lancashire and parts of Yorkshire to combat a spike in coronavirus cases in the north of England. Lucy began to talk about going back to Liverpool "while I still can", fearing that Merseyside might be next. It was still difficult to obtain a coronavirus test and the "test and trace" system for tracking contacts of COVID-19 sufferers was under constant criticism in the media.

As Jonah's 62nd birthday dawned bright and sunny it seemed that the weather was about the only cheerful thing in his world – and even that brought its own problems for those blessed with a large garden with beds and borders and vegetable patches that needed watering! As he prepared to log off and join the others for the special birthday tea that Peter and Lucy had prepared, he looked round the computer screen at the members of his team, with whom he was conducting a final video conference to sum up their day's work.

'Doesn't anyone have anything that can help us move this case on?' he pleaded. 'Andy?' The sergeant shook his head. 'Monica? – Alice?'

'No, sir.'

'Is there still no news on that facial reconstruction?'

'They said they'll probably be able to get started on it on Monday, sir,' replied DC Joshua Pitchfork.

'What about dental records?' Jonah asked in a last-ditch attempt to find that something had been achieved that day. 'Who was looking into those?'

'I've nearly finished ringing round all the practices,' Alice told him. 'I started with the Headington ones, like you said. 'Unfortunately, they all seem to have a policy of destroying records ten years after the patient's last appointment. They all seem to have had a clear-out in the run-up to GDPR. Several of them said that, up until then, they used to keep them for thirty years.'

'So, if we do get more evidence that the body is Marieke Cornelissen, there's going to be no chance of proving it from her dental records,' Jonah muttered. 'I wish the people who drew up this data protection legislation would take future police enquiries into account! What are her family going to think – assuming we manage to track them down – if we end up telling them: this is probably your daughter or sister or cousin or whatever, but we can't tell for sure because we've thrown away all the records that might have helped us to do a proper identification?'

There was a knock at the door. Glancing down at the time in the corner of his computer screen, Jonah brought the meeting to an end and closed the videoconferencing app. He swung his chair round and looked up at Lucy, who was peering cautiously into the room.

'Tea's ready!' she announced.

When they entered the kitchen, the radio news was on, featuring a discussion on the merits of face-coverings as a means of reducing the spread of COVID-19. Seeing that everyone was now present for their meal, Bernie snapped it off, cutting off in mid-stream the protestations of a Conservative MP who considered that any further compulsion in this respect would be an infringement of his civil liberties.

Peter and Lucy had spent most of the afternoon preparing a good spread of finger foods for Jonah's special meal. Peter had made sausage rolls and quiche, while Lucy had opted for vegetable samosas and salad, to "moderate our intake of cholesterol". She took up her usual place next to Jonah and asked him what he would like her to feed him with first. Jonah diplomatically opted for a samosa accompanied by cucumber and spring onions.

'Lucy's decided to go back to Liverpool on Saturday week,' Peter told him. 'Bernie's going to drive her up, so you'll have to put up with me looking after you for the day.'

'I'm sure I'll be able to bear it,' Jonah grinned back, 'but I'm disappointed to lose my girlfriend again so soon. You hardly seem to have been here any time.'

'I know!' Lucy groaned. '*I'd* like to stay longer too, but Dom and Ibrahim say COVID cases are rising again in Liverpool, and Mariam doesn't know if she'll be able to come back at all, because Blackburn is in the local lockdown area. I want to go back before they decide to stop anyone going into Liverpool. Actually, I'd go this weekend if it wasn't that I thought I'd better not go off to the other end of the country until a bit longer after you and Mam were exposed to the virus. If one of you had it asymptomatically then I could theoretically be a carrier now.'

'What will Mariam do if she isn't allowed to travel?' Jonah asked. Mariam was one of Lucy's housemates and a fellow-medical student.

'Well, the lectures are all going to be online anyway,' Lucy told him. 'It's the practical side that's going to be difficult. That's why I want to be up there, not down here, when term starts.'

VICTIM STATEMENTS

'Ruth has been worrying that Dom and Ibrahim won't be eating properly with the girls away,' Bernie chuckled. 'I keep telling her that they're just as capable of cooking as Lucy and Mariam, but she won't have it. She's been taking them food parcels and offering to do their washing for them!'

'As if *we* do *their* washing!' Lucy snorted. 'Aunty Ruth seems to be living in a time-warp; but at least she's come round to the idea of Dom and Mariam going out together, at last. I think she's sort of grateful that he's found a nice modest girl who doesn't flaunt her body everywhere – even if she is a Muslim instead of a good Catholic!'

'And she seems confident that, having her brother living with her will prevent any hanky-panky going on before the wedding!' Bernie added with a grin.

TWO STEPS FORWARD, ONE STEP BACK

'You're right, Lucy: she is living in a different age.'

They cleared away the savoury course and Peter disappeared into the larder for the cake. He returned a moment later carrying  a masterpiece of his own creation. It was in the shape of a policeman's helmet, covered in blue icing with a white chocolate star, iced with the initials E₁₁R, acting as the police badge.

'No candles this year, I'm afraid,' Bernie said. 'Blowing them out is forbidden.'

'Even when we're all from the same household?' asked Jonah. 'I'm sure that's allowed.'

VICTIM STATEMENTS

'It probably is,' Bernie conceded, 'but I'm not taking any risks. I think we could sing *Happy Birthday* though, if we don't get too close to one another while we do it.'

10. BACK TO WORK

'I'm home!' Yvonne called out as she closed the front door behind her. Silence. Leo probably had his headphones on and couldn't hear her, but Trevor usually came to meet her when she arrived home from work. The taxi was on the drive, so he couldn't be out on a call. Perhaps he was in the garden.

She went upstairs to put her work overall in the linen basket and wash her hands. You couldn't be too careful with this coronavirus about. Perhaps she ought to have a complete change of clothes and wash the ones that she had worn to work? But Trevor never got changed after he'd being driving people in his taxi; he'd probably think she was making a fuss. The health and safety briefing at work hadn't said anything about that – just wear a face mask, sanitise often and put on clean overalls every day.

She found Trevor sitting on their bed, surrounded by pieces of paper. He looked up as she entered the bedroom. 'Oh! You're back!'

'Yes,' she answered brightly. After her first morning back at work, she was feeling better than she had for months. At last, some sort of normality seemed to be returning to their lives. 'I did call, but you mustn't have heard.'

'We've got to cut back,' Trevor said, as if she had not spoken. 'We're spending too much and there's not enough coming in. Look at this credit card statement! How can you spend so much at the supermarket? How much can three people eat, for God's sake?'

BACK TO WORK

'It's not just food,' Yvonne defended herself. 'It's washing powder and toothpaste and hoover bags and soap – and – and car shampoo for your taxi, and-'

She dropped her bag down on to the dressing table and slumped into the chair. Her high spirits had evaporated. She reached for a tube of moisturising cream and began massaging it into hands that were dry and cracked after repeated applications of sanitiser.

'Well, we'll just have to use less of them,' Trevor growled. 'Or can't you find cheaper brands?'

'I already do,' Yvonne protested. 'Well, apart from a few things. You know Leo won't eat things if they're not the sort he likes.'

'Well, he's going to have to learn. We can't go on like this,' Trevor insisted.

'But now I'm back off furlough, we'll have more money coming in,' Yvonne argued, 'and I'm going to be working extra hours all week this week – they told us that this morning – so that'll mean overtime. We've got to give all the offices a deep clean before everyone gets back to work.'

'That's not going to be enough. I'm still not getting as many call-outs as I used to, and we've got behind on things while we were both off. We've just *got* to cut back or we won't be able to start paying back on the electric and the gas and the rent and the funeral loan and–' He hurled bills down one by one on the dressing table in front of his wife to emphasise his words.

'About the funeral,' Yvonne interrupted, 'Chrissie Hughes says we can get that paid for us. I've filled in the–'

BACK TO WORK

'Chrissie Hughes?' roared Trevor, grabbing her by one shoulder and twisting her round in her seat so that he could look her in the face. 'What have you been telling her about our affairs? This is private – family stuff – nothing to do with Chrissie Hughes and that – fu – that husband of hers.'

Yvonne's eyes opened wide and she swallowed hard, biting back tears.

'Well?' Trevor demanded. 'Tell me!'

'Nothing,' Yvonne pleaded. 'I only said the funeral cost a lot and she said they got theirs paid for, and we could too. That's all. There's a website where you can apply. I filled it in. I thought I was helping.'

'Oh, go and get us our lunch!' Trevor pushed her away and busied himself with gathering up all the papers and stuffing them into a brown envelope. 'And next time you're shopping, just remember what I said about cutting back!'

Yvonne got to her feet and stumbled out of the room. As she passed Leo's bedroom, she heard the door click shut. He must have been listening to their row. How much did he know? He mustn't be allowed to realise that they were in debt. She fumbled her way downstairs and along the hall to the kitchen.

She got a sliced loaf out of the cupboard and put it on the table. Then she went to the fridge and brought out cheese and ham to make sandwiches, and a two-litre bottle of Coca-Cola. Leo sidled in as she was buttering the bread. She smiled at him and he grinned weakly back.

'Get the plates out for me, would you love?'

BACK TO WORK

Leo obediently crossed the kitchen and fetched three plates from one of the base units. He set them in place on the table and then went back for glasses.

'Would you like tinned fruit for afters?' his mother asked him, trying to make normal conversation and hoping that he would not notice how shaken she was feeling.

'Yeah, OK. What sort?'

'You choose.'

Leo knelt down on the floor and opened another of the cupboards. 'Is pineapple OK?'

'Yes. That'll be fine.'

'Shall I dish it up?'

'If you like.'

He got out three bowls and distributed the pineapple rings between them, while Yvonne finished making the sandwiches.

'That's great, love,' she said warmly. 'Just leave those over there until we're ready for them. Now, could you go and tell your dad the lunch is ready. He's upstairs.'

Lunch was a subdued and uncomfortable affair. Leo ate in silence, watching his parents with anxious eyes. Yvonne tried her best to keep Trevor happy, but he seemed determined to find fault with everything.

'This is the sort of thing I mean,' he said, snatching up the Coca-Cola bottle. 'How much did this cost?'

'It was "buy one, get one free",' Yvonne pleaded.

'But why do we need any of it?' demanded Trevor. 'What's wrong with water?' He ostentatiously got up and strode across to the sink to fill his glass from the tap. Leo followed his father's movements with his eyes as he sipped his own coke guiltily.

Yvonne was relieved when a call came through for Trevor to pick up a fare from the hospital out-patients department. He gulped down the last of his pineapple and headed for the door, shouting back over his shoulder, 'remember what I said, both of you: we've got to stop wasting money!'

Leo seemed to be following his father out of the room, then he hesitated in the doorway and finally came back and started clearing the dishes from the table. 'I'll wash up if you like.'

'Thanks love.' Yvonne stared at her son. It was unusual for him to volunteer to help with the housework. 'You wash and I'll dry.'

They worked in silence. Several times, Leo opened his mouth as if to speak and then appeared to change his mind. Then, at last, he turned round from the sink and looked Yvonne in the face.

'Are we broke?'

'No, of course not!' Yvonne responded quickly. 'Things are just a bit tight at the moment, that's all.'

'It just seemed … Dad said …'

'Dad's worried because he isn't getting many call-outs for his taxi, but now I'm working again, everything will be fine. Don't you worry!'

'Are you sure?' Leo looked at her with anxious eyes.

'Yes. I'm sure.'

'Good. Is it OK for me to go round to Ben's house now?'

'So long as his mum doesn't mind you being there, go ahead.'

BACK TO WORK

Leo tipped the water out of the washing up bowl and dried his hands on his jeans. 'Bye then!'

Yvonne finished drying the dishes and then went back upstairs. She went into the bedroom and opened her underwear drawer. She took out the vodka bottle and the small glass that she had stowed at the back, and set them down in front of her on the dressing table. She hadn't had a single drink for … it must be three weeks – probably nearer four – not since the anniversary of her dad's death. She'd even got through Harry's birthday without touching a drop! Even though she'd been feeling so bad that she couldn't eat or sleep for days.

They couldn't really be buying too much food; she never felt hungry these days. It was Trev who expected his proper cooked dinner every day. He ate more than she and Leo combined! *And* he was as fussy as Leo if he found gristle in his sausages or the curry sauce wasn't exactly to his liking! He had no right criticising her for spending too much!

She unscrewed the bottle, but before she could pour a measure into the glass, she heard an insistent ringing tone from inside her bag, which was still lying on the dressing table where she had left it when she arrived home. Putting the bottle back down, she reached into the bag and brought out her phone.

She stared down at the screen, hesitating over whether to answer. It was Jean, one of the few women who had been at the Alcoholics Anonymous meeting that she had gone to back in March – just before Lockdown had stopped all in-person meetings. Yvonne had successfully fended off their requests

– or it had felt more like demands – for her phone number, but she had weakened enough to accept theirs. Then, at a low point a week or two later, she had made the mistake of phoning Jean while Leo and Trevor were out taking their daily permitted exercise; and now Jean had her number and would keep ringing to see how she was. More often than not, Yvonne rejected the calls, but it seemed rude never to answer, when the woman was only trying to help.

She just didn't seem to understand that the AA meeting had all been a mistake. It was just an impulse brought on by depression following Harry's death and a suggestion from Chrissie that she might need help to stop now that the emergency was over. Anyone would drink under those circumstances, but it didn't mean she had a drink problem.

VICTIM STATEMENTS

And now she could prove it! If you didn't count the rum – which was only because that was how her dad would have liked to be remembered – she hadn't had a drink for months! Not since that AA meeting really.

Yvonne swiped the phone to answer the call. Maybe Jean would see now that she wasn't an alcoholic. She'd just been going through a bad patch, but now she was back in control.

'Hello Jean! I'm sorry I took a while to answer, I've been busy. It was my first day back at work today.' Yvonne spoke brightly, determined to sound upbeat and as if she didn't have a care in the world. 'How are you?'

'I'm very well, thank you. How are you?' Jean was a stockbroker – whatever that meant – and always spoke in this strange, rather formal way, more as if

BACK TO WORK

Yvonne was a client than a friend. That was another problem with the AA meeting: everyone seemed very different from Yvonne. They probably all had degrees and office jobs, and there hadn't been a black or brown face in sight!

'I'm fine. Like I said, I'm back at work now, and Trevor's taxi business is looking up too.' Yvonne continued to paint the rosiest possible picture of her life, in the hope that Jean would accept that her ministrations were unnecessary.

'That's good. You do sound better than last time we spoke. I was ringing to let you know that we'll be starting face-to-face meetings again this week. There's one tomorrow lunchtime, if you'd like to come. It's in the church hall where you came before. Probably most of the people you met then will be there, so it'll be a good opportunity–'

'I'm sorry, I'm working tomorrow. I won't be finished in time,' Yvonne cut across her quickly. 'It was very nice of you to invite me, but really I don't – I mean, I made a mistake. I don't need – I'm on top of it now. It was just a rough patch, because of Harry being killed. You know – depression and all that. I'm fine now. I haven't had a drink since … oh! It must be nearly two months ago.'

'That's great!' Jean said warmly. 'You're doing very well. Lots of us have been really struggling during Lockdown. It would be lovely if you could come to a meeting and tell us about how you did it. It's always encouraging to hear people's success stories – it gives everyone's morale a boost. There's an evening meeting on Thursday, if that would be better for you.'

BACK TO WORK

'No, I can't go out in the evening. It's Trevor's busiest time for the taxi and someone needs to be there for Leo.'

'That's a pity. How about one of our online meetings? I can give you a number to dial in, if you still don't have internet access.'

'That's very kind of you, but I really don't think … Oh! I think that's Trevor back. I've got to go now. Thank you so much for ringing, but I'm sure I'll be OK now.'

Yvonne put away her phone and turned back to the vodka bottle still standing there on the dressing table in front of her. She put out her hand and then withdrew it again. She had boasted to Jean that she had not had a drink for months and didn't need any help with staying dry. If she had one now, she wouldn't be able to say the same next time she rang. But one small shot wouldn't be really drinking! It was only alcoholics who had to stay clear of it altogether, and she wasn't an alcoholic; she just needed a drink now and then, when things got really bad. And nobody could say she hadn't been through some bad things in the last few months!

She picked up the glass and was about to pour a measure into it when she heard the door opening. Trevor really was back now! Hastily, she screwed the top back on the bottle and stowed it away with the glass at the back of the drawer, carefully arranging bras and briefs over them so that they were invisible even when the drawer was pulled out.

She got up and walked to the top of the stairs. 'Hi Trev, would you like a coffee?'

The next day, Yvonne's employer offered her more additional hours on her shift. Thinking that Trevor would be pleased at the thought of even more overtime payments, she jumped at the prospect of increasing her contribution to their family finances. His hostility, when she rang him to let him know that he would have to get lunch for himself and Leo, since she would not be back until mid-afternoon, was, therefore, a disappointment.

'What if I get a call-out?' he demanded. 'You should be back to look after Leo.'

'He's thirteen,' Yvonne pointed out. 'We've left him on his own before. 'And I'll be back by three – three thirty at the latest. I thought you'd be pleased. It's all money in the bank.'

VICTIM STATEMENTS

'That's all very well,' Trevor grumbled, 'but a mother's place is looking after her kids. I suppose this is your way of proving you don't need me.'

'No!' This assertion shocked Yvonne. She lowered her voice and tried to sound conciliatory. 'It's nothing like that. I just want to do my bit to help. I know it's not your fault you haven't been earning while we've been in lockdown. It's just lucky both my jobs were eligible for furlough. I don't understand why yours wasn't. It isn't fair, but it's not your fault. When things are back to normal ...'

'Alright, alright, Trevor growled. 'Cut out all the chitchat. I've got the message. I'm off to make us lunch. What about you? When will you eat?'

'Oh, I'll grab a sandwich somewhere. I'm not sure. Or maybe I'll wait till I get back. Like I said, it'll only be three or so.

BACK TO WORK

Now I've got to go, the supervisor's giving me a dirty look for being on the phone. Coming sir!'

Yvonne blinked in the bright sunshine as she stepped out into the street at the end of her shift. She felt strangely calm and energised, despite it being the end of a gruelling eight hours of mopping, polishing and – most importantly – disinfecting. It was good to be back at work. The other girls had seemed genuinely pleased to see her, and, now that it was more than six months since Harry's death, they were no longer so stilted in what they spoke to her about for fear of upsetting her. Several of them had lost relatives or friends to COVID-19, and she was no longer unique – and hence frightening – in her grief.

She walked briskly to the bus stop and positioned herself carefully two metres away from a young Asian woman in a hijab who was already waiting there. They exchanged nods and hidden smiles beneath their face masks and then fixed their eyes on the road, waiting for the bus to arrive.

Then she saw them! They were walking along the pavement towards her. Any moment now, they would come right up to her. Her heart began beating faster and she felt her cheeks burning beneath the facemask. No! it couldn't be them; she must be imagining it. They would come closer and she would see that they were just perfectly ordinary strangers.

But then the woman appeared, stripping off her facemask as she emerged from a shop on the other side of the road. She called out to the two men and waved her arms. 'Terry! Shane! Over here!'

The Butler brothers – and it must be them or it would be too much of a coincidence – waved back and stopped on the edge of the pavement waiting to cross.

Yvonne's head was spinning, she gasped in air, breathing more and more rapidly as she fought for breath through the stifling facemask. She put out her arm and grasped the metal pillar at the end of the bus shelter, bending her head downwards, hoping not to faint.

'Are you alright?' It was the young Muslim woman, who came closer and gazed anxiously into her face. 'There's a seat here. Come and sit down.'

VICTIM STATEMENTS

She gestured towards a row of narrow seats inside the bus shelter. Nodding her thanks, Yvonne felt her way over to the nearest one and collapsed on to it.

'Shall I call an ambulance?' the woman asked.

'No, no,' Yvonne shook her head vigorously and then regretted it because the movement increased the feeling of light-headedness. 'I'll be fine. I just had a bit of a shock, that's all.'

'Well, if you're sure …?'

'Yes, yes, I'll be fine,' Yvonne repeated. She was feeling a little better now, and managed a weak smile. The woman's eyes smiled back as she continued to watch Yvonne's face anxiously for a few moments before retreating again to the other end of the shelter.

BACK TO WORK

Looking across the street, Yvonne saw the Butlers disappearing inside a café on the other side of the road. They seemed so normal! Nobody would guess that they were out on bail, having been charged with murdering a sixteen-year-old boy. *They* didn't look as if they thought about Harry's death every day or woke up in the night from dreams of seeing him hanging there in the hall! And they didn't appear to be racked with remorse for what they had done, either.

A bus pulled up and the Asian woman got on. Yvonne hesitated. She wasn't sure that she was ready yet to stand up, still less to climb on to the bus. She decided to pretend that she was waiting for a different service.

The bus moved off. Yvonne continued to sit with her head bowed. She was feeling a little better now – now that the Butlers were no longer visible and any danger of them passing close had receded. It would be ten minutes before the next bus came. There was an off-licence only a few doors down the street. She could pop in there and be back in time for the bus. She deserved a small drink after the shock she'd had – anyone would agree. It wasn't right, those Butler brothers being out of jail and wandering around Oxford like that!

Trevor was out when she got home. Leo told her that he'd been busy around lunchtime, ferrying people who were taking up the chancellor's offer of half-price meals during August in his "Eat Out to Help Out" scheme, designed to boost

BACK TO WORK

hard-hit pub and restaurant businesses after their lengthy enforced closure.

Grateful for her husband's absence, Yvonne headed upstairs and into their bedroom. She would just have one small drink to steady her nerves after her shock at seeing the Butler gang in town, and then she'd start making plans for something really nice for Trevor's dinner – something that he'd really enjoy. And then, maybe she could tell him about what the woman on the debt counselling helpline had said about how to sort out their money problems.

11. EAT OUT TO HELP OUT

Trevor turned up the music on the car radio. It helped to calm his nerves and drive out the intrusive thoughts about their mounting debts and Yvonne's drink problem. He had close on an hour's journey ahead of him, alone in the taxi, on his way to pick up a businessman returning from Chicago.

Normally, he enjoyed the airport run – of which there had been far too few in the last six months – time to think and to enjoy the classical music that he loved (but which neither Leo nor Yvonne could understand) in the empty car in one direction, and stimulating talk about foreign travel, business deals or academic conferences with interesting passengers in the other. But right now, he would have preferred to be collecting late-night revellers from a night-club or doing the school run for a child with learning difficulties. He did not relish time to think when his thoughts were all black ones. He would rather have busy roads and chattering passengers to keep his mind from running over and over the same dilemmas, seeking a solution while knowing that there was none possible.

Travelling north on the eastern by-pass, he drove under a bridge and remembered that this was the road to Shotover, where they had found that body not so long ago. That friend of Yvonne's – Chrissie Hughes – seemed to be mixed up in it somehow. It was a while now since there'd been any news about that. The police had asked for information about some woman with a funny name. They'd said the body was female, so presumably it was her. Funny that they hadn't confirmed that yet. But they always waited until they'd informed the relatives, didn't they? Perhaps they couldn't find them.

He reached the large roundabout at Headington and moved over into the right-hand lane, labelled A40(W). The traffic was still lighter than normal. He would most likely be early for the flight – unless things were different when he got closer to London. At least an airport run was a good earner. In fact, over all he'd had a good week so far. If only Yvonne could be prevented from wasting all his hard-earned cash on booze, they might be able to pay enough to the loan company to stop the debt rising any further.

Yvonne! What was he going to do with her? She'd promised faithfully to knock off the drink. And, to be fair, she hadn't had one for weeks before that day when he'd found her in bed in the afternoon with the smell of it on her breath and some trumped-up excuse about it being her father's anniversary or some such nonsense!

He was nearly at the junction with the motorway now: left to Birmingham, straight on to London. He dragged his mind back to the road. He pulled out to allow a lorry to join from the slip road on the left. The two carriageways divided, and he gently steered the car round to the left, climbing up and over the motorway and then gliding down to join the London-bound M40.

There was more traffic now, which was good. Watching out for slow lorries ahead and reckless motorcyclists overtaking on the right kept his mind occupied. He looked down at the clock on the dashboard. Yes, he was definitely going to be early. He slowed down a little – no point paying parking charges that could be avoided.

Why didn't Yvonne think like that when she was shopping? He'd told her often enough that they had to cut back, and she'd promised to be more careful. What had got into her head to buy that bottle of vodka yesterday? Why had she even gone into the off-licence? She kept boasting about how much overtime she was earning, but there was no point if she drank it all away, was there?

Of course, she was sorry – she always was – and she promised not to do it again. She had some story about bumping into the men who killed Harry and needing a drink to steady her nerves afterwards. Was that true? It was no excuse, but it was a disgrace if it had happened. That policeman – the big one who kept coming round checking up on them – had told them they wouldn't be allowed near them. But then, the other policeman – the detective – had said that Harry would be safe, and that hadn't meant a thing, had it?

He took his right hand off the wheel and slammed a fist down on his seat in frustration. The car veered to the left and he hastily gripped the wheel again with both hands to right it. Concentrate on driving, he told himself; that's all that matters.

But how could Yvonne have done it! Couldn't she see what she was doing? Didn't she realise the effect her drinking was having on Leo? And how were they ever going to pay off their debts if she carried on like this? Thank God, she had slept it off by the morning and she'd managed to get off to her early-morning cleaning job on time.

But she should have known better! He shouldn't have to come home expecting his dinner on the table only to find his wife lying comatose on their bed, surrounded by empty vodka bottles. At least she'd had the sense to do it in their bedroom, out of the way of Leo – but what if he'd happened to come in? What would he have thought, if he'd seen his mother in that state?

Trevor had taken the bottles straight to the wheelie bin, smuggling them out of the house in a black bin-liner. He'd told Leo that his mum wasn't well and sent him out for sausage and chips from the chippy on the corner. He mustn't know. He must never find out that his mother was a drunk!

EAT OUT TO HELP OUT

And couldn't she see that? Didn't she realise how important it was for Leo – for the whole family – that she had more self-control? She'd managed it before. She hadn't touched a drink for three months. Why had she started again now, when things were just beginning to get a bit better? Now that he was working again, they'd soon be back on their feet – if only she didn't throw it all away!

But maybe it was *his* fault. She shouldn't have to go out to work – or maybe just a little job while Leo was at school, to pay for a few extras that were nice to have but not essential. Was that what had started her drinking? If he earned more, she wouldn't have to be up before dawn, cleaning offices, and then out again cleaning rooms for spoiled students with more money than sense. He shouldn't have let her find out about that loan. It had only set her worrying and taking on more overtime than she could cope with.

And what was it she'd said about filling in a form online for compensation? That interfering Chrissie Hughes must be behind it! Why couldn't she leave them all alone? Whatever happened, she mustn't get to know about Yvonne's drinking. She was a teacher; she'd probably report them to Social Services and they'd come and take Leo away from them.

Perhaps if he told Yvonne that, she'd drop that Chrissie and let them get on with things by themselves. She didn't seem to understand! This was a private matter, not something to go chattering about to the nosey wife of a police officer.

He'd talk to her that evening. He'd tell her he was sorry for being angry with her and he'd explain about how important it was for her to stop drinking and he'd promise to help her. Whatever it was she needed, he'd do it.

Maybe he ought to do the shopping so she wouldn't be tempted to buy booze when she was in the supermarket. And he could drop her off at work and pick her up when she was finished, so she couldn't call in at the off-licence like she had yesterday. And he'd stop having a beer with his supper, so she wouldn't have to watch him enjoying it, when she couldn't have a drink.

He smiled. He felt much better, now that he had a plan. They could do this. Yvonne wanted to change; he knew that. If he just did a bit more to help, she'd soon be over it and they could get back to how things had been before.

Before what? Before those thugs had killed Harry. They were the ones to blame! It wasn't his fault for not earning enough or for not being understanding enough or for letting Yvonne know that they were in debt. *They* were the ones who had ripped their family apart and broken Yvonne's heart.

And what were Chrissie Hughes's husband and the rest of his police cronies doing about it? Bugger all! No, worse than that – they'd let them all out on bail, so they could terrorise Yvonne in the street and, who knows? Maybe kill another poor black kid who didn't know any better than to get mixed up with them!

Taking advantage of Trevor's lunchtime appointment at the airport, Yvonne had arranged to meet with Bernie and Chrissie at a pub in nearby Iffley. They sat outside at wooden tables, basking in the sunshine while eating their half-price pub meal. Bernie secretly believed that the ham salad and rhubarb crumble that Peter had prepared for his meal with Jonah and the two grandchildren was probably more appetizing, but this was a neutral venue and handier for Yvonne to get to on foot.

Not wanting to leave Leo to eat his meal at home alone, Yvonne had brought him with her. He sat with Gavin at one table, while his mother had what she described to him as a "girls' gossip" two metres away around the next one. Gavin did his best to put the boy at his ease, but Leo's responses were languid and monosyllabic. He kept glancing over towards the table where his mother was deep in conversation with Bernie, anxiously watching as they passed

Yvonne's smartphone from one to the other and pored over pieces of paper.

'Your mum seems to have recovered from her migraine,' Gavin commented. 'Does she get a lot of them?'

'No – yeah – it depends.' Leo sounded flustered.

'Stress often makes them worse – or so I've heard,' Gavin ventured. 'She'll have had a lot to worry about lately, what with Lockdown and the trial being delayed and everything.'

'Yeah, I guess.' Leo reached for a sachet of tomato sauce and squeezed it over his chips. Then his head jerked round suddenly at the sound of Bernie's raised voice.

'Think of Leo!' she was saying. 'Do it for him.'

Then she moderated her tones and Gavin could no longer catch the words.

EAT OUT TO HELP OUT

Leo remained sitting bolt upright staring across at his mother and her new friend. Catching Gavin's eye, he shrugged and began shovelling chips into his mouth.

'How's the basketball coming on?' Gavin asked.

'OK.' Leo continued to concentrate on his food, keeping his eyes down, except when making furtive glances towards his mother's table.

'I suppose you'll have more time to practice now there's no schoolwork for a while.' Gavin suggested, still trying valiantly to make conversation.

'Yes,' Leo mumbled through a mouthful of beefburger. Then he swallowed and looked Gavin in the eye for the first time. Unexpectedly, he asked, 'What are they talking about?'

'Your mum and her friends?' Gavin looked across at the other table in some confusion. 'Oh, just the sorts of things women do talk about when they get together. They're probably swapping knitting patterns and sharing cake recipes.'

'I don't think that other one's sharing recipes,' Leo said, inclining his head briefly in Bernie's direction. 'The one with the short hair and glasses. I've seen her before. She's with the police, isn't she? She came round when Harry was killed – with that weird policeman who goes around in a wheelchair. Is she going to arrest Mum?'

'She's DCI Porter's personal assistant,' Gavin admitted, 'but this isn't police work. She's just here as a friend. What makes you think anyone would be wanting to arrest your mum?'

There was a long silence while Leo gathered three chips together and speared them with his fork. Then he looked up briefly and Gavin saw tears forming in his eyes, before he lowered his face again and stuffed the chips into his mouth. Gavin waited patiently.

At last, Leo swallowed the chips and, without raising his head, he muttered, 'There was this letter. It said unless Mum and Dad paid thousands of pounds to someone, they'd ...' He seemed to be struggling to remember the right words. 'It said "legal action". That means a trial, doesn't it? In court, with a judge and everything – like they're supposed to be doing with the guys who killed Harry. Are Mum and Dad going to prison? Is that what-?'

'No,' Gavin interrupted firmly. 'It's nothing like that at all.'

Leo stared back at him. 'But I saw the letter!'

'Which wasn't addressed to you, was it? If your mum and dad had wanted you to know about it, they'd have told you.'

'They left it just lying around on the table,' Leo defended himself. 'It wasn't like I went through their things or anything – like Dad does sometimes with my stuff!' he added indignantly.

'No. I know,' Gavin said gently, regretting his words of criticism. The boy was clearly upset and anxious and didn't need a lecture on respect for his parents' privacy. 'Look, I know what was in that letter, and believe me, it's got nothing to do with anyone going to prison. The legal action that it's talking about isn't that sort of thing at all.'

'What *does* it mean then?'

'It's … there are two different sorts of courts,' Gavin explained. 'Those men who killed your brother are going to be tried in a *criminal* court. That's for people who break the law. This letter is talking about the *civil* courts, which is where two people can't agree about something and they want a judge to decide who's right.'

'So, what's that woman doing here then?' Leo demanded, pointing with his knife towards Bernie. 'Why's she got that laptop out?'

'She's helping your mum to fill in some difficult forms,' Gavin explained. 'That letter you read was about some money that your dad borrowed. Bernie's helping your mum to sort out a way of paying it off.'

'And if Dad doesn't pay back the money, will *he* go to jail?'

'No. Nobody's going to jail. That's what I meant about the difference between civil courts and criminal courts. Even if they did take out a civil action against your dad – which is very unlikely – the judge would just order him to pay back the money he owes at so much a week. He couldn't send him to jail.'

'Are you sure?'

'Yes. I'm a police officer, aren't I? It's my job to know about the law.'

'I suppose so. Do you think Mum knows all that – about the different sorts of courts and stuff?'

'I'm sure she does now,' Gavin replied confidently. 'Even if she didn't before, Chrissie and Bernie will have explained it all to her.'

'So why is she …? I mean … Oh, forget it!' Leo hid his face in a glass of coke.

'She's worried about the money,' Gavin told him, 'and wasn't it Harry's birthday recently? That probably set her thinking about him again – I mean, thinking about him more,' he corrected himself quickly, 'because of course, she'll have been thinking about him all the time. It's a big thing, losing a son. That's something you need to remember – if your mum seems a bit …'

Gavin trailed off into a confused silence as it occurred to him for the first time that he had been seeing the impact on Leo of his brother's death exclusively in terms of its effect on his parents, and principally on his mother. How had he managed to forget that Leo must also be grieving the loss of a brother?

The two of them had shared a room. They had most likely shared secrets that they kept from their parents. Perhaps they had shared their hopes and dreams. Leo must feel very much alone now, with nobody close to his own age in which to confide. Had Yvonne had a drink problem before Harry's death? If so, then Harry would have been the only person in the world with whom Leo could discuss it.

'She made a cake.' Leo's voice broke through Gavin's distracted musings and brought him back to the present. He hastily turned his attention back to the boy, who went on, 'with seventeen candles on it. She made us sing Happy Birthday. It was creepy.'

'It was just her way of remembering him,' Gavin told him. 'Everyone's different when it comes to losing someone close.'

'She didn't make a cake for *my* birthday!' Leo mumbled almost inaudibly. 'Dad went out and bought one in the end. And he got me a new pair of trainers, only they weren't the right size.'

Gavin couldn't think of anything to say. For several minutes they ate their meal in silence. Leo finished his burger and pushed the plate away.

'PC Hughes?' he said in a small voice.

'Yes?'

'You won't tell anyone, will you?'

'Tell them what?'

'About what I said – about Mum forgetting my birthday and Dad getting the size wrong.'

'No, of course not.'

A waiter in mask and visor silently approached their table and took away their plates, replacing them with bowls of ice cream.

'Only I don't want people to think ...,' Leo continued, 'They might think there's something wrong with her, and there's not!'

'It's OK,' Gavin assured him, 'I won't even tell Chrissie. And ...' He paused, unsure how to go on. Kenny would have done this so much better. With all his years in the scouts, he knew how to talk to teenage boys. 'And … and you mustn't think your mum doesn't … It messes with your head when someone dies the way Harry did. It'll be a while before she …,' he stumbled, unable to find the right words to tell the boy that his mother still loved him. To his annoyance, he found his own eyes welling up with tears. Damn this grief business! Why did it always hit you at the worst possible time?

'Yes, PC Hughes,' Leo said politely, lowering his own eyes, presumably out of embarrassment at Gavin's display of emotion.

'Call me Gavin. I'm not on duty today. See? I'm not wearing my uniform!'

EAT OUT TO HELP OUT

Gavin wiped his face with a paper napkin and smiled across the table in an attempt to lighten the mood.

'That other policeman wasn't wearing a uniform when he came round asking questions about Harry,' Leo pointed out seriously.

'No, well he's a plain clothes police officer,' Gavin told him, glad of the change of subject. 'Detectives don't wear uniforms. They need to be able to follow suspects without being recognised, and that sort of thing.'

'I suppose nobody'd guess a crip in a wheelchair was a policeman, would they?' Leo mused.

'No, they wouldn't,' Gavin agreed, pleased at having successfully distracted the boy from his worries, but unsure where this conversation might be going. Did Leo know that "crip" was a derogatory term used to abuse disabled people? Should he tell him not to use it?

'So, is he just pretending, then – to put people off guard?' Leo asked, sounding more cheerful than at any earlier point during the meal.

'No.' Gavin wasn't sure whether or not to welcome this neutral topic of conversation, which seemed at last to have diverted the boy from his worries about his parents. What would Jonah himself want him to say about his condition? 'Someone shot him in the back – years ago: you'd have only been a baby then or you might have heard about it on the news. He was quite famous for a while.'

'I suppose he was probably quite old when it happened,' Leo suggested thoughtfully. 'So, it won't have been so bad for him. I think I'd rather be killed, like

Harry, than stuck in a wheelchair like that.'

'He wasn't all that old,' Gavin protested. 'I suppose he must've been about my age.' Leo gave him an I-rest-my-case look. 'OK, yes, I know I must seem old to you, but that's not how it feels to me – or not most of the time!' he added with a laugh. 'I will admit I'd rather leave running after criminals in the street down to younger officers who can do it without getting out-of-breath and red-in-the-face! But seriously, it doesn't make any difference how old someone is.'

'So, do you think he'd rather be dead, too?'

'No!' Gavin's heart lurched as the thought occurred to him suddenly that Leo might have been considering taking his own life. 'That's what I mean – however bad things are, there's always plenty to live for. And old people aren't any different from young ones – we'd all rather hang on and have a bit more of life, even when it's tough.'

'I wouldn't want to carry on living if I couldn't play basketball,' Leo said decidedly. Gavin gave an internal sigh of relief – so he was only talking about the hypothetical wheelchair situation, after all.

'There are wheelchair basketball teams,' he pointed out. 'Or you might find all sorts of other things to enjoy that you'd never thought about before. You just never know. Anyway, you're not likely to ever be in that position, are you? So, I wouldn't think about it, if I were you.'

Leo sat looking at him, stirring his Neapolitan ice cream into a pinky-brown mush with his spoon.

EAT OUT TO HELP OUT

'Mum said she wished *she* was dead,' he said suddenly.

'I'm sure she didn't really mean it,' Gavin replied at once. 'Or she only meant it for a moment or two, while she was feeling bad about losing Harry. It was a terrible shock for her, finding him the way she did. It's bound to take time for her to … Look!' He glanced over at the next table, inviting Leo with his eyes to follow his gaze. 'See there?' he went on earnestly. 'Your mum's getting help from Chrissie and Bernie *because* she's thinking about the future – for your whole family. She's not thinking about dying – she wants you all to carry on living for a long, long time. And she's finding out how to pay back the money your dad had to borrow to pay for things while he wasn't working, so as you'll all be able to enjoy it.'

VICTIM STATEMENTS

As soon as lunch was over, Yvonne hurried Leo away, anxious that they should both be at home when Trevor returned. Bernie, Chrissie and Gavin watched them go, standing by their chained-up bicycles.

'How did you get on?' Gavin asked.

'Pretty well, I think. I've shown her how to apply for more compensation from the CICA and given her more info on their Universal Credit entitlement, but we didn't have time to fill in the applications, so who knows whether she'll carry through on them.'

'How did she seem in herself? The boy was a bit on edge. Do you think she's been drinking?'

'She wasn't drunk just now,' Bernie replied cautiously. 'She was very on-the-ball in fact. She'd remembered to bring her payslips and child tax credit records and all the other stuff that I asked her for. But I'm afraid I probably wouldn't recognise the signs.'

'No, well … I suppose at least she looks a lot better than back in April when she could hardly get out of bed.'

'Oh, she's quite different from that,' Chrissie assured him. 'She was telling us about all the things she's been doing to try to sort out their debts. She rang the helpline, and they've written on her behalf – in fact, I think they've got a pet solicitor who did it for them, so it'll be all official – proposing a plan for repaying the loan. They've got a rent holiday agreed with the Housing Association and Yvonne's got an account with the local Credit Union.'

'That's good,' Gavin nodded.

'The big problem seems to be Trevor,' Bernie put in. 'Yvonne says he's dead against asking for any help from anyone. I tried to explain that this isn't about charity, it's only what they're entitled to, but she just keeps saying that he won't see it that way.'

'She seems very positive about being back at work this week,' Chrissie said hopefully. 'And she says Trevor's been getting regular bookings for his taxi now that things are opening up again. I think if it wasn't for this loan with its ridiculous interest rate, they'd be doing OK financially.'

'And once their compensation comes through, they should be able to pay that off,' Bernie added. 'If only she finishes putting in the application!'

'I just hope she's remembering to give Leo a bit of TLC as well,' Gavin murmured. 'I got the impression he's feeling like he's got the weight of the world on his shoulders at the moment.'

Mindful of Gavin's words concerning Leo, Chrissie invited Yvonne round for a chat a few days later – they were neighbours, after all, as well as both being members of that club that nobody would have wished to join: bereaved mothers of sons who had suffered a violent death. Trevor was working and Leo was round at a friend's house. The two women sat in the garden drinking lemonade and eating slices of Chrissie's homemade carrot cake while they talked inconsequentially. It was all very peaceful.

But Chrissie was on a mission. She knew that Gavin was worried about Leo's state of mind, and she could see that, although she was putting on a good face, Yvonne was still not as much at ease as she would like people to think. After several unsuccessful attempts at steering the conversation naturally in the direction of her friends drinking habit, she decided that there was nothing for it but to take the bull by the horns.

'Did you get to that AA meeting you said you were going to?'

'Oh!' Yvonne seemed flustered. 'Well, yes I did as a matter of fact. It seems like ages ago now.'

'Did it help at all?'

'I'm not sure,' Yvonne hedged. 'They gave me some leaflets and told me about this thing called the twelve steps. They wanted me to go back, but then the meetings all stopped when Lockdown happened.'

'That's a pity.' Chrissie left the sentence hanging in the air, hoping that Yvonne might elaborate further.

'I did try a Zoom meeting a couple of months back. 'One of the ladies from the meeting took my phone number and she rang and invited me.'

'That was nice of her.'

'Yes. I suppose it was. But I didn't go again. It was all old white men talking about things I didn't understand.'

'What sort of things?' Chrissie was puzzled.

'There was this one who said working from home was good because it meant he wasn't expected to take clients for a drink. And then this other one said something about a thing called a – a – a *conference dinner* and how difficult it was to refuse the wine there. I knew one of them – he's the Principal of the college where I clean. I didn't dare say a word!'

What about the lady who invited you?' Chrissie asked. 'Wasn't she there?'

'Yes, she was. She was quite nice, I suppose, but … She's like the rest of them. She's got a degree and all sorts of other qualifications and she keeps using words I don't understand. I just don't fit in!'

'Maybe there would be another group you could join?' Chrissie suggested. She was unsure how these things worked.

'Oh, there are lots of meetings,' Yvonne told her. 'They said that, at first, I ought to go to as many as possible – one of them said at least three times a week! But I can't do that! Trev would be sure to find out and he'd be cross that I'd been talking to other people about … Anyway, I know now. I don't need them. I've got the drinking under control. It was only Harry being killed like that that made me – you know – for a while. That's all.'

Chrissie pondered on this statement. Should she accept it at face value or should she point out that Leo's story about his mother's migraines had not fooled her. It was a difficult tightrope to walk. If she pressed Yvonne too hard, she might lose her confidence and have no further opportunity to exert any influence. She was still trying to think what to say next when Yvonne resumed her self-justification.

'I did have a little wobble,' she admitted. (Chrissie wondered if she had somehow read her mind regarding the migraines.) 'But that was just worrying about how we were going to pay back that loan. I'm sure everything will be just fine when that's all sorted out. And there's the trial, too,' she added after another moment's thought. 'Do you know when that's going to be?'

'No.' Chrissie shook her head. 'I'm sorry. We haven't heard anything about that either – but now the courts are open again, it won't be much longer, I'm sure.'

12. TRIALS AND TRIBULATIONS

The days and weeks dragged on. The weather remained warm, but became less settled. Warm and sunny became hot and muggy with occasional rain. Everyone was grateful that it was now permitted to meet with people outside their own household indoors as well as in the open air. They became accustomed to wearing masks in shops, pubs and churches, as well as on buses and trains. Some office workers were back in their offices, while others gladly continued to work at home. Was this the "new normal"?

Then, as the August days slipped away amidst staycations and cut-price meals out, the cases of COVID-19 slowly began to rise. Scientists started to talk about a "second wave", while the more hopeful said that it was simply that more people were being tested. There was speculation in the press about the likely effect of reopening schools in September, and questions were raised about a plan to administer coronavirus tests to students. Would children have to wear face masks? Would teachers be provided with PPE for close-contact activities? How would social distancing be achieved in classrooms full of young children?

Chrissie sighed as she read yet another directive from the Department for Education. When the school closed in July, the head teacher had told the staff to "take time off to re-charge your batteries", but that didn't take into account all the planning that was involved in making the school safe for all children to return full-time after the summer holiday. Chrissie was glad that her class had only primary-age children in it, which meant that she did not have the problem of assessing which should be required to wear masks and which were exempt. Several of them would definitely have objected strongly to having their faces covered. It was going to be hard enough to get them all into the new daily routine without imposing such a frightening and restricting measure on them.

She pushed away her laptop and got up to make herself another cup of coffee. She should think herself lucky to be in a school that already had small classes and a high staff-student ratio. And at least she wasn't the Head, having to organise getting contractors in to put up Perspex screens and mark out two metre distances on the floor, while trying to balance an ever more precarious budget.

She would see tomorrow what her classroom looked like with all the new arrangements in place. Then the day after that, the children would be back. At least with them all in school, she would no longer have to plan every lesson twice – once for delivery in school and again for those learning at home.

The kettle boiled and she poured water over instant coffee granules in a mug; proper coffee was reserved for when Gavin was at home and they could justify putting on the filter machine. She was just bending down to return the milk jug to the fridge when the landline phone rang. She hastily closed the fridge door and went out to the hall to answer it.

'Good morning,' said an efficient-sounding voice at the other end, 'is that Mrs Christine Hughes?'

'Ye-es, speaking,' Chrissie replied suspiciously, expecting the voice to go on to tell her that they were working in her area and would be pleased to come round to quote for replacement windows, cavity wall insulation or perhaps a new driveway.

'My name is Marcia. I'm employed by Thames Valley Police.'

'Do you want Gavin?' Chrissie cut in. Her heart had speeded up at the mention of the police. Had something happened to Gavin? No! More likely just a colleague wanting to speak to him – a query on his overtime form or an irregularity regarding expenses. 'He's not in at the moment, I'm afraid,' she gabbled on as she fought down the fear that this was not a problem with the pay-run but *that call* – the one that every police wife dreaded. 'He's on duty today. If it's urgent, you could-'

VICTIM STATEMENTS

'No, Mrs Hughes. It's alright. Either of you will do. As I was saying, I'm a Witness Care Officer with Thames Valley Police. My job is to keep witnesses and victims of crime informed about their cases when they are coming to court. I'm pleased to be able to tell you that the trial of the man accused of killing your son has been scheduled to begin on-'

'You've got a date?' Chrissie interrupted, unable to remain silent as relief that Gavin was safe and delight that their long wait for justice might soon be at an end flowed over her.

'Yes. I know it's been a long time for you both, but the court is now fully open and we're trying to address the backlog of cases. Shane Butler will go on trial on October the nineteenth. Have you been told that it will be a joint trial with his brother and sister-in-law and another man? They're all accused of drugs offences and of a second murder.'

'Harry Whittle? Yes, I know about that. Harry's parents are neighbours of ours. Have you spoken to them yet?'

'I'm afraid that's confidential information. I was only mentioning the other murder because I wanted you to realise that this will be a complex trial and may go on for some time – several days at the very least, possibly a number of weeks. I didn't want you to think it would all be over in the one day.'

'You must be gentle with Yvonne,' Chrissie said anxiously. 'She's in a very fragile state at the moment. You do know that she found him hanging there in their house?'

'Yes, Mrs Hughes. I've had sight of the case file. I know all about what happened. I can assure you that I will take all of that into account when I speak to Mrs Whittle. But what I'm ringing you for today is to let you know that I'm going to be your point of contact throughout the lead-up to the trial and right through to the verdict and sentencing. If you have any questions about the process, you can come to me and I'll explain things for you. I'll give you my number now, if you've got something to write down with.'

'Yes, of course. I'm ready. Fire away.'

Chrissie noted down the number on the pad that they kept by the phone.

'And my name again is Marcia Williams. If ever I'm not available, this number will get you through to one of my colleagues and they'll either be able to answer your queries themselves or they'll take a message for me.'

'Thank you. Now about the Whittles-'

'I've told you; I can't talk about other clients.'

'No, but I just wanted to say: they've been under a lot of strain recently. Yvonne was furloughed for months and Trevor drives a taxi, so he didn't have any money coming in at all during lockdown. And all that's on top of losing Harry.'

'We'll be very careful,' Marcia assured her. 'Now, if I can just go through a few things with you?'

'And Leo,' Chrissie cut in, determined to make sure that Marcia was fully appraised of the Whittle's home situation. 'Don't forget him.'

'Leo?'

'Harry's younger brother. He's twelve, I think – no, Gavin said he's had a birthday so he must be thirteen now. He's a very lonely young man, I think.'

VICTIM STATEMENTS

'Thank you, Mrs Hughes. We'll bear what you say in mind, but I do need to take you through a few things so we can assess what your needs are regarding the trial. You won't be called as a witness, but you do have a right to submit a statement about the impact that this crime has had on you. We have a joint statement from you and your husband on file, but that was made some time ago, so you may want to update it – particularly if you feel that you've had ongoing problems due to Kenneth's death.'

'Kenny, everyone called him Kenny.'

'I'm sorry – Kenny's death. You don't have to decide now; there's plenty of time. Have a think about it and let me know when you're ready. Do you have a copy of the statement you made or would you like me to send you one?'

TRIALS AND TRIBULATIONS

About twenty minutes later, Chrissie put down the phone and went back to her cold coffee in the kitchen. Marcia had been very kind, but it had still felt a bit like an interrogation. So many details to convey to her: their availability to visit the court in advance of the trial and to meet with the prosecutor, her email address, and Gavin's, for documents to be sent to them, confirmation that they did not need them in another language or in braille or audio format, confirmation that they would not need special arrangements in order to access the court building.

Never mind! They had a date at last; that was the main thing. She put the coffee mug in the microwave to re-heat it and hunted for her mobile phone in her bag. She must ring Yvonne to find out whether she had received a similar call and, if not, to warn her to expect one.

Marcia's efficient formality would most likely be intimidating for Yvonne, who would see her as an authority figure and hence to be feared.

She sat down at the kitchen table and keyed in Yvonne's mobile number. After only a few rings, she answered, more cheerfully than Chrissie remembered her sounding before.

'Hi Chrissie! I was going to ring you: the funeral expenses have come through! They just paid them into our bank account just like that! I could hardly believe it!'

'That's great,' Chrissie agreed warmly, then, a little anxiously, 'Does Trevor know yet?'

'Yes. I was afraid he'd be cross, but in the end, he just said it was about time we got something back after all the tax he's paid. So, now we've nearly paid off that awful loan and once my salary comes in at the end of next month, we *will* have paid it. I can't tell you how relieved I am!'

'Yes, that's great,' Chrissie repeated. 'Now, I was ringing about something else. Has anyone been in touch to talk to you about the trial?'

'No? What about it?' Yvonne's voice changed suddenly. Now it was filled with anxiety and suspicion.

'They've fixed a date for it to start,' Chrissie told her. 'They rang me just now. I expect you'll get a call later. It's going to be the nineteenth of October.'

'I see.'

'It was a very nice woman called Marcia rang me,' Chrissie told her, sensing her uncertainty. 'She took me through my options: we can watch it all, if we like, or we can wait until it's all over and then they'll tell us what the outcome was. She's going to arrange a visit to the court, so I can see where I'll be sitting, and where everyone else will be, in advance. I expect she'll ring you too, or it may be someone else from the Witness Care Unit.'

'Are you going to be a witness then?' asked Yvonne, snatching in alarm at the word "witness". 'Will we have to stand in the witness box, like in the TV shows, and answer questions?'

'No, it's just what they call the unit. Marcia's what they call a Witness Care Officer, but she works with victims and their families too.'

'Officer? Does that mean she's a police woman?'

'No, she's a civilian member of staff,' Chrissie explained patiently. 'I mean, she's employed by the police, but she's not a police officer. And she's in a separate unit that only deals with looking after people like you and me who aren't familiar with courts and legal procedure.'

'I see.' Yvonne did not sound very reassured. Chrissie began to regret having rung her. Probably Marcia, or another of the trained staff from the Witness Care Unit, would have known how to give Yvonne the news without alarming her so much and could have answered her questions better.

'Like I said,' she reiterated, 'she seemed very nice and she offered to come round to talk to me and Gavin about what's going to happen. Try not to worry about it. Just ask her all about it when she rings.'

After she'd finished her call, Chrissie put down the phone on the table, next to her still untouched mug of coffee. Then she picked the mug up in both hands and sat with her elbows on the table sipping thoughtfully. It was so easy to do what you thought was for the best, only to discover that you had only made things worse!

She looked towards the abandoned laptop and the notepad on which she had been scribbling notes for this week's lessons. What was it that she'd been doing when Marcia rang? She closed her eyes and tried to concentrate, but the only thing that she could think about was the trial and what it would mean for her and Gavin. It would be a relief for it all to be over with – giving them *closure* as people said these days – but as soon as the date was announced publicly, Kenny would be back in the news. His face would appear unbidden on newspaper front pages and television news screens. They might get reporters outside their house again hoping to get a few soundbites on how they were feeling now or trying to snap a picture of them going about their lives. One thing this business had certainly done for her was to cure her of any desire she might ever have had for becoming a celebrity!

Should she ring Gavin to tell him the date of the trial? No, his police contacts would be sure to let him know, and if not, it would be time enough when he got home from his shift that evening. What then? She looked guiltily across at the laptop again. Those lesson plans wouldn't write themselves! But first she would ring Bernie and let her know that Yvonne had got her compensation. She would be pleased to hear that her efforts had borne fruit.

'Hi there, Chrissie!' Bernie sounded genuinely pleased to receive her call.

'I've been meaning to ring you. Have you heard they've fixed a date for the trial?'

'Yes, someone from the Witness Care Unit rang me only a few minutes ago. That was what I was ringing you about – well, sort of. I rang Yvonne Whittle and she told me she's got the funeral costs from the CICA. I thought you'd like to know.'

'Yes, thanks, that's great. Hey, Jonah! Did you hear that? Yvonne's got her compensation.'

'That *is* good news,' Jonah agreed. 'And it's good news about the trial too. They told me about it this morning. I've just been going back through the files, refreshing my memory with all the things the prosecutor is going to need for making the case in court.'

'Oh yes, that's something else,' Chrissie put in, remembering Yvonne's anxiety about being called as a witness. 'Will you need Yvonne to testify? She's working herself up into a bit of a state about the prospect.'

'It's not down to me,' Jonah told her. 'The prosecutor makes those decisions. If she's in a bad enough state that her testimony could damage the prosecution case, then maybe they'll do without, but it would be usual for the person who found the body to be called to give an account of what they saw.'

'Wouldn't the first responders' testimony be more relevant?' asked Bernie. 'They'll be able to give a much more coherent account than poor Yvonne.'

'Well, I'm certainly willing to put that to them,' Jonah conceded, 'but, as I said, it's not my decision.'

'Thanks. I appreciate that.' Chrissie paused. There wasn't really any more to say, but it seemed a bit abrupt to end the call so soon – not to mention that she would then have no excuse for not getting stuck into those pesky lesson plans! 'How's your other case going? Are you any closer to finding out who the body in the woods belongs to?'

'No,' Jonah replied dismally. 'You'll have seen the facial reconstruction that we put out in the media? That sparked a lot of interest from the public, but so far none of it has led anywhere. Well, not quite: we *have* managed to re-unite one or two people with loved-ones who weren't so much missing as just not keeping in touch. And we've got half a dozen outstanding missing persons from places as far afield as Barnstable and Whitehaven who fit the description, but there's no DNA available to test them for a match with our body and no reason to believe that they ever came to Oxford.'

'What about that nurse that you were looking for?' Chrissie asked. 'Have you found her yet?'

'Yes!' Jonah sighed. 'All along, I was convinced that she was the most likely candidate – except that the date of her disappearance didn't really fit in with some of the other evidence – but, again, no DNA, so we couldn't confirm it. But then last week the Dutch police got back to me to say they'd found her.'

'Really? So, where had she been all this time?'

'Living a blameless and unsensational life in Eindhoven,' Jonah replied wryly. 'I interviewed her over the phone. She's been there for the last eight years, working in the hospital there. She didn't see the appeals for her to come forward because she was so busy with this COVID business and was avoiding watching the news reports.'

'So, she had nothing to do with the body?' asked Chrissie with a touch of disappointment in her voice. She knew how important it was to police officers that they were able to solve the cases that they were involved in and see justice done.

'None at all,' Jonah confirmed. 'She just happened to go for a walk there shortly before she left the country to go travelling – presumably some years after the body was buried there. She hadn't realised that that was where her lanyard went missing, and since she didn't need it any more, she didn't make much effort to find it.'

TRIALS AND TRIBULATIONS

'How disappointing for you,' Chrissie said, unconsciously adopting the sympathetic tone that she would have used when one of her class tried hard but could not master a skill. Never mind, I suppose at least that means you can eliminate her from your enquiries,' she added, trying to put a hopeful spin on the news. 'Anyway, I'm sure you're busy, so I won't keep you any longer.'

For the rest of the week, Chrissie was too much taken up with her job to think about the Whittles. Once she was back in school, the children in her class became her all-consuming priority. It was always difficult at the beginning of the Autumn term when they had been out of school for five weeks and were having to get back into a routine of daily lessons, most of them with a new teacher who was not familiar with their individual quirks. This year it was doubly difficult: some of the children had not been in school for over six months; some had experienced distressing events, such as the death or serious illness of a family member; others found it hard to understand why they were not allowed to touch or hug their friends.

So, it was not until Saturday that she had time to think about Yvonne again.

'I think I'll pop round this afternoon,' she told Gavin over lunch. 'It's easier to see how someone is face-to-face than on the telephone. I don't like the sound of how you say she seemed when you called the other day.'

'But is it for us to keep checking up on her like this?' Gavin protested mildly. 'I called in on her because you asked me to, and it seemed reasonable to be checking that she'd been informed about the trial and everything, but what excuse do you have for going round again? She may start thinking we're stalking her!'

'But you said you thought she'd been drinking again,' Chrissie protested. 'If you're right, we need to nip it in the bud before it gets out of hand again.'

'But it's not all down to us,' Gavin argued. 'And if we keep interfering, she may decide she's had enough and stop talking to us altogether. We can't *make* her get help for her drinking.'

'No, but we can show we care – give her the opportunity to ask for help. I'll think of an excuse, so it doesn't look too obvious that we're worried about her.'

The taxi was on the drive a few hours later, when Chrissie arrived at the Whittles' house, carrying a large shopping bag, which bulged round a square-looking object concealed inside. The doors were open and there was someone leaning inside apparently doing something under the back seats. When she got closer, she could see a long electrical cable snaking out from the house through the open front door and she recognised Trevor Whittle vacuuming the car. It had never occurred to her before, but obviously a taxi needs to be kept scrupulously clean inside and out – especially during a pandemic.

She hesitated over whether or not to call out a greeting to him as she walked carefully round the car to reach the front door. He was engrossed in his work and clearly had not seen her. He might not like being interrupted and feeling obliged to make conversation. On the other hand, if she said nothing, he might think she was sneaking in to speak to his wife behind his back. She compromised by waving though the windscreen as she squeezed past between the car and the house. He did not look up.

She faced another dilemma when she reached the open front door. How should she make her presence known? To reach the door knocker, she would have to step inside the house, which seemed a bit presumptuous. Should she call out to let Yvonne know she was there? But what if she were out of earshot? What if she were upstairs in bed with another of her "migraines"? And whatever she did to attract attention would almost certainly reach Trevor's ears and he would wonder why she had not spoken to him first.

VICTIM STATEMENTS

Before she had made up her mind what to do, she heard footsteps on the stairs. Leo appeared.

'Do you want Mum? She's getting the washing in. I'll get her.'

Without waiting for a reply, he headed off into the kitchen. Chrissie put down the bag on the doorstep and bent down to take a large rectangular cake tin out of it. She waited with both hands holding the tin, clutching it hard against her front.

'Chrissie! I wasn't expecting you.' Yvonne hurried down the hall to greet her. The kitchen door blew closed behind her with a bang.

Chrissie smiled towards her. 'I'm so glad you're in. I was wondering if you could help me out?' She held up the cake tin. 'I've been all on edge ever since I heard about the trial starting next month; and when I'm nervous, I always bake things to take my mind off whatever's worrying me. And now, I've got such heaps of stuff I don't know what to do with them all. Gavin and I are never going to be able to eat everything. So, I was wondering: could you take these scones off my hands? I thought, with you having a growing boy in your house, you'd probably be able to make use of them.'

Yvonne gazed down as Chrissie lifted the lid of the tin to display a dozen or more date scones, which she had hastily baked that afternoon. 'That's very kind of you,' she began.

'It's so hard to remember that it's just the two of us now,' Chrissie went on, speaking quickly to prevent the "but" which she sensed was hovering on Yvonne's lips, 'and, of course, there always used to be Kenny's scout troop who would always eat up anything that we couldn't manage. None of our neighbours have kids, so you and Leo are my only hope – really!'

She thrust the tin towards Yvonne, taking the opportunity of this close encounter to study her friend's face for signs that she had been drinking. No, her eyes were bright and clear and her hair was neatly braided. The hands that took hold of the cake tin gripped it firmly with no sign of a tremor. Perhaps Gavin had been wrong in thinking that she was back on the booze. Or perhaps it had been an isolated incident brought on by the shock of hearing about the trial.

'Well, thank you very much.' Yvonne smiled amiably, but did not invite Chrissie in. 'I'm sure we'll all enjoy these. It's very good of you to think of us.'

She took a step back, as if planning to close the door. Chrissie, who had retreated to a two-metre distance after handing over the tin, stepped forwards again.

'Gavin told me you said Marcia rang,' she said quickly, determined to prolong the conversation long enough to give Yvonne an opportunity to ask for help if she wanted it. 'How did that go? I was all in a dither afterwards, thinking about watching the trial and wondering what it would be like.'

'It was OK. Like you said, she was very nice.'

'That's good.' Chrissie was running out of things to say. It was clear that Yvonne was waiting for her to go. 'Well, I suppo-'

'What's going on?' Chrissie jumped at the sound of Trevor's voice behind her. Turning round, she saw him looming over her with the vacuum cleaner in his hand.

'Oh! It's you!' he exclaimed. Then, as if remembering his manners, 'good afternoon, Mrs Hughes. Can we help you?'

'Chrissie's brought us some of her homemade scones,' Yvonne explained, holding them up for him to see. 'I'll just go and put them away, and then I can give you back the tin,' she added, glancing rapidly towards Chrissie and then turning to go.

Chrissie stood aside to allow Trevor in with the hoover. He put it down in the hall and began winding up the flex.

'I was just saying to Yvonne that I'm in two minds about the trial,' Chrissie said. 'I want to be there to see what happens, but I'm not sure I want to hear all the details all over again. It gives me nightmares sometimes just thinking about it.'

TRIALS AND TRIBULATIONS

'I'm going to be there alright,' Trevor growled. 'I want to see the bastards put away for life. I don't suppose they will be though. Probably be out in a few years, looking for some other poor kid to get their claws into.'

'I'm afraid you may be right,' Chrissie agreed, pleased that Trevor seemed a little more friendly towards her than usual. She racked her brains to think of a way of convincing him that she was on their side, with the hope that he might be willing to accept their help. 'I could hardly believe it when they were allowed out on bail.'

'It's a disgrace!' Trevor finished winding up the electric cable and stood up straight. Chrissie was suddenly struck by his size, enhanced by his being the height of the doorstep above her. She did not fancy the Butler brothers' chances if he were to encounter one of them alone. If she had been charged with killing Harry Whittle, she would have preferred to be remanded in custody, safe from those powerful arms and hands, which looked as if they could strangle a man with ease.

'Here you are!' Yvonne had returned and was standing on the step holding out Chrissie's cake tin. She took it and put it back in the bag. 'Those scones look lovely,' Yvonne went on. 'It was ever so good of you to think of us.'

'I'm just pleased to see them go to a good home,' Chrissie smiled back, waving away her thanks. 'I get carried away when I start baking and don't think where it's all going to go, and I hate the idea of wasting food.'

'Yes, well, thanks again. We appreciate it.'

TRIALS AND TRIBULATIONS

They all stood there. Yvonne took hold of the door as if she would like to shut it but didn't like to appear rude. Trevor stood behind her gazing down at Chrissie over his wife's head. Chrissie wondered if she ought to go, but felt dissatisfied at how little her visit had achieved.

'Was Marcia able to tell you whether you'll be called as a witness?' she asked in the end.

'She wasn't sure,' Yvonne told her, 'but she said she thought, if I didn't want to, they wouldn't make me.'

'That's good,' Chrissie nodded.

'And she's going to take us round the court the week before the trial, so we can see what it'll be like,' Yvonne went on.

'What a lot of fuss!' Trevor snorted. 'Why do they have to bother with all that nonsense? What difference can it make seeing the place beforehand? Why can't they just get on with it?'

As September progressed, it became increasingly difficult to ignore the steady, and then accelerating, rise in COVID-19 cases. As deaths also began rising again in the second half of the month, all attempts at brushing away suggestions of a second wave as scaremongering had to be abandoned. The idea that the figures were merely a reflection of improved testing started to look like dangerous wishful-thinking.

Chrissie found little time to think about the upcoming trial. Her job became all-consuming as she found herself once more juggling with remote as well as in-person teaching. Some parents decided that they would prefer to keep their, possibly vulnerable, children at home rather than expose them to the risk of mixing with others in school. Sometimes, a whole class or larger group would be told to self-isolate because one of their number had tested positive. Several members of staff became infected and one was admitted to hospital.

Her conscience smote her when a call came through from Yvonne one afternoon after school. Gavin was working a long shift that day and she was taking advantage of his absence to catch up on a few jobs.

'I hope this isn't a bad time,' her friend began apologetically.

'No, not at all,' Chrissie assured her quickly, pushing aside the sugar-paper shapes that she had been cutting out in readiness for a craft activity with her class the following day. 'How are you? It seems like a long time since I saw you.'

There was a long pause and she began to wonder if Yvonne had rung off. Then, 'I'm sorry to be a nuisance,' came the tentative voice again. 'It's just …'

'Yes?' Chrissie gazed at the pile of exercise books that were lying on the table waiting to be marked.

There was another pause and Chrissie thought she heard Yvonne swallowing and then a bang like something hard being put down on a wooden surface.

'You know the trial?' Yvonne's voice came again at last.

'Yes?' The washing machine at the other side of Chrissie's kitchen beeped, announcing that its cycle had finished.

TRIALS AND TRIBULATIONS

'They say I've got to be a witness!' Yvonne burst out.

'I thought you'd been told you wouldn't have to.'

'Yes. That's what I thought too, but this important lawyer says I've got to. And I don't want to. Marcia took me round the court yesterday and showed me where I'd have to stand – right in the front! And the men who killed Harry are going to be right there in front of me! I didn't sleep a wink last night thinking about it.' Yvonne's speech became faster and faster until she ran out of breath and shuddered to a sudden halt.

'Did you tell Marcia how you felt about it?'

There was the sound of rapid, jerky breathing and a tinkle as of glass on glass, then a gulp followed by more quick breaths.

VICTIM STATEMENTS

'Are you OK?' Chrissie asked anxiously.

Another gulp and then Yvonne answered. Ignoring her friend's last question, she continued to speak in fitful phrases punctuated by shallow gasps for air.

'Well – I'd already said I'd rather not do it – but that big lawyer said – he said – he said the jury might think – might think – I – I was hiding something if I didn't! So, then I couldn't say no, could I?'

'I – I –.' Chrissie struggled to think of anything to say. 'What does Trevor think about it?' she asked at last.

'He doesn't understand at all!' Yvonne wailed, apparently close to tears. 'He says – he says – he wishes they'd let *him* in the witness box. He'd soon tell the judge what to do with *those animals* that killed Harry!' another gulp and another tinkle of glass. 'But that lawyer says it's got to be me, because I was the one who found him. He said their lawyer might try to say that *I* did it. Do you really think they would?' She sounded scared now.

'I suppose they *might*,' Chrissie said cautiously, 'but I'm sure the judge and the jury wouldn't take any notice if they did,' she added quickly. 'Look, I'm really not the right person for you to talk to. I don't know any more about these things than you do. What did Marcia say about it?'

'I didn't like to ask. I mean, that important lawyer was saying that was what was going to happen and I didn't think ... I mean, I wouldn't want to ... I'm sorry, I shouldn't have rung.'

'No, no, of course you should. I'm just trying to think ...' The washing machine beeped again, as if it were impatient at not yet having been emptied. Chrissie gazed longingly at the pile of exercise books and yearned for some instant solution to Yvonne's dilemma. 'I'm sure Gavin told me once about witnesses giving evidence by video link, if they didn't want to face the defendants. I'll ask him about it if you like. Would that help, do you think?'

'Would you? Thank you so much!' Yvonne slurred. 'Thanks! I feel much better now. I suppose I'd better go now. You must be busy. I'm sorry if I interrupted anything.'

'No, no not at all,' Chrissie lied joyously, seeing liberation at hand. 'It was lovely to hear from you. Just try not to worry. I'm sure everything will work out fine.'

She ended the call and sat looking indecisively from the exercise books to the sugar-paper shapes. Now, where was she …? Before she had made up her mind which task to attack first, the washing machine gave a final indignant beep and clicked off. That settled it! She would hang out the clothes first and then get back to preparing for the next day's school before making a start on their evening meal.

She emptied the machine and carried the washing basket out into the back garden. The shadows were lengthening, but there was still some time before it would get dark. She looked upwards and studied the sky. There were a few fluffy white clouds, but nothing to signify rain overnight, and the forecast had been for more dry weather tomorrow.

She began pegging out Gavin's uniform shirts and trousers. The black polo shirts and combat trousers were much easier to care for than the crisp white shirts and smart office-style trousers of Gavin's early days in the force. They didn't show the dirt nearly so badly and the creases fell out as they dried on the line. How would she have managed the pile of ironing if there had still been a fresh shirt to wash for every day of the week – two if the uniform hadn't been updated before Kenny joined.

Nevertheless, there had been something nice about those freshly-laundered white shirts. It made her feel proud to see Gavin going out with one of them on under his uniform tunic – which she always made sure was brushed clean of dust and dandruff.

'Let me help you with those!'

Craig was home. Chrissie hauled her mind back out of her nostalgic daydream and turned to greet him.

'Thanks. I hadn't realised it was so late. I'd better be getting the dinner on as soon as we've done this.'

Craig stepped forward and began dextrously pegging clothes on the line. His time in the army had given him all sorts of domestic skills which he liked to use to help Chrissie to whom he felt indebted for giving him a home.

'I was thinking about the trial,' Chrissie told him. 'I'm wondering whether I ought to ask for time off work to go and watch.'

'Of course, they'll let you go, if you want to,' Craig said decisively. 'Why wouldn't they?'

'That wasn't what I meant,' Chrissie explained. 'It's not if they'll let me, it's more … well, I don't really think I can justify asking for time off in term-time, when so many staff have been off self-isolating and the kids need so much help catching up with the work they missed last term and then there's Kathleen Burrows still in hospital with COVID and-'

'But it's what's right for *you* that counts,' Craig insisted. 'There won't be another time. If you'd like to be there, then you go.'

'That's just it!' Chrissie sighed. 'I don't know if I do want to be there. Gav says it could go on for days – weeks even – and most of it won't be about Kenny, it'll be to do with the drugs offences and with them killing Harry Whittle. His mum was on the phone just now. That was what got me thinking about it all. She's worried about having to testify. I'd like to be there for her, but I don't see that I'd be allowed to do anything for her. I wouldn't even be in the same room as her. They told us, the public will all be in a different court room watching the trial by a video link. I don't know! Maybe I could ask to sit with her while she's waiting to be called.'

'Isn't that her husband's job?' Craig asked dismissively. 'Look Chrissie: isn't it time you stopped trying to put everyone else's lives right and looked after yourself a bit?'

13. MISSING PERSON

September passed with no further progress being made in the case of the Shotover Skeleton. Various other cases demanded attention and the quest for the identity of the body was pushed on to the back burner, with the hunt through the missing persons files a "filler" to be taken up in between more pressing demands on the team's time.

But on the last day of the month, when Jonah made his daily call to Andy Lepage, who was keeping an eye on things in the office while his superior continued to work from home, he was greeted with a promising development.

'Alice Ray's come up with a missing person who seems to fit our Shotover corpse rather well,' Andy reported. 'It's a Jane Turnbull. She went missing late at night on the last day of Eights Week in 1983. Her vital statistics match with our skeleton and we've got a photo of her that isn't too far off how the facial reconstruction came out. D'you want me to send you the file?'

'Yes,' Jonah agreed eagerly. 'Can you scan it and email it to me – I assume it hasn't already been digitised?'

'No, sir. If it had, I guess we'd have found it earlier. I'll get Jennifer to send it to you right away.'

Jonah ended the call and went in search of Peter, passing through doors which opened automatically in response to a wireless signal from the keypad on the arm of his chair. He found him in the garden, holding the ladder while Bernie picked apples from one of the big old trees that grew there.

'I'm sorry!' she called down. 'Did you need me? You could have used the intercom.'

'No, it's OK,' Jonah called up to her. 'It's Peter I was looking for. He drove his chair across the grass and positioned it where he could talk easily to his friend. 'Cast your mind back to 1983. Do you happen to remember a missing person case from that summer – Eights Week to be precise?'

Peter frowned in thought. 'That's a good long time ago. Nothing immediately springs to mind. Can you tell me any more about it?'

'The name was Jane Turnbull. According to Andy, her description matches the reconstruction of those bones we unearthed on Shotover.'

'Jane Turnbull,' Peter murmured slowly. 'No, the name doesn't ring a bell.

Do *you* remember it?' His voice grew suspicious. Was his friend just testing him? 'You were working with me in 1983. Anything I was involved with, you'd know about too.'

'No, I don't. That's why I was hoping you might. Never mind; Andy's sending the file across, maybe that'll help.'

'You need to bear in mind we had two kids under three in 1983,' Peter went on, 'so life was all a bit of a blur for me that year!'

'Jonah wouldn't remember that one,' Bernie joked. 'He likes to think he never fails to solve a case. This Jane Turnbull must be a missing person who was never found or she wouldn't be a candidate for your unidentified skeleton, so he'll have blotted it from his memory to preserve his aura of infallibility!'

Jonah opened his mouth to refute this allegation then thought better of it, merely directing a hard look towards the leafy canopy above.

'Now, hold on to that ladder; I'm coming down!' Bernie called.

Peter sprang to attention and grasped the ladder more firmly in both hands as his wife descended carrying a large basket containing huge red-flushed green apples.

'The Bramley's doing well this year,' she observed. 'You'd hardly know I'd been picking, the number there are still up there. I can see our freezer's going to be full of apple pies again this winter.' She stepped off the bottom of the ladder and turned to address Jonah. 'Let's go inside and I'll make us a brew, and you can tell us all about this Jane Turnbull and why you think she may be the body in the woods.'

By the time they were all three settled in the living room with steaming mugs of tea in front of them, the scanned pages of the case file had arrived in Jonah's email inbox. He displayed them one-by-one on the screen attached to his chair.

'This is the photograph that her parents provided. I see what Andy means – it *does* look rather like the reconstruction from the skull of our skeleton.'

A brief interlude of fumbling with the keypad brought up a second image on the screen. Peter and Bernie peered over Jonah's shoulder to see them better.

'Mmm,' Bernie agreed. 'I see what you mean. The reconstruction makes her look a bit plumper, but the set of the eyes is about right and the shape of the nose.'

'She still doesn't look in the least familiar, though,' commented Peter. 'I don't think it can be a case that I was involved in. Was there any suggestion of foul play? We probably wouldn't have been given a missing person case unless there was some suspicion that it might turn out to be murder. I mean – that's what Richard's team specialised in, wasn't it?'

'I don't know. I haven't read the file yet, have I?' Jonah began flicking through pages of notes on the screen. 'Let's see … Her father raised the alarm when she didn't show up for work on the Monday, but she was last seen alive on the previous Saturday – the final day of Eights Week.'

He scrolled down, his lips moving silently as he read rapidly to himself. 'Oh! I see why Andy thinks this might be her.

She worked at Lichfield College, so there's a connection with the owner of that cuff-link we found.'

'Lichfield?' Peter asked, suddenly taking more interest.

'That's right. That's what I was saying, it's the same college as-'

'Did she work in the kitchens?'

'Yes, I think that's what it says. Just let me check … Yes! Her father, Harold Turnbull, was the head chef there and he presumably got her the job.'

'That's right!' Peter said slowly. 'I remember interviewing him in the kitchen there. He stood there with his apron on and a big cleaver in his hand, threatening to go round to her boyfriend's and force him to tell us where she was.'

'So, he blamed the boyfriend for her disappearance?' Jonah asked at once.

'Yes. Don't you remember? We ended up having to get a restraining order put on him. He actually did go round to the boyfriend's house later on and tried to force his way in. I remember Richard trying to persuade him – the boyfriend that is – not to press charges for criminal damage.'

'I don't remember any of that,' Jonah said in a tone that hinted that perhaps Peter was exaggerating the seriousness of the incident. '*Was* the father charged in the end? And what about the boyfriend? Was there any truth in the idea that he was culpable in any way?'

'Nothing that could be proved exactly, but there was strong circumstantial evidence. Come on, Jonah! You must remember! We dug up the boyfriend's garden looking for the body. I'm sure you were there. You brought the girl's sister over from uni to look at the house and tell us if any of her clothes were missing.'

'Did I?' Jonah frowned in thought. 'I don't remember. Where was this house? And which uni was it?'

'The house was in East Oxford – off Cowley Road – not far from where we lived,' Peter told him. 'It's all coming back now! The boyfriend was a plumber and we found traces of blood in his van. The sister was at uni somewhere in London, I think. I'm sure you drove over there and picked her up.'

Jonah resumed scrolling through the pages of notes, trying to find something that would jog his memory. It was supremely frustrating not to be able to recall something that his old colleague apparently now remembered clearly.

'Yes, you're right,' he said at last. 'Debra Turnbull, aged twenty, training to be a teacher at Whitelands College in Putney. Oh! I remember now! I'd just passed my sergeant's exams and I'd been sent on a residential course at Hendon. Someone – presumably someone with a complete ignorance of the geography of London – had the bright idea that I could collect the girl on the way back. I spent hours queuing in traffic on the North Circular!'

'That explains why you don't remember us interviewing the father in the college kitchen,' Peter agreed. 'It's not something I'll forget in a hurry!'

'So, what happened in the end?' Bernie asked. 'Was the boyfriend charged?'

'No,' Peter shook his head. 'Or at least, I think he was, but then a witness came forward who'd seen her leaving the house the evening she disappeared –

after the time he was supposed to have killed her. In the end, there just wasn't enough evidence to prove he'd done it, and they dropped the charges to avoid him being tried and acquitted. They hadn't relaxed the double jeopardy rule back then, so they couldn't risk prosecuting without a watertight case. When you looked at it, the evidence was all just circumstantial. We had a pretty good idea that's what happened though.'

'If only we'd found the body then, we might have been able to convict him,' Jonah added.

'But if she was killed by her plumber boyfriend, that doesn't explain how a Lichfield College Boat Club cuff-link came to be buried with her,' Bernie pointed out. 'And surely it can't be a complete coincidence that she worked at that same college. There has to be a link between the link and the murder.'

'Maybe she had another boyfriend who was a member of the boat club, and he gave her the cuff-link,' Jonah suggested, his agile mind springing into motion. 'If her main boyfriend found it, he may have seen red and killed her, and then taken the body to Shotover in his van.'

'There was a knife missing from the boyfriend's kitchen,' Peter added. 'We assumed he must have stabbed her with it. Was there any sign of that on the body?'

'I don't think so, but we've only got bones, remember. They couldn't tell us cause of death. She could've died from soft-tissue injuries without it leaving any signs on the skeleton.'

MISSING PERSON

'How did you know about the missing knife?' Bernie asked. 'I mean – I assume the boyfriend didn't tell you?'

'No, the sister did,' Peter explained. 'It was one of a set that her parents gave her. I told you: her father was a chef. He probably thought it was the sort of thing that no home should be without.'

'How did the boyfriend explain it?'

'He got very flustered,' Jonah told her. 'I can picture him now, sitting in the interview room while our team was going through his house and digging up his garden. He said he didn't know anything about the knife set. He never used it himself and he always worried that Jane might hurt herself on them.'

'Self-harm d'you mean?' demanded Bernie.

'No, more just accidental. He said he didn't like having sharp knives like that in the house; it was asking for trouble.'

'And yet they found traces of blood and skin under his fingernails – what? four days, was it? – after his girlfriend disappeared,' Peter put in. '*And* the neighbours reported hearing raised voices that night too.'

'We had a strong case against him,' Jonah agreed. 'If only we'd found the body then!'

'The way we pieced it together was that she got back from serving dinner at the college on that Saturday Night. It was a special Eights Week do and it finished late. They had a row–'

'Which we now know may have been to do with some relationship that she had with the owner of that cuff-link,' Jonah cut in.

MISSING PERSON

'For whatever reason,' Peter continued, 'they rowed and he attacked her with the knife. He probably didn't intend to kill her, but that's how it turned out. In an attempt to cover it up, he bundles her into the back of his van and takes her off somewhere–'

'Shotover Hill, as it turns out,' Jonah interjected.

'Shotover Hill or wherever,' Peter agreed. 'Then he cleans up the house and the van and washes his hands, not very well,' he added with a smile. 'I think we can assume that he didn't sing *Happy Birthday* twice while he was doing it! – and waits for someone else to raise the alarm.'

'It says here that there were only minute traces of blood in the kitchen,' Jonah added, reading from his screen. 'The pathologist said that if she'd been stabbed to death there, he would have expected there to be more.'

'Even after he'd cleaned the place up?' queried Bernie.

'As far as I recall, the point he made was that the amount of blood found was consistent with the boyfriend's story about an accidental injury from some time earlier,' Peter explained. 'It was one of those cases where the suspect was able to construct a version of events that fitted the evidence so well that a jury would be almost sure to decide that there was *reasonable doubt*.'

'And that cuff-link only increases the level of doubt,' Jonah added gleefully. He enjoyed a challenge. 'I think it's time we made a concerted effort to make contact with the 1983 Lichfield College boat crews!'

MISSING PERSON

'Don't you need to inform her family first?' Bernie asked. 'I mean, if word gets out that you're asking people about this Jane Turnbull again …?'

'Bernie's right,' Peter agreed. 'Hadn't you better start by establishing a positive ID for your skeleton? What about dental records? Or DNA?'

'OK, OK, I'll get Andy on to it,' Jonah conceded, 'but as soon as we get confirmation that those bones *do* belong to Jane Turnbull, I'm going to get back on to that Alumni Office and force them to give us names and addresses.'

He had hardly finished his call to Andy Lepage, giving detailed instructions for his next move, when the phone attachment on Jonah's wheelchair buzzed to signify an incoming call. It was Gavin.

VICTIM STATEMENTS

'I'm sorry to bother you on a working day, he apologised. 'I know you must be busy, but Chrissie asked me to ring. She's anxious about Mrs Whittle. Apparently, she's working herself up into a bit of a state about giving evidence at the trial. Is there any way she could be excused from testifying?'

'As you know, it's not my decision,' Jonah answered. 'I can talk to the prosecutor, but at the end of the day, it's his call, not mine. Besides, her appearance might well sway the jury in favour of conviction.'

'Not if the defence convinces them that she's a drunk whose evidence can't be relied on. There were officers on the scene almost right away, weren't there? Why can't they testify instead?'

'OK, I'll talk to the prosecutor,' Jonah conceded, 'but I think they've got their minds made up on that score. The impact on the jury of hearing a mother describing how she came home to find her son murdered is just too good to miss.'

'Well, I hope they've got a plan for what to do if she takes a bit too much Dutch courage and collapses in the witness box,' Gavin muttered with uncharacteristic anger. 'It may be all just a game to them, but for the likes of the Whittles it's life and death.'

'OK. I've got the message; I'll do my best,' Jonah promised. 'Now, I'll have to go, there's another call waiting.'

The new caller was unexpected: it was Professor Weldon, speaking in a rather tired voice, but sounding surprisingly cheerful for a man whom they had been led to believe was at death's door only a few weeks before.

VICTIM STATEMENTS

'I gather you wanted to speak to me again,' he said. 'I'm sorry it's taken so long, but my wife only just remembered to give me the message.'

'It's very good of you to call,' Jonah replied. 'How are you? I heard you'd been in hospital with COVID.'

'That's right,' the professor confirmed, 'not at all a pleasant experience, but I'm a lot better now – just a bit short of breath occasionally. Now, what was it you wanted to ask?'

'We've got a list of names for the boat crews from Eights Week 1983,' Jonah told him, 'but the Alumni Office is being cagey about giving us addresses. I was hoping you might remember something more about them if I went through the list with you – maybe hearing the names would jog your memory.'

'I'm willing to give it a go. Fire away.'

'Thank you. Just a mo, while I find the list.' Jonah screwed up his eyes in concentration as he searched for the file on his computer. 'I won't be a minute,' he continued, 'just give me a – ah! Here we are! According to this, the first eight comprised Jeremy Scott-Urquhart, Timothy Plumstead, Giles Kingman, Gerald Leslie, Graham Weldon, Charles Rawlins, Peregrine Milton, Julian Palmer, and Anthony Pulborough. Do any of those names ring a bell with you?'

'Milton! Of course! Peregrine Milton. I'd been worrying about what his surname was ever since you asked me about the 1983 crew, but it just wouldn't come. Sign of old age, I suppose. Now let's see …'

Jonah waited patiently without speaking. At last, the professor continued.

VICTIM STATEMENTS

'Julian was the president of the club, but you knew that already. Who was it you said rowed at number six?'

'Charles Rawlins.'

'He must have been the chap with the long red hair that kept flopping about. It was very off-putting for me sitting right behind him. No idea what happened to him after he left, I'm afraid.'

'Can you remember anything about their relationships?' Jonah enquired. 'Who was friends with whom – any girlfriends – that sort of thing?'

'Julian always tried to be friends with everyone. Looking back, I suppose he was probably rather insecure and desperate to be liked.'

'But no special friends?' Jonah prompted.

'Not that I knew of. There *were* three of them who did a lot of things together.

MISSING PERSON

Number six – the chap you say was Charles Rawlins – was one of them. Yes! I remember now. Charles, Gerald and Jeremy! They fancied themselves as the three musketeers: all for one and one for all and all that. I remember Jerry–'

'Is that Jeremy or Gerald?' interrupted Bernie, who was taking notes.

'Jeremy. Jeremy had a car, which was very unusual for an undergraduate at that time. It made him pretty popular with a lot of people, because he could give them lifts to places they wouldn't have been able to get to otherwise. But he wouldn't *lend* it to anyone except for his two best buddies, Gerald and Charles – said those were the only people he could trust with his *motor* as he insisted on calling it.'

'So, if one of those three got into some sort of trouble, the others would help him out?' Jonah asked.

'Yes, definitely.'

'Did any of them – or any of the other boat club members come to that – have a girlfriend who worked at the college?'

'One of the domestic staff d'you mean?'

'That's right,' Jonah confirmed. 'Especially someone who worked in the kitchens.'

'I think Peregrine Milton may have done. I vaguely remember him getting some ragging about something of that sort. I don't know her name or anything though. Tony – the cox – was notorious for picking up random women. So, I wouldn't put it past him to have had a fling with one of the staff. There were some quite young ones who served at dinner.'

MISSING PERSON

'That just leaves Timothy Plumstead and Giles Kingman,' Jonah remarked, glancing down at his list. 'What do you remember about them?'

'Nothing at all, I'm afraid,' Weldon sighed. 'The names don't even sound familiar. I suppose that means there isn't anything particularly remarkable about them, but that's not much use to you, is it? I'm sorry. I feel I ought to be able to tell you a lot more than I can.'

'No, no. Every little helps, as they say,' Jonah assured him. 'I'm very grateful to you for ringing. You've given me some useful leads to follow up.'

'Do you really think one of them killed a woman and buried her in the woods?' Weldon asked. 'Do you know who she is, yet? Was it one of the college staff?'

'We don't know for sure yet,' Jonah told him. 'So don't mention it to anyone, but yes, we do suspect that the body may be that of someone who worked at Lichfield College back in the eighties. Now, I'd better not take up any more of your valuable time. If you do happen to remember anything more about any of the rowing club members – especially about their social lives and girlfriends – please let me know.'

Jonah ended the call and looked round at Bernie and Peter with a satisfied expression on his face. 'Next stop the Alumni Office,' he declared.

Daisy Gregg, the Alumni Engagement Officer, was working from home, but she agreed to a video call with Jonah. He failed to charm out of her the addresses or contact details of any of the living members of the 1983 boat crews, but she did confide the information that Julian Palmer had died in 2015 and that letters sent from the Alumni Office to Gerald Leslie had begun to be returned to sender "not known at this address" some twenty years or so ago. Then she forwarded to him a quantity of back issues of the Lichfield College alumni magazine, and suggested that he might find what he wanted in the annual updates that graduates sent in, detailing their latest news.

Jonah thanked her politely, silently cursing Data Protection legislation and her employer for having trained her in it so well. Then he called Andy Lepage.

'I've got a couple of dozen copies of the *Lichfield College Magazine* that I'm going to send on to you,' he told him. 'Get the team to have a read of them, particularly the news items from graduates who matriculated any time between 1979 and 1982. You're looking for information that might help us to find anyone off that list of boat club members that we've got. The other thing I want you to do is to search the 2015 registration records for Julian Palmer's death. If we can find out where he died, we may be able to track down his family and find out if he still had his pair of cuff-links. And while you're on to the records office, you could do a search for Gerald Leslie's death. He went off the radar round about the turn of the century, but he may not be dead, just not interested in keeping in touch with his old college.'

'Right-io!' Andy replied cheerfully. 'I'll get on to that right away.'

'And what about those dental records?' Jonah asked, sensing that he was about to end the call. 'Any joy there yet?'

'No. The dental practice that she was registered with merged with another one in the nineties, so it took a while to find the right person to talk to. Then, when I did, they told me they have a policy of destroying patient records ten years after the last time they had contact with that patient.'

'What! Even when the patient has been reported as a *missing person*?' exploded Jonah.

'Well, they weren't to know that,' explained Andy. 'As far as they knew, this was just a patient who'd probably moved away years ago without informing them. It's not like a GP practice, where patients have to transfer their registration when they move.'

'Well, get on to her GP then and see if they've got anything that would help to identify her,' Jonah told him. 'And double-check her missing person file, in case there's anything in that we could use.'

'Right you are, sir. I'll get on to it right away.'

Jonah ended the call and looked up at Bernie. 'That wretched GDPR has a lot to answer for,' he growled. 'How're we supposed to find out what happened when all the records have been destroyed and we aren't allowed to know where the people who might remember live?'

The first week of October saw the first substantial progress in the Shotover murder case. Further scrutiny of the skull suggested that the victim had undergone orthodontal work. Jane Turnbull's GP records, while not containing enough detail to confirm identity, did provide sufficient evidence of agreement that Jonah felt able to make contact with her family to raise the possibility of her body having been found.

Neither of her parents was still alive, so Jonah broke the news to her sister.

'What now?' she demanded over the phone from her home in Bristol, where she lived with her husband and three children. 'When are you going to charge that bastard who killed her?'

'I have to emphasise,' Jonah told her, 'that nothing is certain. We haven't been able to make a positive identification yet. One reason that I'm ringing is to ask if you would be willing to supply a DNA sample to help us to know whether the remains that we've found really do belong to your sister.'

'Yes, yes, of course,' Debra replied brusquely. 'Whatever it takes. What do I do?'

'I'll arrange for someone to call round to take the sample,' Jonah told her. 'Now, while we're talking, there's one other thing that you might be able to tell me, which could help with our enquiries. Do you know if your sister had a relationship with anyone at the college where she worked – one of the students, perhaps?'

'No.' Debra Carr, as she was now, spoke confidently. 'The only person she had eyes for was that cretin, Adrian. She was completely infatuated with him, in spite of everything he did to her. She left him any number of times, but she always went back. She never even looked at anyone else.

Meanwhile, the team had been busy hunting for news of the whereabouts of members of the 1983 rowing crews. It turned out that two of them lived in the Oxford area: Anthony Pulborough, the First Eight cox, was a fellow of Holy Cross College; Jeremy Scott-Urquhart, now the owner and CEO of a public-relations company, had settled in the village of Horspath, a few miles to the east of the city.

Jonah decided to tackle Dr Anthony Pulborough, Fellow in Geography, first. He telephoned him at work and made an appointment to meet him at his home in Marston. He was a small rotund man, bald on top with wispy white hair and pale blue eyes. He invited them in, hurrying on ahead to open the door to a cluttered sitting room, filled with antique furniture. He pushed a high-backed easy chair out of the way to allow Jonah's wheelchair room to enter.

'Can I get you a drink?' he asked, gesturing towards a well-stocked cocktail cabinet, which stood between a huge grandfather clock and an ornate writing desk.

'No thank you,' Jonah replied briskly. 'We won't be here for long. We'd just like to ask you a few questions about your time as an undergraduate at Lichfield College.'

'Mustn't drink on duty, I suppose,' the don smiled back. 'Presumably you don't mind if I do?'

'By all means – go ahead.' Jonah returned the smile, reflecting that anything that might loosen the little man's tongue was likely to work to their advantage.

Pulborough helped himself to a generous measure from a bottle of single malt Scotch before sitting down in a velvet-covered armchair. Jonah was no expert, but he guessed that the whisky was not a brand that would be found readily on his local supermarket shelves.

'As I said on the phone, we're trying to find the owner of a pair of cuff-links, which were commissioned by the college Boat Club in 1983. Professor Weldon has a pair, and he tells us that all the other members of the first and second crews that year bought a pair too. Is that right?'

'Yes. I've still got mine.' Pulborough put his hand in his pocket and drew out a small box. He opened it and held it out for Jonah to see. 'I looked them out after your call. But why the sudden interest in them?'

'We have one of a pair and we're rather keen to unite it with its owner,' Jonah replied. Bernie held up the evidence bag as he continued. 'It was found at a crime scene, which makes us think that he could be an important witness.'

'How exciting!' Pulborough downed the remainder of his whisky and replaced the glass on top of the cocktail cabinet. He leaned forward and asked in a confidential whisper, 'and what *was* the crime? Do tell!'

'Murder,' Jonah replied, moving his chair back a little and colliding with a chaise longue. 'A murder that could easily have happened back in 1983, when you and your rowing friends were all up at Oxford. So, it's rather important for me to contact you all to eliminate you from our enquiries. Did you keep in touch with any of the others?'

'Let me see … Well, there's Jeremy, of course: we meet up a couple of times a year usually – Christmas and the college garden party in the summer, but that's had to be cancelled this year. He lives locally – Horspath. I can give you the address.'

'Thank you, but he's already next on our list to visit. What about the others? Do you know where we could find any of them?'

'Weldon has a chair here in Oxford. You'd be able to find him through the Chemistry Department.'

'Yes, we've already spoken to Professor Weldon.'

'Have you? Have you? I haven't bumped into him in person for years – it's almost as if he's avoiding me!' Pulborough shook his head as if in bewilderment. 'He's got a fellowship at Lichfield, you know, and yet I haven't seen him at any of the gaudies.'

'Anyone else?' prompted Jonah.

'Giles and I swap letters at Christmas. He's living in the States now. He's landed a professorship at Notre Dame University in Indiana – or Noter Dame, as our American friends call it,' he added enunciating the name in an exaggerated way to emphasise the ignorance of correct French pronunciation exhibited by the Yanks.

'Thank you. That's very useful. We'll be able to contact him though his department. That's Physics, isn't it?'

'That's right. I can see you've done your homework.'

'Any others? Charles Rawlins, for example? Or Gerald Leslie?'

'No.' Pulborough shook his head. 'I haven't heard from either of them for years. Charles invited me to his wedding … when was that …?' He drummed his fingers on the arm of his chair and screwed up his eyes in concentration. 'I can't remember,' he said at last, 'but it was a while back – early-nineties at a guess. I fancy he's divorced now, but don't quote me on that.'

'Did you go to the wedding?' Jonah asked. 'Where was it?'

'No. I have a feeling I was abroad at the time. There's a lot of fieldwork involved in my discipline. As to where it was … let me see now… Surrey, I think, or maybe Hampshire. Aldershot rings a bell, but don't quote me on that.'

'Thank you, that's very helpful – anyone else?'

'No, I can't think of anyone.'

'How about Timothy Plumstead?' suggested Jonah, glancing down his list.

'No. I'd forgotten all about him, to be honest. I never knew him very well, even when we were both up at Lichfield. He was a bit of a loner, didn't mix much. I have a feeling he went into the City, but don't quote me on that.'

'Thank you. That gives us a possible starting point, at any rate. Now that only leaves Julian Palmer, out of the First Eight. Do you know anything about what happened to him?'

'Why, he's dead! Didn't you know?' The don stared at Jonah with a look of great surprise on his face.

'Yes, *we* know. I wanted to hear what *you* knew about it,' Jonah told him. 'Did you go to his funeral?'

'No. I only heard about it through a notice in the paper. We lost touch after his divorce. I'm afraid I rather took the wife's side. He treated her very badly by all accounts. Anyway, after that he became a bit of a recluse. His father gave him a house on the family estate – Norfolk, I think that was – and he hardly stirred from there, after that.'

'And when was this divorce?' Jonah enquired.

'Oh, way back! They hardly seemed to have been married five minutes. It was obviously a mistake from the start. Julian was never cut out to share his life with anyone – too self-centred. As soon as poor Lucinda tried to strike out on her own a bit, he was down on her like a ton of bricks. I won't speak ill of the dead, but I will say this: most of his friends disowned him after what he did to her. And the court agreed: she got a very generous divorce settlement, by all accounts.'

'Thank you. That's all very useful to know. You don't happen to know where I might find *Mrs* Palmer, by any chance?' Jonah asked, treating Pulborough to one of his most charming smiles.

'No, I'm afraid not. I'm pretty sure she sold up the house they had together and moved back up north to wherever it was her family were, but I can't remember where that was.'

'Alright. You've been very helpful. Now there's just one more thing I'd like to ask you.' Jonah turned the screen on his chair round to face Pulborough. 'Have a look at that face and tell me if you've ever seen that woman.'

Pulborough leaned forward and peered at the photograph of Jane Turnbull, which Jonah had brought up on the screen. 'No,' he said, shaking his head, 'I can't say I have. Who is she?'

'Think back to when you were an undergraduate at Lichfield,' Jonah prompted. 'Did you ever see her around the college?'

'No,' the don repeated, 'I don't think so. Is she the victim? You did say this was a murder enquiry, didn't you?'

'We aren't sure yet,' Jonah told him, 'but we think she might be. Are you sure you've never seen her before?'

'Well, if you're talking about when I was up at Lichfield, I certainly couldn't swear to it. I couldn't swear to much from back then, to be quite honest!'

Pulborough laughed. 'Quite apart from the passage of time, undergraduates aren't noted for their sobriety or their chaste lifestyle, are they? I could have gone out with her once or twice, for all I'd remember! What's her name?'

'Jane Turnbull,' Jonah told him. 'Does that name mean anything to you?'

'Not a thing!' Pulborough declared. 'Like I said – but don't quote me on this – I really don't think I ever met the girl. Now, would you like me to give Jerry a ring and arrange for you to meet him? He'll probably be able to help you better than I can. He's bound to know where Charles and Gerald are. They used to go round together all the time when we were undergrads.'

MISSING PERSON

The following morning, Bernie and Jonah pulled up outside Jeremy Scott-Urquhart's period cottage in the picturesque village of Horspath. It was smaller than might have been expected for the residence of a successful business executive, but perhaps he favoured elegance over grandeur.

Inside, when he invited them in through the low doorway, it was all exposed beams and horse brasses. Bernie felt sure that, if she were to poke her head into the kitchen, she would encounter bunches of herbs hanging to dry over a range and possibly strings of onions or even a home-cured ham or two.

'My second wife's idea,' he informed her, seeing her gazing at an antique-looking wood-burning stove in the fireplace of the sitting room, which took up the whole of one side of the house, with windows at front and rear. 'I never use it. The central heating is quite adequate, and these days, they're considered to be terrible polluters – all those particulates they're supposed to be pumping into the atmosphere! Now sit down, both of you, and tell me what this is all about.'

Bernie moved one of the armchairs to make more room for Jonah's wheelchair, and then sat down in it. Scott-Urquhart selected a two-seater sofa under the back window. Was this a chance choice or had he deliberately arranged for the strong morning sunlight to be pouring in behind him making it difficult to read his face?

'I believe your friend Dr Pulborough told you that we're hunting for everyone who bought a pair of these cuff-links,'

Jonah began. Bernie held up the evidence bag. 'Do you still have yours?'

'I do indeed,' Scott-Urquhart smiled back. He reached over to an occasional table and picked up a jewellery box identical to the one that Pulborough had shown them. 'Here they are, if you'd like to see them.'

Bernie applied hand sanitiser before taking the box from him and looking inside. Then she nodded to Jonah before closing the box again and handing it back.

'Excellent!' declared Jonah. 'We now have three pairs accounted for, but that leaves twenty-one more that we haven't traced – or twenty and a half to be more precise!'

'So, how can I help you?'

'Have you kept in touch with any of the other people who had a pair?' Jonah asked. 'We'd like to speak to each of them to eliminate them from our enquiries.'

'No. The only one I ever see these days is Tony Pulborough.'

'What about Charles Rawlins and Gerald Leslie? I gather you and they were friends.'

'Poor Gerald committed suicide. He was always a bit of a melancholy type. That was a good while back now.'

'You don't happen to have an address for his family, do you?'

'No.' Scott-Urquhart shook his head. 'I sent my condolences to his parents, of course, but I don't have the address any more, and I think they moved after that anyway.'

'Do you at least remember whereabouts they lived?' Jonah pressed him.

'I'm really not sure. Nottinghamshire maybe or could be Staffordshire, but, as I said, I think they moved after Gerald died.'

'So, he was living with them when he took his own life?' Jonah pounced on this crumb of information.

'Yes. He had some sort of breakdown after he went down from Oxford and went back home to recover, but ... well it seems he never did.'

'If you were such good friends, I would have thought you'd have visited him there,' Bernie observed, 'which makes it strange that you don't remember which county it was in.'

'Now that's where you're wrong,' Scott-Urquhart replied smoothly, still smiling. He appeared to be enjoying the interrogation. 'It was Gerald and Charles who were the great friends. I was only ever on the periphery. They shared rooms in Lichfield and did everything together. I think they felt sorry for me and allowed me to join in out of pity.'

'Why would they feel sorry for you?' asked Jonah.

'No particular reason,' the businessman replied airily. 'I was a bit gauche in those days. Awkward in company – especially female company. They took me under their wing and helped me to find my feet. I was in the year below them and they helped me to settle into college life. That was all there was to it. We weren't great friends, whatever you may have heard.'

'And after you came down?' Jonah queried. 'Did you keep in touch with Charles Rawlins at all?'

'For a bit, but we drifted apart. I've no idea what he's doing or where he is now.

I've had as much as I can do keeping on top of my own affairs without harping back to my old university days! My first wife screwed me for all she could get when we divorced, and then there were school fees and university fees and … and then wife number two turned out to be just as money-grabbing as the first one. I can't think why I was so foolish as to allow myself to be caught a second time! I should have known better, but–.' He stopped abruptly and looked sheepishly towards Bernie. 'I'm sorry: I suppose you two are probably…?' he glanced across to Jonah with an unconvincingly innocent expression on his face.

'No, sir,' Bernie said firmly. 'My relationship with DCI Porter is purely professional.'

VICTIM STATEMENTS

'Getting back to Charles Rawlins,' Jonah put in. 'Dr Pulborough thought his wedding took place in Surrey or possibly Hampshire. Were you invited too?'

'Not that I remember. When would that have been?'

'Dr Pulborough thought it was the early nineties.'

'Ah well, that would explain it. I would have been in the throes of my first divorce round about then. It's no wonder I don't remember anything about it. I was in no mood to go round accepting invitations to other people's *happy occasions*!'

'I see.' Jonah was silent for several seconds, pondering what he had heard. 'Now, getting back to 1983,' he resumed eventually, 'do you remember any of your set having a relationship with one of the domestic staff at the college?'

MISSING PERSON

'Good Lord no!' Scott-Urquhart's tone was full of derision. 'What makes you ask that?'

'We have reason to believe that the remains of a young woman which were found recently in a shallow grave on Shotover Hill are those of this woman, who worked in the college kitchens when you were an undergraduate there and who disappeared on the day of your Eights Week dinner in 1983.'

Jonah rotated his computer screen to display the photograph of Jane Turnbull. 'Do you recognise her?'

Scott-Urquhart made a big show of peering at the screen, twisting his head to view the face at different angles. Then he looked up and smiled again. 'No!' he said glibly. 'I've never seen her before. What makes you think that any of my "set" as you put it had anything to do with her?'

'One of your very distinctive cuff-links was found with her body,' Jonah told him. 'We can only assume that a member of the boat club gave it to her.'

'Well, as you can see, it wasn't me.' Scott-Urquhart waved his hand in the direction of the jewellery box. 'As you've seen, both my cuff-links are still present and correct. Don't you think it's much more likely that she stole the cuff-link from some chap's room?'

'*Did* any of those cuff-links go missing round about that time?' Jonah asked at once.

'Not that I know of, but you know students! Whoever it belonged to probably thought he'd just misplaced it. Undergrads are always losing things, but they usually turn up again in the end. Now, I don't like to hurry you, but I do have a rather urgent video conference coming up in a minute or two, so if we're done now…?'

Jonah and Bernie withdrew, leaving the executive with one of Jonah's cards and the usual appeal to get in touch if he were to remember anything else that might be of use to the investigation.

'Do you trust what he says?' Bernie asked, as they drove back home. 'He seemed too smooth-talking to me, but maybe that's just my prejudice against his type.'

'I'm not sure. I think he may be hiding something from us, but I'm not sure what. And his description of his relationship with Rawlins and Leslie doesn't match Weldon's "all for one and one for all" idea at all, does it?'

'That's exactly what I thought,' Bernie agreed.

'But, of course, it could be Weldon who's got it wrong,' Jonah mused. 'He could even be deliberately misleading us.'

'I hope it isn't Graham Weldon who killed her. I rather like him – much more appealing than those two Public School types we've just interviewed. I wouldn't be surprised if the two of them were in it together!'

'Pulborough did seem keen to be the one who rang Scott-Urquhart to arrange for us to go round,' Jonah agreed thoughtfully, 'which meant that he already knew that we'd be wanting to see the cuff-links. How do we know for certain that the ones he showed us weren't the same pair that we saw at Pulborough's house?'

'We could pay Pulborough another visit and ask to see them again,' Bernie suggested.

'We could … but let's keep that option in reserve and just bear in mind that things may not be everything that they seem. If the two of them were both involved in the murder, then it's better that they think they've put us off the scent. We've still got another four members of the first eight crew to talk to yet – if we can track them down!'

'Not to mention the second eight and boat club officials and whoever snapped up those few spare ones that Our Graham told us about,' pointed out Bernie. 'And we haven't established who the body actually is yet!'

'That's where you're wrong,' Jonah crowed, as they turned into their drive. 'Andy has just texted to say they've got a positive ID based on the DNA sample that Debra Carr gave us. We'd better get over there this afternoon and break the news before it leaks out to the tabloids.'

Debra Carr led them into the lounge of her unassuming semi-detached house and stood with her hands clutched together in front of her. She was a small woman with brown hair, showing grey at the roots. She was wearing a navy-blue skirt suit and sensible shoes.

'Please, Mrs Carr, sit down,' Jonah urged gently.

'So, it is her?' She perched on the edge of an armchair, still clasping her hands together nervously. 'Jane was murdered, wasn't she? I always *knew* she hadn't just run away!'

'Yes, I'm afraid you're right. Mitochondrial DNA extracted from the skeleton on Shotover Hill is a match to yours. That together with your sister's medical records, makes it almost certain that it is her body that was buried up there.'

'I see. So, what now?' She looked up at Jonah, wide-eyed.

'We need to gather more evidence first,' Jonah told her. 'Would it be alright for me to ask you some questions about her – to help us out find out how she died?'

Mrs Carr nodded silently.

'I may have to come back to you later with more questions,' Jonah began, 'but for the time being, I'd just like to know whether she ever spoke to you at all about her work at Lichfield College.'

'Not really,' she shook her head. 'She didn't particularly enjoy it, but it was a job, and they weren't that easy to come by back then.'

'Did she ever speak about getting to know any of the students?'

'No. She worked in the kitchens. She wouldn't even meet the students.'

'Are you sure?'

'Yes! I told you all this before.'

'We were just wondering… We have reason to think that she may have been in some sort of relationship with one of the undergraduates. Are you sure she didn't say anything about that to you?'

'No! And she wouldn't. She was besotted with that creep, Adrian. I told you! He treated her like dirt, but she just couldn't keep away from him. She'd go home to Mum and Dad when things got really bad, but then, a few days later, she'd go running back to him and they'd make up, and then it'd all start all over again. She'd never have looked at another man – she wouldn't have dared!'

'So, she never complained about any of them bothering her?' persisted Jonah, unwilling to give up on his current pet theory. 'Maybe she had eyes for nobody except her boyfriend, but that might not stop one of the students getting a crush on her. None of them gave her any presents, for example?'

'No. Nothing like that.'

'I see,' Jonah nodded. 'That's cleared that up then. Thank you. Now, will you be alright? Would you like us to wait with you until …?'

'No – no thanks – I'll be fine. Jason will be back any minute. His school's on the other side of town, so he sometimes gets held up in the traffic, but he's not usually much later home than me. In fact – here he is!'

14. WITNESS FOR THE PROSECUTION

'Trev! Tre-ev!'

At the sound of his wife's voice, Trevor Whittle looked up from his task of mowing the lawn in their small back garden. Yvonne was standing in the kitchen in her slippers, calling out through the open door. He released the handle of the electric mower and the engine stopped.

'What is it?' he called back.

'It's the trial!' Yvonne sounded as if she were about to break down in tears. 'They've put it back to November!'

'What? But they said it was starting next week. You've booked time off! How can they?' Trevor strode across the garden towards the house. 'How do you know? Who told you?'

'They rang just now. I'm not sure exactly who it was. Someone from the court, I think.' Yvonne retreated into the kitchen to make space for him to enter. 'They just said they were sorry about the delay, but some cases took longer than they expected and ...'

Trevor put his arms round his wife as her voice gave way to sobs.

'How could they do this to us?' he growled over her head. 'Can't they see ...?'

He became aware of Leo standing in the hall, holding his ubiquitous basketball and watching them through the doorway. He was about to tell him to go away and leave his mother in peace, when his mobile phone rang. He snatched it up out of his pocket and looked down at the screen.

VICTIM STATEMENTS

'Sorry, sugar dumpling, I'll have to take this: it's work.'

The call was for a pick-up from the hospital. It was one of his regulars: an elderly widower who had to go for routine checks at the Anticoagulant Clinic.

'Yes, Mr Patterson, I'll be right over. Ten minutes – fifteen max.' He helped his wife into a chair and then turned to Leo. 'Your mum's had a bit of a shock. Make her a cup of tea, will you? And then finish the lawn for me. I've got to go now, but I'll be back before lunch.'

Cyril Patterson belonged to the "mustn't grumble" school of thought. Whatever life threw at him, he somehow managed to be unfailingly cheerful. When Trevor poked a masked face round the door of

WITNESS FOR THE PROSECUTION

the waiting area outside the clinic, he greeted him like a long-lost friend.

'Trevor!' he called out. 'How are you? And how are the wife and – how's young Leo?'

He had been about to say "wife and kids"; Trevor could tell. He had only just remembered in time that Harry was dead. It was nearly a year ago now. People were starting to forget. Nearly a year! And those bastards still hadn't been convicted!

'We're fi – well, we're doing as well as – how are you?'

'Oh, much the same! The quacks are still managing to keep me going.'

Trevor helped him up out of his seat and gave him an arm as they walked slowly out to the car.

'You didn't answer my question.' Mr Patterson breathed heavily at the exertion of walking. 'How *are* you all doing? I read in the papers about the trial being postponed. Have you got a date for it yet?'

'Well, we did have,' Trevor informed him through gritted teeth, 'but we've just been told that it's being put off for another month.'

'That's not good.' Mr Patterson clicked his tongue and shook his head slowly as Trevor eased him down into the front passenger seat. 'I'd have thought it'd have been a priority case for them.'

Trevor closed the door and walked round the car to the driver's side. 'Why a priority?' He asked as he strapped himself in. 'Because they killed a police officer?'

'No, because they killed a minor,' Mr Patterson replied emphatically.

WITNESS FOR THE PROSECUTION

'But everyone will say it was Harry's own fault for getting involved in a drugs gang,' Trevor pointed out grimly. 'I expect that's what the judge is thinking – or whoever decides which cases come up first. Harry got in with the wrong people and only got what he deserved when they killed him.'

'A society can be judged by the way it treats its most vulnerable members,' his passenger asserted with conviction. 'And I'd've said that includes youngsters like your Harry, just left school, a bit credulous, eager to please. The bottom line is: he was only sixteen, didn't you say? That's too young to die by anyone's standards.'

They turned on to the Northern By-pass and headed west at a good speed. Although businesses were opening up again, the traffic was still lighter than in pre-pandemic times.

'And how's your wife bearing up?' Mr Patterson seemed determined to delve into their deepest feelings. 'She was the one who found him, wasn't she? That must make it hard for her to…'

Trevor hesitated before answering. With most people he would have resented such intrusive questioning. What right had anyone to know the toll that the events of last December had taken on them? But there was something about his passenger's quiet persistence that disarmed him. He knew that Muriel Patterson – Cyril's wife of almost sixty years – had died four or five years earlier. Their four children were spread around the globe and rarely visited – not at all now, of course. He must be very lonely by himself in that big house.

'Oh! She's up and down a lot – you know!' he replied at last. Then, when Mr Patterson did not comment, he went on, 'having the trial put off again was a blow, but she'd been all keyed up worrying about being a witness, so … I don't know! We'd both like it to be over, but I don't know how she's going to cope with being cross-examined by some clever defence lawyer asking trick questions.'

'Isn't there anyone who can help her? To be more prepared, I mean.'

'They took us for a guided tour of the court,' Trevor told him. 'Showed us where we could sit to watch, and where Yvonne would have to wait to be called into the witness box, and where she'll have to stand to give evidence. I think that only made things worse, to be honest. She's not allowed to watch what happens before they question her. I don't get that.

Surely, as Harry's mum, she has a right to see the whole of his killers' trial?'

'It's the rules,' Mr Patterson told him gently. 'It's so that witnesses don't hear the evidence that other witnesses give, in case it influences what they say themselves.'

'It doesn't seem right to me,' Trevor muttered, 'and it's driving Yvonne crazy, worrying about it all.'

'I'm not surprised. These last few months must've been hell for all of you, but for your wife especially.'

They passed under the A34 dual carriageway and then over the Oxford Canal. There was even less traffic now that they were heading away from Oxford. Trevor did not know how to respond. Conversations in his cab did not usually take this sort of turn. This was very different from, "been on your holidays yet this year?" and "what did you think of the match last night?"

'Did I ever tell you about our youngest – Sally – losing her baby?'

'No. I'm sorry to hear that. When …?'

'Oh, years ago!' Cyril waved his hand to indicate that he was not fishing for sympathy. 'It was two years before they moved to Australia, which was … let's see … nineteen ninety-one. No, I only brought it up because it's the nearest I know to … Well, thinking about your Harry brought it all back. Everyone kept saying, "it's only a miscarriage" and "you'll have other children". I was as bad as everyone else. I couldn't think why she didn't just pull herself together and get on with life.'

Trevor didn't know what to say. This shared confidence made him feel uncomfortable.

VICTIM STATEMENTS

'Her husband – Nick – couldn't understand it either. I think it nearly broke their marriage, but they managed to stick together and she came out of it in the end. But it was a long haul. I remember one evening Nick came round asking my wife to talk to her. She'd been sitting for hours upstairs in the room they'd decorated to be the nursery, just staring at the wall, holding a pair of knitted bootees.'

Trevor remembered the times when he'd found Yvonne sitting similarly in their bedroom, staring at Harry's old school photograph. He remembered his anger at discovering that Harry's clothes were still hanging in the wardrobe that the two brothers shared, instead of having been put in the recycling bin as Yvonne had said she would do. And he remembered taking her by the shoulders and shaking her, trying to make her react to his presence, trying to get her to wake up from her inertia and stop wallowing in self-pity.

Cyril sighed. 'But, like I said, they came through in the end. They've got two kids now – both grown up and in good jobs down under. They came over for Muriel's funeral – two fine strapping lads!'

He put out a bony blue-veined hand and rested it briefly on Trevor's thigh. 'I can't imagine what you and your wife are going through right now, but one's thing's certain: you'll both pull through a bit easier if you can keep talking. Muriel and I talked about everything together. That's the worst of being on your own – having things to say and nobody to say them to.'

They pulled up outside a large detached house on the outskirts of Eynsham. Trevor reversed the taxi into the drive so that Cyril would not have far to walk to the front door. He jumped out and went round to help his passenger out.

'I hope I haven't bored you with my reminiscences,' Cyril apologised, as they walked slowly together to the house. 'You're a good listener, Trevor. I always enjoy a ride in your cab.'

Trevor pondered on Cyril's words as he drove home – later than he had expected because two more calls came through while he was on his way, and he had to divert to pick up passengers and deliver them to their destinations. Had he been too hard on Yvonne? Was Cyril being serious when he said that it had taken his daughter two years to come to terms with losing her baby? And *that* was only a miscarriage. Nothing like as bad as having your teenage son brutally murdered!

But that was no excuse for her drinking. Depression he could understand. Hell! He felt depressed himself – anyone would in their situation – but why couldn't Yvonne see that she was only making things worse? That interfering policeman had given her the number for AA. He thought she was an alcoholic! Who else might there be who was thinking that way? What about the neighbours? Did they think that too? Couldn't Yvonne see that she was ruining her reputation allowing people to see her like that?

But they were wrong – all of them! Alcoholics were smelly old men begging for money in the street. Yvonne couldn't be one of them – not his beautiful wife!

He'd just have to keep a closer eye on her, that was all. If he did all the shopping and took her to and from work every day then she'd have no reason to go out, so she wouldn't be able to buy the booze and she wouldn't be able to drink it. But he couldn't be around all the time, could he? He had to work. He needed the work more than ever with all that debt to pay off. He'd tried to keep it from Yvonne. He didn't want to worry her. But she'd found out anyway. So, she must know they couldn't afford to spend on anything they didn't have to – and yet she was wasting their precious cash on her bloody vodka!

He gripped the steering wheel tighter as anger threatened to overwhelm him. Why couldn't she see what she was doing? Why didn't she just stop!

WITNESS FOR THE PROSECUTION

He was nearly home now. He must calm down. He must go up to her and reason with her, quietly, calmly. He must make her see how important it was for her to stop the drinking and… Maybe she ought to go back to the GP and ask her to increase the strength of those antidepressants that she'd prescribed for her. Yes! Of course! Why hadn't he thought of that before? That must be what was wrong. The pills weren't working, so she was trying to top them up with alcohol. It was so simple when you thought of it that way. If he could solve her depression then she'd stop drinking!

He parked on the drive and hurried over to the front door. 'Hi darling! Sorry I'm late! I got a couple of more calls while I was out!'

No reply. No sound at all. He went inside and peered into the lounge. It was deserted; so was the kitchen. Where was everyone? He went to the foot of the stairs and called up, 'Leo! Are you up there?'

Still no response, so he climbed the stairs and put his head round his son's door. Leo was sitting at his desk with his headphones on, music blaring at full blast. Trevor walked over and plucked them off his head.

'Where's your mum? It's gone lunchtime.'

'Sorry Dad. I didn't notice the time. Mum wasn't feeling good, so she asked me to get the lunch for you, but I forgot. She's having a lie-down.'

Trevor strode across the landing to their bedroom. He flung open the door and stared in. There she was, sitting on the end of the bed, drinking vodka straight from the bottle! He stormed across the room, slamming the door closed behind him, and made a grab for it. She turned her head and looked up at him with a puzzled expression on her face, as if she were trying to remember who he was.

'This has got to stop!' he raged. 'You can't go on like this!' Then, in a lower, more measured tone, 'Think of Leo. How must he feel, seeing his mother like this? And we can't afford to be wasting our money on – on –'

He stared down at the vodka bottle in her hand. 'We've got to be more careful with money. You saw how much we owe, didn't you?'

He sat down next to his wife and put his arm round her, moving a piece of paper that lay there to make room. It had words on it in her neat handwriting, but the lines had all been scored out. An elaborate doodle rose up out of the initial capital and swirled across the top of the paper and down the right-hand side. She had been writing something – but what?

Yvonne leant on his shoulder, her head under his chin. He could feel her cheeks wet against his neck.

'I'm sorry!' she sobbed. 'I do try – really I do! But … I can't stop thinking … I keep seeing him – Harry – just hanging there. And that lawyer – you know – at the court, saying I'd have to answer questions about it – about finding him. I just don't think I can!'

'Just try not to think about it,' Trevor murmured, hugging her to him. 'I know you'll do just fine, but it's not for weeks yet, is it? Let's cross that bridge when we come to it, eh?'

'I'm sorry,' she repeated. 'I know I'm being silly, but I can't stop feeling that way.'

'Well one thing that I'm sure would help is if you stop all this – this …!' Trevor grabbed hold of her hand and waved the vodka bottle in front of her face in frustration.

'I know, I know!' Yvonne sobbed. 'It's just so hard. I keep thinking about having to stand there in front of everyone answering questions and then …'

'It's simple,' Trevor told her, forcing himself to speak in a low, calm voice. 'We'll just make sure there's no alcohol in the house – ever. Then you won't be able to have a drink every time you start worrying about it.'

He took the bottle from her hand. She did not resist.

'Let's start by throwing this away,' he went on. 'Is there any more you've got hidden anywhere?'

Yvonne shook her head. Then, seeming to come to a decision, she looked up at him briefly, before leaning forward and pulling out a drawer in her dressing table. She dropped her hand back into her lap as if this effort was as much as she had energy for and sat staring at the drawer. Trevor put down the bottle at the back of the dressing table out of his wife's reach and fumbled in the drawer. Behind a jumble of hair elastics, combs and almost-finished lipsticks, he found another bottle of vodka, the seal still intact.

'Right! I'll take this. Is that the lot now?'

Yvonne nodded.

'Sure?'

She nodded again.

'OK. Now, here's what I'm going to do.' Trevor picked up both bottles and walked over to the door. 'I'm going to empty these down the sink. And I'm going to get my six-pack of lager from the fridge and I'm going to throw that out too, so you can see I'm not asking you to do anything I'm not doing too – OK? We'll have no alcohol in the house from now on. Then you can't hit the bottle every time you're feeling down. And you've got to promise me that you won't go buying any more – understand? Do – you – understand?' he added emphatically, seeing the blank stare that Yvonne was giving in response to his speech.

'Yes,' she murmured. He took a step towards her. 'Yes, yes I understand.' She cowered back as if she were afraid of him.

VICTIM STATEMENTS

'I'm sorry. I didn't mean to shout at you. I just need to be sure you won't … I'll just get rid of these and then I'll be back. You lie down and get some rest.'

Yvonne watched him go, closing the door carefully behind him to deter Leo from looking in. Not that he would: he always kept away when she had one of her "headaches". What must he think of her? It was a pity his year group had been sent home after a teacher tested positive. If it hadn't been for that, he wouldn't have been at home today. He'd missed so much school this term! It was hardly worth having the school open again.

She crawled up the bed and lay down with her head on the pillow. The room was over the kitchen and she could hear Trevor clinking glasses and rummaging in the cutlery drawer. He must be getting lunch. Tears started again as she reflected that she ought to have had it ready for him when he returned. He was working to support them. The least she could do was to have his meals ready for him when he got back! She was useless as a wife – and as a mother! They'd be better off without her. Trev was right: she was wasting their money on alcohol and embarrassing Leo and …

'Here you are, sugarplum!' Trevor was back with a plate of sandwiches and two glasses of water. 'Try and eat some of these, while we talk things through.'

He put down the tray and helped her into a sitting position, propping her up with pillows like an invalid. She smiled weakly and reached obediently for a sandwich. She watched her hand as if it did not belong to her. It shook as she grasped the food and it took all her willpower to bring it up to her mouth so that she could take a bite.

'That's better.' Trevor laid the plate down on the bed and settled himself down next to her, leaning back against the bedhead. 'Now let's just-'

'I'm sorry!' Yvonne interrupted. 'I know I've let you down. I am trying – really, I am. It's just …'

'No. No. You haven't let us down. You've been through a bad time and you let it all get to you, that's all. Now we just have to work out the best way to deal with it.'

'They said at AA that I need help from a higher power,' Yvonne said tentatively, grasping the unexpected opportunity to admit to Trevor that she had spoken to people outside the family about her drinking. 'But I'm sure they're wrong,' she added quickly, sensing her husband's body tensing at the word "AA". 'I can deal with it – I mean, *we* can deal with it – I'm sure.'

'You've been to AA?' he demanded. Then, more quietly, 'when?'

'Oh, ages ago – before lockdown. I only went to one meeting. I realised at once it was a mistake. You're right, we don't need people telling us how to-'

'No.' Trevor seemed to be making a conscious effort to relax and stay calm. 'No. We've got to face facts. Maybe you do need help. Let's … let's keep an open mind. But, a *higher power*? What do they mean by that? God?'

'They said it was up to me to decide,' Yvonne told him, grateful for his interest. 'One of them said it was the AA group that was his higher power. One of them said something I didn't understand about cosmic energy. There was one who said she prayed to God when she wanted a drink and He helped her not to. She asked me if I believed in God and I told her we'd had the boys christened. And then that made me think about when Harry was born and ...'

She dissolved into more tears. Trevor put his arm round her and hugged her close.

'Maybe *I* could be your higher power,' he suggested hopefully.

'Yes, maybe,' Yvonne sniffed. She had wanted to be able to talk to Trevor about her addiction, but now that it came to it, she wished he would go away and leave her in peace. He was so strong. He didn't understand the compulsion that sometimes came upon her to blot out the world and drift into oblivion. She was glad when his mobile phone rang and he had to go out to another pick-up.

WITNESS FOR THE PROSECUTION

She lay back and closed her eyes. She did not have the energy to finish the sandwiches. The next thing she knew, Leo was calling through the closed door, 'I'm going to the park with Dylan! I've left a note for Dad.'

'OK, love,' Yvonne croaked back, her mouth dry. 'Be back by five!'

'OK!'

She rubbed her bleary eyes and pushed herself up on one elbow. Leo's footsteps clumped down the stairs and then a few moments later the front door banged. Yvonne looked at the alarm clock next to the bed: half past three! Where did all the time go these days? She rolled over and felt the surface of a piece of paper beneath her. It was the one she had been working on while Trevor was out: the statement that the woman from the police – or was it the prosecution service? – had told her she should write.

It was supposed to tell the judge about how she had been affected by Harry's death. She'd called it an "impact statement", which made it sound like a car crash or something. Finding Harry like that hadn't "impacted" her; it had destroyed her! Living without him wasn't like getting whiplash; it was like being in a nightmare that she could never wake up from. It was constant pain, but she didn't want the pain to go away because that would be a betrayal of Harry's memory.

But if she wrote all that, the judge would think she was mental! And Trev would be angry if that was read out in court, because he thought they ought to be strong and not show people she wasn't coping. And what if Social

Services read it and thought it meant she wasn't a fit mother for Leo? Perhaps it would be better just to forget about the whole thing … and yet, people ought to know! The judge ought to know what those *animals* had done to them. He ought to take it into account when he set their sentence. She ought to try.

Trevor brought pizzas home with him for their evening meal. They ate them in the lounge with the boxes open on their laps. Yvonne still didn't feel hungry and passed most of hers over to Leo.

'I've got to go out again at six-thirty,' Trevor announced as he handed round cans of lemonade. 'I've got another airport pick-up booked. It's a nice little earner, but it means I'll be out until nearly nine – at best.'

'That's fine,' Yvonne answered, secretly pleased, and then secretly guilty for being pleased. 'We'll manage, won't we Leo?'

Leo grunted something unintelligible and carried on eating his pizza.

After Trevor had left, Yvonne sat in the living room with a pad of paper in front of her and a pen in her hand, determined to make some progress with the "Victim Personal Statement" that the woman from the support agency had told her she could submit to the court. She clicked the button on the top of the pen nervously, trying to decide how to start.

'Harry meant the world to me,' she wrote slowly. No! That would sound as if she didn't care about Leo too. 'My son Harry was only sixteen when he was killed.' No. She crossed out the last word and replaced it with "brutally murdered". 'He had his whole life in front of him. He did not deserve to die so young. I think of him every day. I would do anything to bring him back.'

She sat back in her chair and closed her eyes in an attempt to think better. What else could she say? That woman had said she ought to talk about how Harry's death had affected her. Wasn't it obvious? How else could a mother be affected by her son's death?

Perhaps Chrissie Hughes could help: she must have been asked to make a statement too. Yvonne's heart started beating faster as another thought struck her. What if Chrissie said things that made people think that she hadn't cared as much for Harry as Chrissie cared for her Kenny? She was a teacher. She would know how to write things. Everyone would believe her.

She got up and closed the door so that Leo would not overhear, before sitting down again and punching Chrissie's number into her mobile phone. It was answered almost immediately, almost as if Chrissie had been waiting for a call.

'Hello Yvonne!' She sounded pleased and perhaps a bit relieved. 'How nice to hear from you! How are things? I suppose you heard about the trial being put back to November?'

'Yes. Your husband was kind enough to call in to check we knew. It was about the trial that I was ringing – well, sort of.'

'Yes?'

'Have they asked you to write a – a "Victim Personal Statement"?' Yvonne read out the words carefully, to make sure she got them right.

'Yes. I must get round to it. I'm afraid I keep putting it off.'

'Do you really? I'm the same. I keep starting and then I can't think what to say.'

'You're doing better than me then.' It was almost as if Chrissie was relieved to hear that Yvonne was struggling with this apparently simple task. 'I haven't even thought about it. I've just pushed it to the back of my mind. I think I was hoping Gavin'd do it; but I should have known he wouldn't want to. He's not very good with words – or at least he always *says* he isn't.'

'He must know what sort of thing they want, mustn't he?' Yvonne suggested. 'Being a police officer, I mean. Won't he have heard them read out?'

VICTIM STATEMENTS

'I don't know. I suppose he *may* have done.' Chrissie sounded unsure. 'Tell you what! Why don't we have a go at writing ours together? It may be easier if we can bounce ideas off one another.'

'Now?' asked Yvonne eagerly. 'Trev's going to be out until about nine, so you could come round now.'

'Sorry. I can't go out. Gavin could be in any minute and He'll need his dinner.'

'Oh! Sorry. I should've thought.'

'No. That's alright. Why don't you come round to ours? The dinner's in the slow cooker, so there's nothing for me to do with it, and Gavin's as likely to be two hours as two minutes. That's policing for you: there always seems to be something that crops up just before the end of his shift!'

'OK – if you're sure,' Yvonne asked anxiously. 'I don't want to be …'

'You won't be,' Chrissie assured her. 'I'll be glad of the company – and grateful for the nudge to write that statement!'

To Yvonne's surprise, writing her statement became much easier when she had Chrissie there to prompt her with ideas and suggest different ways of expressing her feelings. She was educated and knew the right words to use and all sorts of tricks to make the statement come alive. And it was such a relief to be able to talk about Harry with someone who understood what he meant to her! Trev was a typical man and didn't like discussing his emotions – he would probably have denied having any! And Leo was too young. Anyway, she wouldn't want to burden him with her troubles: being a teenager was hard enough without that.

'How about putting a paragraph or two at the beginning introducing Harry to the judge?' Chrissie suggested, after she had typed up their first draft on her laptop. 'Perhaps a little story to help them understand what he was like and why it matters so much that he isn't here anymore.'

'What sort of story?'

'Well, how about a memory of him that makes you proud of him or where you were all happy together.' Yvonne continued to look puzzled, so Chrissie went on. 'I think *I'm* going to start with how Kenny always wanted to be a police officer, right from when he was tiny. He used to play games with his toys, arresting the bad ones and putting them in jail. He'd have liked this little chap.'

WITNESS FOR THE PROSECUTION

She reached across and picked up a teddy bear in police uniform, which had been watching their endeavours from a shelf above the table.

'Someone left him on the spot where Kenny was killed,' she explained. 'We don't know who. The kids in my class have named him Leo. L-E-O for Law Enforcement Officer. I thought it was a clever idea.'

'Yes,' agreed Yvonne. '*I* wouldn't have thought of that.' Then, after a pause, 'I wonder what *my* Leo would think of it!' She laughed. 'He'd probably pretend to be really cross about it and swear us to secrecy – and then go round boasting about it to his friends. You know how boys are.'

'I certainly do,' chuckled Chrissie. 'When Kenny was a teenager, he made a big song and dance about how awful it was having to wear clothes that I'd knitted for him. He claimed that none of the other boys had mums who knitted and it made him look stupid. But then, one of his friends' mums asked me for the pattern for the hat I'd made for him and she told me her son wanted one too – to stop Kenny boasting about how he'd got the only one like it!'

'Harry was just the same,' Yvonne giggled. 'He was always complaining about my food, but then I found out he'd been telling the boys at school that I was a professional cook and had won prizes.'

'Had you?'

'Well, only a little baking competition for the mums and toddler group I used to go to with Leo; but I put the certificate up on the fridge and read out the words to Harry and he must have taken it seriously. He *was* only six at the time.'

Chrissie laughed. Then she fell silent, staring down at the teddy bear in her hands. 'Kenny was so pleased when they accepted him in the police cadets,' she murmured. 'Let me show you the photo.'

She got up and walked across the kitchen to get out a photograph album from a drawer.

'I've been re-organising our photos,' she told her friend. 'This album is just about Kenny – his life story, if you like.'

She turned the pages, looking for the picture that she wanted. Yvonne gazed as photographs flicked past of a baby, then a toddler, a schoolboy and a teenager. Uniforms seems to play a large part in this boy's life: cub scout uniform, school uniform, scouts, and then …

'Here it is!' Chrissie held out the album so that Yvonne could see a large print of a teenage boy – he must have been about Harry's age – dressed in police cadet uniform, smiling self-consciously at the camera. 'We were so proud of him – Gavin especially. I suppose it was nice for him to think that Kenny wanted to follow him into the police service. I was pleased too, but a bit of me would have liked him to have chosen teaching. I'm sure he'd have made a good teacher. He always handled his scout troop really well.'

'Harry never really knew what he wanted to do when he left school,' Yvonne murmured. 'Trev thought he ought to stay on and do A' levels, but Harry wasn't clever like that. He was better doing things with his hands. And then these men offered him a job – horticulture, they told him it was. They said they'd teach him all about it. How was he to know they were crooks and it was cannabis they were getting him to grow?'

'Of course, he didn't,' Chrissie agreed vehemently. 'They're very vulnerable at that age, because they can be very naïve and yet they think they know better than their parents and couldn't possibly come to them for advice!'

'But the jury will think-'

'No, they won't,' Chrissie cut in quickly. 'The judge will make sure they don't. The bottom line is: he was only sixteen. *Nobody* deserves to die at that age – nobody! Now, you were thinking about some story to put at the beginning of your statement – something to give the judge an idea of who Harry was and what he means to you.'

'I don't know,' Yvonne said slowly. 'He wasn't like your Kenny. He didn't do things like scouts and police cadets and all that.'

'I'm sorry. I didn't mean to imply … You don't have to do that sort of – of – I mean, it's not *public* achievement that counts it's … For example, there's a little girl who was in my class last year. She has cerebral palsy and she couldn't talk – or at least only single words, not sentences – and then all of a sudden, things just seemed to click with her and her speech came on by leaps and bounds. She was the one who thought of the name Leo for the police bear, in fact. Or is there something that Harry used to do for you that you miss now he's not there? Did he make tea for you on Mother's Day or …?'

'There's this mug he made for me at school,' Yvonne remembered. 'That was for Mother's Day. The writing's almost worn off now, but it said "For Mum" and three kisses.'

'OK then, why not write about that? Everyone will be able to identify with a little boy making a present for his mum. Actually, I think that's better than my ideas for Kenny. There'll be lots of people talking about him being a police hero, but my statement ought to be about – about – why – we – why we – miss him – so – much!'

Chrissie unexpectedly dissolved into tears. Yvonne looked round in alarm, unsure what to do. She spotted a box of tissues on the windowsill and brought them over. She set them down on the table in front of her friend and then, casting aside all thought of social distancing, sat down next to her and put her arm awkwardly round her shoulders.

VICTIM STATEMENTS

The sobs subsided as quickly as they had come and Chrissie blew her nose and gave an embarrassed laugh. 'I'm sorry, Yvonne; I don't know why that set me off.'

There was the sound of a key in the front door lock, followed by voices in the hall. Yvonne leapt up and hurried round to resume her place on the far side of the table. That must be Gavin arriving home. She wasn't sure what the rules were about meeting indoors at the moment – they seemed to change every week – but she was sure that it must be illegal to touch someone from outside your own household.

Chrissie got up to greet her husband, who was accompanied by the black police woman who had visited their house with him on several occasions.

WITNESS FOR THE PROSECUTION

Yvonne couldn't remember her name. She looked hardly any older than Harry.

'We had a bit of trouble attending a road traffic accident,' Gavin explained, as he beckoned his colleague into the kitchen. 'A van mounted the pavement and hit a pedestrian and her husband went for the driver. Stella here got caught in the cross-fire. I brought her here to clean her up a bit before she goes home.'

Studying the young woman more carefully now that she had stepped into the light, Yvonne saw that she had dust in her hair and a streak of blood down one side of her face. Her uniform was also dirty, as if she had been rolling around in the road.

Chrissie was all sympathy and solicitousness. 'Oh, you poor thing! Come upstairs with me and I'll help you get sorted out.'

VICTIM STATEMENTS

Yvonne got to her feet too. 'I'd better go. Thank you for all your help.'

'No, no, don't go yet.' Chrissie turned back and waved her back to her seat. 'Stay and have dinner with us. There's plenty. I always make too much when I use the slow cooker. She turned to Stella. 'Why don't you stay too? You could ring your gran, so she won't be worrying about you.'

'I – I – that's very nice of you,' Stella stammered. She looked towards Gavin and then back to Chrissie. 'Yes, thank you, that would be very nice – if you're sure?'

'Of course, I'm sure!' Chrissie declared. Then, turning to Yvonne, 'and you'll stay too, won't you?'

'Well, I've already eaten,' Yvonne said weakly, remembering the pizza. But she had allowed Leo to eat most of hers in the end and the smell from the slow cooker had been making her hungry all evening. 'But that seems a long time ago now,' she added, seeing Chrissie smiling at her expectantly. 'So, thank you very much. I'd love to stay. But I must be back before nine.'

'That's settled then.' Chrissie escorted Stella upstairs to the bathroom and Gavin sat down diagonally opposite Yvonne at the table. He smiled across at her.

'It's always best to let Chrissie have her head when she gets these motherly fits on her,' he confided. 'Resistance is useless, as they say!'

Yvonne smiled back uncertainly. 'She's been helping me with my victim impact statement,' she told him. 'I couldn't think what to say.'

VICTIM STATEMENTS

'I'm no good with words myself,' Gavin nodded. 'I leave all that sort of thing to Chrissie.'

'She's very clever. She came up with all sorts of things I'd never have thought of.'

'Yes. I'm very lucky to have her.'

They sat in silence. Yvonne tried to think of something to say. It seemed rude just to sit there staring across the table.

'What happened?' she asked in the end. 'With the accident you were telling us about.'

'Like I said, we got a call to attend an RTA. When we got there, there was a woman lying on the ground with a crowd standing round her and a white van was stopped with one wheel up on the pavement. While I was on my knees helping the casualty, a fight broke out in

512

the crowd. Stella intervened to stop it and she got knocked over in the scrum.'

'How awful!' Yvonne's eyes opened wide. 'What was the fight about?'

'A witness said she'd seen the van driver on his mobile phone just before the van mounted the kerb. The victim's boyfriend went for the driver and a couple of other bystanders joined in attacking him.'

'I suppose it's understandable they'd be angry. Was the woman badly hurt?'

'It's not understandable for them to use racist language against a police officer performing her duty to restore public order,' Gavin replied curtly, 'or for them to fling that officer against a brick wall. And it wasn't helping the woman, diverting me from assessing her injuries and making her comfortable until the ambulance arrived.'

VICTIM STATEMENTS

'No, of course not,' Yvonne agreed quickly.

'Luckily there was another patrol car not far away, and they got there in time to break up the fight before anyone was seriously injured.'

'So, the woman who got knocked down? Was she OK?'

'The paramedics took her to A and E just to be on the safe side, but they reckoned she was just winded. They said she'd be covered with bruises in the morning, but no bones broken. It was a low-speed impact in a thirty-mile-an-hour zone. To be honest, I'm more concerned about Stella. It may have brought back memories of seeing Kenny killed. It must've been similar in a way – except that then it was deliberate. In this case, I reckon the driver lost concentration and just didn't notice the bend in the road. It was unlucky it was right by the queue for a takeaway. He'll most likely get a fine and lose his licence for a bit.'

'I don't think he ought to ever be allowed to drive again,' Yvonne declared. 'He could've killed someone.'

'Yes, he could,' Gavin agreed. 'But it'll be for the courts to decide.'

'When it eventually gets to court!' Chrissie chimed in, catching his words as she and Stella re-entered the room accompanied by Craig, who had stayed in his room, out of the way, while Chrissie and Yvonne were talking. 'I've almost got past believing it'll ever happen, after all the postponements we've had.'

'We were talking about the driver in our RTA,' Gavin told her. 'But you're right: this off-on business with the Butler gang trial is very wearing on the nerves.'

VICTIM STATEMENTS

'I keep psyching myself up to give evidence and then the news comes through it won't be for another few weeks,' Stella agreed. 'I'm really dreading it, but I want to get it over with too.'

'Do you really?' Yvonne looked up at her, surprised. Police officers were supposed to be confident and self-assured, but PC Gilbert looked no different from the young women that she worked with at the office cleaning company. 'I thought it was just me!'

'Sit down Stella and I'll dish up.' Chrissie took charge. 'Gav! Can you sort out drinks for everyone?'

Soon they were all sitting round the table enjoying chicken curry accompanied by naan bread.

WITNESS FOR THE PROSECUTION

'Are you *really* nervous about the trial?' Yvonne asked Stella. 'I'm petrified, but I thought you …?'

'I'm petrified too,' Stella smiled back. It'll be my first time and I'm terrified I'll mess up and let Kenny down.'

'That's just exactly how I feel!' Yvonne felt a warm wave of relief go through her body. 'I'm afraid I'll get confused and say the wrong thing and make the jury think they probably didn't do it, after all.'

'I'm not even sure why they need me to give evidence,' Stella added. 'It's not as if I saw the man's face.'

'They'll need you to explain what you and Kenny were doing there in the first place,' Gavin told her. 'And why you didn't see the car coming until it was too late. And, the fact that you were in the process of arresting Harry is what links the two murders together: the prosecution case is that they killed Harry to prevent him identifying them as the gang that was employing him to grow the cannabis plants. It's all just part of building up a picture of what happened for the jury.'

'Don't you worry,' Chrissie said, reaching out to pat Stella's hand. 'I'm sure you'll do splendidly. You've got a lovely clear speaking voice.'

'Why can't they just read out the statement I made to the police?' Yvonne asked. 'Or, surely the ambulance people could tell the jury what happened. They got there quite quickly. Why does it have to be me?'

'Gav?' asked Chrissie when nobody answered her friend's question.

He sighed, apparently reluctant to speak. 'Well,' he said at last, 'you were the person who found him, which is a significant event.'

'Maybe it's to do with an alibi,' suggested Stella. 'Maybe it's important that you tell the jury what time it was when you got home.'

'But I'm not sure exactly!' Yvonne's eyes opened wide.

'Don't worry about that,' Gavin said quickly. 'The 999 call you made will have been logged and the ambulance crew will have noted their time of arrival. All you'll need to say is about how long it was before you called for help. And if there's anything you don't remember, just say so. It won't matter. In fact, it will probably make your evidence more convincing, because nobody remembers everything that happens to them.'

'Are you sure?'

'Yes,' Gavin told her firmly.

VICTIM STATEMENTS

Gavin and Chrissie cleared away the plates.

'There's no pudding,' Chrissie apologised, 'but I thought we could have some of my date and nut cake with coffee – unless anyone has a nut allergy,' she added anxiously.

Stella and Yvonne assured her that the cake sounded delicious and they were neither of them allergic, but Yvonne looked down anxiously at her watch.

'I really think I ought to go,' she said. 'I must be back before Trev gets home. Thanks ever so much for everything, and especially for helping me with my victim statement.'

'You're welcome,' Chrissie smiled back. 'It was good for me to have a reason to get down to thinking out ours.'

She escorted Yvonne to the front door while Craig took charge of the new coffee machine that he had bought Chrissie for her birthday and Gavin fetched more plates. Then she came back to the kitchen and reached down a large cake tin from one of the wall cupboards. Soon they were all settled back in their seats with mugs of coffee and generous slices of cake in front of them.

'I think you ought to make a victim impact statement too, Stella,' Craig said unexpectedly.

'But I'm not a victim!' Stella protested. 'They're for family and people who were injured. I was only doing my job.'

'But you've been impacted, haven't you?' Craig insisted. 'The flashbacks, the insomnia, … that's all down to seeing what happened to Kenny. The judge ought to take that into account when he's deciding how long to put the bastards away for.'

'He's right,' Chrissie agreed. 'You *are* another victim.'

'But ... but ...,' Stella struggled to find the right words. 'But it shouldn't have affected me like that. I'm a police officer. We have to be able to deal with seeing things like that. I don't want people to think I'm not up to the job. Although ... maybe I'm not. Maybe I ought to resign.'

'No!' the other three chorused in unison.

'No,' Gavin repeated firmly, giving Craig a warning look. 'You're a first-rate police officer. And you wouldn't be human if seeing another officer crushed to death didn't affect you. But I think you're right,' he added, looking round at Chrissie and Craig again. 'It's probably best not to go overboard about ... things. It's a lot better than it used to be, but there are still a few people in senior ranks who'd say *if you can't stand the heat, keep out of the kitchen*. And we definitely don't want to lose you.'

15. GUILTY UNTIL PROVED INNOCENT

Jonah's attention, meanwhile, was directed towards Adrian Chivers, the boyfriend with whom Jane Turnbull had been living when she disappeared and who had been the chief suspect when that disappearance had been investigated back in 1983. Life did not appear to have treated him kindly – but then, when you looked at his long criminal record, perhaps he had done little to encourage kindness. He had spent several spells in jail for assault and had, on more than one occasion, been given restraining orders to protect women with whom he had been in a relationship.

His plumbing business had collapsed not long after the case against him for Jane Turnbull's murder was dropped. He had left Oxford, probably in an attempt to escape from neighbours who believed that he was, nonetheless, guilty. After a nomadic life, settling for short periods in various towns across the Southern half of England, he had ended up sharing a flat with his widowed brother, Frederick, on the ninth floor of a tower block in Reading. It was there that Jonah and Bernie sought him out for questioning.

'You'd better come in,' he grunted when he opened his front door and saw them there. 'Excuse the mess. I'm doing a clear-out. My brother died and his daughter wants to take his things.'

'I'm sorry to hear that.' Jonah followed him into the living area which was strewn with cardboard boxes each partially filled with personal items of all sorts: photographs, clothes, DVDs, a table lamp. 'Was it COVID?'

VICTIM STATEMENTS

'Yes.' Chivers nodded his grizzled head. 'We both got it, but Fred, he had COPD[7].'

'I'm sorry,' Jonah repeated. 'I realise this isn't a good time, but we do need to talk to you about Jane Turnbull. You remember her, I suppose?'

'Remember!' Chivers sat down heavily in a worn armchair with cigarette burns in the upholstery. 'As if anyone ever gave me the chance to forget! I suppose you think you've got some new evidence and you're going to pin her murder on me at last. Well, for the last time, I never touched her. She just

---

[7] Chronic Obstructive Pulmonary Disease: a term covering a number of lung conditions that cause breathing difficulties.

walked out on me and never came back. End of!'

'I don't disbelieve you,' Jonah said quietly. 'I'm here because we've discovered her body and you, as possibly the last person to see her alive, may be able to help us work out how she ended up where she did.'

'And where was that then?' growled Chivers. 'Not in my back yard, like you thought, anyway.'

'No,' Jonah agreed. 'Her remains were found in a shallow grave in woodland on Shotover Hill. You may have heard reports about it on the news.'

'No. I don't watch the news. So, how d'you know it's her, then?'

'DNA from the body matches with her sister. There's also evidence from dental records and the measurements of the skeleton. We're confident it's her. Do you

527

have any idea how she came to be buried up there?'

'Well, I didn't bury her, if that's what you're thinking. I told the truth back then, and I'm telling it now: she just walked out on me. I never hit her or stabbed her – and I didn't bloody well cart her up to Shotover and bury her! Why can't you just leave me alone?'

'I'm sorry, Mr Chivers,' Jonah said again, 'but I'm afraid we do need to ask you some questions, because there's some new evidence turned up and we don't know what it means. Could you have a look at this, please?'

Bernie held out the evidence bag containing the single cuff-link. Chivers looked at it suspiciously and then reached out his hand and took hold of it. 'What's this then?'

'It's a cuff-link that was found in amongst Jane Turnbull's bones,' Jonah informed him. 'Have you ever seen one like his before?'

'Nope!' Chivers handed the bag back to Bernie. 'It's not mine, I can tell you that for nothing. I never had nothing like this. Cuff-links! My dad had some for his Sunday best shirt, but what would I want with 'em?'

'Jane never mentioned that she'd found one?' suggested Jonah mildly. 'It's one of a set belonging to the Lichfield College Boat Club. We wondered if she might have picked it up when she was working there.'

'If she did, she didn't tell me,' Chivers replied defiantly. 'I told you: I've never seen anything like this before. If this was with her body, then don't you think it was the guy who owned it what killed her?'

'Yes,' Jonah agreed quietly. 'That's exactly what I think, which is why I was hoping you'd be able to help me to find him.'

'How would I know?' Chivers shrugged his shoulders and pushed away one of the cardboard boxes with his foot. 'Some fancy man she was seeing, I suppose.'

'And you've no idea who that might have been?' pressed Jonah gently. 'You hadn't found out that she was seeing someone else? That wasn't what you argued about the night she disappeared?'

'No, it wasn't!'

'What was the row about then?'

'Nothing! I don't remember. She got upset about something and walked out back to her mum. She was always doing it. It didn't mean nothing.'

GUILTY UNTIL PROVED INNOCENT

'Her blood was found in your van,' Jonah pointed out.

'Yeah! I explained all that last time. She cut her hand on a new freezer we was bringing back from the shop. It's all there in your police files – look it up! Forensics went all over the freezer and found blood there too. You've got nothing on me – nothing! Why can't you leave me in peace to sort out my brother's things?'

'I'm sorry,' Jonah repeated again. 'I know this isn't a good time for you, but we do have to try to find out who killed Jane. And if it wasn't you – as I'm actually quite inclined to believe – don't you want the real killer to be brought to justice?'

'Justice! Don't talk to me about justice! Whatever happened to *innocent until proved guilty*? Everybody thinks I did it. What are the chances of you finding out who it really was after all this time? All that's going to happen is I'm going to have reporters following me round, talking to the neighbours, writing about how I've got away with murder all these years.'

'Well, we have to try,' Jonah told him. 'I'll leave you my number. If you think of anything – maybe someone that Jane talked about from the college – give me a ring.'

'What d'you think?' Andy Lepage asked when Jonah related this interview to him that afternoon. 'Is he telling the truth? Does he really know nothing at all?'

'To be honest, I'm inclined to think he is,' Jonah replied. 'He has every reason to fabricate some story about Jane having an affair with someone from the college – suggesting that she was off to see her lover on the day she disappeared. And yet, he maintains she wasn't and she didn't. He still says she was going back to her parents.'

'Maybe he just isn't bright enough to think all that through,' suggested Bernie. 'He didn't strike me as exactly Mensa material!'

'You'd think anyone would have picked up more on the cuff-link,' Jonah insisted. 'It was an obvious pointer to her having a lover at the college. And we more or less handed that idea to him on a plate.'

'So, you think the murderer is one of the Lichfield College boat crew?' asked Andy.

'I do,' Jonah nodded. 'And the next thing I'm going to do is to have a little talk with Professor Giles Kingman of Notre

Dame University.' I've got a Skype call booked with him in … two minutes ago. You can sit in on that, if you like.'

'Good morning, Inspector – or I suppose it's afternoon for you,' Professor Kingman greeted them warmly when Jonah and Andy logged in to the videocall. 'What can I do for you?'

Jonah studied the face that looked out from his computer screen. Kingman appeared to have worn better than his boat club colleagues. He could easily have been younger than his sixty years. His full head of hair was still an attractive shade of dark brown and his bearded face had no obvious wrinkles.

'I need you to cast your mind back rather a long way,' he told his interviewee. 'To Eights Week in 1983 to be precise. There was a special dinner at the college on Saturday evening. Do you remember that?'

'That would be the end of my second year,' the professor replied thoughtfully. 'Yes, I remember. We'd done rather well on the river, so it was a celebration. Why the interest after all these years?'

'Were all the members of the boat club there?' Jonah asked, refusing to be cajoled into revealing any more information at this stage in the interview.

'As far as I remember, why?'

'And were you all wearing your special boat club cuff-links?'

'Cuff-links? What *is* this? I thought you said this was a murder enquiry.'

'It is,' Jonah smiled back, 'and one of the pieces of evidence in that enquiry is a cuff-link that was commissioned for the Lichfield College Boat Club in 1983 and presumably worn by a club member. Do you have a pair yourself?'

'Yes, I do actually. I wear them when I want to flaunt my Oxford credentials in front of someone who might be considering supporting our research. American billionaires are often touchingly impressed by anything that appears to be English and traditional. The college crest looks suitably mediaeval and when they see the crossed oars, they immediately assume I rowed in the Boat Race! But I still don't see-'

'A single cuff-link has turned up among human remains in a shallow grave on Shotover Hill,' Jonah told him. 'We assume that its owner must know how they got there.'

'Aaah!' Kingman nodded slowly. 'I get it now. You think one of us killed whoever it is and buried the body, dropping a cuff-link as he did it.'

'Something like that,' Jonah admitted, 'which is why I was wondering whether all the boat club members were wearing theirs at dinner that night.'

'So, the murder took place before dinner on Saturday of Eights Week?'

'Perhaps. But you haven't answered my question.'

'As far as I remember, yes, we all had them on. Julian made it clear he expected us to wear them. He'd made such a thing of getting them made for us specially. I certainly didn't notice anyone who wasn't – or who was one short.'

'Thank you.' Jonah paused for a moment in thought. 'Now, can you tell-'

'I suppose you need proof that I've still got both of mine,' Kingman interrupted. 'Shall I send you a photograph, with today's newspaper in the picture so that you can be sure it's not an old one from before I lost one of them?'

Jonah gazed back, observing that the professor had a twinkle in his eye. He was clearly more intrigued than frightened by the questioning.

'The time-stamp from your camera-phone will be quite sufficient,' he grinned back.

'Not so dramatic though, is it? I was rather looking forward to my photo being Exhibit B, when it all comes to court.' His face suddenly went serious. 'But I shouldn't joke, should I? Someone's been killed, haven't they? Am I allowed to know who?'

'A young woman by the name of Jane Turnbull,' Jonah told him. 'She worked in the Lichfield College kitchens. Her father was Head Chef.'

'I didn't know her.' Kingman shook his head slowly. 'Or at least, not that I remember. It was a long time ago now. But I don't think I ever met any of the kitchen staff. Did she serve at table as well, do you know?'

'I don't think so. But she may have done. I've got a picture of her here, if you don't mind taking a look.' Jonah pressed buttons to display Jane's photograph on both his screen and Kingman's.

Kingman stared at it intently, then shook his head. 'No. I don't remember ever seeing her before.'

'Did any of the other boat club members have friends among the domestic staff?' Jonah asked. 'One explanation for how she came to have the cuff-link would be if she was in a relationship with one of them.'

'No. I don't think so.'

'OK. Now I've been told that Jeremy Scott-Urquhart, Charles Rawlins and Gerald Leslie were very close: "the three musketeers" was how one person described them to me. Is that how it seemed to you?'

'Yes, I think that's a fair description,' Kingman nodded. 'They were certainly great buddies. You don't think they murdered this woman together, do you?'

'Just trying to get a picture of how things were, that's all,' Jonah assured him. 'Can you tell me anything more about them – or about any of the other boat club members? Leslie and Rawlins shared a room – is that right?'

'Well, a set of rooms: a lounge and two bedrooms, yes. Jeremy didn't live in college. He wanted somewhere that he could keep his car, so he rented a shared house with some students from Brasenose – or was it Corpus? Anyway, it was out Headington way – Quarry Road, I think.'

'So, not with the other two musketeers then? Why do you think that could have been?'

'I think they didn't want to be so far out. It's far more convenient to be in college.' Kingman thought for a moment. 'And there was Charles's double-bass to consider!' he added with a grin. 'It sometimes seemed to rule his life. He was always trying to cadge lifts to take it to places. He was in some sort of chamber orchestra or something. They used to rehearse in the college chapel. He wouldn't have wanted to lug it all the way from Headington every week, would he?'

'No, I don't suppose he would,' Jonah agreed. 'And speaking of Charles: you don't happen to have his contact details, by any chance?'

'No, I'm afraid not. I didn't really keep up with any of them after I moved to the States.'

'OK. Let's go back to the 1983 Eights Week dinner. What happened after it was over? Did you all just go back to your rooms or …?'

'No, we all went to the Bird and Baby afterwards for a few drinks.'

'The Bird and Baby?' queried Andy.

'It's an old nickname for the Eagle and Child,' Bernie informed him. 'You know – on St Giles – just across the way from the Lamb and Flag.'

'You're probably too young,' Kingman smiled. 'I expect all the student slang has changed by now.'

'When you say "all", who exactly do you mean?' asked Jonah.

'All the first eight, probably quite a few of the second eight too. I wasn't that keen actually, but I didn't like to say "no". I had a couple of drinks and then managed to extricate myself and went to bed. I was tired after all the rowing. I wasn't really up to a pub crawl.'

'About what time was that?'

'Nine-thirty – ten o'clock. I wasn't keeping track of time, and it's a long time ago. I hope you're not expecting me to go into the witness box and swear to any of this.'

'No, no, I just want to build up a picture of what went on. Did anyone else leave when you did?'

VICTIM STATEMENTS

'Graham had already gone. I'm not even sure if he came with us to the pub at all. You should ask him. He's still in Oxford – or back in Oxford, I'm not sure which. He managed to land a fellowship at Lichfield – lucky beggar!'

'Thank you. We've already spoken to Professor Weldon.'

'Have you? How is he?'

'He's had coronavirus,' Jonah told him, 'but he's on the mend now.'

'Poor chap! Well, give him my good wishes if you're speaking to him again.'

'You were telling us who else went to the pub and when the party dispersed,' Jonah reminded him.

'Just before I left, Jerry, Charles and Gerald suggested seeing how many different pubs they could have a drink in before closing time. They headed off together to the Lamb and Flag, and I escaped under cover of going with them. I think Julian tagged along too. Who else are you interested in?'

'How about Anthony Pulborough and Timothy Plumstead?'

'Anthony definitely didn't participate in the pub crawl. Now I come to think about it, he and I walked back to college together. I don't know about Timothy. I don't remember if he was there at all. He wasn't the sort of person who made his presence felt – very quiet, never said much.'

The following morning, as they were about to start breakfast, an email dropped into Jonah's inbox with a photograph attached, featuring a pair of Lichfield College Boat Club cuff-links lying on the front page of the South Bend Tribune dated 14th October 2020. Evidently, Professor Kingman had not been able to resist the temptation to make his contribution to the investigation as dramatic as possible.

'Or else he's smart enough to realise that it's important to prove that his cuff-links aren't the same as any of the others that we've been sent pictures of,' Bernie observed in answer to Jonah's wry smile. 'If he were lying about having both of his still intact, he could've got one of the others to photograph theirs and send him the pic.'

'Well, let's suppose for the time being that none of the people we've interviewed so far *has* given us a forged photograph, what does that tell us?' Jonah pondered. 'Giles, Graham, Anthony and Jeremy all have a full complement of cuff-links, so it

GUILTY UNTIL PROVED INNOCENT

can't be theirs that got buried with Jane Turnbull, but that doesn't mean they weren't involved in killing her – or at least in burying her.'

'You're thinking it might be some sort of conspiracy?' asked Peter.

'I'm thinking it could be. Lugging a dead body about isn't that easy. Neither is digging a grave, even a shallow one.'

'My money would be on the three musketeers,' Bernie declared as she poured out tea from a large brown pot. 'Unless she was killed up on Shotover, they'd need transport to take the body up there. As far as we know, Jeremy Scott-Urquhart is the only one with a car. And he seemed a slippery customer to me. He was definitely at odds with everyone else when you asked him about his relationship with Charles and Gerald. I bet the cuff-link belongs to one of them and he's distancing himself from them before you find that out.'

'Didn't you say that Gerald Leslie took his own life?' asked Peter, buttering a slice of toast. 'That would fit in with him being involved. He couldn't live with himself and killed himself out of remorse.'

'You're right,' Jonah agreed, perhaps a little reluctantly. 'That would certainly fit the facts as we know them so far. But equally, the cuff-link could belong to any of the others. It may not even be one of the first-eight rowers: we haven't even started looking at the second eight or the other hangers-on!'

16. CHRISTMAS IS COMING

'You asked to see me, ma'am?' Gavin felt nervous as he entered Inspector Tracy Burton's office. His doings did not often come to the attention of anyone more senior than his sergeant.

'Yes Gavin.' Tracy smiled back reassuringly. 'Sit down and relax. There's nothing to worry about. I just wanted to go through the report you wrote about the incident when you and PC Gilbert attended that RTA a few weeks back. We've got two cases going to the magistrates' court out of that, and I wanted to be sure I knew what the issues are.'

'I see, ma'am.' Gavin tried to remember what he had put in his report and to gauge where it might have been defective. Tracy was seven years his junior, but she was a university graduate and well-known for being good at her job and not one to suffer fools gladly. He pulled out the chair that she had indicated and sat down, facing her across her desk.

'Relax, Gavin,' she repeated. 'This isn't the Spanish Inquisition. And it's *Tracy* or, if you really can't bring yourself to use first names, *Inspector*. I'm not the Queen, you know!'

'Yes ma- Tracy.' Gavin wondered if she was laughing at him, but her smile looked friendly rather than mocking. She was trying to put him at his ease – he hoped!

'As I was saying,' she continued, 'the driver of the van – an Arthur Greenshaw – has been charged with careless driving. So far, he hasn't taken up the opportunity to plead guilty, so we've got the case coming up next month. The chances are he will plead guilty before it comes to court, but we need to have all the evidence clear to make sure that the aggravating circumstances are taken into account: using a mobile phone, for example. Your report gives the name of a witness who saw him holding it – did you see that yourself?'

'No. We didn't arrive until after the incident. The driver had got out of the van by then. I found the mobile on the passenger seat of the van after he was taken away.'

'Do you think the witness can be relied upon?'

'I think she'll stick to her story. She was very definite about what she'd seen.'

'Good. Now about the other charges.' Tracy paused, apparently in thought. 'Matthew Johnson is being charged with

VICTIM STATEMENTS

racially-aggravated common assault for his attack on PC Gilbert.'

'I don't think Stella will like that,' Gavin ventured nervously. 'She wanted us to drop the charges – with him being upset about his girlfriend being injured and everything.'

'I'm afraid we can't do that – especially with Greenshaw insisting on pressing charges for Johnson's assault on him. It would send out all the wrong messages if we treat an attack on one of our officers as less serious than one on a driver who had just run down a pedestrian. And it's especially significant when you take into account the language that he used. His verbal abuse against an ethnic minority officer would probably have been sufficient to justify a charge of threatening behaviour, even if he hadn't attacked her physically.'

'Will she have to give evidence in court?'

'Maybe. Or it may be better if you do. With any luck, he'll plead guilty with the mitigation that he was distraught after seeing his girlfriend hurt and it'll all be settled with a fine and maybe a bit of community service. The important thing is demonstrating that abuse of police officers is unacceptable, whatever the circumstances. So, can I leave it to you to explain to Stella what's going to happen and why?'

'Yes, I'll have a chat with her.'

'Thanks. I'll let you know when we've got a date for the hearings.'

Gavin got up to go, but Tracy called him back. 'I thought you might like to know: that break-in you attended down Cowley Road – a Mrs … Langdon?'

'Yes?'

VICTIM STATEMENTS

'Her son got in touch and asked us to stop the investigation. It turns out the only thing that was missing was some money she had in a kitchen drawer. He says, he took it for safe-keeping because she was getting forgetful and he was afraid she'd lose it.'

'Stella will be pleased,' Gavin smiled. 'She said all along it was just Mrs Langdon getting confused.'

'The son also apologised for being rather short with you and said to tell you he was getting the window fixed.'

'Well, I suppose that's something good come out of it. Will that be all?' Gavin turned to go again.

'Yes – except … I was sorry to hear about the trial being postponed again.'

'Thanks.'

'It must make things very difficult for you and your wife.'

CHRISTMAS IS COMING

'And for Stella. She keeps psyching herself up to give evidence, and then it doesn't happen. Still, once this new November lockdown is over …'

'Yes. Let's hope it does the trick, although I can't say I'm as optimistic as Boris and his mates seem to be. Personally, I'd be cancelling Christmas if it was up to me!'

'There were more fireworks going off last night,' Bernie commented as she dressed Jonah on the first day of the new lockdown. 'I suppose it was people making the most of them while they're still allowed to meet together.'

'So much for starting the lockdown on 5th November,' muttered Jonah. 'I thought the idea was to put a stop to firework parties, not to bring them forward.'

I suppose it's human nature, if they'd already bought the fireworks,' Bernie sighed. 'And we're getting such mixed messages from the government. Stay at home for four weeks so that you'll be able to hug granny when she comes round for Christmas dinner. How does that make any sort of sense? I suppose they think the virus is going to declare a Christmas truce and play football with us in no-man's land!'

She settled Jonah into his wheelchair and he immediately started checking his emails. He smiled at the sight of a message from Andy Lepage, which had come through late the previous night.

'Andy's been speaking to another of the Lichfield rowing crew,' he announced. 'He tracked down Peregrine Milton via the British Embassy in Peru and he's been talking to him on the phone. He says he'll brief me about it this morning.'

'But not until after breakfast,' Bernie warned. 'And I mean Andy's breakfast, not yours! If he was up at midnight speaking to this Peregrine fellow, he won't be wanting you pestering him at the crack of dawn. I'm sure he'll ring you when he's ready.'

Jonah didn't have long to wait. Andy knew his boss well enough to make ringing him to report his news the first job of the day. He sounded upbeat as he related what he had found out.

'Peregrine Milton is a member of the British diplomatic mission in Lima,' he told them. 'He's married with a grown-up son. He was in the second year of a history degree in 1983.'

'Yes, yes' Jonah interrupted impatiently. 'But what does he remember about that Eights Week dinner – and the cuff-links?'

'I was coming to that.' Bernie could imagine the grin on Andy's face as he spoke. Lucky for Jonah, his sergeant was familiar with his single-mindedness when there was an investigation underway. 'He said that he remembers the dinner, but not the pub crawl afterwards. But then he admitted that he must have been drinking that evening, because he spent the night dossed down on the floor of Timothy Plumstead's room, rather than walking back to his lodgings in Summertown.'

'Does he have contact details for Plumstead?' Jonah cut in. 'If they were buddies?'

'No. He claims he didn't know him that well. It was only that he was a first-year, which meant he was entitled to a room in college. Apparently, first and final year students were guaranteed somewhere in college if they wanted it, but second years often had to find their own digs. He did offer to put us in touch with Gerald Leslie's family, though. He went to the funeral and kept in touch with his mother afterwards.'

'Now that's useful! Did he give you the address?'

'No. He said he'd contact them first. He was afraid it would be too much of a shock having the police turning up without warning. Apparently, his mother is quite frail now.'

'OK.' Bernie could hear the dissatisfaction in Jonah's voice. His instinct would have been to interview Mrs Leslie the moment he had finished his conversation with Andy. Not that he wasn't capable of biding his time and playing a long game when it was part of a plan to further an investigation, he just didn't like having to wait when there was an obvious course of action open to him. 'Go on, then. What about Milton's cuff-links? Does he still have them?'

'Not with him in Peru, but he doesn't remember getting rid of them. He says they must be packed away somewhere in his family home in Norfolk. His son Christopher's living there while his parents are abroad. He's training to be a solicitor with a firm in Swaffham. Milton said he'd ask him to have a look for them for us.'

Jonah grunted. More delay!

'I showed him the photo of Jane Turnbull, but he didn't recognise her. *However*,' Andy paused dramatically, 'he did admit to having had a brief liaison with the daughter of one of the scouts. Apparently, she used to come in at weekends to help her mother with her cleaning duties. I don't suppose it's relevant, but if we could track her down, she might know if any of the other domestic staff had relationships with students at that time.'

'Perhaps,' Jonah sounded dubious. 'What was her name?'

'Unfortunately, he couldn't remember. He thought she was called Bridget, but then he decided it was Brenda.'

'Her surname would be more use,' Jonah grumbled. 'I can't go to the college and ask them for the address of an ex-employee who had a daughter whose name could have been Brenda or maybe it was Bridget, can I?'

'No sir. I only mentioned it because it does suggest that students did sometimes get into bed with domestic staff at the college.'

'Anything else?'

'Well, it's only Milton's personal opinion, but he did say that he thinks something happened to Gerald Leslie that Trinity term.'

'What sort of thing?'

'He didn't know. He just said that he seemed to change suddenly. Apparently, he'd always been a cheerful type – life and soul of the party sort of guy – and then suddenly he lost all interest in things. Milton said that, looking back, it must have been the start of his clinical depression, but nobody talked about that sort of thing in those days.'

'Hmmm,' Jonah mused. 'Are you thinking what I'm thinking?'

'Possibly, sir.'

CHRISTMAS IS COMING

'I'm thinking that finding yourself mixed up in the death of a young woman, and concealing her body in a shallow grave where it might be discovered any day, might well dampen your spirits somewhat.'

'Yes, sir. That's how I was reading it too.'

Peregrine Milton was as good as his word. Two days later, an email arrived containing the address of Gerald Milton's mother, Joyce, and an email address for his sister, Caroline Brown. They were living together in the family home in rural Derbyshire. Caroline readily joined a Zoom meeting with Jonah, apologising that her mother, while keen to help, could not cope with the new technology.

VICTIM STATEMENTS

'Her eyesight is failing,' she explained, 'and her hearing's not too good either, to be honest. She'd only get confused and that makes her anxious. She's completely compos mentis,' she added hurriedly. 'It's not dementia or anything like that. And she loves talking about Gerald. You'll be welcome to come up here and speak to her once this lockdown is over.'

So, Jonah booked an appointment for the first week in December, when they expected to be allowed to travel outside their immediate neighbourhood again. Meanwhile, he emailed the photograph of Jane Turnbull and an image of the cuff-link for Caroline and her mother to look at.

Caroline rang the next day. Jonah got the impression that his investigation was a welcome break from her confinement with her mother, while her husband, who was working from home, shut himself up in his study all day.

'I showed mum the pictures you sent,' she told him. 'I'm afraid she didn't recognise the girl, but she did remind me that Gerald broke up with his girlfriend earlier that year – before the Easter holidays. He didn't seem particularly upset about it, but it occurred to me that he might have taken up with someone else on the re-bound?'

'Yes, perhaps,' Jonah agreed. 'Do you know the name of this girlfriend? And how long they'd been going out together?'

'Tracey. I remember because I'd never come across the name before. Mum and I had a bit of a giggle about it behind her back. I don't think I ever knew her surname. Gerry met her in their first year, and it must have been quite serious because he invited her to stay during that summer – to meet the family, so to speak!'

'And the relationship lasted until the middle of his second year,' murmured Jonah. 'Do you have any idea what precipitated the break-up?'

'I assume he just got tired of her,' Caroline answered dismissively. 'She wasn't really very suitable for him. She was nice enough,' she added quickly, 'but they had so little in common. She'd been to a comprehensive school in Croydon. Her father was a bus driver! She was like a fish out of water when she came to stay with us.'

Jonah had studied Google maps in preparation for the anticipated trip to Derbyshire to visit the family and knew that the Leslie family home was a large

Georgian house, set in its own grounds with a stable block at the back. He smiled as he imagined a bus-driver's daughter from one of the less salubrious of London's suburbs trying to hold her own amid conversations about huntin', shootin' and fishin' or the difficulty of finding good servants these days.

'Dad tried his best, bless him,' Caroline went on. 'But I could tell he wasn't sorry when they split up. I think he'd been having nightmares about what the shareholders would think if Gerry married her. Mum always did a lot of entertaining on behalf of the business and, of course, Gerry's wife would have been expected to, as well.'

'You don't think your brother's depression could have been caused by the breakdown of that relationship?' queried Jonah.

'Oh no! He was well out of that, and he knew it. He was on great form that Easter. That's why it was such a shock when he tried to kill himself in the summer.'

'Did he?' Jonah was immediately alert. 'How?'

'He tried to hang himself from the light-fitting in the ceiling of his room. Of course, it broke and he just got a few bruises where he fell down. But it gave us all a shock. He was very low all summer, but then he seemed to buck up a bit when it was time to go back to Oxford. No! it was a bit before that. A friend of his came to stay: Charles something. He was very good fun. I quite fancied him myself at the time, but he wasn't interested in dating Gerry's little sister!'

'Did he say *why* he wanted to take his own life?' Jonah asked cautiously. 'Was there anything in particular that had made him depressed?'

'Well, he certainly didn't confide in me! I think he told Mum and Dad that it was pressure of work: he wasn't as clever as the other people on his course; he was afraid of failing his exams; that sort of thing.'

'But you think there must have been something more?' suggested Jonah.

'He never seemed that bothered about exams before,' she replied. 'So, I always thought it was probably an excuse. At the time, I assumed it was some girl who'd turned him down – not Tracey, someone else – but, who knows?'

'Now, before I let you go, can I just ask about the cuff-link? Do you remember your brother having a pair like the one I showed you?'

'No. Mum didn't recognise it either. I'm sorry.'

'Not to worry,' Jonah said as if it were unimportant, 'just let me know if either of them happens to turn up, will you? Just for the record.'

He ended the call and looked up at Bernie, who had been taking notes of the interview. 'What's the betting that the reason his family never saw those cuff-links is because he'd lost one of them before he went home that summer?'

'I said it would all end in tiers!' Bernie declared a few weeks later, gazing at a map on her computer screen, which showed a bright patchwork of colours signifying the level of restrictions in operation in each area of England. 'What's the point of boasting that the lockdown is over when practically everywhere is in Tier 3?'

'*We*'re not – yet,' Peter pointed out, 'and neither is Liverpool.'

'That's only because they didn't kick up a fuss over being put into Tier 3 back in October,' Bernie retorted scornfully. 'It's a slap on the wrist for Andy Burnham[8] over the stink he kicked up in Greater Manchester. We'll all be in Tier 3 by Christmas, which will allow Boris to say that it's only local COVID outbreaks that are preventing us all from hugging Granny and having parties.'

'That's a very cynical view,' Jonah commented, 'but I suspect you may be

---

[8] The Mayor of Greater Manchester stood out against a local lockdown, demanding more help from central government for businesses affected by such restrictions.

right that they'll have to back down in the end and cancel the big Christmas getaway idea. My guess is that the Scilly Isles and the Isle of Wight are about the only places that will escape. As far as I'm concerned at the moment, the worst thing is that Derbyshire is in Tier 3, so I've had to put off our visit to Mrs Leslie and her daughter until the New Year. I'm certain that Gerald Leslie was involved in Jane Turnbull's death, and they could hold the key to the whole case.'

'They'll keep,' Peter put in seriously. 'I'm more concerned about the state of the crown court lists. The Butler Gang trial has been put off yet again. I know Gavin and Chrissie were hoping it'd all be over by Christmas. If anyone has a right to complain about things being put off to the New Year, its them!'

CHRISTMAS IS COMING

'Them and the Whittles,' Bernie agreed. 'Christmas is going to be pretty miserable for them as well, lockdown or no lockdown.'

Gavin and Chrissie were indeed feeling let down – once again – by the criminal justice system. They had received an apologetic call explaining that the recent lockdown, and a new risk assessment of the court buildings, had led to overrunning of earlier cases, with the result that theirs had now been moved to a date in January.

'I never thought it would be more than a year before it was all over,' Chrissie moaned.

'It feels like longer,' Gavin agreed morosely. 'Every time I go out, I see those fairy lights at number forty-two and it takes me back to last Christmas and the way we were taking our decorations down when everyone else was putting theirs up.'

'I know,' Chrissie nodded. 'They always go a bit over the top with those plastic reindeer and that blow-up Father Christmas, but this year, they've got those flashing lights all over the wall as well. And fancy putting them all up in November!'

'The Morrisons at number thirty-six have got theirs up as well,' Gavin told her. 'I wish they wouldn't, but you can't blame them: there's been stuff in the newspapers about putting decorations up early being good for morale.'

'Yes,' Chrissie nodded. 'They keep saying we all need something to cheer us up after so many months of COVID. But it doesn't cheer me – it just makes things worse. And I don't see how all those people who lost family to the virus will be cheered up by a bit if tinsel and some illuminated reindeer, either!'

'I suppose it's different for us,' Gavin mused, trying to be fair to his neighbours, 'with Kenny being killed just before Christmas. They don't have the two things together in their minds in the same way.'

'And it doesn't help with keeping the lid on the children's over-excitement,' Chrissie continued, as if she had not heard him. 'They're all chattering about having their grandparents round for Christmas dinner and seeing uncles and aunts they haven't met since last Christmas, and I keep worrying about how disappointed they're going to be when the government is forced to announce that mixing over Christmas has been cancelled, after all!'

'Oh yes! I've been meaning to tell you …'

'Tell me what?' Chrissie asked as Gavin hesitated.

'Lorraine's invited us for Christmas. She says, she knows we won't be feeling like making a big effort this year, so she's ordered a bigger turkey than usual and she wants us both to go up there and stay with them for a couple of days.'

'Aren't they in Tier 3? Can't you just tell them it's too risky?'

'I don't like to – not after I was so rude to her when she came to help after Kenny died. She *is* only trying to be kind.'

'I know, but I honestly don't think I could face spending Christmas in someone else's house – not this year – not our first Christmas after Kenny died.

576

Maybe if *I* give her a ring, woman-to-woman …?'

'No,' Gavin said firmly, 'she's *my* sister. I've got to do it. I was thinking of volunteering to be on duty on Christmas day – if you'll be OK at home without me?'

'That's a good idea,' Chrissie agreed, brightening up a little. 'She can't argue with that. And I'll be fine. Craig will be here to keep me company, if I want any. And he won't insist on trying to cheer me up if I don't! And speaking of Craig: what do you think we ought to get him for Christmas? I'd like to give him something big, but what if he doesn't get us anything much? I mean, I've no idea what he'll be expecting. I don't want him to think we're patronising him. What d'you think? He could do with a new suit. He's still only got that old one of Kenny's that we gave him.'

'Does he though?' Gavin asked mildly. 'He doesn't wear it for work. I know he's the boss of the mail order side of things, but he wears overalls like the rest of the packers. He won't need a suit unless he goes for another job interview somewhere else. And he seems happy enough there, so I can't see that being for a while.'

'So, what do you think he'd like?'

'I don't know,' Gavin shrugged. 'He never seems to need anything. I suppose he's got used to managing without much, what with living on the streets for so long.'

'I suppose we could give him vouchers, so he can buy what he wants himself,' Chrissie mused. 'But then it's so obvious how much you've spent, and what if he doesn't get much for us? I don't want to make him feel bad.'

CHRISTMAS IS COMING

'Oh, do stop worrying about it.' Gavin advised, shaking his head in frustration at his wife's anxiety. 'I thought you were knitting him one of your fancy pullovers, anyway. Isn't that enough?'

'That's different.'

'Yes – and better. He can't put a price on it, so he can't be offended that it doesn't match up to whatever he may or may not have got for us. Just give him that – or make him some of your homemade biscuits to go with it, if you want to do more.'

'Yes, that's an idea!' Chrissie brightened up. 'I'll do that. He likes my caramel shortbread. Or I could make a big batch of fudge and give some to Wayne and Dean's boys – and Leo Whittle, too. I'd like to give him something, in case Yvonne … did you know she forgot his birthday this year?'

'Yes, he told me, but I was sworn to secrecy. How did you find out?'

'Yvonne told me. She was dreadfully upset about it. She said she's going to try to make it up to him at Christmas. I just hope that doesn't mean getting them into more debt. I promised her one of my Christmas cakes. I told her I'd made too many, now that the homeless party is definitely off this year, and she'd be helping me by taking one off my hands. I don't know if she believed me. But she said she'd have it and she looked sort of relieved.'

'She'll be upset about the trial being put back again,' Gavin observed glumly. 'I hope it doesn't set her drinking again – that and Harry's anniversary. Christmas is going to be really tough for her this year.'

CHRISTMAS IS COMING

'Maybe we could invite them round for Christmas dinner – or maybe for tea,' Chrissie suggested.

'Not if you're giving them a Christmas cake,' Gavin pointed out. 'And I'm going to be on duty, remember?'

'Boxing Day, then. We're allowed to socialise for three days, aren't we?'

'I'm sorry, Chrissie.' Gavin put his arm round his wife's shoulders. 'I just don't think it'd work. Trevor wouldn't like it, for a start. And if Yvonne does relapse, the last thing young Leo is going to want is anyone from outside the family seeing her in a state. I really am sorry, but I think you need to let this go. You can't fix everyone's lives. Sometimes you just have to back off and let them get on with it by themselves.'

VICTIM STATEMENTS

A few streets away, Yvonne was doing her best to get on with the monumental task of preparing for a Christmas that would inevitably be like none that had gone before. After her failure to make an effort for Leo's birthday, she was determined that he would not miss out on a proper Christmas celebration, however lacking in festive spirit she felt herself. Money was still tight, but thanks to Chrissie Hughes and her friend, that awful loan had been paid off. Once coronavirus was over, they'd be able to start paying back the arrears on their rent and other bills. The poor boy deserved to have a nice time after everything he'd been through.

She had got their artificial tree down from the loft and set it up in the living room. Now she was struggling to fix a tinsel star to the top, which was an inch or two higher than she could reach.

'I'll do that.' She turned at the sound of her son's voice. He came over and took the star from her. She hadn't noticed how tall he had grown in the last year. He seemed to tower above her as he reached up and attached the star to the top branch with ease.

'Would you like to finish this for me?' she asked, thinking that he might enjoy decorating the tree. 'It's all in this box. Just be careful with the lights.'

'OK.' Leo turned and began rummaging in the box, looking for all the familiar ornaments from previous years. Was he pleased to have been asked? It was so difficult to tell when he said so little, whatever mood he was in.

17. FESTIVE SEASON

Yvonne became sleepily aware that there was an alarm going off in the room. She reached out and picked up the clock that lay on the small cupboard next to their bed. It was still dark, but on these winter mornings that was no guide to the time. Three a.m.! More than an hour before her usual working-day time, and her job had been on hold again since the beginning of November, so usually they got up much later now. Why was the alarm going off? Of course! It was Christmas Day.

She rubbed the sleep out of her eyes and climbed carefully out of bed, trying not to disturb Trevor who lay beside her, apparently still asleep. She fumbled under the bed for her slippers and then felt her way across the room to the door, picking up a large sock filled with small gifts from the dressing table as she passed it. Then she crept along the landing to Leo's room.

Hanging from the door handle was an identical sock. Just one! There had always been two before, neatly labelled with the boys' names, so that Santa would know which presents to put in each. No label this year – just a single sock hanging forlornly on the door. Taking a deep breath to calm her nerves, Yvonne laid down the full sock on the floor outside the door and took away the empty one. She tiptoed back to her room and climbed into bed beside Trevor, who seemed to sense her disquiet and took her in his arms.

'Happy Christmas,' he murmured in her ear. 'You feel shivery. I know something we could do to warm you up.'

'No, Trev. I'm not in the mood. Just a cuddle, OK?'

'OK.'

Yvonne snuggled her head into Trevor's shoulder. 'It seemed strange not having a stocking for Harry,' she murmured. 'I suppose it must have been the same last year, but I don't remember. Did I do a stocking for Leo last year?'

'No. You were out of it all last Christmas. I found the stash of stocking-fillers you'd bought and gave them to Leo, but we didn't bother with hanging up stockings and filling them up at midnight.'

'What happened to that new bike we bought Harry, so he could get to work quicker? I don't remember seeing it after …'

'I took it back to the shop. When I told them he was dead, they refunded the money.'

FESTIVE SEASON

'I suppose we could've kept it for Leo.'

'His bike was OK and I'd maxed out our credit cards. And there was the funeral to pay for.'

'Yes, of course. The funeral.'

Three hours later, another alarm went off in another part of Oxford. Bernie reached out from under the bedclothes and silenced the ringing. She got up and went across to the door to switch on the light. Then she came back and stood over the bed, looking down at her still-snoozing spouse and announcing, 'Happy Christmas!'

Peter opened his eyes and looked up at her. 'Happy Christmas!' he smiled back.

VICTIM STATEMENTS

'I'll go down and start sorting out his nibs,' Bernie said. 'I suppose you'll have stuff to do for the dinner.'

'Not quite yet! It's a smaller bird than usual, so I need to be careful not to overcook it. I don't think I've ever done Christmas dinner for just the three of us before.'

'Mmm,' Bernie nodded as she tied the cord of her dressing gown. 'It will certainly feel strange not having Lucy here. I know it all makes sense her staying up in Liverpool, but … well it'll just seem very peculiar, that's all!'

'Everything's going to be odd. It looks as if we're booked up all day with Zoom meetings, instead of having Stan and Sylvia for dinner and the grandkids coming over in the afternoon and taking Jonah over to St Albans to see Nathan and Georgia on Boxing Day and …'

FESTIVE SEASON

'... and your Hannah ringing up while we're eating our dinner or just when we're in the middle of a game with Ricky,' Bernie laughed. 'At least this time, we've got everybody booked in to appointments in an orderly fashion!'

When Chrissie came downstairs on Christmas morning, she was surprised to hear the strains of *Deck the Halls* emanating from behind the closed kitchen door. Opening it, she saw that the table was laid for breakfast. Paper serviettes printed with holly and ivy patterns had been cleverly folded into crowns, which stood proudly on each place setting; there were new mugs with *Merry Christmas* printed on them in red and green lettering; and the effect was completed by a centrepiece of greenery hung with tiny silver bells. The singing was coming from a CD player, standing on the work surface next to the coffee-maker, which was accompanying the carols with its own burbling and wheezing music.

'Would you like some toast?' Craig greeted her. 'I hope you don't mind,' he added, looking anxiously across at the table. 'I know you don't want to do Christmas this year, but I thought we ought to just mark the day a bit. I can turn the music off if you don't like it.'

'No, yes, it all looks lovely. Thank you.' Chrissie sat down in her usual place at the table. She picked up the mug and turned it round in her hand, discovering that, on the other side, it had her named. 'Toast would be lovely, and these mugs are super. Thank you.'

FESTIVE SEASON

'You don't have to be polite about them,' Craig grinned back as he put slices of bread into the toaster. 'I found your stash of mugs at the back of the cupboard when I was getting the plates out just now. I wouldn't have got them if I'd known you had so many already.'

'No,' Chrissie insisted. 'It's nice to get new ones. Every one is special, because of who gave them to me. They're mostly from the children at school – and some really old ones that Kenny got me, back when that was about all his pocket-money would stretch to. I always told him you could never have too many mugs, and it's still true – honestly!'

'Anyway, I'm glad I got you something else as well,' Craig smiled back, evidently not totally convinced by Chrissie's protestations. 'It was too big to wrap, so I've left it in the front room. You can see it later – after you've had breakfast. I hope there'll be time before Gavin goes out. I know he's working today.'

'Time for what?' Gavin asked, catching the end of the conversation as he came in, already dressed in his police uniform.

'Craig was just telling me that he's left a mystery present for both of us in the front room,' Chrissie told him. 'And he's got us these personalised mugs too.' She got up, glancing towards Craig before heading for the door. 'While the toast's doing, I'll go and get our presents for you. They're not much – just some home-made things. We didn't want to – well, we weren't sure what you usually … I'll go and get them.'

Gavin sat down and appeared to be admiring his mug. Craig brought the coffee jug across and poured it for him.

FESTIVE SEASON

'It's a pity you have to work today,' he observed, 'but I suppose someone has to do it.'

'Yes,' Gavin nodded, 'and I haven't taken a turn for a long time, because I usually managed to get out of it on the basis of helping with the homeless party. My sergeant has always been very understanding about the Christmas lunch. So, with that not happening this year, it's my turn.'

'And it beats sitting round reminiscing about Christmases past,' suggested Craig.

'Yes, that as well.'

The toast popped up. Craig put the slices on two plates and refilled the toaster. Then he brought the plates across to the table for Gavin and Chrissie. 'What time have you got to go?'

'Half an hour. Don't worry, there'll be time to see this mystery present of yours.'

'It's nothing really,' Craig reddened. 'I just wanted to do something to show that I do appreciate what you've both done for me. And I'm sorry I haven't always been easy to live with.'

'Nonsense!' Chrissie was back, carrying two gift-wrapped parcels. 'You've been a model lodger: keeping your room spotless and helping with the housework. I don't know what we'd do without you!'

She put the parcels down on the table in front of him. 'Go on! Open them!'

Craig tore the paper off the smaller parcel to reveal a rectangular tin, red with a snowflake pattern on it and the words Merry Christmas on the lid. He opened it and discovered half a dozen pieces of shortbread topped with caramel and chocolate.

'Thank you!' He smiled towards Chrissie. 'My favourite! Not that *all* your baking isn't delicious,' he added quickly.

Then he turned his attention to the other package. It felt soft and squidgy in his hand and he guessed that it must be one of Chrissie's knitted creations. He unwrapped it carefully and took out a chunky sweater knitted in brown wool. He held it up against his chest to show that it fitted and smiled at Chrissie. 'Thank you! It's just what I need,'

'I thought it would keep you warm, cycling to work on these cold winter mornings,' she smiled back.

Craig pulled off the fair isle pullover that he was wearing (one of Kenny's) and put on his present. It fitted perfectly. On impulse he put his arms round Chrissie and kissed her cheek. 'Merry Christmas, Chrissie.'

'Merry Christmas Craig. And thank you for …,' she looked round at the table, '… all this.'

Gavin had been buttering his toast while Craig was opening his presents. Now he got up, half-eaten slice in hand, and gestured towards the door. 'Shall we go through and see this mystery gift? Or I may have to go out before I find out what it is!'

They trooped through to the lounge. Craig threw open the door dramatically, then stepped back to allow Gavin and Chrissie through first. They entered the room and looked round. In one corner (the spot where they usually put the Christmas tree, but Craig had no way of knowing that) there was something new. It was a tall display cabinet: triangular to fit neatly into the corner, a small cupboard at the bottom, open shelves in the middle and two glass-fronted shelves at the top.

Gavin walked across to examine it closer. Still holding his toast in his right hand, he ran his left hand over the surface. 'Did you make this?'

Craig blushed red. 'Well, Wayne helped. And they let me have space in their workshop while I was doing it.'

'It's perfect!' Chrissie declared. 'We said we needed somewhere to keep Kenny's swimming medals and things, but then lockdown started and we never got round to getting one. I'm so glad we didn't, now, because this is much nicer than anything in the shops.'

She picked up two photographs of her son, which stood on the windowsill, and moved them to one of the shelves of the new cabinet. 'There! Now let's finish breakfast and then I'll go upstairs and find his scout badge and that trophy he won at school and ...'

'And his Queen's Police Medal,' Craig added. 'That ought to go in the middle, because it's the most important.'

'Gavin's got a medal too,' Chrissie told him. 'Where've you put it Gav?'

'It's only a long-service medal,' Gavin said quickly. 'It only means I've been in the force for more than twenty years and kept my nose clean. It's nothing special.'

'Still, it'd be nice to have it in there next to Kenny's medal, wouldn't it?' Chrissie said. She turned to Craig. 'Will you help me sort Kenny's things out and arrange them, later? I won't be able to reach those high shelves.'

FESTIVE SEASON

After lunch was over, Yvonne, Trevor and Leo all stood round the Christmas tree gazing down at the pile of gaily wrapped parcels beneath it.

'There's more than I was expecting,' Yvonne commented. 'I thought this year we wouldn't have many presents to unwrap, but what with Susan's hamper and the box of stuff Michelle sent, it's come to a lot.'

'Well normally Michelle doesn't come over until Boxing Day,' Trevor pointed out, so her presents never go under the tree. And Susan!' He laughed as he thought of his scatty older sister, perhaps the only person in the world to have sent belated Christmas cards in January. 'Well, this must be a record for her! Shall we start with her hamper? There may be something in it that we could have for dinner.'

VICTIM STATEMENTS

'I don't think I'll want any dinner after that lunch,' Yvonne smiled back. 'I ate far more turkey than I ought to have done, but it was very good, though I say it myself.'

'You excelled yourself,' her husband agreed, 'didn't she, Leo?'

'It was very nice,' he mumbled dutifully, 'but I'd still like to see inside the hamper.'

Trevor cut the tape that held the stout cardboard box closed and lifted up the lid. Inside, there was a rectangular wicker basket. He took hold of it and lifted, while Yvonne held the box down. It was a tight fit, but eventually it came out. Leo lifted the lid and peered in. Nestling on a bed of finely-shredded paper were two bottles, several glass jars and an assortment of cardboard packets. Trevor immediately took one bottle in each hand

and lifted them out. He examined the labels carefully, before holding one of them out to Yvonne.

'Elder flower cordial,' he said. 'We've never had that before. Why don't you get some glasses and we'll all try some? And while you're doing that,' he added holding the other bottle close to his chest, 'I'll take care of this.'

Leo stared after this father, who disappeared into the hall. What was he going to do with the wine? Maybe it needed to be kept cool in the fridge, like Champagne. Or maybe he didn't want Mum opening it right away and maybe having a bit too much and spoiling the day. They hadn't had wine with their dinner for weeks now. Was that because they couldn't afford it or was Mum trying to cut down at last?

VICTIM STATEMENTS

'Here you are, love!' his mum was holding out a small glass towards him. It was one of her special ones from the glass-fronted cupboard next to the window. He wasn't usually allowed to touch them. 'Go on! Try it!'

Leo took the glass and sipped cautiously at the clear liquid. It was sweet and tasted a bit of oranges.

'Do you like it?'

'It's OK, but I think I'd rather have some coke.'

'Go on then. There's some cans in the kitchen. You don't have to finish that, if you don't like it.'

'No, it's OK, just nothing special.' Leo tipped his head back and emptied the glass before heading off in search of the coke.

He found his father engaged in stowing the bottle of wine on top of one of the kitchen wall cupboards, where it would be out of sight, and out of reach, of his wife. When he saw Leo, he stepped hastily down from the chair that he was standing on. He looked embarrassed.

'It's your Aunty Beatrice's birthday in a few weeks,' he explained. 'I thought we'd keep this to give to her. It's not the sort of wine we like, but I know she does. You don't need to mention it to your mum. She might not like the idea of passing a present on, but I know Bea won't mind, and we are a bit strapped for cash at the moment.'

'And you don't want Mum …,' Leo began. Then he changed his mind. He had had a feeling that Dad was taking him into his confidence about Mum's drinking, but maybe it was all just about the money. 'OK,' he amended. I won't tell her.'

VICTIM STATEMENTS

He picked up his can from the counter and led the way back to the living room, where his mother was busily sorting through the other items in the hamper. She looked up when they entered.

'There's some posh jam and marmalade,' she informed them, 'and some biscuits and a little Christmas pudding, which will be nice for our dinner today.'

She put the lid back on the hamper and pushed it away under the coffee table. 'Now let's see what else we've got … Here you are, Leo! This says it's from your Aunty Michelle.'

'It's probably another of those awful jumpers she always gets me,' Leo groaned, taking the parcel and tearing off the wrapping paper. 'At least this time, I don't have to pretend it's what I always wanted!'

FESTIVE SEASON

He was proved right. His mother's sister had sent a Christmas jumper with a reindeer face on the front, complete with a red pompom for a nose. 'Doesn't she remember that she's already given me about a million of these?'

'She probably thinks you'll have grown out of them by now. Don't worry: we won't make you wear it. Now, here's her present for you, Trev. Go on! Open it!'

Leo watched as his father took the gift and began to unwrap it. It looked like a bottle. Aunty Michelle usually gave her brother-in-law whisky for Christmas. Yes! There it was: a large bottle with tartan on the label.

'I'll put this away somewhere safe,' he grunted, getting up.

'That's a good idea,' Mum said brightly, watching him go and then turning to Leo. 'And why don't you take that jumper upstairs and put it in a drawer, Leo – while your Dad's doing that?'

'I – I'll wait in case there's anything else that needs to go upstairs,' Leo protested weakly.

'No. It'll be better to clear the decks a bit in here now. There's hardly room to swing a cat. Go on! Don't worry, you won't miss anything.'

Leo got up and left the room. He raced upstairs, threw the jumper down on his bed and then hurried back down again. Why was Mum so keen to get him out of the room? Did she know what Aunty Michelle's present to her was? He could guess. It was usually either vodka or some weird fancy drink like sloe gin or cherry brandy. Was Mum afraid that Dad would confiscate it, whatever it was? He did seem to be being a bit funny about anything alcoholic this year, and they hadn't even had the usual glass of wine with their Christmas lunch.

Leo and his father reached the lounge door at the same time. Neither of them had closed it when they left, but it was shut firmly now. Opening it, Leo saw his mother sitting with an open parcel on her lap. She looked up and smiled. 'Look what Michelle got me: a big box of chocolates!' She lifted the lid and held them out. 'Go on: take one!'

When Gavin arrived home that evening, he found Yvonne and Craig sitting together on the sofa with a large cardboard box, now almost empty, in front of them.

VICTIM STATEMENTS

'What do you think?' Chrissie asked, pointing towards the display cabinet, which was now full of photographs, trophies and framed certificates. 'I've managed to fit all the important things in, and I thought we'd keep all our family photograph albums in the cupboard at the bottom.'

Gavin inspected the display. His own long-service medal was displayed alongside Kenny's Queen's award in the centre of the shelf closest to his eye level. Flanking those were various scouting awards, including Kenny's Queen's Scout certificate, and a letter of commendation for leading a Duke of Edinburgh's award group.

'It looks great,' he told them, 'but I'm not sure about having my long-service award in there. It's not as if I did anything to deserve it. I just stuck it out for twenty years, the same as anyone could have done. It's not like Kenny's-'

'But that's not true!' Craig interrupted. 'I've never seen any other police officer taking such an interest in the homeless people or checking up on kids like that Whittle boy or-'

'And plenty of officers *don't* stick it out, as you put it,' Chrissie added. 'They wouldn't have an award if it wasn't an achievement. I want it there, for everyone to see, because you deserve it. And anyway,' she added, seeing that Gavin was about to protest again, 'it needs to be there for Kenny's sake. He joined the police because he wanted to be like you!'

Yvonne turned over in bed again, but she just couldn't make herself comfortable.

VICTIM STATEMENTS

She was too hot under the duvet, but as soon as she threw it off her, she started shivering. She wondered if she dared get out one of those miniature bottles of liqueurs that had accompanied the chocolates in her present from Michelle. They were so close – hidden at the bottom of her makeup bag on the dressing table – but Trevor might wake, if she got out of bed. He would take them from her, and then she would lose the assurance that they gave her – the certainty that, if the cravings became unbearable, she would be able to have a drink. Not to get drunk. She was never going to allow herself to do that again, but just one drink, just enough to give her that warm glow that would set her up to face the day. Or, in the present situation, to calm her fluttering heart and soothe her to sleep.

FESTIVE SEASON

That Christmas pudding had helped. Until she breathed in the delicious brandy smell and then took her first spoonful, she had forgotten that feeling that she got when taking that first delightful sip! They said that all the alcohol was driven off in the cooking, but it certainly had given her a pleasant buzz. What a pity it hadn't lasted. If only she dared get out and have just one mouthful from one of those tiny bottles! But if Trev saw her drinking, he'd be angry. And anyway, she'd promised. But one little taste couldn't matter, could it?

Somehow, she managed to drift into, if not sleep, at least a kind of drowsiness. She hardly noticed when Trevor slipped silently out of bed and crept out, carrying his clothes to the bathroom to get dressed so that he didn't disturb her. That was kind of him. He was good like that, when he could see that she wasn't well. She'd cried a lot last night, she remembered now, thinking about all the Christmases they'd had before, when the two boys were little. He probably thought that it was those thoughts that had kept her awake, tossing and turning until the small hours.

Well, he was probably right, wasn't he? It wasn't anything to do with needing a drink. She was just feeling down because it was Christmas and Harry wasn't there to share it. She'd only thought about the liqueurs because they'd looked so interesting and she knew that they'd sometimes helped her out of her despondency over losing Harry last year. It was nothing to do with the Christmas pudding. That was ridiculous! Everyone said there wasn't any alcohol left once it had been cooked.

FESTIVE SEASON

She swung her legs over the side of the bed and sat up. Immediately her head began to swim. She closed her eyes, counted to ten and then opened them again. It was very dark, but there was just enough light coming in under the door for her to make out the shapes of the furniture. She switched on the bedside lamp and at once everything felt far too bright. She blinked several times and wiped her hand across her forehead, preparing to stand.

As soon as she got to her feet, the light-headed feeling began again and she reached out to steady herself against the dressing table. She breathed deeply and closed her eyes again. The bag containing the miniatures was right there, beneath her left hand. Almost without thinking, she opened it and reached inside. Her hand closed around one of the tiny bottles and, before she had time to think about what she was doing, she had the top off and was putting her head back to sample the sweet, fruity concoction. My, that felt good!

She looked down at the label: rhubarb gin. Whoever would have thought rhubarb could taste so good? The bottle was half empty, after only a mouthful. She might as well finish it, now she'd started – or was that Trevor coming back? At the sound of footsteps on the stairs, she hastily tightened the cap again and thrust the bottle back into the bag. Not a moment too soon: she had been right, here was Trevor with a breakfast tray.

FESTIVE SEASON

'I'd like to go for a walk this afternoon,' Gavin announced as he dried up the last of the dishes, following their Boxing Day lunch of cold turkey sandwiches and warmed-up Christmas pudding. No alcohol in their pudding, and no brandy butter to accompany it either. Chrissie's familiarity with the rules regarding the homeless people's Christmas Party, meant that she was scrupulously careful about the ingredients of the many puddings that she prepared in the run-up to Christmas every year.

Gavin didn't mind. He had seen too many of his colleagues injured by drunks brawling in the street – and too many of them drinking to excess in an attempt to combat the stress of long hours and increasingly little job satisfaction. He would treat himself to a can of lager while they watched an old film together that evening, but he preferred to keep a clear head during the day.

'I've got a present for Wayne and Dean's two boys that I'd like to drop off.'

'I've got some shortbread for them, too,' Chrissie nodded. 'And some for the Whittles. We can call in at theirs on the way.'

They set off, clad in coats, gloves and woolly hats (two of Chrissie's finest knitted creations). It was not as sunny as Christmas Day had been, but the wind had moved round to a south-westerly direction and it was no longer quite so bitingly cold as it had been. Gavin carried a mysterious parcel wrapped in brown paper and tied with string, while Chrissie had her shortbread concealed in a canvas shopping bag. She wondered what it was that Gavin had got for the boys, but he seemed to want to keep it secret, so she did not pry. She would find out soon enough and it would make it more exciting for the boys if she was genuinely surprised when the Big Reveal came. Children could always sense when the grown-ups were pretending.

The silver taxi glinted in the winter sunshine as they approached the Whittles' front door. Trevor was clearly keeping it clean and polished in readiness for more passengers once the new "Kent variant" of the virus receded and Oxford came out of its "Tier 4" restrictions. It must be a very worrying time for the self-employed whose business fluctuated wildly as regulations came and went, and public confidence waxed and waned. Trevor must have expected to make a bit over Christmas, with everyone wanting taxis to take them to and from boozy get-togethers, but then the five-day relaxation of the rules had been reduced to one and all mixing was forbidden in places such as Oxford where COVID-19 was now spreading rapidly again. Thank goodness Bernie had managed to get that compensation for them! That was one debt at least that would not be hanging over them anymore.

Gavin reached up to ring the doorbell, then stepped back to wait for an answer.

'Just put the box down there,' he instructed. 'Better not to get too close, just in case.'

Chrissie stepped forward and placed another red and white tin on the doorstep. She glanced up at the frosted glass in the door, hoping to see someone approaching inside, but there was no sign of life.

'Do you think they heard? Shall I ring again?'

'If you like,' Gavin shrugged, 'but they're probably just busy.'

'Or maybe Yvonne isn't well,' Chrissie nodded grimly, 'but Trevor or Leo could answer.'

She pressed the bell again and heard it buzzing loudly in the hall. Whatever reason they had for not answering, it could not be that the bell wasn't working. She stepped back to stand beside her husband, waiting.

They were just about to continue on their walk, leaving the box of shortbread on the step when the door opened and Trevor looked out.

'Happy Christmas!' Chrissie called to him from two metres distance. 'I brought you all a little present.' She pointed towards the festive tin. 'It's nothing much

– just some shortbread that I baked myself. I thought Leo might like it.'

Trevor bent down and picked up the tin. It looked very small in his large, muscular hands. 'Thanks. I'm afraid Yvonne can't come to the door right now. She's having a lie down. Christmas took it out of her – you know!'

'Oh yes!' Chrissie nodded. 'I quite understand. Give her our love and I hope she's feeling better soon.'

'Thanks. I will,' Trevor mumbled. Then he nodded towards Gavin, as if acknowledging his presence before closing the door again.

'Looks like Yvonne's got another of her migraines,' Chrissie observed as they walked back out to the road.

'Not surprising,' Gavin replied. 'Christmas is the worst possible time for alcoholics. Everyone's expected to drink too much and it's really hard for them to say "no".'

'So, you *would* class her as an alcoholic? I thought probably she was just … I don't know! Well, just drinking to dull the pain of losing Harry.'

'I'm not sure it matters what you call it,' Gavin shrugged. 'Alcoholism, depression, grief: they're all just words.'

They turned into Lewes Road and were soon approaching the house where Wayne and Dean lived with Carl and Harry – not forgetting Star! There was a holly wreath hanging from the door knocker and fairy lights surrounding the porch. Through the window, Chrissie could see a Christmas tree covered with tinsel, baubles and more lights, topped by a gold angel blowing a long trumpet.

VICTIM STATEMENTS

Gavin put up his hand to ring the bell, but before he could press the button, the door opened and Carl beamed up at him.

'Hello, Constable Hughes,' he called out. 'I saw you coming!'

'Would you like to see my presents?' Harry was there too, pushing his way past his brother to speak to the visitors. 'I've got a Lego castle and a tennis racquet a-'

'And *I've* got one too,' Carl interrupted. 'Daddy Dean says he'll take us to play tennis in the park when it opens up again.'

'And Star's got some presents too,' Harry broke in again. 'She's got a new harness and a squeaky ball and-'

'Boys, boys! What going on?' Wayne appeared, looming over them in the doorway like a giant. 'Hello Mr Hughes –

FESTIVE SEASON

Chrissie! What brings you here? Not official police business, I hope!'

'No, not at all,' Chrissie laughed. 'We've just got some little presents for you and the boys.' She put a box of shortbread down on the ground near the front door and stepped back. Gavin did the same with his odd-shaped parcel.

They stood watching from a distance as Carl and Harry fought over who should open which present. After a few moments, Wayne intervened, insisting on being given both of them.

'Thank you. It's very kind of you to think of us.'

'Go on,' urged Gavin, 'open it!'

'Let me do it!' shouted Harry, reaching up to snatch the intriguing package from his father's hand.

VICTIM STATEMENTS

'No, Harry,' Wayne said firmly. 'You go and get Daddy Dean, and then we'll all open it together.

'Daddy Dean! Daddy Dean!' Harry disappeared, his voice fading as he ran down the hall in search of his other father.

'What's all the excitement?' Dean came round the side of the house with Harry trotting in his wake. He had been engaged in essential bicycle maintenance in the back garden and he was wiping dirty hands on an oily rag. 'Hello, Chrissie. Harry said something about presents. You really shouldn't have – but it's very nice of you.'

'Can I open it now?' demanded Carl.

'The box is just some shortbread that I made,' Chrissie explained, 'but I'm all agog to see what Gavin's put in that parcel!'

FESTIVE SEASON

Wayne sat down on the doorstep with the package on his lap. He carefully untied the string and folded out the brown paper to reveal two lengths of thin dowel wrapped in bright yellow and red striped fabric.

'What is it?' asked Dean.

'I know! I know!' crowed Harry excitedly. 'It's a kite, isn't it Mr Hughes? You've made us a kite – like you said you would.'

'That's right,' Gavin nodded. 'It's for you all to share.'

'Can we go and fly it now? Will you take us up the hill?' Harry looked up hopefully at Dean, who shook his head.

'Sorry, Harry. It's too late. It'll be getting dark soon. Maybe tomorrow – if the weather's OK.' Dean turned back to Gavin. 'Thank you. The boys will love it.'

VICTIM STATEMENTS

'Oh, it's nothing,' Gavin mumbled. 'It was something for me to do.'

18. NEW YEAR

New Year's Day dawned cold and cloudy, but Jonah was in a buoyant mood. He had a Zoom meeting booked with Gerald Leslie's sister and mother, and Caroline had promised that she had something of importance to reveal. Her email had come through the previous day, requesting the meeting and saying that she had "found something that you ought to see". She also said that her mother, Joyce, was keen to be included, and that she was now completely at ease with online meetings after having participated in several over the Christmas period. That was good. Who better than Gerald's mother to remember the unfortunate undergraduate who had taken his own life? And who would have a greater desire to learn why he had fallen into such deep despair?

Both women must have been eager for the meeting, because they were already in the "waiting room" when Jonah logged on. Bernie, who was acting as host, immediately admitted them and two faces appeared side-by-side on Jonah's screen.

'What is it you wanted to show me?' he asked them, after the preliminary greetings were over.

'Er … yes,' Caroline said, sounding less confident all of a sudden. 'Well … My daughter, Melinda, came over for Christmas Day, and …'

Jonah studied her face on the screen as she continued to hesitate.

'They went up in the loft,' her mother put in. 'That's where all Gerald's things are. We didn't have the heart to throw them out, but we didn't want to be staring at them all the time either. It takes two to manage the ladder, and I'm no use for that sort of thing these days.'

'Yes, we went up and got down some of Gerry's things,' Caroline continued. 'And we found this!'

Jonah stared as she held up a small object, moving it around uncertainly in front of her in an attempt to bring it into focus on the webcam.

'Does it mean that he had something to do with killing that woman?' Mrs Leslie asked anxiously.

'Not necessarily,' Bernie answered quickly. 'There could be plenty of other explanations.'

'And there *is* just the one?' Jonah asked, still staring intently at the single cuff-link, which Caroline continued to hold up.

'Yes,' she confirmed. 'We hunted through all his things and there was no sign of the other one.'

'Well,' Jonah said slowly, 'as Dr Fazakerley said, 'this doesn't *prove* anything. He could have lost the other cuff-link at any time – or it could have been mislaid after he died. However, it is very suggestive, given where we found the other link.'

'He was never the same after that Trinity term,' Mrs Leslie told him. 'I always thought something must have happened, but he would never answer any of my questions.'

'So, you think he may have had something weighing on his mind?' Jonah suggested.

'Yes, that's exactly how he seemed. Do you think he killed her, and then couldn't live with himself afterwards?'

NEW YEAR

'Mum!' Caroline sounded shocked. 'Don't say that sort of thing. He wouldn't! Gerry wasn't like that.'

'I don't mean he set out to kill her.' The older woman reached out and Jonah thought she must be taking hold of her daughter's hand, low down, below the range of the camera. 'It could have been an accident. Young people together. A few drinks too many. Larking about. Doing silly things. Something goes wrong, and someone falls and hits their head or … what if they were on the river? I remember punt parties when I was up at Oxford. It would have been-'

'Mum! Stop it!'

'Caroline – darling – we've got to face facts. Something awful must have happened. Gerald was never the same after that summer, and something like this would explain it, wouldn't it? I don't want him to have been mixed up in hiding this girl's body, any more than you do, but at least it would explain why he couldn't live with himself – instead of … well, instead of me thinking it must be all my fault.'

'Mrs Leslie,' Bernie intervened again, 'families always blame themselves when someone takes their own life, but I'm sure you did everything you could have done.'

'That's what I try to tell myself, but I always think … what if I'd encouraged him to confide in me more when he was little? He might have told me what was wrong. Or could I have paid for him to have more counselling sessions or …?'

'We've been through all this loads of times,' Caroline intervened. 'You did everything you could.'

'I know. I know. But it would still be a comfort to know *why* he did it – and for it not to be anything I did.'

'We think that your son – probably with a group of his friends – was there when a young woman called Jane Turnbull died.' Jonah took control of the conversation. 'We don't know how she died or where. All we know is that she ended up being buried in a shallow grave on Shotover Hill, together with a cuff-link that looks very much indeed like the pair to that one your daughter just showed me. Her parents are both dead now, but her sister would very much like to know what happened to her. And, if she was unlawfully killed, it's only right that whoever did it is brought to justice.'

He paused for a few seconds, gazing straight into the camera.

VICTIM STATEMENTS

'We'd like to help,' Mrs Leslie said at last. 'What do you need us to do?'

'Just to answer a few questions, and to tell me anything you can remember about your son and his friends when he was in Oxford. He shared rooms with a Charles Rawlins. Do you remember him at all?'

'We met him a couple of times, when we drove Gerald up to Oxford, and then he came to stay with us that summer – the summer that Gerald's depression started. Only we didn't talk about depression back then. We just said he was down in the dumps and told him to stop worrying about his exams.'

'Mum!' Caroline protested mildly. 'What did we just say?'

'You don't happen to know where this Charles is now, by any chance?' enquired Jonah.

'No. I'm sorry.' Mrs Leslie shook her head. 'I do remember that he went into the City after they graduated – working for a merchant bank, I think. He offered to find Gerald a job there too, but nothing ever came of it.'

'Presumably you didn't find any address book or a diary or anything like that in with his things?' Jonah asked hopefully. 'Or anything else that might tell us about his friends?'

'No, I'm afraid not.' Caroline shook her head.

'He had a big clear-out not long before he died,' her mother added. 'I suppose I ought to have seen it as a warning sign. He threw away all his old lecture notes and all sorts of paperwork from Oxford. He said he didn't need any of it and it was just cluttering up the place.'

VICTIM STATEMENTS

'So, you think he may have wanted to forget his time in Oxford?' suggested Jonah. 'Or perhaps to destroy documentary evidence of something that happened then?'

'Yes,' Mrs Leslie agreed. 'That's exactly how it seems now, but I never thought at the time. It was only when I read the note he left that I realised how he must have been feeling.'

'I don't suppose you still have the note?'

'Yes. I do. I've got it here. I thought you might want to see it. Shall I read it to you?'

'Yes please,' Jonah smiled back. He was liking this unexpectedly astute and efficient old lady more and more.

Mrs Leslie put on a pair of reading glasses and held up a piece of pale blue writing paper in front of her.

NEW YEAR

'Dear Mum and Dad,' she began, 'I'm sorry but I just can't live with myself anymore. It's all my fault, nothing to do with you. Please try not to mind too much. Love, Gerald.'

She stopped abruptly and dabbed her eyes with a tissue, which her daughter passed to her.

'Thank you, Mrs Leslie,' Jonah said gently, trying to give her time to compose herself before asking any more questions. 'That's very helpful. It gives us an idea of his state of mind just before he died.'

'Would you like a copy of the note?' Caroline asked. 'I could email you a photograph of it, if you like.'

'Yes. That would be useful. Thank you.' Jonah paused, trying to decide whether there was anything to be gained by continuing the conversation. The two women appeared to have told him all they knew about Gerald Leslie's time in Oxford. 'I think that's all for now. Thank you for your time. You've both been very helpful.'

Bernie ended the video conference and then looked towards Jonah. 'What do you think?' she asked. 'Is Gerald our murderer?'

'Well, I certainly think that he's the owner of our cuff-link! But I don't see how he could have killed Jane Turnbull and buried her body up on Shotover Hill without some help. He couldn't get a dead body out there by himself. He'd need a car and at least one other person to help carry her.'

'Unless she went up there with him while she was still alive,' suggested Bernie.

NEW YEAR

'They'd still need transport,' Jonah insisted. 'Unless everyone's been lying to us about what they did after the Eights Week dinner, he was still in central Oxford until late that night. A bus – even assuming they were still running at that time of night – would only get them as far as Headington, and nobody, however far under the influence, sets off on a three-mile bicycle ride at eleven at night!'

'So, are we looking at our Jeremy, the useful friend with the car?' suggested Bernie.

'Who was living out in Headington that year,' agreed Jonah, smiling broadly, 'in Quarry Road, according to Giles Kingman.'

'Which is but a short step away from where they found the body!' Bernie exclaimed, suddenly enlightened. 'So, he'd most likely be familiar with Shotover and realise that they'd be able to hide the body there.'

'Precisely! So, now I think we need to make a concerted effort to track down Charles Rawlins. I'll get on to the Alumni Office again and put it to them that they'd be impeding a murder enquiry if they don't hand over his contact details, and let's have another chat with our friend Professor Weldon and see if he can remember anything more about who did what on the night of the boat club dinner.'

'What about Jeremy Scott-Urquhart?' asked Bernie. 'Aren't you going to interview him again?'

'Not yet. Let him carry on thinking we believed everything he told us. When we confront him with his lies, I want to have more evidence to put to him, in the hope that we can force him to change his story.'

NEW YEAR

Things moved on quickly from that point, despite the announcement of another national lockdown, which ended any hopes that Jonah may have had of travelling to Derbyshire to see for himself the debris of Gerald Leslie's short life. Daisy Gregg at the Alumni Office accepted that, now that it was certain that an employee of the college had died in suspicious circumstances, possibly helped on her way by one or more of its undergraduates, the police had a legitimate reason for demanding the names and addresses of those whom they suspected of being involved. She agreed to provide contact details for all the members of the 1983 rowing eights.

VICTIM STATEMENTS

While he was waiting for this information to come through, Jonah called Graham Weldon again to ask what he could remember about the evening of the Saturday of Eights week 1983. He confirmed Kingman's statement that they had gone to the pub together after dinner. He had gone home after only a few drinks, but most of the others stayed on longer. Did they wear their cuff links to the pub? Yes, they were all still dressed in formal wear after having been to dinner in college. Had anyone lost a cuff link? Not that he noticed. What about Gerald, in particular? Did he have both cuff links on when they went to the pub? Yes, he thought so, but he couldn't swear to it.

A video interview with Charles Rawlins the following day proved more fruitful. Rawlins, it turned out, was now a stockbroker and gentleman farmer living in Surrey. There were photographs of horses and watercolours of rural landscapes on the wall behind him in what he described as his "home office". Also visible were a music stand and shelves stacked high with sheet music.

'What can I do for you?' he asked. He seemed rather nervous, but then people were often nervous at being interviewed by the police.

'We're investigating the death of a young woman in Oxford nearly thirty years ago,' Jonah told him. 'We think you may be able to help us. You were a member of Lichfield College Boat Club in 1983, weren't you?'

'Yes. That's right.' Rawlins seemed a little calmer now. He very sensibly kept his answers short and did not volunteer additional information.

'And you had a pair of the special cuff-links that the president of the club had made that year?'

'Yes, I did."

'Do you still have them?'

'No, I don't think so. It's a long time ago.'

'That's a pity. Most of the other members of the first eight still have theirs. We're rather interested in finding out which of you lost one on the night of 28th May 1983 – the Saturday of Eights Week. Can you enlighten me on that point?'

'No. I'm not aware of anyone losing a cuff-link.'

'Never mind. Now, my assistant is going to share her screen with you.' There was a pause while Bernie, through the magic of computer technology, displayed the photograph of Jane Turnbull alongside the rectangles containing each person's face. Rawlins stared at it impassively.

'Do you recognise this woman?'

'No.'

'This is Jane Turnbull,' Jonah told him. 'In 1983, she was working in the kitchens at Lichfield College. She went missing on the night of 28th May and her body was found recently in the woods over on Shotover Hill. We have reason to believe that she met with someone from the Boat Club that same evening. Are you *sure* you don't remember seeing her with one of your rowing buddies?'

Rawlins stared back in silence.

'I see you're a musician,' Jonah commented, with apparent irrelevance. 'What instrument do you play?'

'The piano,' Rawlings answered. Then, seeing that his inquisitor was not satisfied, he added, 'and the treble recorder.'

'And the double-bass?' enquired Jonah.

'What makes you say that?' Rawlins snapped back, strangely agitated by this line of questioning. 'And what is it to you, anyway, *what* I play?'

'One of your friends mentioned it. I gather you played in a band?'

'It was a string ensemble. Look can we get back to whatever it is you wanted to ask me about? I haven't got all day, you know.'

'I was just thinking about how difficult it must have been getting a double-bass around to gigs,' Jonah continued, ignoring his protests. 'You were lucky to have Jeremy Scott-Urquhart as a friend. His car must have been very useful.'

'Yes. It was. But how is this relevant to your investigation?'

'Everything is relevant until proved otherwise,' Jonah said smoothly. 'But since you don't want to talk about it, let's turn to something else. Poor Gerald Leslie: you are aware that he killed himself, I presume?'

'Yes, I did hear.'

'Any idea why?'

'None at all. Mind you, he was always nervy. Even at school he was always getting into a flap about things.'

'You were at school together?'

'Oh yes! And prep school before that. We'd been friends for years before we came up to Oxford.'

'And after you both came down? Did you keep up your friendship?'

'Well, I tried to help him, but he was going downhill rapidly. Just couldn't get his act together at all. And then … Well, presumably something tipped him over the edge, a girl I expect.'

'Did he have any girlfriends at all while he was up at Oxford?'

'No, not really. Not that I remember. Nothing that lasted, at any rate.'

'Could he have been going out with Jane Turnbull?'

'No. I don't think so. I think I'd have known.'

'But he might have wanted to keep it secret, with her being only one of the domestic staff,' Jonah suggested.

'Well, if he did, he succeeded. I certainly wasn't aware of anything going on,' Rawlins declared. 'And you'd think I would, seeing as we were sharing rooms that year.'

'Ah yes! So, it wouldn't have been possible for Mr Leslie to bring anyone back to his room without you knowing?'

'No. I'd have been bound to hear them, even if I was in bed.'

'And did either of you bring any guests back on the night of the Eights Week dinner in 1983?'

'No!'

'OK. Now, please would you describe to me exactly what you did do after that dinner?'

'It was years ago. How do you expect me to remember?'

'Just try your best. You all sat together at dinner: you and the rest of the first eight crew, celebrating your success on the river. You moved up three places in the table that year. Afterwards, it would be natural to go for a few drinks together.'

VICTIM STATEMENTS

'I suppose someone's already told you that's what happened,' Rawlins growled. 'Yes, we went for a few drinks and then came back to college and went to bed.'

'Where did you drink?'

'The Lamb and Flag.'

'Oh! Professor Kingman thought it was the Eagle and Child.'

'Maybe it was then,' Rawlins sounded annoyed. 'I don't remember. I think we went on to a few pubs – you know how it is with students – and then we opened a bottle of wine when we got back to college.'

'Who's "we"? Did you invite the whole rowing eight back to your room?'

'No, of course not,' Charles retorted irritably. 'It was me and Gerald and Jeremy – and Julian turned up later. Or was it Jeremy who came later? I can't remember. It got very late – after midnight – and we'd all been drinking, so Jeremy stayed over in our rooms.'

'Ah yes! He lived out in Headington, didn't he? Quarry Road, was it?'

'No, just round the corner from there: Old Road.'

'Yes, I know it,' Jonah replied, carefully controlling his features to avoid showing the delight that this statement provoked in him. 'It's the one that goes on out and crosses the by-pass, isn't it?'

'Yes, that's right, but Jerry's house was the other way – further in towards the city.'

'I see,' Jonah nodded. 'Sorry, I interrupted you. Go on. You were telling me about what you did that night.'

'That's all there is to it. We had a few glasses of wine and then we all went to bed. Julian went back to his room and

Jerry spent the night on the sofa in our sitting room. That's all there was to it. And then we all woke up the next day with massive hangovers.'

'I see. And you're sure there wasn't anyone else there? You didn't meet anyone on the way back from the pub and invite them to join you?'

'No. It was just the four of us.'

'I see,' Jonah repeated. 'So, you're absolutely sure that Jane Turnbull – the woman whose picture I showed you – didn't come back to your rooms with you?'

'Quite sure.'

'Then, how do you account for the fact that one of your friend Gerald's cuff-links was found with her body?'

Rawlins' mouth dropped open. He was clearly unprepared for this. Jonah had been half-expecting him to have been briefed about the significance of the cuff-links, and to have a story ready. Perhaps Scott-Urquhart had been telling the truth when he declared that he did not know how to contact his old friend.

'Perhaps he gave it to her,' he suggested at last. 'It was the sort of thing he would do, if he fancied her.'

'When?'

'What d'you mean? How would I know?'

'When did he give it to her? You were all still dressed for dinner when you went to the pub. We have a witness who tells us that included everyone wearing their special cuff-links. You and he were together for the whole time from dinner until you went to bed. So, when did he have the opportunity to meet Jane Turnbull and give her one of his cuff-links?'

VICTIM STATEMENTS

'Later, maybe – I don't know!' Rawlins thought for a few moments, before continuing angrily, 'anyway, how can you be so sure it *was* Gerald's cuff-link? Lots of people had them. It could have belonged to any number of people.'

'No, not *any* number, only twenty-four. And we know that in 1983 the only people who had them were the current members of the Boat Club.'

'Well, if it was Gerald's, maybe he dropped it in the street on the way back to our rooms. We were all pretty pissed by then. None of us would have noticed. And this girl – this Jane Turnbull – could've picked it up.'

'Yes, that's quite possible,' Jonah agreed equably. 'Well, thank you for your time, Mr Rawlins. I don't think I need detain you any longer.'

19. BIRTH AND DEATH

Leo was woken by the sound of his parents moving around on the landing. He reached for his phone to check the time. Only seven-thirty! That was early for a Sunday. Usually, they liked to have a lie-in, unless Dad was booked to take a passenger to an early flight. That was Mum going downstairs already. What was up?

He rolled over and closed his eyes again. Normally on this date he would have been up early, restless in his anticipation of what was to come. But after last year … better not to expect anything, so as not to be disappointed.

He couldn't stop listening though. His father's footsteps followed his mother's downstairs. Then there was the faint sound of clinking crockery from the kitchen. Silence for a while and then footsteps on the stairs again. They were whispering outside his room now. What was going on?

The door burst open and there was Dad, wearing a striped apron and a chef's hat. He bowed ceremonially then stood upright again, holding the door open for Mum to come in with a breakfast tray. She was wearing a black dress and a frilly white apron. Her hair was braided neatly beneath a white maid's cap and her face was made up with red lipstick.

'Happy birthday!' they chorused.

'Sit up,' Dad commanded, striding over to the bunk bed, where Leo was lying and arranging the pillow to make it into a support for his son's back.

Then Mum stepped forward and placed the tray on his knees – rather awkwardly because of having to bend low under the upper bunk. They had talked about taking off the top bunk – Harry's bunk – now that Leo had the room to himself, but that had never come to anything. They often talked about doing things that never got done. Like last January, when Leo had been promised a big birthday party to celebrate becoming a teenager and, in the end …

He gazed down at the tray. It looked like the sort of breakfasts that they had had when they stayed at a guest house in Bournemouth one summer. There was a plate of fried food: bacon, a sausage, egg and beans. Next to it was a smaller plate with a round of toast cut into triangles. There was an individual pat of butter and a tiny pot of marmalade.

'I'll put your orange juice down here, so it doesn't get spilt,' Dad said, placing a glass on the desk.

'Would you like cereal?' Mum asked. 'We got a variety pack so you can choose which you'd like.'

'Thanks. Does it have Coco Pops?'

'Yes, I checked, because I know you like them. I'll bring them up.' She turned to go. 'But eat your fry-up while it's warm.'

'Umm.' Leo looked round uncomfortably. 'Er ... Dad! Do you think you could take this tray and put it on the desk? I think I'd rather sit up to eat. It's a bit cramped in here.'

'Yes, of course.' Dad reached in and took back the tray. 'We must get round to taking that top bunk off,' he went on. 'Let's do that later this morning, shall we?

'OK.' Leo cut into his sausage. 'Dad?' he mumbled as he chewed. 'How's Mum?'

'She's fine. What d'you mean?' Dad demanded sharply.

BIRTH AND DEATH

'Nothing. Only, I was afraid she might…' Leo trailed off, wishing that he'd never said anything. This was probably going to mess up everything.

'She'd fine,' Dad repeated firmly. 'And she's trying to make up to you for last year. It was tough for her having your birthday so soon after Harry died. She's making a big effort this time – so mind you let her know you appreciate it!'

Mum was back, with the tiny packet of Coco Pops a bowl and a little jug of milk.

'Here you are! I'll put them down here and you can eat them when you're ready. Now, come on, Dad! We've got things to do.'

'Thanks Mum. This is all … very nice.' Leo said, trying his best to sound pleased. It was nice that they were trying to make his day special, but he'd really rather have just had the cereal and maybe a can of coke to wash it down. And breakfast in bed wasn't really very comfortable.

'Eat your breakfast,' Dad said, following Mum out of the door. 'And then get dressed and come down. We've got a few things to show you.'

Leo's heart gave a lurch. He'd heard reports of families getting into debt through spending too much on presents over Christmas. What if Mum and Dad had splashed out on things for him because they were feeling guilty about forgetting his birthday last year? Nothing more had been said about that threatening letter that he'd seen, but Dad had kept reminding Mum that they had to cut back. He'd been doing all the shopping lately too. Was that because he didn't trust Mum not to spend too much?

BIRTH AND DEATH

He ate his food at top speed, anxious to get finished as soon as possible, as if finding out what they'd got for him sooner would somehow reduce the amount it had cost. Then he tore off his pyjamas and pulled on his clothes before racing downstairs.

Mum and Dad were in the kitchen eating their own breakfast of tea and toast. They got to their feet when he burst in. Mum swallowed her last mouthful of toast and Dad stepped towards him with his slice still in his hand.

'All ready?' he asked heartily. 'Then follow me!'

He led the way into the living room. There was the Christmas tree, still standing in front of the window, where passers-by would see the lights at night. They'd never left it up until his birthday before, but everyone seemed to be keeping their decorations up for longer this year. It was something about keeping cheerful despite the third Lockdown and the rising numbers of COVID cases.

Pinned to the picture rail along one side of the room was a long banner: *Happy Birthday Leo*, it proclaimed in shiny gold letters. Under the tree was a pile of parcels wrapped in colourful paper. Leo stood, staring round in silence.

'Go on!' Mum urged. 'Which one do you want to open first?'

Leo got down on his hands and knees and reached under the tree. The first parcel felt soft and squidgy in his hand. He looked at the label: Happy Birthday Leo, love Mum and Dad.

'Thanks!' he said, thinking that he would get his gratitude over with before opening the gift, just in case it was a disappointment and he wasn't able to put the right enthusiasm into his voice once he knew what it was.

He tore off the paper and out fell a pair of shorts and a football jersey in the claret-and-blue colours of his team.

'It's last year's strip,' Mum said anxiously. 'And they're not new. I hope that's OK?'

'It's awesome! Thanks Mum.' Leo got up and gave her a hug.

'Chrissie's friend, Bernie, found them for me online,' she explained. 'You can get all sorts of things there.'

'Go on,' Dad urged again. 'See what else you've got.'

Leo dived back under the tree and pulled out the remaining parcels. A strangely-shaped one turned out to be a DVD about the history of West Ham Football Club and a large bag of popcorn.

VICTIM STATEMENTS

'I thought we could watch it this evening,' Dad said. 'We could pretend we're at the cinema.'

'We've got choc-ices in the freezer,' Mum added, 'for half-time.'

'Go on! What about the rest?' Dad reminded him.

Leo returned to the task of present-opening. He unwrapped a CD of gospel music from Aunty Beatrice: not much good, but better than the slim paperback that she'd sent last year. It had been intended to help him after Harry's death, but he hadn't been so much interested in whether Harry was in heaven as when Mum was going to get back to normal.

Aunty Michelle had sent a bar of Fairtrade chocolate and Aunty Susan's gift was a bottle of aftershave, "because you're a young man now". Finally, there was a long thin package with no label on it.

'Chrissie brought that round,' Mum explained. 'She said her husband made it – you know! PC Hughes.'

Leo tore open the wrapping paper and some pieces of wood fell out. There were some scraps of thin material too: pale blue and dark purply red – West Ham colours! He stared round at Mum and Dad. 'What is it?'

'It's a kite!' Dad picked up the wooden rods and started fitting them into pockets in the fabric. 'See! This is how it goes together. I used to have one when I was a kid. I can't think why we never got one for you before.'

'Chrissie says Shotover Hill is a good place to fly it,' Mum added. 'She said they used to take their Kenny up there when he was your age.'

VICTIM STATEMENTS

'It's very nice of them,' Leo mumbled, hoping that they wouldn't insist on a kite-flying expedition. What if his mates saw him with it? It was the sort of thing only little kids did. 'I'll take these upstairs,' he added, gathering up all the presents in his arms. 'Thanks Mum – Dad.'

At lunch time, Mum made sandwiches and opened a bag of crisps. They pulled crackers, which Dad had saved from Christmas, and wore the paper hats from inside them. Then, Mum told him to close his eyes and Leo waited while she moved around behind him. There was the sound of a match being struck. Then her footsteps on the tiles of the kitchen floor as she returned to the table.

BIRTH AND DEATH

'OK!' she called, 'you can open them now!'

It was a cake – a big round one, orange with thin black stripes like his basketball, but in place of the manufacturer's name it said, in black lettering, *Happy Birthday Leo*. Round the edge a circle of candles burned.

'Mum! That's great! Did you make it?'

The candles flickered as his breath passed over them. Mum nodded. 'Yes. Do you like it? It was Chrissie's idea. She asked what you were interested in, and I told her you were into basketball, and she came up with this.'

They sang *Happy Birthday*, just like when Harry was alive, and then Leo blew out his candles. He was too old to believe in making wishes, but he made a secret one anyway – just in case! Please keep

Mum like this forever. Don't let her start drinking again – ever!

The telephone rang just as Mum was cutting the cake. 'I'll get that,' said Dad, getting up. 'It's probably just a cold-caller. That's all we seem to get on the landline, these days.'

He went into the hall, closing the door behind him. They could hear the rumble of his voice as they ate their cake. It must be more than an automated message claiming that their Amazon Prime subscription had just been renewed.

'February!' He sounded angry now, but then his voice dropped to a murmur again. Leo strained to hear what he was saying, but it was too indistinct. Something about *a disgrace* and *a mockery*, but nothing to explain what it was that Dad was angry about. Then there was a click as he put the phone down. Seconds later, he was storming back into the kitchen.

'They've cancelled the trial again!' he raged.

'Cancelled it?' quavered Mum.

'Postponed it then – to 9th February!'

'February? But it was supposed to be next week. I've arranged for time off in case I have to be there in the morning before my shift's over.'

'You'll have to ask them to move it.'

'But why? I mean, why have they changed it?'

'They *said* the judge was ill,' Dad shrugged. 'Just can't be bothered more like! I don't think they *want* to have it. It's only a black boy been killed, after all!'

'It's Kenny Hughes too,' Mum pointed out nervously. 'I mean, they'd want to prosecute someone who killed a police officer, wouldn't they?'

VICTIM STATEMENTS

'Then why can't they get on with it and get it over with?' demanded Dad.

Leo finished his cake in silence and then slipped away into the garden. He found his basketball and practised dribbling it around the paved path that surrounded the small lawn. A few minutes later, Dad came out.

'Come along Leo!' he called. 'I'll drive you over to Shotover Hill and we'll have a go with that kite of yours!'

Yvonne watched them go from behind the Christmas tree with a feeling of relief. Trev was frightening in this mood: frustrated and angry but with nobody to take it out on. Perhaps an afternoon in the open air with Leo would calm him down. Leo looked scared as well. He

670

must find all this chopping and changing of dates unsettling too. What a pity the call had come through on his birthday and spoiled it for him.

She went back into the kitchen and began clearing away the debris from their birthday lunch. She put the remains of the cake into a tin to keep it fresh, and began washing up the plates and cutlery. 9th February! That made another four weeks to wait – another four weeks to worry about what she would say when she was called into the witness box. And it put off by four weeks the time when she would see Harry's killers sentenced to prison.

Chrissie Hughes must have had a telephone call too. How was she feeling about this new delay? Yvonne dried the last glass and put it away. Then she reached for her mobile phone and found Chrissie's name in her contacts list. It rang out for what felt like ages and then clicked through to voicemail. Chrissie must be busy. Maybe they were still eating their lunch.

Not knowing quite how it happened, she found herself in the bedroom, sitting on the end of the bed with her makeup bag on her lap. The liqueur miniatures were in there – down at the bottom, hidden beneath lipsticks and powder compacts. She had been forced to find a new hiding place, now that Trevor knew about the underwear drawer. She still hadn't touched them, even though there had been lots of times when Trevor was out and she could have had a little tipple to cheer herself up. It would be ungrateful to leave them languishing there for ever. Michelle had intended them for her to drink. She ought at least to try them!

20. CASE CLOSED

'Now Mr Scott-Urquhart, I'd just like to check that you understand that you are here voluntarily to answer questions in relation to the murder of Jane Turnbull in 1983.' Jonah gazed across the table at his interviewee, who looked calmly back.

'Yes,' he replied, 'I understand.'

'And you also understand that this interview is being recorded on video and may be used as evidence in future criminal proceedings?'

'Yes. I understand. I have nothing to hide. Ask away!'

'Good.' Jonah martialled his thoughts. 'Let's start with your car. You were unusual, as an undergraduate, in having a vehicle at your disposal when you were up at Oxford. Where did you keep it?'

'I could park it outside the shared house where I lived. That's why I chose not to take rooms in college.'

'And is that where it was on the Saturday of Eights Week 1983?'

'Yes. I imagine it was.'

'So, how did you get into the city for the Eights Week dinner? It's a good way from Headington, isn't it?'

'Not so far for a fit twenty-year-old. I will have walked. There's nowhere to park near college anyway.'

'So, you dressed yourself up in a penguin suit and fancy shirt – including those special cuff-links,' Andy Lepage intervened in a slightly mocking voice, 'and walked down Headington Hill to go to the dinner?'

'No.' There was contempt in Scott-Urquhart's voice. 'I was already down there for the rowing. I'd left my dinner jacket in college and I changed into it there.'

'In the rooms that Charles Rawlins and Gerald Leslie shared, by any chance?' asked Jonah.

'Yes. They let me keep some of my things there, so I didn't have to keep going back and forth to Headington.'

'In exchange for you letting them use your car?' suggested Andy.

'No. There was no agreement of that sort.'

'But they did sometimes borrow your car?' Jonah pressed him. 'Or, was the person who told us about that mistaken?'

'Yes, yes, Charles and Gerald did sometimes borrow it. What does it matter?'

'If it was used to transport a young woman's body from Lichfield College up to the woods on Shotover Hill on the night of Saturday 28th May 1983, then it matters a great deal,' Jonah told him.

'Are you suggesting that Charles or Gerald killed that woman? That's absurd!'

'Tell me about that evening,' Jonah urged. 'You were all at the dinner. What did you do after that?'

'We went for a few drinks at the Lamb and Flag.'

'The whole boat club or just you and a few friends?'

'We all went, but people started drifting away after a bit. I went back with Charles and Gerald to get changed, and I think we had a few more drinks there. Then I went home.'

'Quite a feat!' Andy commented. 'Walking all that way after … let's see now… a glass or two of wine with your dinner, then drinking in the pub till closing time, and then a few more drinks with good old Charles and Gerald.'

'I was a phenomenal drinker in those days – I could take it. Drink hardly used to affect me at all back then.'

'But your friend Charles says different.' Andy's voice had a touch of menace in it. 'He says you spent the night on their sofa.'

At this, Scott-Urquhart showed the first signs of nervousness. He looked from Andy to Jonah as if trying to gauge their reactions.

'That's not how I remember it,' he said at last, 'but it was a long time ago. I did sometimes doss down on their floor overnight, but I don't remember doing so after that Eights Week dinner.'

'Very well,' Jonah took over again. 'You went home, either on Saturday night or perhaps Sunday morning. When was the next time you saw your friends Charles and Gerald?'

'I don't know – Monday morning I should think – on the river. We went rowing every morning before breakfast.'

'Now, going back to your car,' Jonah suddenly switched tack, 'I've heard that your friend Charles had a double-bass. Did he ever use your car to transport it to places?'

'He may have done. Why do you want to know?'

'I just wondered. What model was it – the car, I mean?'

'A Ford Escort.'

'The saloon version or…?'

'No. It was an estate.'

'So, the double-bass must have fitted easily. What a useful friend you must have been for him!'

CASE CLOSED

'Look,' Scott-Urquhart glared across the table, 'what has any of this to do with this woman's death? Why do you keep harassing me? I've told you: I never saw her in my life and I don't know how she got hold of one of our cuff-links!'

'I'm just trying to get a feel for what things were like among boat club members back then,' Jonah replied smoothly. 'Thank you for being so patient. That's all for now. One of our uniformed officers will show you out.'

'What was all that about a double-bass?' demanded Andy, after PC Callum McLaughlin had led their interviewee away.

'Giles Kingman told me about it,' Jonah replied, smiling enigmatically. 'But when I asked our friend Charles about it, he got strangely agitated. I'm rather curious to know why.'

VICTIM STATEMENTS

'Perhaps he was just afraid you'd ask him to play something,' suggested Andy facetiously. 'I can't see what it has to do with Jane Turnbull's disappearance.'

'Don't you now?' Jonah was smiling more broadly now.

'I think I get it,' Bernie put in. 'Are you thinking that a small woman might fit inside a double-bass case?'

'Precisement!' Jonah declared, taking on the accent of fictional Belgian detective Hercule Poirot. 'Hastings, you display a perspicacity most remarkable!'

'So, let me get this straight,' Andy said slowly. 'You think that Gerald killed the victim and his friends helped him to conceal her body by putting it in the double-bass case and taking it up to Shotover Hill in Scott-Urquhart's car?'

'Yes, in a nutshell,' Jonah confirmed. 'Or at least, it could have been Charles or

Jeremy who killed her, or they may all have been responsible for her death. All we know is that Gerald must have been there when they buried her, so that his cuff-link somehow dropped into the grave with her, and Charles must have been involved because of the double-bass and Jeremy was the only one with a car to get her from Lichfield to Shotover.'

'But if they stick to their stories, we'll never get a conviction,' Andy sighed.

'No. So we'll have to try to persuade them to *change* their stories.' Jonah thought for a moment. 'Andy! I'd like you to go and pay Charles Rawlins a visit at home. Take Alice Ray with you – she could do with the experience. Show him Jane's photo again. See if you can't persuade him to tell us the truth. Meanwhile, I'm going to have another little chat with Professor Weldon, in case he can remember anything else about that night.'

'Can I get you some tea?' Mrs Rawlins asked politely as she led Andy upstairs to her husband's office. 'Or coffee, perhaps?'

'No thank you, Mrs Rawlins. We're fine. This won't take long. It's just a few i's that need dotting and t's that need crossing. We'll only be a few minutes.'

'If you're sure …?' They reached the landing and she led the way across it to a white-painted door, firmly closed. 'I'd better just check that he isn't in a videoconference,' she said in the low voice.

She opened the door quietly and peered round it cautiously. 'There's a police officer here to see you. Can he come in?'

Andy couldn't hear the reply, but it must have been in the affirmative because she threw open the door and gestured to him to go inside.

'I'll leave you to it,' she murmured, closing it behind him.

Andy stood gazing round at the room. To his right, there was a large desk under the window, with a computer and three monitors on it. Another wall was lined with filing cabinets. The wall opposite the desk was adorned with three expensive-looking pictures, interspersed with photographs of a younger Mrs Rawlins with a horse. To the right of the desk, standing up in a corner of the room, there was a double-bass! Its bow hung on one of the tuning pegs, suggesting that the instrument had only recently been in use.

VICTIM STATEMENTS

'Take a seat, officers!' Charles said genially. 'To what do I owe the pleasure?'

'We'd like to have another chat about the night of the Eights Week dinner, back in 1983,' Andy told him. 'We've been speaking to a few other members of the boat club and we just want to get everything clear in our minds.'

'It's a long time ago,' Charles protested mildly. 'If there are discrepancies it's only to be expected. Was there anything in particular you wanted to know about?'

'We now have reason to believe that one of your friends, Gerald Leslie, lost one of his cuff-links that night,' Andy told him. 'There seems to be agreement among all the people we've talked to that he had them on when you were all in the pub after dinner. So, we're wondering if you could throw any light on how it came to go missing after that.'

'You really think I can remember a missing cuff-link after all this time?' Charles asked in a tone of mild derision. 'As I told your superior, Gerald and I went back to our rooms, had another few drinks and then went to bed. He must've dropped a cuff-link on the way – and presumably that woman you keep harping on about picked it up.'

'We don't think so,' Alice put in. 'We have reason to believe that Jane Turnbull was in your rooms with one or both of you that night. She was seen out in the streets at just the time when you would have been returning from your pub crawl. Do you deny that one of you invited her back with you?'

'Yes, of course I-,' Charles began. Then he stopped short and appeared to be thinking. 'Can I have another look at that photograph?'

Alice promptly took out a copy from her pocket and handed it to him. He stared down at it.

'Yes, I suppose that might be her,' he murmured. 'She looked different that night. She had a big bruise on her face – here!' He put his hand up to his own right cheekbone. 'And she was holding one arm as if it hurt her. She was in a hurry and not looking where she was going. She bumped into us. Gerald asked her what had happened to her and she said her boyfriend had hit her. Gerald was all for going round to their house and teaching him a lesson, but she said "no" she just wanted to get away from him. Gerald insisted on taking her back to our rooms with us.'

CASE CLOSED

'And how long did she stay?' asked Andy.

'I don't know exactly. Like I said before, we'd all been drinking and we had more when we got back. I think Gerald took her into his room with him, but I'm not sure. It's all very hazy – you know how it is. All I know is, she was gone by the morning. The last I saw of her, she was very much alive and giggling over some sort of joke Gerald had made.'

'Are you saying that Gerald may have *given* her the cuff-link that night?' asked Alice.

'Perhaps,' Charles shrugged, 'or maybe it just came off and got caught in her clothes or something. I'm just telling you what I remember. I didn't see her after Gerald took her into his room, promising her a good time. I went to bed at that point and woke up with the mother of all hangovers in the morning – by which time she was gone.'

'He could be telling the truth,' Jonah murmured, when Andy related this conversation to him on his return from Surrey. 'However, I doubt it. He's trying to pin everything on Gerald, because *he* can't challenge his version of events; but there's no way one person on their own could have got a body up Shotover Hill – even assuming that they had the use of a car.'

'And how could he even have got the body *to* the car?' Bernie agreed. 'From any of the student rooms, he'd have had to carry it across the quad and someone could easily have looked out of a window and seen him doing it.'

CASE CLOSED

'Yes, of course!' Jonah shouted. 'Yes. You're right. And who do we know with rooms in college who was up and about that night? Time to talk to Professor Weldon again, methinks!'

He punched buttons on the keypad on the arm of his chair and soon they all heard the ringing tone sounding out from the mobile phone attachment.

'Hello? Inspector Porter?'

'Professor Weldon! Do you have a few minutes? I just have a few more questions about your friends from the boat club.'

'Fire away. Always happy to help.' Weldon spoke cheerfully, sounding less tired than last time they had spoken.

'Do you happen to remember Charles Rawlins having a double-bass?'

'Come to think of it – yes, I think he did. Why?'

'You don't by any chance remember what sort of case he had for it?'

'No, I'm not sure I ever saw it. Is it important?'

'Probably not. Now, cast your mind back to 1983. Is there anything else – anything at all – that you remember about the Saturday night of Eights Week – or the Sunday morning?'

'No. I've told you everything I could remember already.'

'Are you sure? I'm not asking about what you and your friends did. I'm interested in any unusual occurrences at all: things that went bump in the night, voices in the quad in the early hours, anything at all out of the ordinary.'

'The quad...?' Weldon went silent, apparently thinking. Jonah waited patiently for him to go on. 'There was something funny went on that year –

probably a Sunday, but I couldn't be sure it was that week. I had rooms in Overton quad that year. I looked out of the window and there were Charles and Gerald carrying the double bass in its case! It was you mentioning the double-bass that reminded me.'

'And that was strange because…?' Jonah prompted him.

'It was so early in the morning – before breakfast. They seemed to be struggling to lift it. They looked the worse for wear, so they'd probably had a heavy night of drinking, which fits with it being a Sunday. Any other day they'd have been heading for the river – and I'd have been going there too.'

'Excellent!' Jonah purred. 'And were they alone, do you know? Or was anyone else with them?'

VICTIM STATEMENTS

'Let me…yes! Jeremy was with them. I can see him now! He seemed annoyed with them about something. He kept getting ahead of them and then coming back to chivvy them along. It was rather comical – like an old Laurel and Hardy sketch.'

'Where did they take it?'

'I don't know. They went through the cloisters, as if they were taking it to breakfast in hall, but obviously, once they were inside the building, I couldn't see which way they went.'

'So, they could've been making for the kitchen door out into the gardens and then to the road?' Jonah asked eagerly.

'Yes. They could have been,' Weldon confirmed. 'In fact, I think they must have done that, because, if they'd been at breakfast, I'd probably have asked them what they were up to.'

'And this could all have taken place the day after the Eights Week dinner?'

''I *could*, but it may have been at a different time altogether. So, don't expect me to stand up in the witness box and swear that was when it was.'

'Understood,' Jonah nodded. 'But it was definitely that year? Could you pin it down to Trinity term?'

'It was definitely the 1982-83 academic year, because that was the only year I had a room in Overton quad. I can't say for certain that it was Trinity Term – sorry!'

'Not to worry!' Jonah assured him cheerfully. 'You've been a great help all the same.'

He ended the call and turned to look at Andy and Bernie. 'I'm pretty sure I know what happened. The only question is whether we have any chance at all of proving it. Andy! I want both of our friends Jeremy and Charles brought in for questioning under caution. Let's see if we can catch them out in a lie and force the truth out of them.'

'Now, Mr Rawlins,' Jonah said for the tenth time, 'will you please consider your position carefully. 'You have admitted that you and your friends took a young woman back to your rooms on the night of Saturday 28th May 1983, and that it was probably Jane Turnbull, who went missing that same evening. We have a witness who saw you and your two friends carrying a heavy double-bass case across Overton Quad, from your rooms the following morning. In my mind, it is obvious what was in that case.'

CASE CLOSED

'My double-bass, of course,' Charles replied, glancing nervously towards his solicitor, who sat silently next to him in the interview room. 'It's a heavy instrument.'

'So heavy that two fit young men struggled to lug it across the quad?' enquired Jonah sceptically. 'I've had my officers experimenting. We've got hold of a full-size double-bass and a nice strong carrying case to fit it. Any of my officers can carry it across our car park single-handed. The whole lot only comes to about 30 kilos.'

'I don't know!' Charles was becoming flustered now. 'I don't even remember this. Your witness has probably got it all wrong.'

'My client is not obliged to answer any of these questions,' the lawyer pointed out stiffly. 'It is my opinion that you are on a fishing trip, because you lack any evidence to substantiate your accusations.'

'OK then,' Jonah conceded. 'Let's admit that it's going to be difficult to prove what happened after all this time. So, now I'm appealing to your client's better nature.' He turned to address Charles, making eye-contact before continuing. 'Mr Rawlins, we have the remains of a young woman. Her family have been grieving her disappearance for nearly forty years. Her parents died without ever knowing what became of their daughter. Her sister is anxious to know how she died. In the name of humanity, show some compassion and tell us what happened that night.'

A flicker of something crossed Charles' face – was it remorse? Regret? Sadness perhaps? Then it was gone. With another rapid glance towards his solicitor, he said impassively, 'no comment.'

In the next interview room, Andy and Alice were faring little better with Jeremy Scott-Urquhart. He, too was well-aware that silence was his best policy when it came to questions about what had happened on that fateful night in 1983. Andy decided to ramp up the pressure.

'Look Mr Scott-Urquhart,' he said, leaning forward in his seat (but taking care not to come closer than the statutory two metres), 'we know that Jane Turnbull was with you and your friends that night. We know that, after she entered Lichfield College that evening, she was never seen again. It is quite clear to me that something happened to her while she was there, and I'm asking you to fill me in on what it was.'

'I can't help you, I'm afraid. All I can say is that any woman who may have been in those rooms that night was still alive and well when I left to go back to my lodgings. If things got out of hand after that, it's nothing to do with me.'

'Your friend Charles remembers it differently,' Andy told him. 'He says that you stayed in their rooms overnight.'

'Then he's remembering it wrong,' Jeremy insisted. 'Whatever happened was nothing to do with me.'

'So, you admit that something happened?'

'I don't *admit* anything. I'm just saying that, whatever Charles and Gerald may have got up to, I wasn't involved.'

'Oh, but you were,' Andy said, putting as much menace into his voice as he could. 'Because the dead woman's body couldn't get up to Shotover Hill without some sort of transport – and we believe that she made that journey in your car.'

'What a vivid imagination you have, sergeant!' Jeremy replied, but Andy could see that his armour was slipping. This was a last-ditch attempt to remain detached and scornful of the accusations against him. He hurried to press home his advantage.

'It's not my imagination,' he replied calmly, 'it's evidence. We have a witness who saw you helping your friends to carry a double-bass case from their rooms to your car the morning after the victim disappeared, and we have reason to believe that it contained her body – or were you all just taking the bass for a joy-ride?' he finished, sarcastically. 'Perhaps stringed instruments enjoy an early morning trip into the countryside! What do you think?'

'I – I – I don't know what you're talking about!'

'Ah, but I think you do.' Andy felt in his bones that this suspect was about to give in – if only the solicitor didn't intervene and persuade him to remain silent. 'You may not have had a hand in killing her, but I'm quite sure you helped with hiding her body afterwards.'

'No!' Jeremy yelped. Then he looked round in confusion, as if he didn't know where the sound had come from. 'I mean – yes, you're right. I *did* go back to my lodgings that night, like I said, but Charles rang me the next morning – quite early – all in a flap, saying that the girl had died in her sleep. He was convinced that the police would think that they'd killed her somehow – and anyway, it was against college rules to have a woman in their rooms overnight, and they would both be sent down. I agreed to come with the car and see what I could do.'

'Good,' Andy leaned back in his chair and smiled in satisfaction. 'Now we're getting somewhere. Tell me what you did then.'

Jeremy took a deep breath and then let it out in a long sigh. He glanced apologetically towards his solicitor, who nodded back at him. Then he turned back to Andy.

'I parked the car in Goose Lane. There's a gate from there into the college gardens. Gerald met me there – you can only open the gate from the inside. He was in a right state, gibbering about waking up and finding her lying dead in the bed next to him. He kept saying over and over again, "I never touched her. I never touched her." I couldn't make out what he was going on about, except that this woman that he'd befriended was there, in their rooms, dead.'

'What exactly do you mean, *befriended*?' asked Alice coldly.

Jeremy looked at her for the first time. He appeared to be studying her face and did not answer for perhaps ten seconds.

'We stumbled across her on the way back from the pub,' he answered at last. 'Literally. She wandered out of a side street and Gerald crashed into her. She was crying and the side of her face was all swollen and bleeding. Gerald fancied himself as a knight in shining armour and he insisted on bringing her back to their rooms to look after her. We'd all had a skinful and it seemed like the gentlemanly thing to do at the time.'

CASE CLOSED

'You found a vulnerable young woman in distress in the streets and you thought the *gentlemanly* thing to do was to take her back to your rooms?' Alice exclaimed scornfully. 'I suppose you thought she needed a good seeing to, to cheer her up!'

Andy shot a warning look at his colleague, cutting in calmly with another question. 'Did she say how these injuries had happened?'

'Eventually. She told us her boyfriend had hit her. She said she was on her way back to her parents, but she'd missed her last bus. Gerald said she could sleep on their sofa and then get a bus home in the morning. I do honestly think he was trying to help her – whatever happened after that.'

'And what did happen?' asked Andy.

VICTIM STATEMENTS

'To be quite honest, I don't remember much about that night,' Jeremy confessed. 'We'd all had a lot to drink and Charles insisted on opening a bottle of wine after we got back to college. I must have managed to stay upright long enough to walk back home or I couldn't have got that telephone call, could I? But I don't remember anything about it. I just remember Gerald bending over the girl dabbing her face with a wet handkerchief, and Charles saying she must have some brandy because it was good for shock. Oh yes! And she said she mustn't have too much to drink because she hadn't had any dinner.'

'So, going back to that Sunday morning,' Andy prompted. 'What happened after Gerald let you into the garden?'

CASE CLOSED

'We went through to his rooms and, sure enough, there was the girl lying dead on the sofa. They'd carried her there from Gerald's room and put a blanket over her, but I looked under it and there she was. She looked awful!' He shivered at the recollection. 'Her face was cold and stiff and she was a funny grey colour. I could see at once she was dead.'

'Why didn't you call the police?' demanded Alice. 'Or an ambulance?'

'We were scared. Nothing like this had ever happened to us before. Gerald was in tears and Charles wasn't much better. They were convinced that people would think they'd killed her.'

'Didn't it occur to you that they may have done?' Alice asked icily.

'Not for one moment! You must believe me! I knew them!'

'Never mind about that.' Andy threw Alice another warning glance. 'Tell us what you did next.'

'We decided that we needed to get the body out of college, so nobody would know she'd spent the night there. We wrapped it in a blanket, but Charles was afraid we might be seen carrying it out to the car. Then we hit on the idea of putting it in his double-bass case. She was only a tiny thing and we managed to squeeze her into it.'

'Her body wasn't stiff then?' Alice asked. 'You could bend it to fit the case?'

'It was stiff in places. Her face felt hard, like I said, and I remember having a bit of trouble bending her elbows, but no, rigor mortis hadn't set in, if that's what you're asking.' He turned back to Andy. 'That's about it, really. We carried the case out to the car and drove up to

Shotover and dumped the body in the woods there. We thought it'd be found soon enough and people would assume that she'd had a heart attack while she was walking out there or something. We never thought it would be so long before...'

'I see.' Andy sat for a few moments studying his face. Then he shook himself, as if coming to a decision. 'Right then, Mr Scott-Urquhart. I think that's all for now. An officer will escort you back to the cells while DC Ray puts what you've just said into a written statement, which you'll be asked to check and then sign. You can show it to your lawyer before you do so, if you like.'

'And then, will my client be free to go?' enquired the solicitor.

'That will be up to the Senior Investigating Officer,' Andy told him. 'He may have more questions to ask.'

When Andy poked his head round the door of Interview Room 2, he saw that Jonah was still battling to break Charles Rawlins' silence and being thwarted at every turn by sulky "no comment" responses to his questions.

'Sir?' he called out quietly. 'Can I have a word?'

Jonah turned his chair round and glided silently out into the corridor, leaving Bernie facing the stubborn Rawlins across the table.

'What is it?' he asked in a low voice, as soon as the door closed behind him.

'Scott-Urquhart has admitted taking the body up to Shotover in his car and hiding it there,' Andy whispered back. 'He says they met her on their way back to college that night, took her back to their rooms and plied her with drink. He claims she died in her sleep and Rawlins rang him at his lodgings to ask him to bring the car down. I don't know how much of it to believe, but...'

'But that'll certainly put the pressure on our friend Charles,' Jonah nodded. 'Good work, Andy!'

It didn't take very long for Charles' resistance to crumble after that. With his friend having confessed to moving the body, it was impossible to maintain his silence. After conferring briefly with his lawyer (who presumably advised him that a continued refusal to answer questions might be interpreted by a jury as a sign of guilt) he admitted that Jane Turnbull had stayed the night in their college rooms. He continued to maintain that Jeremy had also been there all night, and he insisted that the plan to hide the body rather than reporting the death to the authorities was his. Whether these discrepancies were attributable to honest differences in remembrance or to deliberate lying, who could tell?

'And finally,' Jonah said, looking his interviewee straight in the eye, 'can you remember what you were each wearing that morning?'

'No.'

'Gerald wasn't still wearing his dress shirt with the cuff-links?' Jonah suggested.

'No, of course not! He was in his pyjamas when he found the girl was dead. And then he just grabbed whatever clothes he could find. Jeans and a tee-shirt, I should think.'

'And what was she wearing? Had she got undressed to go to bed?'

'No.' Charles paused and seemed to be thinking. 'No. She was still fully-dressed. I think she must have passed out as soon as she got into Gerald's room. She was looking pretty grim by that time, I have to admit. I don't think she was used to drinking that much wine.'

'And Gerald's shirt, with the cuff-links, did you happen to notice it that morning? Was it in his room when you went in to see the dead woman?'

Unexpectedly, Charles put his head back and laughed. 'You're still banging on about that cuff link, are you? Shall I tell you what really happened to it?'

'Yes please,' Jonah replied politely, as if he were accepting the offer of a biscuit with his coffee. 'If you'd be so kind.'

'The stupid bint swallowed it! It somehow dropped into her wine glass while Gerald was pouring some for her and she just gulped it down! She coughed a bit – choking – and then she took another swig and down it went! Gerald only realised when it was too late. I can see his face now, staring as if he couldn't believe what had happened and shouting out, "you've drunk my cuff-link!" all indignant.'

After several hours of interrogation, Jonah allowed them both to return home.

'OK Andy, I'll leave you to prepare the file for the CPS,' he said as they made their way out to the car park. 'Go home and get some rest and then get on to that first thing tomorrow.'

CASE CLOSED

'Right you are, Sir. What do you think will happen to them? There's no chance of a murder charge sticking, is there?'

'Not a snowflake's chance in Hell,' Jonah agreed. 'Preventing a Lawful and Decent Burial, Obstructing the Coroner, maybe Perverting the Course of Justice, but probably not. They'll probably get suspended sentences and nothing much will change for them. I can't see Jane's family feeling they've got justice for her.'

'I suppose they'll have to admit it wasn't the boyfriend who did it, now,' Andy suggested hopefully. 'Maybe it'll do *him* some good being vindicated at last.'

'Too late for that.' Jonah shook his head gloomily. 'The damage has already been done. Who knows how he would have turned out if he hadn't had all that suspicion hanging over him all his life? And that's what those two don't appreciate,' he added, jerking his head in the direction of the police car in which Jeremy Scott-Urquhart was sitting, waiting to be driven back to his luxurious cottage, so different from the cramped and untidy flat in Reading where they had interviewed Adrian Chivers. 'They still think that all they did was to conceal the fact that a woman died in their rooms – most likely from alcohol poisoning after they plied her with drink on an empty stomach. They don't realise the impact that covering that up has had on other people.'

21. JUSTICE?

'From an early age, Kenny knew what he wanted to be when he grew up.' Chrissie's voice cracked as her mouth suddenly became very dry. She bent down and picked up the bottle of water that she had left on her seat when she rose to address the court. 'I'm sorry,' she mumbled, looking anxiously up at the judge as she took a deep draught.

'Please, Mrs Hughes, take your time. These gentlemen aren't going anywhere.' The judge was a woman of indeterminate age with wisps of hair peeping out from beneath her wig, steely grey to match the steely expression with which she glared at the Butler gang sitting, well-spaced-apart at the side of the court. She looked down benignly on Chrissie and smiled kindly. 'Take a few deep breaths and start again when you're ready.'

'From an early age, Kenny knew what he wanted to be when he grew up,' Chrissie resumed, reading carefully from the paper that she held in her left hand, while still clutching the water bottle in her right. 'He wanted to follow his father into the police force. I remember how proud he was the day he wore his police cadet uniform for the first time. He always wanted to help other people – particularly young people.'

Chrissie paused and took another mouthful from the water bottle.

'The day he died was just a normal day on duty. He was working with a young trainee constable. Their job was to guard the back entrance of a house where cannabis was being grown, while other officers raided the premises through the front door. They had just apprehended a boy who had run out of the house, when it all happened. As PC Gilbert described so well, here in court last week, Kenny gave her the opportunity to make her very first arrest. She was busy handcuffing the boy when a car came speeding towards them. Kenny's first thought was to save his young colleague and the boy whom she was arresting. He pushed them out of the way of the vehicle, with the result that he was himself crushed by it.'

In the silence that followed this dramatic account, Chrissie became aware of the sound of her own breathing and her heart seemed to be pounding far harder than normal. She closed her eyes and took in a slow, deep breath before continuing.

VICTIM STATEMENTS

'This was just before Christmas in 2019. Everyone else was putting up decorations, buying presents and going to parties. We were taking our decorations down, giving away the presents we'd got for Kenny and waiting and waiting to hear that the man who'd killed him had been found.'

For the first time, Chrissie raised her eyes from her prepared statement and looked towards Shane Butler, sitting handcuffed to a man in uniform. He stared back at her with deep-set brown eyes beneath thick black brows. His expression did not show any hint of remorse. He looked bored, as if he was impatient for the proceedings to be over. Chrissie hurriedly turned her attention back to the judge.

'Thanks to the hard work of DCI Jonah Porter and his team, and to Craig

Manson and members of the Oxford homeless community, who provided the evidence they needed to bring a prosecution, this man *was* found. I hope that this means that he will never put any other family through what we have been forced to endure.'

She reached the foot of the first page and moved it to the bottom of the sheaf of papers in her hand.

'At this point, it would be natural to enumerate all Kenny's good qualities and to tell you all how much society has lost by his early death. I could talk about the work he did with the scouts, about all the young people that benefitted from his help and encouragement with the Duke of Edinburgh Award scheme, about the half marathons that he ran for charity. I could tell you how brave, intelligent and kind he was.'

VICTIM STATEMENTS

Chrissie paused and looked round the court, first at the judge, then at the four members of the Butler gang, and finally up at the public gallery and the video camera that was relaying the proceedings to journalists in the next room. Gavin was up there, sitting with Craig and Stella. He was staring straight ahead and refused to meet her gaze. Craig, however, smiled down at her and raised his hand in a thumbs-up gesture.

'But, while I'm proud of the young man that my son grew up to be, that's irrelevant in considering the enormity of the crime that was committed when he was smashed against a brick wall and left to die,' she resumed, speaking faster and more passionately now. 'I've worked all my life with children that a lot of people considered worthless because they couldn't do the things that Kenny did. For some of them, learning to write their own name was as hard as running a marathon. Very few of them could aspire to joining the police service. People sometimes write them off and think they'll never achieve anything. And yet every single one of them – just like Kenny – is unique and special and valuable.'

She paused dramatically and looked directly into the judge's eyes. 'So, Your Honour, in passing sentence on Mr Butler and his associates, I would ask you to remember that the value of a young life cannot be measured by what they have done or what they might have done if they had lived, and that every death leaves an unfillable hole in the lives of those left behind.'

'Thank you, Mrs Hughes,' the judge smiled down kindly. 'That was very eloquently put. And now I believe you have another statement to read out?'

'Yes.' Chrissie looked round nervously at the public gallery. Yvonne Whittle was there, sitting next to Trevor on the front row. 'Mrs Whittle has asked me to read out her statement for her.'

'In your own time then, proceed.'

Chrissie moved another piece of paper to the bottom of the pile and stood for a moment staring down at the first page of the document that she had helped Yvonne to write. She glanced nervously up at the public gallery again. Yvonne's eyes were lowered as if she could not bear to watch. Trevor was staring straight ahead. Would he approve of what she was about to read out? Had Yvonne showed it to him, as she had promised she would? Chrissie cleared her throat and began to read, slow and stilted at first and then with more animation, trying to express the feelings that she had seen in her friend as they chose the words to express her grief.

'When he was eight years old, Harry brought home a mug that he had painted at school. It was a present for me for Mother's Day. There were flowers on the front and round the back he'd painted the words "For Mum" and three kisses. I still have that mug. The flowers have all worn off now, but I can still read, on the back, "For Mum" in bright red letters, and see those three kisses. I cry every time I see it, because it reminds me of my beautiful son.'

Chrissie stopped for another draught of water and a quick glance towards the gallery. Her heart soared as she saw that Trevor had put his arm around his wife's shoulders. They had been so worried that he might have been angry at hearing her feelings put into words and read out in public.

'Harry wasn't ever top of his class at school. He didn't win prizes or break records. He was just an ordinary boy, like lots of others. When he left school, he wanted to make his own way in life. He wanted a job. He wanted to earn money and be independent. A man that he thought was his friend offered to pay him to look after some plants. He said he would teach Harry horticulture. Harry thought he was being kind.'

Chrissie looked towards Terence Butler, the leader of the drug-dealing gang. With the black beard which normally dominated his features covered by a face mask, there was a clear family resemblance with his younger brother,

Shane. He stared back at her impassively.

'By the time Harry realised that there might be something wrong with the business that he had got drawn into, he was too deeply involved to be able to get out. He was scared of the Butler brothers and the thugs that they employed, and scared of being sent to jail if he was caught by the police. So, he just kept on working for them and bottling up his worries, because he was afraid of what would happen to him if he told anyone about them. He didn't even dare to talk to me or his dad, he was so scared.'

Chrissie moved the top paper to the bottom and stood for a moment studying the words on the next page. Then she looked up at the judge again.

'He never meant to do anything wrong,' she continued, trying to put into her voice the earnestness with which Yvonne had emphasised these words to her. 'All he ever wanted was to earn money so that he could save up and start out in life on his own. He was only sixteen years old. He had never done drugs. He was very naïve and he trusted people. And,' Chrissie continued, fixing the Butler brothers with her hardest stare, usually reserved for the most egregious behaviour of the most wayward members of her class and speaking slowly and deliberately, '**he *never* grassed up the men who tricked him into breaking the law.**'

She waited for this statement to sink in before continuing, 'so, even by their low standards, there was never any reason to end his life in the dreadful way that they did. He was just a boy, although he was trying to be a man. He was an important member of our family, and we all – myself, his dad and his brother Leo – miss him more than we can ever say. I think about him every day. Sometimes I struggle to get out of bed in the morning, because the weight of missing him holds me down and I'm tempted to turn over and close my eyes and shut out the world. I feel that I have failed as a mother. I should have protected my son from men like these. I should have asked more questions about his job. I should have checked up on who he was working for.'

Chrissie stopped, lowered the sheaf of papers and looked up at the judge again. 'These are Mrs Whittle's words,' she said in a low voice, 'not mine.'

'Yes,' the judge nodded. 'I understand. Carry on.'

'But I know that I have to get up and get on with my life as best I can,' Chrissie resumed, reading the words carefully. 'I have to do it for the sake of my husband and my one remaining child. I worry about Leo, in case he falls into the hands of people like this too. I'm grateful to the police for catching Harry's killers and I hope that they will be stopped from ruining the lives of any more families in the future.'

Chrissie folded the papers in her hands to indicate that she had finished and stood with eyes lowered waiting.

'Thank you, Mrs Hughes,' the judge said kindly. 'Perhaps you would like to join your husband in the public gallery now.'

There was a low murmur of talking among the watchers in the gallery as Chrissie made her way up to join them. The judge sat in silence making notes with a fountain pen. Then she looked up to check that Chrissie was back in her place and nodded to an usher, who called for silence.

The sentencing took a lot longer than Chrissie had expected. There were multiple offences to be taken into account: causing death by dangerous driving, failing to stop and report an accident, perverting the course of justice, numerous drug-related offences and, of course, murder. The murder of Harry Whittle, that is. The jury had concluded that there was insufficient proof of Shane Butler's intention to kill to justify a guilty verdict in the case of Kenny's death.

Chrissie found her mind – and her eyes – wandering as she listened to details of terms of imprisonment for each offence and each offender. Looking across at Yvonne, she saw that she, too, seemed to be finding it hard to concentrate on the judge's words. Then suddenly it was all over and a court official was calling out, 'Be uprising!' as the judge stood up and walked out of the court.

Chrissie looked at Gavin in bewilderment as they scrambled to their feet. Was that it then? Was this the end of it all?

'Eleven years for causing death by dangerous driving is quite steep,' she heard Jonah saying to Peter and Bernie, 'when you consider he pleaded guilty. I reckon the judge didn't really agree with the jury letting him off that murder charge.'

'He got life for Harry's murder anyway,' Peter pointed out, 'so the other sentences are pretty academic really.'

'More a matter of sending out the right signals to the public,' Jonah agreed. 'Of course, if the jury had brought in a guilty verdict for Kenny's murder, it would have changed everything. Shane Butler would have been looking at a whole life order for killing a police officer in the course of his duty.'

'Thirty-two years minimum, isn't that far short of a whole life order,' Bernie observed. 'He must be about forty, so he'll be in his seventies before there's any chance of release.'

'Hold on there!' Peter protested. 'That's my age. I don't like the idea that you're writing me off as over-the-hill. I'm looking forward to a good few more years yet!'

'Excuse me.' Yvonne had sidled up to them and was looking anxiously towards Jonah. 'Can you tell me exactly what that all means? Are those men all going to prison?'

VICTIM STATEMENTS

'Yes,' Jonah told her. 'They've all got life sentences, which means that, even if they're released – and that won't be for years and years – they'll always only be out on licence and they can be sent back if they break any of the conditions. And Terry Butler's wife has been given life for perverting the course of justice, because she provided an elaborate alibi for her husband and brother-in-law. She was just as guilty of killing Harry as the others, even though she wasn't even there at the time.'

'There you are!' Trevor broke in. 'What did I tell you? They're all being put away. You don't need to worry about meeting them in the street any longer.'

'Yes,' Yvonne murmured. 'That's good. But somehow it feels...'

'Yes,' agreed Chrissie. 'It's all a bit of an anti-climax, isn't it? This is supposed

JUSTICE?

to make us feel better, but I'm not sure it does really.'

A court official appeared and began ushering them out, apologising for the need to hurry, to allow time for cleaning the public gallery ready for the next hearing. As they stepped out into the cold of the freezing February air to resume their normal lives, the mechanism of criminal justice continued relentlessly on its way.

THANK YOU

Thank you for taking the time to read Victim Statements. If you enjoyed it, please consider telling your friends or posting a short review. Word of mouth is an author's best friend and much appreciated. Thank you,

Judy

ACKNOWLEDGEMENTS

I would like to thank many Facebook friends, especially those from the *Pesky Methodist* group, for commenting on ideas for developing this book. Liz Parkinson's comments on some draft sections were particularly valuable.

I am grateful to Gillian Gilbert for reading the manuscript, giving helpful comments and pointing out typographical errors.

I am grateful to *Support After Murder and Manslaughter* (https://samm.org.uk/) for giving their permission for me to dedicate this book to them and their work with families bereaved through murder or manslaughter and for pointing me in the direction of the report *Review into the Needs of Families Bereaved by Homicide* by Louise Casey, which was invaluable in

ACKNOWLEDGEMENTS

understanding the added trauma that the criminal justice system may impose on such families when they are at their most vulnerable.

I am indebted to the authors of a wide range of internet resources, which I have used for researching the background to this book. In particular, personal stories from *Care for the Family* and *Police Care UK* provided insight into the varied experiences of families affected by injury or sudden death. Other online sources include:

- OpenStreetMap (https://www.openstreetmap.org/)
- Alcoholics Anonymous (www.alcoholics-anonymous.org.uk/)
- Behind Blue Lines (www.behindbluelines.co.uk/the-podcast/)

VICTIM STATEMENTS

- Thames Valley Police (www.thamesvalley.police.uk/)
- The Ministry of Justice (http://www.gov.uk/moj).

The FutureLearn course "Identifying the Dead", which I took in 2016, provided useful information about the work of forensic anthropologists in identifying human remains.

I consulted a number of publications during the writing, including:

Forensic Anthropology: A Comprehensive Introduction, Natalie R Langley and MariaTeresa A Tersigni-Tarrant (editors), Taylor & Francis Group 2017, ISBN 978-1-4987-3612-1

Treating PTSD: A Compassion-Focused CBT Approach, Shirley Porter, Routledge 2018, ISBN 978-1-138-30333-1

ACKNOWLEDGEMENTS

Understanding Victims of Interpersonal Violence: A Guide for Investigators and Prosecutors, Veronique N Valliere, Routledge 2020, ISBN 1-4987-8048-3

The Witness Charter, © Crown Copyright 2013, Produced by the Ministry of Justice.

Victim Personal Statements: A Review of Empirical Research, Julian V Roberts and Marie Menikis, Report for the Commissioner for Victims and Witnesses in England and Wales, 2011.

Every effort has been made to trace copyright holders. The publishers will be glad to rectify in future editions any errors or omissions brought to their attention.

DISCLAIMER

This book is a work of fiction. Any references to real people, events, establishments, organisations or locales are intended only to provide a sense of authenticity and are used fictitiously. All of the characters and events are entirely invented by the author. Any resemblances to persons living or dead are purely coincidental.

Many of the locations and institutions that feature in this book are real. Their inhabitants and employees, however, are purely fictional. In particular:

- You will search in vain for Chichester Road, Lewes Road or Arundel Road in Rose Hill;

- Lichfield, St Luke's and Holy Cross colleges are all fictitious and none of

DISCLAIMER

their members are based on real people at Oxford University or anywhere else;

- None of the police personnel are based on any officers from Thames Valley Police or any other police service;

- None of the hospital staff described here are based on real people, whether employees of the John Radcliffe Hospital or any other;

- The school where Chrissie Hughes works is imaginary as are the staff and students.

MORE ABOUT THE CHARACTERS IN THIS BOOK

This book is the third of a trilogy of stories about Gavin and Chrissie Hughes in the aftermath of the sudden death of their son, Kenny. The first in this series, **Weed Killers**, was published in 2020. The second, **Lost in Lockdown**, came out in Spring 2021.

Many of the characters in this book feature in the fourteen **Bernie Fazakerley Mysteries**:

1. **Two Little Dickie Birds**: a murder mystery for DI Peter Johns and his Sergeant, Paul Godwin.
2. **Murder of a Martian**: Peter and Jonah solve a double murder and Peter meets Martin Riess for the first time.

MORE ABOUT THE CHARACTERS

3. **Grave Offence**: Peter investigates an assault and a suspicious death, while Jonah is in rehab in the spinal injuries centre.

4. **Awayday**: a traditional detective story set among the dons of Lichfield College.

5. **Death on the Algarve:** a mystery for Bernie and her friends to tackle while on holiday in Portugal.

6. **Mystery over the Mersey**: a murder mystery set in Liverpool.

7. **Sorrowful Mystery**: Jonah investigates a child abduction and Peter embarks on a new journey of faith.

8. **In my Liverpool Home**: Bernie and her friends return to Liverpool to investigate a suspicious death in Aunty Dot's Care Home.

9. **Organ Failure**: a body is discovered under the organ in St Cyprian's Church and Jonah is called in to investigate.

10. **Rainbow Warrior**: One of their friends is injured in a hit-and-run incident and Jonah is convinced that this is attempted murder.

11. **Admission of Innocence**: Father Damien calls Peter and Jonah out of retirement to solve a murder case and prevent a miscarriage of justice.

12. **Lethal Mix**: Three of Lucy's student friends are injured in an anti-Muslim hate crime in Liverpool. Jonah, Peter and Bernie assist Merseyside Police to bring their attacker to justice.

13. **A Secret Gardener?** Bernie's friend Martin discovers a body in the Fellows' Garden of his Oxford College.

14. **Crowd of Witnesses**: Jonah decides to write his memoirs, beginning with a murder investigation from 1982.

Bernie Fazakerley, Peter Johns and Jonah Porter also appear in two other novels:

- **Changing Scenes of Life**: Jonah Porter's life story, told through the medium of his favourite hymns.

- **Despise not your Mother**: the story of Bernie's quest to learn about her first husband's past.

   And there's a book of short stories, in which Peter narrates his side of the story:

- **My Life of Crime**: the collected memoirs of DI Peter Johns. This includes some episodes that appear in other books, but told from a new

VICTIM STATEMENTS

perspective, as well as some completely new stories.

You can find all these books on Judy Ford's Amazon Author page:

www.amazon.co.uk/-/e/B0193I5B1M.

Visit the Bernie Fazakerley Publications Facebook page.

www.facebook.com/Bernie.Fazakerley.Publications

Follow Judy Ford on Twitter:

@JudyFordAuthor

You can find some of the recipes from this book on the Bernie Fazakerley Publications website:

https://sites.google.com/view/bernie-fazakerley

GLOSSARY OF UK POLICE RANKS

Uniformed police

Chief Constable (CC) – Has overall charge of a regional police force, such as Thames Valley Police, which covers Oxford and a large surrounding area.

Deputy Chief Constable (DCC) – The senior discipline authority for each force. 2nd in command to the CC.

Assistant Chief Constable (ACC) – 4 in the Thames Valley Police Service, each responsible for a policy area.

Chief Superintendent ('Chief Super') – Head of a policing area or department.

Police Superintendent – Responsible for a local area within a police force.

Chief Inspector (CI) – Responsible for overseeing a team in a local area.

VICTIM STATEMENTS

Police Inspector – Senior operational officer overseeing officers on duty 24/7.

Police Sergeant – Supervises a team of officers.

Police Constable (PC) – 'Bobby on the beat'. Likely to be the first to arrive in response to an emergency call.

Police Community Support Officer (PCSO) – A uniformed civilian member of the police service.

Crime Investigation Department (CID) – Plain clothes officers

Detective Superintendent (DS) – Responsible for crime investigation in a local area.

Detective Chief Inspector (DCI) – Responsible for overseeing a crime investigation team in a local area. May be

GLOSSARY OF UK POLICE RANKS

the Senior Investigating Officer heading up a criminal investigation.

Detective Inspector (DI) – Oversees crime investigation 24/7. May be the Senior Investigating Officer heading up a criminal investigation.

Detective Sergeant (DS) – Supervises a team of CID officers.

Detective Constable (DC) – One of a team of officers investigating crimes.

These descriptions are based on information from the following sources:
[1] Mental Health Cop blog, by Inspector Michael Brown, Mental Health co-ordinator, College of Policing. mentalhealthcop.wordpress.com/, accessed 31st March 2017.
[2] Thames Valley Police website, www.thamesvalley.police.uk, accessed 31st March 2017.

GLOSSARY OF OXFORD UNIVERSITY JARGON

This glossary is by no means exhaustive. A fuller list of Oxford terminology may be found on the University website.

Coming up – Arriving at Oxford at the beginning of term

Commemoration Week - the 9th week of Trinity Term, so called because of the events that take place to commemorate the benefactors of the university.

Commemoration ("commem") Balls – formal dances held by some of the Oxford colleges during Commemoration Week.

Eights – Intercollegiate rowing races.

Eights week – The week in Trinity Term when intercollegiate rowing races take place.

GLOSSARY OF OXFORD JARGON

Fellow – A member of staff holding a Fellowship at one of the colleges. Fellowships may be Tutorial (teaching) or Research.

Finals – Also known as "Schools". Both terms are abbreviations of "Final Honours School". These are the examinations taken by undergraduate students at the end of their final year of study.

Gaudy – A college event for old members. Most colleges hold one each year during the summer vacation.

Going down – Leaving Oxford at the end of term

Gown – Members of the university are entitled to wear gowns that indicate their level of scholarship. The term may also be used to refer to the university community as a whole, as in "Town and Gown" which expresses the, sometimes uneasy, relationship between the residents of Oxford and the members of the university,

Greats – The commonly-used term for *Literae Humaniores*, which is an undergraduate degree programme comprising classical languages (Latin and Greek), philosophy and ancient history.

Hall – the dining hall of a college. This term may also be used to denote the evening meal ('dinner') served there. 'Formal Hall' means that staff and students are required to dress formally in gowns when attending.

High Table – The table in a college dining hall, often on a dais, at which the Head of House and Fellows dine.

Hilary Term – The second term of the university year, which starts in January.

GLOSSARY OF OXFORD JARGON

Isis – The part of the River Thames that runs through Oxford.

Master – The principal of a college. Each Oxford college is headed by a senior Fellow. Each college uses its own terminology for this. Titles include: Master, Principal, President, Rector, Dean, Warden, Provost.

Michaelmas Term – The first term of the university year, which starts in October.

Schools – Also known as "Finals". Both terms are abbreviations of "Final Honours School". These are the examinations taken by undergraduate students at the end of their final year of study.

Scout – A college servant responsible for cleaning. Each scout is usually assigned to a specific part of the college. A student may refer to "my scout" meaning the scout responsible for cleaning his or her room.

Staircase – The older Oxford colleges are designed on a 'staircase' system, in which a group of rooms is accessed by a staircase that opens on to one of the quadrangles around which the college is built. Typically, rooms are identified by a combination of the name of the quad, the number of the staircase and the room number within the staircase group.

Subfusc – Formal attire worn by students and academics on formal occasions, including matriculation, examinations and graduation.

Trinity Term – The third term of the university year, which starts in April.

Tutor – A member of staff (or a postgraduate student) who gives tutorials to undergraduate students.

GLOSSARY OF OXFORD JARGON

Tutorial – A session in which one or two (or occasionally more) students are taught by a Tutorial Fellow or some other person appointed by their college. Typically, this involves students preparing work in advance and talking about it during the tutorial.

Tutorial Fellow – A member of staff holding a Tutorial Fellowship at one of the colleges

The Union – The University debating society, which also has a building housing a library, bar and various other facilities for its members.

WHO'S WHO

The Hughes Family

PC Kenneth Hughes Killed by Shane Butler in 2019

PC Gavin Hughes Kenny's father.

Christine Hughes Kenny's mother.

The Whittle Family

Harry Whittle Killed by the Butler gang in 2019

Yvonne Whittle Harry's mother.

Trevor Whittle Harry's father.

Leo Whittle Harry's brother

The Butler Gang

Shane Butler Terry's brother.

Terence (Terry) Butler Shane's brother.

Holly Butler Terry's wife.

Stuart Hatton Works for Terry and Shane.

Wayne and Dean's family

Wayne Major Married to Dean

WHO'S WHO

Dean O'Brien Married to Wayne

Carl Foster Their adopted son

Harry Foster Their adopted son

Bernie's "Family"

Bernie Fazakerley Married to Peter. Formerly Fellow in Applied Mathematics at St Luke's College. Jonah's Personal Assistant.

DS Richard Paige Bernie's late husband. Father to Lucy.

Lucy Paige Bernie's daughter.

DI Peter Johns Bernie's current husband. Retired police officer.

Angela Johns Peter's late wife.

Hannah Potter Peter's daughter. Married to Laurence.

Laurence Potter Married to Hannah.

Edward (Eddie) Johns Peter's son. Married to Crystal.

Crystal Johns Eddie's wife.

VICTIM STATEMENTS

Ricky Johns Eddie's son. Peter's grandson.

Abigail Johns Eddie's daughter

Emily Potter Hannah's daughter

Amber Potter Hannah's daughter

DCI Jonah Porter Married to Margaret.

Margaret Porter Jonah's late.

Reuben Porter Jonah's son.

Nathan Porter Jonah's son.

Friends of the family

Stan Corbridge Married to Sylvia.

Sylvia Married to Stan.

Father Damien Rowland Priest at St Cyprian's Church.

Celeste Gilbert Grandmother to Leroy, Daniel and Stella

Police Personnel (alphabetically)

Sergeant Malcolm Appleton

Penelope Black Forensic anthropologist

WHO'S WHO

Chief Superintendent Alison Brown

Dr Michael Carson Forensic Pathologist.

DCI Anna Davenport

PC Stella Gilbert

Sergeant Pamela Gregson Custody Sergeant

DS Andrew Lepage

Ruby Mann Senior SOCO

DC Alice Ray

DC Joshua Pitchfork

DCI Jonah Porter

PC Callum McLaughlin

Jennifer Moorehouse Civilian staff member.

PC Louise Otterbourne

PD Q General purpose Police Dog.

PC Melanie Stanton Dog Handler

PC Ben Timpson

ABOUT THE AUTHOR

Like her main character, Bernie Fazakerley, Judy Ford is an Oxford graduate and a mathematician. Unlike Bernie, Judy grew up in a middle-class family in the South London stockbroker belt. After moving to the North West and working in Liverpool, Judy fell in love with the Scouse people and created Bernie to reflect their unique qualities. She has worked in academia and in the NHS.

As a Methodist Local Preacher, Judy often tells her congregation, "I see my role as asking the questions and leaving

ABOUT THE AUTHOR

you to think out your own answers." She carries this philosophy forward into her writing and she hopes that readers will find themselves challenged to think as well as being entertained.

www.ingramcontent.com/pod-product-compliance
Lightning Source LLC
Chambersburg PA
CBHW070533030726

47505CB00001B/20